DEC 0 9 2014

ALSO BY BRENDA NOVAK

HISTORICAL ROMANCE

Of Noble Birth
Through the Smoke

CONTEMPORARY ROMANCE

Whiskey Creek Series: The Heart of Gold Country
When We Touch (prequel novella)
When Lightning Strikes
When Snow Falls
When Summer Comes
Home to Whiskey Creek
Take Me Home for Christmas
Come Home to Me

Dundee, Idaho Series
A Baby of Her Own
A Husband of Her Own
A Family of Her Own
A Home of Her Own

Stranger in Town
Big Girls Don't Cry
The Other Woman
Coulda Been a Cowboy
Sanctuary
Shooting the Moon
We Saw Mommy Kissing Santa Claus
Dear Maggie
Baby Business
Snow Baby
Expectations

D1595687

ROMANTIC SUSPENSE

The Bulletproof Series
Inside
In Seconds
In Close

The Hired Gun Series
White Heat
Killer Heat
Body Heat

The Last Stand Series
Trust Me
Stop Me
Watch Me
The Perfect Couple
The Perfect Liar
The Perfect Murder

The Stillwater Trilogy
Dead Silence
Dead Giveaway
Dead Right

Every Waking Moment

Cold Feet

Taking the Heat

HONOR BOUND

GLENVIEW PUBLIC LIBRARY
1930 Glenview Road
Glenview, IL 60025

A NOVEL

BRENDA NOVAK

NEW YORK TIMES BESTSELLING AUTHOR

PREVIOUSLY PUBLISHED AS *THE BASTARD*

Montlake
Romance

This is a work of fiction. Names, characters, organizations, places, events, and incidents are either products of the author's imagination or are used fictitiously.

Text copyright © 2011 Brenda Novak

All rights reserved.

No part of this book may be reproduced, or stored in a retrieval system, or transmitted in any form or by any means, electronic, mechanical, photocopying, recording, or otherwise, without express written permission of the publisher.

Published by Montlake Romance, Seattle

www.apub.com

Amazon, the Amazon logo, and Montlake are trademarks of Amazon.com, Inc., or its affiliates.

ISBN-13: 9781477824832
ISBN-10: 1477824839

Cover design by Laura Klynstra

Library of Congress Control Number: 2014905352

Printed in the United States of America

To Hilary Sares, a fabulous editor, a wonderful friend, a wise brainstorming partner and all-around wonderful person. Thank you for your support, expertise and enthusiasm.

Chapter 1

Cornwall, England
February 1794

The Baron St. Ives was an ugly little man.

Jeannette Boucher could hardly pull her gaze away. Standing next to her, perched on skinny, shapeless legs, arms behind his back, abdomen swelling in front of him, he reminded her of a pelican. Three reddish chins hung low over the top of his collar while powder from a ringletted wig dusted the shoulders of his lavish gold-embroidered coat. Despite Jeannette's own diminutive size, he barely cleared the top of her head.

". . . into which holy state these two persons present come now to be joined . . ."

God, help me, Jeannette prayed as beads of nervous sweat trickled down her back. Her wedding dress was laced too tight. Dizziness almost overwhelmed her as she eyed her future husband again.

At least forty years beyond her own eighteen, Lord St. Ives looked back at her through heavy-lidded, lashless eyes. White flakes congealed in the creases of his face, contrasting with the purplish veins that burst like blossoms on his cheeks. Something occasionally twisted his lips into what a less perceptive soul might have interpreted as a smile. But not Jeannette. She was too young to be so fooled, too acquainted with happiness. She could not mistake Percival Borden for anything other

1

than what he was: a sick old man, as unfamiliar with gaiety as she was with its opposite.

Until the Revolution, of course. The Revolution had changed everything.

Wetting her lips, Jeannette tried to draw air into her lungs. She didn't want to swoon, dared not give away her desperation. She and her family had barely escaped war-torn France with their lives. Her parents and younger brother deserved a reprieve from the terrible hardships they had suffered. Jeannette was determined to give them that.

But she had never expected her heart to fight so tenaciously against the tether of her will. Even now, hemmed in by innumerable bodies, she was tempted to flee, to part the nuptial witnesses like the Red Sea and run for her life.

"Wilt thou have this man to be thy wedded husband . . ."

The words of the ceremony slipped in and out of her consciousness. It wasn't until a hush fell over the church as those crowded inside strained to hear her response that she knew the vicar had asked the question that would make her the wife of a man she did not love.

For an awkward moment she could not speak. Throat dry, voice gone, she glanced at the twinkling prism created by an errant ray of sunshine that had penetrated the cloudy sky outside to filter through the stained-glass window. Dust motes danced like fairies in that light, twirling, shimmering in vibrant array. *To be so free . . .*

Lord St. Ives's hand tightened on hers, and Jeannette forced her gaze back to the tall, gaunt vicar. But it wasn't until she pictured her parents' worried expressions that she managed a weak, "I will."

Minutes later, it was over. The baron kissed her with slack lips, clasped her fingers in his small, manicured hand, and, turning her to face the rows of pews behind them, presented his new bride to the congregation.

Faces beamed at Jeannette—strangers all, except her parents and brother, who nodded their approval while standing to watch the new couple parade down the aisle.

Jeannette heard many murmur of her youth and beauty as she passed, but more spoke of the ball awaiting them that evening at Hawthorne House. Her new husband was no small man among those in the county, his wedding no obscure event in Cornwall.

"What a joy to see you properly wed!" her mother gushed as soon as St. Ives turned away to accept the felicitations of his friends.

Jeannette was glad to stand in the warmth of the sun. At least it felt familiar, despite the intermittent rain. The church interior, beautiful in its way, with an abundance of marble and stained glass, had been so cold.

Unable to think of an appropriate response to her mother's fabricated brightness, Jeannette turned to her father.

"I am proud of you," he whispered in their native French. "You have chosen well. Lord St. Ives may not look the handsome gallant, but he comes from some of the finest blood in all of England. Our cousin Lord Darby has assured me of that, no? And he is rich as a king. You will always be well cared for."

Jeannette struggled to swallow the lump that swelled in her throat. "Yes, Papa."

Her thirteen-year-old brother, Henri, stood watching them with a gentle, pained expression. She managed a smile when she caught his eye, but before she could speak to him, her new husband drew her toward a fancy, gilt-edged coach waiting at the head of a line of lesser conveyances. A team of four huge horses pranced while their driver, dressed in burgundy livery, held the matched beasts in check, and several footmen stood at attention.

"Thank God that is over with," St. Ives muttered.

As one of the footmen helped her inside, Jeannette wondered if her husband expected some kind of response, but she had no idea what to say to such a rude remark.

The baron climbed in behind her and took the opposite seat. "But a man must marry, eh?" He reached out and squeezed her knee, his grin a picture of eager anticipation.

Trying not to notice how his dull gray eyes measured every detail of her body, Jeannette quelled the urge to shrink from his touch and stared out at the many guests who would soon be joining them again.

"Will you miss France overmuch?" he asked.

The carriage lurched forward, forcing her to brace herself with a hand on one side. Rain over the past several days had left the streets full of ruts and mud, making the coach sway dramatically as they began their journey.

For politeness's sake, she wanted to say that she wouldn't, but knew her husband would interpret it for the lie that it was. "*Oui*," she admitted at last.

"France's loss is my gain." His lips curved into another of his odd smiles, revealing teeth yellowed with age and tobacco.

Jeannette's stomach tightened into a hard knot. For a moment she wished her governess had not taught her such excellent English—she understood him only too well. Fearing she might disgrace her family yet, she made no reply.

Thankfully, her new husband said nothing more, and they rode in silence the three miles to Hawthorne House.

Lieutenant Crawford Treynor stiffened as his mother welcomed him with a kiss. Her smile looked contrived amid the elegant features of her face, an expression Treynor didn't recognize. But then, he'd seen little of Lady Bedford over his lifetime—and wished to see even less.

Her slender fingers plucked at the braid on his uniform. "You grow more handsome every year." Reseating herself, she picked up a gold-handled letter opener and an ivory envelope from a pile of correspondence on the table next to her. "Come, sit down."

The drawing room where his mother received him was only half as luxurious as her husband's home in Devonshire. Even so, it lacked little by way of creature comforts. Compared to the poverty Treynor had known as a child, this cottage, with its ornate cornices, carved mantel and fine furniture, looked like a castle.

He followed her to the settee but remained standing, his hands clasped behind his back. He planned to stay no more than a quarter of an hour, just long enough to fulfill his duty toward the woman who had given him birth.

"How did you know I was in Plymouth?" he asked, using polite conversation to fill the abyss between them.

"Certainly not from your infrequent letters." She placed the letter opener on top of her papers and arranged her expensive, stylish gown before looking up at him. "You send me little more than the weather or general war information. Nothing I can't learn from reading the *Times*."

"My apologies. Perhaps I shall do better in future," he said, but his sense of obligation did not extend that far. Although he sometimes wished he could put the past aside, he knew he could not. The ill treatment he had received at the hands of the brawny farmer she'd paid to raise him had left too many scars.

His mother grimaced. "Forever the gentleman, aren't you? Tell me, has anyone the power to penetrate that cool reserve?"

"You already know the answer to that."

Her eyes narrowed. "So you still blame me. Tell me, what else could a woman in my position have done with a bastard son? Have you forgotten that my first duty is to my husband?"

Treynor shrugged. She'd managed to take excellent care of herself along the way, but he wasn't willing to argue. "Certainly you didn't ask me here to dredge up the past."

"No." Her pale blue eyes held a cynical gleam that seemed to pierce right through him. "But that is why you finally came, is it not? Hoping I would do just that?"

Tensing, Treynor studied the delicate clutter that surrounded them. He wanted to appear aloof and unconcerned, as if his manner could deny the hammering of his heart. "You've kept your secret for twenty-eight years. I would not expect you to part with it now."

"How thoughtful."

He ignored the icy undercurrent, refused to let her bait him as she had in years past. "What brings you to Plymouth?" he asked, idly stroking the wing of a porcelain bird sitting on a table nearby.

The verbal feint made her laugh. "A wedding." She stood and glided to the bell pull. "Lord Percival Borden, the Baron St. Ives, married this afternoon."

"Did he now?"

"He did. Will you at least sit? And have tea?" She arched an eyebrow at him, making her invitation a challenge.

Treynor decided a few more minutes in her company couldn't hurt. He strode to the chair across from her and paused before taking a seat. "Are the wedding festivities over? I hope I'm not keeping you."

Chuckling without mirth, she moved back to her own seat. "Sit down. My headache would detain me even if you didn't. Besides, I have decided to tell you."

The bald statement plucked Treynor's breath away. "About my father? I'm waiting."

She waved the question aside and, still smiling, changed the subject. "At the wedding I met the family of another officer who serves on your ship. They mentioned that their son was in port and would be attending the ball tonight. That's how I knew you were in Plymouth."

The hope that she might actually provide him with the information he'd craved since his youth held Treynor prisoner, as she knew it would. "And who were they?"

"The Viscount Lounsbury and his wife, Eleanor."

"Ah. Cunnington's parents." He didn't bother to conceal his dislike for the lieutenant he served under, but neither did he elaborate on it. Miles Cunnington was a sadistic bastard. Not that his mother would care. Titles and privileges meant far more to her than character.

"You don't like him?"

She'd heard the underlying disdain in his response. But before he could answer, a sallow-faced butler knocked and entered the room pushing a cart bearing an elaborate tea service. He stopped at his lady's side and, at her gesture, poured two cups.

"You can go now, Godfrey. See that you close the door tightly on your way out."

Although Godfrey had been with the family for years, even traveled with Lady Bedford on this and every other trip, he bowed with brittle formality, scarcely acknowledging Treynor's presence, and withdrew without a sound.

"Back to Cunnington," she said. "What is it you hold against him?"

"Besides his arrogance? And the fact that his father's title is the only reason he is where he is today?"

"Do I detect a bit of jealousy? Surely you don't hate the entire aristocracy."

"I pride myself on hating only those who merit such emotion," he responded. "The rest inspire little more than contempt."

This time her laughter sounded genuine. "My son is a champion of the common man, then? Sugar? Milk?"

"Neither." Although he longed to head back to Plymouth and the pub where his mates awaited him, Treynor accepted the cup she offered. That he felt obligated to take tea when he had no desire to remain in the room tested his patience. But he had to allow his mother time to show her hand. Perhaps, at last . . .

"How long are you in town?" she asked.

"Weather permitting, we sail tomorrow." He drank his tea in almost one gulp and leaned forward to put his cup on the tray. "Where is the marquess?"

She shrugged. "I'm sure he will be along presently."

"Does he know I am here?"

"I told him you might come."

"And he doesn't mind? How odd. Now that I am an adult, he becomes generous."

"He's getting old. Sometimes power shifts in a marriage, something you might learn for yourself someday."

"I doubt it. I don't plan to marry."

His mother blinked in surprise. "Ever?"

Again, he shrugged, but the tinge of bitterness he heard in his own voice betrayed the depth of his conviction. "I think I have learned enough about the fairer sex to prefer my bachelorhood."

"Don't tell me Mrs. Abbott beat you as often as her husband did."

Treynor flinched at his mother's casual acceptance of the abuse he had suffered as a boy. She cared no more now than she had then. "Since you have asked, Mrs. Abbott was more than kind. She was so desperate for any crumb of masculine attention, I was terrified to be left alone with her." He fixed her with an unswerving gaze. "And her daughter Millicent became singularly determined to seduce me. When I refused her, she told her father I tried to rape her." He tacked a smile to his lips. "Of course Cayle had something to say about that. He got good and drunk and came after me. And I believe you know the rest of the story."

"Yes. You were fourteen when you broke his jaw and left the Abbott farm for good . . . to join the navy." She sipped her tea, watching him over the rim. "Then there's me, of course. You already alluded to the fact that you think me less than a credit to womankind."

"Evidently you feel you had good reason for doing what you did. Whether or not I agree makes little difference now." He tucked the strand of hair that had fallen from the cord holding the rest back behind his ear. "Why not tell me about my father and be done with it?"

Her movements calm and fluid, she took another sip of tea. "Would you like something else?" She motioned to the tray that held scones, clotted cream and gooseberry preserves.

"No. I believe it's time to go." Coming to his feet, Treynor sketched a formal bow. "Keep your secret, Mother. The possession of it seems to agree with you."

He was nearly clear of the portal when her voice rose behind him. "If you must know, he was the stable master. William was in America for nearly two years, and I enjoyed the attentions of our stable master.

He had a fine physique, he was kind and he was loyal to a fault, even if he wasn't always right in the head."

He whipped around to face her. "You're lying."

"Am I? William didn't return when he said he would, not soon enough to claim you were legitimate. I had no choice but to give you up. Certainly even you can see that. Are you happy now, my dear?"

Treynor felt as though someone had opened a trapdoor beneath him. He'd waited his whole life to learn that he was the spawn of a man who'd started having fits and eventually lost his mind?

Once again, his mother had drawn blood. Whether she spoke the truth or a lie didn't matter. Her mocking words proved how little she cared about him.

His hands curled into fists as he fought to tamp down the pain he couldn't believe he still felt. "Good night," he managed through clenched teeth.

A shrill laugh answered him, one that echoed off the walls as he closed the door.

Chapter 2

The ball was every bit as lavish as Jeannette had expected. A tantalizing display of elaborate fare rested on dark walnut tables. Servants shuttled to and from the kitchen, carrying empty platters or returning with full ones. A fountain held court in the center of the room, spewing champagne from the mouths of silver gargoyles. And sprays of fresh-cut flowers adorned every open space and the center of each table, overwhelming the perfume and perspiration of the bodies packed inside until the air smelled more like a funeral than a wedding.

Although Jeannette cared little for such a show of pomp and grandeur, her parents seemed to enjoy it. It was no more than what they'd been accustomed to. For her own part, she could only wait nervously for the hour of doom: the moment, fast approaching, when her husband would lead her away to their bridal chamber.

Maman had attempted to explain all that was expected of a wife. But the few ambiguous kernels of knowledge she had imparted did nothing to quell Jeannette's fear. Duty, patience and long-suffering had much to do with her mother's message, rather than what, specifically, a bride was supposed to do. Jeannette had never experienced so much as a passion-filled kiss. The idea of allowing Percival Borden complete access to her body was beyond repulsive. Just the thought of what he might look like without his clothes made her ill.

Yet tolerate him she must. *Think of what it will mean for my family . . .*

It was growing late and the guests were starting to leave. Those who remained seemed singularly determined to make the revelry last as long

10

as possible, and for that, Jeannette was grateful. Drunken voices tripped over words, creating a steady chorus punctuated by an occasional staccato laugh. Men gorged themselves on what was left of the food and wiped their mouths with their sleeves while those who danced wobbled beneath the effects of the champagne.

Lord St. Ives had brought Jeannette a glass when they'd first arrived, then spent the remainder of his time with his friends—political allies, her father attempted to explain when it began to appear strange that his son-in-law would abandon her so easily. But Jeannette didn't mind. She had no more desire for St. Ives's company than for a cobra in her bed.

The English gentry and lords and ladies that had surrounded her for most of the evening appeared more formal than their French counterparts, but in Jeannette's eyes they were not so different. As the daughter of a count, she had grown up in aristocratic circles. The bloodlines of France and England were so intertwined that one could scarcely stand without the other. But English sympathy for the plight of titled yet homeless Parisian refugees probably had more to do with fear than with loyalty. The seeds of revolution had been sown so close to home, no one really knew what might be reaped—or when such harvest would come.

"Have you been enjoying yourself, *ma petite*?"

She looked up to see her mother studying her with worry-filled eyes. "You look pale. *Es-tu malade?*"

Jeannette glanced around the room, searching for her husband in his brass-buttoned coat, shiny blue-and-gold breeches, light blue stockings and black buckled shoes. Despite his lack of height, he was easy to spot because of his conspicuous apparel. "Just a headache," she admitted with her best imitation of a smile. "It must be nerves. A girl does not marry every day."

"A girl does not marry *so well* every day," her mother reminded her, going along with Jeannette's attempt to be cheerful. "But if it is your wifely duties you fear, do not worry. It will all be over quickly enough. The baron is a childless widower. No doubt he will leave you to yourself once you conceive, eh?"

Inwardly alarmed by her mother's words, Jeannette nodded. Of course the baron would want an heir, but the thought of bearing his babe was as abhorrent as the notion of lying with him in the first place.

"Give him sons, and he will be generous with you your whole life."

"I can only pray that I am so favored by God," Jeannette whispered.

A man wearing a dark green waistcoat, white ruff shirt and black coat approached. "Allow me to introduce myself," he said. "I am Sir Thomas Villard, a close personal friend of your husband."

"*Enchantée de faire votre connaissance.*" Jeannette allowed him to take and kiss her hand.

"My pleasure, I assure you." His warm fingers clasped hers a moment longer than necessary as calculating eyes, eyes that very nearly matched his coat, probed hers. "May I bring you another drink? Your hands are cold."

Jeannette pasted a fresh smile on her face. Thomas Villard was no young man. He had to be approaching forty, but he possessed interesting features. Thick, dark eyebrows arched above deep-set eyes in a thin face that would have been mildly attractive if not for his hawkish nose. "*Merci*, no. Perhaps I am not yet accustomed to the weather here. And this hall bears such a draft."

He glanced at the enormous room with its high ceilings and great, dangling chandeliers. "So it does." Turning to her mother, he bowed over her hand. "May I compliment you on the beauty of your daughter? And her impeccable English?"

Rose Marie beamed. "*Merci, monsieur.* And may I ask how you know the baron?"

"I am a frequent visitor at Hawthorne House. You might say I am like family."

Before he could elaborate, another gentleman approached, holding a brandy in one hand. "I should have known I would find you flirting with the bride, Thomas," he boomed with a boisterous laugh. "Take pity on your poor brother and introduce me."

Thomas Villard sniffed, dabbed a handkerchief to his great nose and complied—but with obvious reluctance. "Lady Lumfere, Lady St. Ives, may I present Richard Manville, my younger brother."

"Sired by different fathers," Richard clarified, which explained more than the difference in their names. While Thomas was tall, angular and clean shaven, Richard was husky with a barrel chest, bearlike hands and a full beard.

"You are both from Cornwall, yes?" Jeannette sensed a certain tension between the two brothers.

"Richard lives in Liskeard. I prefer London, for the most part." Sir Thomas seemed to forget his irritation as his gaze lingered on her once again. "I find country life a bit dull at times, although the baron occasionally entertains, which goes far toward breaking the monotony."

"The way the baron entertains would certainly do that," Richard added and finished his drink. "Myself, I prefer a more . . . conventional existence." He winked at Jeannette and set his glass on the tray of a passing servant.

"Isn't your wife waiting to leave?" Thomas asked.

This pointed question met with another booming laugh. "Don't worry," Richard told him. "I'll not give away your little surprise." Lifting an unlit pipe to his lips, he tilted his head in acknowledgment of the women. "Sleep well tonight, ladies," he said and swaggered off, presumably to find his impatient wife.

Sir Thomas watched his brother go. "Bit of a lout, isn't he?"

Jeannette said nothing. Richard did seem coarse, but she was more concerned with his words than his manner. What had he meant by *I'll not give away your little surprise*?

"I see you have met Sir Thomas, my dear."

St. Ives's voice at her elbow caused Jeannette to turn in surprise—and to cringe when she found him standing so close. "*Oui*, and his brother Richard."

The baron chuckled. "Ah yes, Richard. He is gone now, I believe."

"And none too soon," Thomas added dryly.

"Did he have much to say?" the baron asked.

"*Non*, milord." Her mother answered before she could. "He was anxious to see to the comfort of his wife."

"He forgets himself too easily." Sir Thomas scanned the room once again. "Has our friend Desmond arrived? He is so late now he has all but missed the festivities."

"He is by the door—and looking splendid, I must say," St. Ives responded.

Jeannette followed the line of her husband's gaze to a tall blond man speaking to a group of older gentlemen. Wearing clothes that were almost as extravagant as St. Ives's—a dark red suitcoat with gold stitching over a shiny, gold waistcoat—he wasn't difficult to spot.

As if he could sense their attention, he looked up and met Jeannette's gaze.

"Handsome devil, is he not?" the baron prompted.

"It is difficult to tell at this distance," Jeannette replied when she realized her husband was talking to her. But the way the other man carried himself reminded her of a strutting peacock fanning its feathers for all to admire.

St. Ives laughed. "Perhaps you will agree after you have had the chance to get to know him."

Her confusion, which had started with Richard's strange words earlier, grew deeper, but the baron's expression revealed nothing of his thoughts, and his next question distracted her. "You must be exhausted. Are you ready to retire?"

Jeannette grappled with her failing nerve. "If you will please allow me a moment, my lord," she replied. "I must bid my parents farewell."

"Agatha waits to take you upstairs to your chamber." He indicated a prune-faced maid standing patiently at the bottom of a grand stairway. "I will be up after you have had time to change. Come, Thomas. Shall we greet Desmond?"

Blood rushed into Jeannette's cheeks as Thomas Villard's gaze raked over her once more. By the salacious glint in his eye, she suspected he imagined all that would happen between her and the baron in the next hour. She could tell that it aroused him.

She reached for the comfort of her mother's hand as St. Ives pulled Villard away.

"The time has come, *ma mère*." She struggled to mask the nervousness in her voice as she watched the baron move through the remaining dancers.

Rose Marie patted her arm. "He does not rush you. He is a kind man, no?"

Jeannette couldn't bring herself to formulate an answer that would have no scrap of truth or enthusiasm, so she changed the subject. "Tell me, what did you think of Villard's brother?"

"Richard Manville?" Doubt clouded her mother's expression. "He seems strange . . . But he was deep in his cups."

Her mother was right, of course. What did she expect from a drunken, ill-mannered Englishman? She was simply grasping at anything with the power to divert her mind from the very near future. "Of course."

Rose Marie leaned in. "Are you too frightened to go through with this, *ma petite*?"

"No!" The word came out overly loud; Jeannette feared her mother noted it.

"*Alors*," her mother sighed. "The baron is far too old for you. I told you when he offered for your hand that I would rather see you with—"

"A young handsome man? Maman, a woman with no dowry cannot pick and choose. We could not afford to turn the baron away. And Papa's own cousin, Lord Darby, found him to be a worthy suitor, *n'est-ce pas*? Darby is a powerful man here in England. We can trust him."

"But you are our only daughter. I could not bear it if—"

"Maman," she interrupted again. "'Tis too late. I belong to the baron."

"Of course." Forgetting her earlier display of optimism, her mother fell silent for several seconds. Then she said, "I pray for your happiness, my child."

Jeannette nodded. "I know. Where is Papa? I must hurry."

"*Je ne sais pas*. I have not seen him for half the night. This has been a difficult thing for him, *ma petite*, to see his only daughter wed to a foreigner."

"Tell him to think of it as an end to our uncertainty over the future," Jeannette told her. "We could have fared much worse in our predicament." She eyed the crowd again, but her father was nowhere to be seen. Even Henri had disappeared, which was just as well. She never could have fooled her brother into thinking she was satisfied with her situation and knew her unhappiness would pain him.

"Give my love to Papa—"

Rose Marie's hand latched onto her arm. "Stay. Another few minutes won't make any difference."

Jeannette noticed Lord St. Ives watching her. "I must go. I do not wish to appear reluctant."

"Of course." Her mother released her as the heavy doors of the house banged shut on the heels of some departing guests. The tomblike sound filled Jeannette with dread. Yet, forcing herself to turn away, she moved toward the waiting maid and mounted the curving staircase, saying a silent good-bye to her youth.

Agatha had a bath waiting. Jeannette allowed the maid to assist her with undressing, then sank into the warm water. Even the thought of what lay ahead couldn't silence the contented sigh that issued from her lips as she stretched out. The bath was unusually large, a welcome luxury. She nodded to the maid, who picked up a cake of perfumed soap to wash her as Jeannette extended a dripping leg out of the water.

That, at least, was fair and white. Despite being an only daughter, or possibly because of it, Jeannette had spent much of her time at her family's country estate, riding or roaming the hillsides. Outdoor exercise had left her body a little too lean, perhaps, and the sun had made her complexion slightly darker than the pallor so sought after by most females, but she wasn't one to worry about such details.

The maid's touch eased her headache, but did little to stop her troubled thoughts from returning to the ball.

Richard Manville was a strange one. Drunk or no, his words made her uneasy. And there was something mysterious about Sir Thomas Villard. Possibly that Desmond fellow, as well. With their knowing glances and sly smiles, her husband and his friends behaved as though they shared a great secret, or a joke of some sort.

"Does Sir Thomas visit Hawthorne House very often?" she asked the maid.

Agatha's hands stilled on her shoulders. "No, milady. The master brought 'im 'ome for the first time only a week ago."

"What?" Jeannette nearly sloshed water over the sides of the tub as she twisted around. "But I thought Sir Thomas and my husband have been close friends for some time. He said he is like family!" She knew her husband's servant might hesitate to comment, but Sir Thomas had left her unsettled enough she couldn't help pressing for what information she could get.

The maid began to wring her hands. "Well, per'aps so. I am just a lowly servant, after all. I don't rightly know the master's business—"

"But you do know who visits here, no?" Jeannette reached out to still the woman's agitated movements. "What is it? Is something wrong?"

"No, milady." The maid's round eyes did nothing to convince Jeannette, but there was little she could do to persuade her to speak against her will.

"Tell me something. How long have you been at Hawthorne House?" Jeannette hoped another tack might get Agatha to open up.

The maid readjusted a bone hairpin to keep Jeannette's hair from falling into the water. "Twenty years next month, milady."

"Do you like it here?"

Several drops of water ran off her hands and plinked in the bath before she answered. "It keeps a roof over me 'ead," she said at last.

"And my husband, he is kind?"

From the corner of her eye, Jeannette saw Agatha throw a glance at the door.

"Per'aps we should dry ye off now."

Not really an answer. The maid's lack of a response did not bode well.

Agatha waited with a large towel. Jeannette rose, letting the water run off her body in rivulets. Her husband would arrive any minute; she didn't want him to catch her in the bath. Perhaps if she'd finished her toilette, he'd put out the lamps before he took her virginity.

She shuddered.

"Are ye cold, milady?"

The room was so hot that the maid's face flushed to a bright red while she toweled Jeannette off. A giant fire roared beneath a baroque mantel along one wall, eliminating any hint of the cold drizzle that had begun to fall outside. Still, Jeannette could hardly admit the true reason for her quaking limbs. "A bit," she lied. "I will be warm enough when dressed."

"Aye, and there's a warmin' pan in yer bed."

"Merci."

Jeannette allowed Agatha to help her don the filmy negligee that had been a gift from her mother, then stared, disconcerted, at the high, heavily carved bed with its rich gold trappings.

Unfortunately, her headache was back and rising to new dimensions by the time her hair fell, brushed and gleaming, to her waist. Gazing into a cheval glass, she almost didn't recognize the pale face staring back at her.

"Shall I let Lord St. Ives know that you are ready?" Agatha's solemn eyes met Jeannette's reflection.

Jeannette nodded. She had no choice. She felt like a fox cornered by baying hounds. It didn't help that those hounds were the urging of her own conscience.

The maid closed the door as she left, leaving Jeannette to wait and to pace, her mouth so dry she could scarcely swallow. Tears burned behind her eyes and, despite the fire, her hands remained as stiff and cold as a cadaver's. At least her family's future was now secure, she told herself. Everything was decided, done. The trade had been made when she and the baron exchanged vows. She had only to finish her part of the bargain.

A heavy hand pounded on the door, nearly causing Jeannette to collapse in a heap on the floor. She'd heard no tread and felt completely unprepared to meet her husband, regardless of Agatha's ministrations.

How could she be such a coward? she wondered, feeling ashamed. Would she shrink from her duty to those she loved?

"*Entrez*," she said, steadying her voice.

The word had scarcely left her mouth when the door burst open, but it wasn't St. Ives. It was Henri, and his narrow face was as pale as her own.

Jeannette dragged the heavy counterpane from the baron's bed and used it to cover herself. "What are you doing here? What is the meaning of this?"

Henri didn't seem to notice what she was or wasn't wearing. "Jeannette, thank God I have arrived in time. Come with me. We must leave at once."

"But I cannot—"

"Hush! They were talking about you. The baron is not the man we thought he was. He—he has plans to dishonor you." His dark eyebrows, thick like their father's, drew together as he made an effort to compose himself, but he couldn't quite manage it. "Never mind." He gestured as if he could sweep the confusion away that easily. "The details are too ugly. Come away!"

Jeannette stiffened in surprise. "I understand that you are worried about me, Henri, but Maman and Papa were strangers when they married and—"

"This is different." His lip trembled as he pushed her toward the door. Although as tall as she already, he was reed thin.

"But I am not dressed!"

For the first time, Henri seemed to realize she was dragging the counterpane. His face grew red, but he remained steadfast in his purpose. "There is no time to delay. I heard them . . . outside . . . placing wagers . . ."

"On what? Henri, do not frighten me."

His chin jutted out in defiance. "You have no need to worry. I am your brother. I will not let anything happen to you."

Grabbing his slender shoulders, Jeannette gazed into his big brown eyes and gave him a gentle shake. "Stop this. I am a married woman now. I have no choice but to stay here. You know that as well as I do."

"Listen to me!" His fingers bit into her elbow as though he'd drag her away if he had to. "I have learned the baron cannot father a child, Jeannette." His whispered words came in a torrent. "He is bringing others to your bed, to acquire an heir any way he can. And the men he has chosen are eager for the opportunity, even placing wagers on whose seed will take in your belly!"

At this announcement, all the strength threatened to leave Jeannette's limbs. She gripped Henri's arm for support. Was that what Richard Manville had meant? Why Sir Thomas had fairly salivated at the touch of her? Were they anticipating a turn in her bed? She knew the baron had been married before, that the late baroness had borne him no children . . .

"Come, *vite*!" Henri tugged harder, but she wrenched away.

"No! You must go back down and act as if nothing has happened. Detain St. Ives, if possible, while I leave on my own."

"But Maman and Papa . . . we should all go!"

Jeannette's heart sank. How she wished that were possible. She wanted nothing more than for her whole family to be miles and miles away. But St. Ives would never sit idly by and allow her parents to take her from Hawthorne House. His standing and reputation would be ruined. And, if alerted, he could easily stop them. He had power here in England, knew everyone. "Think, Henri! I belong to the baron. And we are refugees, paupers! All he has to do is deny our accusations and follow through with his plan. Who would stop him, except Papa? And I will not have Papa dueling over me."

"But you cannot go alone! Who will protect you? A woman on her own is not safe."

"I can take care of myself. You know I can. But you must promise me something, Henri."

Agitated and still eager to grab her and leave, he shifted on his feet. "Yes, anything!"

"Do not breathe a word of this to anyone, even Papa, until I am well away."

Warring emotions twisted his face into an agonizing grimace, but he finally sighed and nodded. "Where will you go?"

"To London, of course. Our cousin Darby will help me, I am sure, if only I can get to him. After I am off, tell Maman and Papa where I have gone. The three of you can meet me at Lord Darby's in two weeks."

"But how will you travel so far? You have no money!"

"I will manage. Just do as I say!"

"What choice do I have?" he asked, his bravado crumbling.

"Exactly. Now go, so I can change." She hugged him, a close, poignant embrace, then half shoved him out the door, frantic now lest the baron appear.

"*Au revoir,*" he murmured softly, his somber expression looking years older than his age.

Jeannette couldn't answer for the lump in her throat. She managed a quick wave and closed the door, then dropped the counterpane and flew to the armoire. The maids had placed her gowns and other belongings in the clothes cupboard just that morning, but nothing fancy would do. She needed plain clothing, like the peasant's blouse and skirt she had worn when her father smuggled her out of France. She'd kept them, but would she be able to find them?

A tread outside in the hall made Jeannette freeze at the very moment her hands laid hold of the thick wool skirt she sought. She turned frightened eyes toward the door when she heard the baron's voice. He was seconds away from striding into the room to find her nightgown at her feet, along with almost every other garment she possessed.

"*Who* wants a word?" he asked someone else whose voice Jeannette couldn't quite make out.

She stood, transfixed, expecting the door to swing inward at any moment. But the baron's voice receded along with his steps, leaving Jeannette shaking like one with a palsy.

Another few moments, then. She had been spared another few moments.

Tearing the skirt from the wardrobe, she launched into a new search of the armoire for her blouse—and spotted a corner of white lying on top of her shoes. In her frenzy, she'd knocked the garment down.

Jeannette's fingers flew over the laces and buttons as she dressed. The night they had escaped France, she'd had her family about her. Now she had only herself and a strident inner voice that urged her to move. Now. Fast.

Scooping up the slippers she'd worn with her wedding dress, she flew to the door. Her nerves could not tolerate another moment in the room.

She pressed her ear to the hard wood of the door, trying to hear above the heavy tramp of her heart, but only a few distant voices filtered up to her. She had no idea whether or not it was Henri who had taken St. Ives away, which direction her husband had traveled or when he'd be back. She could only hope that her younger brother would waylay the baron if he hadn't already, while God directed her feet to safety.

Cracking the door, she peeked into the long dark hall before slipping outside. Shadows alerted her to heavy furniture arranged along the left wall, but she couldn't carry a candle, and without one, she feared she'd become lost.

Laughter tinkled on the air, rising from the ballroom below as Jeannette tried to decide the best way to get out. She'd visited Hawthorne House for the first time only that morning. She knew nothing of its mazelike corridors. But heading down the stairs she had climbed with Agatha wasn't a possibility. She had to find another way out.

And she could. In a grand house such as this, double entrances into almost every room facilitated the servants' movements; she was bound to find an exit. Besides that, the lateness of the hour boded well. St. Ives employed many servants and had hired more to help with the ball. Most of the belowstairs help would be too preoccupied with cleaning up or seeing to the remaining guests to notice a plainly dressed woman who could easily be one of their own.

Stuffing her hair up under the crushed bonnet that had been crammed into the pocket of her skirt, she moved cautiously through the darkness. The floor beneath her creaked, the noise stretching her nerves taut, but she didn't slow. Seconds mattered, fractions of seconds . . .

If only she could slip outside, the thick trees surrounding the baron's mansion would hide her. But not for long. She had to get to London and to Lord Darby before her new husband found her.

The corridors of Hawthorne House twisted and turned past so many rooms, Jeannette lost count. Eventually she found the back stairs and headed down into a large, hot kitchen. Pans clanged as a tired-looking slavey washed dishes. A tall man dressed in livery flung orders at several young women busy stacking plates in a cupboard he waited to lock. The pungent smell of onions and roast duck permeated everything, along with the gentler aroma of the baked goods lining a deal table.

Jeannette blended with the bustle as she passed through the pantry, pushing aside baskets of turnips, crates of potatoes and sacks of wheat to find the back door.

Freedom hit her with the first icy blast of the wind. Then silence engulfed her, along with a thick cloaking mist that didn't permit so much as the moon's light to penetrate. She half expected someone to cry out her name, for the entire house to descend upon her. But there was only the fog. And though its fingers were as cool and impersonal as the baron's own, she gladly accepted its embrace as she ran quietly into the night.

Chapter 3

By the time Jeannette stumbled into Plymouth, the fog had turned into thin wispy tentacles mixed with rain. The five- or six-mile walk in the damp, chilly night had been grueling. Every carriage that had rumbled by on the road to town had sent her fleeing into the brush for cover, leaving her scratched and bruised by thorny branches, and her slippers ruined, worn through and caked with mud.

Concentrating on the sound of the rain splashing into puddles, she tried to ignore the scurrying of unseen animals, the presence of which set her teeth on edge. Even when her lungs began to burn and her skirts became sodden and heavy, she pressed on, wondering where to go now that the village rose like a dark giant climbing out of the sea.

Several minutes later, Jeannette wiped drops of rain from her face with her sleeve as she passed through the narrow, cobbled streets. Would she have to spend the entire night without shelter? Plymouth was one of His Majesty's great naval bases and often in the news, but she'd never visited the city before. She'd stayed in London until she'd met Lord St. Ives. Then he'd brought her, along with her parents and brother, to a quaint but expensive inn outside Liskeard.

A drunk man lying amid the garbage in the gutter sat up as she passed by. "Ahoy thar, pretty maid," he cried out.

Startled into a run, she flew around the next corner, hoping to find light and people near the water. Sailors were reputed to be an unsavory lot known for carousing the night away, but their company was better than no company at all.

The street sloped down to meet the wharves and the rest of the fog cleared, giving Jeannette her first glimpse of the night's moon. A mere sliver of light that appeared to curve into a jeering smile, it mocked her fear and her flight. It touched the harbor with a silvery glow that caused the black, inky sea to glisten like a field of crushed diamonds. Large merchant brigs, smaller clippers and a frigate farther out rocked upon the waves. The lanterns attached to their masts looked, from a distance, like so many yellow eyes staring back at her.

Two men approached on a street intersecting her own. Before they could see her, she darted into the shadows to wait for them to pass.

The stench of wet wool and sweat trailed after them. They had to be heading toward the noisy taverns along the harbor. That was the only section of town that had any life at this hour. The light and music tempted Jeannette, as well. She hesitated to visit such disreputable establishments, but she hardly felt any safer on the streets.

In the end, the miserable weather became the deciding factor. She followed them before she could lose sight of their stocky forms, telling herself she'd let them lead her through the streets. She longed for the warmth of a fire and a safe place to rest, if only for a few minutes.

A chorus of music, laughter and male voices swelled as her guides stepped into a pub named, by a crudely lettered sign, The Stag.

A moment later, Jeannette followed.

Glad to escape the rain that was dripping into her face despite her beleaguered bonnet, Jeannette hovered near the entrance, feeling rather conspicuous in her peasant garb. Surely only women of ill repute frequented these taverns. But she would have crawled into a beast's lair if it meant a reprieve from the dark, the wet and the cold.

Although The Stag wasn't crowded, it smelled strongly of ale, wood smoke and foul cheroots. The barmaids were haranguing a few snoring stragglers, trying to get them to remove their slumbering bulks to the rooms upstairs. But judging by the empty glasses cluttering the vacant tables, most had already moved on.

A huge fireplace took up one whole wall. Eager for its warmth,

Jeannette sank down on its hearth and rubbed her freezing fingers before the crackling flames. Her hair lay plastered against her face and neck. And her skirt clung to her shivering body. Ah, for a warm bed, or a change of clothes . . . But she had no coin to purchase either.

Content that she was safe for the moment, she stared into the flames and tried to think. She couldn't stay long, would have to press on come morning. Otherwise, St. Ives stood a good chance of finding her before she reached Lord Darby. And, as her husband, the baron could legally drag her back to his home, beat her, do almost anything he pleased.

Jeannette thought of Henri and her parents and hoped they fared well. No doubt they were worried about her.

How she wished she were back in France, safe in her home. She longed for the life she'd known before the Revolution. But every morning when she opened her eyes to England, she knew those days were gone, probably forever.

Leaning wearily against the stones, she forced back the tears that threatened to spill down her cheeks. Her nose was beginning to run. She reached into her pocket for a handkerchief, but, realizing she didn't have one, shrugged and wiped her nose on her sleeve, too dejected to care.

A clatter brought Jeannette's head up. Guffaws rang out from a group in the corner as a barmaid tried to keep the tankards she hadn't dropped from joining the one she had.

"That ought ter cool yer ardor," she said, swinging her hips as she moved around the table.

Jeannette pushed the straying tendrils of hair out of her eyes. Five sailors, roughly dressed, sat at a table with three others, dressed in the formal blue-and-white uniform of officers in the Royal Navy. Ignoring the overturned cup and spilled ale at their feet, they laughed as mugs of the same brew were placed in front of them.

The girl who delivered their drinks giggled as the man she'd doused pulled her onto his lap. "Not 'ardly," he vowed.

Another barmaid, taking an interest in the revelry, sauntered toward them and leaned so low over the table that Jeannette expected her to knock over more drink.

The sailors didn't notice—the ale, anyway. Their eyes were riveted to what Jeannette could only assume was a spectacular display of cleavage. All except one particular officer, who wore the single epaulette of a lieutenant. Tilting his chair back against the wall, he watched the maid with a scowl.

"What's wrong? Don't ye like what ye sees?" she teased, singling him out.

Another young man with short-cropped hair spoke up. "Ah, don't mind Lieutenant Treynor, Molly. He's been dour all night. Besides, he's not all he's cracked up to be." He shot the officer in question a quick smile, as if to soften his quip, but the man called Treynor merely shrugged.

"Well, I'm not askin' 'im ter marry me," Molly retorted.

The others hooted with laughter.

"'E's in love then? Got a jealous wife?"

"No," the young sailor replied. "He's just too concerned with his duty to enjoy a good romp. At least one he'll tell about." He winked. "A lieutenant's got a lot on his mind, you know."

The man called Treynor set his chair back on all fours with a bang. "Indeed. I must make sure you gentlemen make it back to the ship come morning, along with the beef we were sent for."

"You know you can trust us, Trey," the younger man said. "Anyway, the *Tempest* puts in at London before we head back out to sea. If I was going to desert, I'd do it there, where I have family." He stood and took the barmaid's hand. "Come on, Mol. My coin's as good as his, and I'll keep you warmer."

Molly paused, her reason obvious, at least to Jeannette, who had never seen a more handsome man than the lieutenant. White, straight teeth gleamed between full lips. A slight cleft in his chin and a strong, square jaw complemented a rather crooked smile. Brows a shade darker than his sandy-colored hair arched above light eyes. Although Jeannette couldn't determine the exact color of those eyes, they seemed intelligent and expressive, even from across the room.

"That's the way of it, then?" the maid asked with obvious disappointment.

"I'm not worthy of your charms, Molly love," Treynor answered with an unexpected grin. "Go and enjoy yourself with Dade. He's a much younger man and will no doubt be quicker, if not more to your liking."

The sailors chortled at Treynor's insult, and someone close enough to Dade nudged him in the ribs.

"I wish ye'd let me be the judge o' that," the girl sulked, but when Dade appeared wounded, she curved her lips into a grudging smile. "Oh, all right. 'Tis gettin' late, and I'm not one ter plead fer a man in my bed. Most o' the time, the likes of ye are beggin' me!"

"No doubt." The lieutenant agreed amiably enough, but Jeannette couldn't help wondering if he was merely being kind.

Molly and Dade moved away from the table with the other maid and the man who'd captured her. The four of them headed to the stairs as Treynor got up. Impressive by any standard, he stood a head taller than his comrades.

After throwing a few coins on the table, he turned to the officers who remained. "I'll expect you up at first light."

"I'll be there. But will they?" Another of the officers hitched a thumb at the departing sailors. "Why you'd let 'em go a-whorin' on their last night of shore leave is beyond me."

Treynor chuckled. "If only for the chance, I have no doubt you'd be trailing a skirt as well. Anyway, I'd rather they have their fun here. The *Tempest* looks like a bawdy house whenever we put in." Tossing back the remainder of his ale, he left the room with only a slight sway in his step to reveal that he, too, had indulged in his share of drink.

As Jeannette watched him go, a plan formed in her head. The sailors were leaving early in the morning and, according to the man called Dade, they were heading straight to London, which would probably take about two days.

Any other form of transportation would take at least a week.

Rain thrummed on the windows of the baron's drawing room, slapping the glass and cascading down in sheets. The wind howled through the eaves as well, bending the trees against the house and drawing Percy's attention to the dark night beyond.

His bride had gone missing more than three hours ago. But she was out there . . . somewhere.

"Will you not answer to these charges?" the count demanded when he didn't speak.

Percy turned from the window and once again faced his bride's family. "It's rubbish, of course. No more than the wild imaginings of your boy here, I suspect. What other answer could there be?"

Henri stood in the middle of the floor, his face flushed. "I imagined nothing, *monsieur*. Those men talked of my sister. I heard them say 'Jeannette' and make"—his eyes darted back to his parents—"certain disrespectful remarks regarding her beauty and . . . 'ripeness.'"

"Mon Dieu!" The count jumped to his feet while his wife remained on the sofa, crying. "I demand an explanation!"

"The charges are ridiculous." St. Ives ignored Henri and directed his comments to Jeannette's father instead. "Whoever the boy heard—and he gives no names—could have been drunk and talking about their own lustful fantasies. Surely you can see that."

"I see nothing, *monsieur*, only that my daughter is missing. My son"—the Comte de Lumfere motioned to Henri—"seems to offer the only clue."

Percy drew himself up to his full height, however lacking he knew that to be. "I beg your pardon, sir. Does my reputation not count for anything in France? Does the blessing your own cousin, Lord Darby, gave this wedding not stand as a witness in my favor?"

"Until I get my daughter back safely, I care little for a man's reputation, or another's recommendation."

The baron strove to keep a tight rein on his temper. It had been a humiliating, disastrous evening. But at least the Bouchers had come to him with their accusations instead of adding to his problems by simply disappearing as their daughter had.

"I realize how difficult this must be for you." Percy kept his voice as level as possible. "But please try to understand my own dismay. This unfortunate misunderstanding has poisoned my wife against me. Do you not see? We are both victims."

The Comte de Lumfere grunted. "Jeannette would not have offended you without good reason."

Percy eased himself into a chair, trying not to wince at the pain such movement caused his gouty foot. He was so tired; they were all tired. It was getting late. The guests who had traveled long distances slept in the east wing. The others had departed. Even most of the servants had retired for the night. Except for the steady rain outside, the crackle of the fire to his right and the echo of their own conversation, the house was quiet.

"She was misled. It is as simple as that," Percy insisted when he felt capable of sounding calm. "And I am as concerned as you. We must find my wife before something terrible happens."

"We *will* find her, *monsieur*, and when we do, we will surely get to the bottom of this matter—"

A brisk knock interrupted. At Percy's command, Sir Thomas and Desmond entered, pulling a sopping Richard Manville along with them.

The baron came to his feet as quickly as he could. "Sir Thomas? What have you here? You're supposed to be searching for my wife."

"That's him," Henri exclaimed, pointing a finger at Richard. "That is the man I heard talking about Jeannette."

"Mr. Manville?" Percy asked.

"*Oui.* 'Tis him. I swear it is."

Sir Thomas nodded. "I am afraid the boy is right. My brother has a confession to make."

Percy looked to Manville. "Spit it out, man. What went on here this night? I have never been accused of such heinous crimes and would dearly love to hear the truth of it. What have you to say?"

Manville doffed his hat and twisted it in his hands. The effects of the drink he'd imbibed earlier had worn off, or Thomas had sobered him up. Percy didn't know which. At this point, neither did he care.

"I didn't mean any harm," the big man mumbled. "I was only havin' some fun, tryin' to get the fellows' blood up, you know."

Percy made a sound of incredulity. "Having fun? Do you know what damage your 'fun' has caused me?"

Richard's gaze darted to Henri before returning to Percy. "I am afraid so. It is my words that caused your new wife to run off, is it not?"

"You maligned my honor and spoke of my bride with disrespect!"

Manville nodded, his eyes now focused on the carpet. "I am terribly sorry, milord. I will help search for her, do anything I can to make amends—"

"But he wasn't alone in it," Henri piped up. "There were others placing wagers as if . . . well . . . as if what Mr. Manville said about Jeannette was not shocking at all."

"I take full responsibility," Richard said without argument. "It was all my doing, my own strange sense of humor. And look at the grief I have caused."

Jeannette's father opened and closed his hands in an obvious effort to keep himself from throttling Richard. After a moment, he gained control and offered Percy a stiff bow. "I apologize as well, Lord St. Ives, for our momentary lack of faith. But now that we have learned the truth, I hope you will not fault our daughter for reacting as any other virtuous woman would in the same circumstance. I assure you, she is a good girl, just as a young bride should be."

Hallelujah. Percy breathed a sigh of relief and returned the bow. "No need to worry. Once we have found my lady, we simply need to convince her of her mistake and all will be well, eh?"

Tapping his cane on the floor like a gavel, the baron turned to Thomas, Desmond and Richard. "I want the three of you back out there searching, all night if necessary. There is no telling the dangers that might befall a woman alone. My young bride could be set upon by highwaymen or brigands or worse—"

"My lord?"

It was Henri who interrupted. Percy paused long enough to give the boy a chance to speak, but he'd heard just about all he wanted to hear from him already.

Henri looked hesitant, but at his father's nod, he finally said, "My sister is on her way to London, *monsieur*. We were to meet her there in two weeks' time."

Percival Borden smiled. "Why, thank you, Henri. We will certainly find her more quickly now that our search has some direction. Sir Thomas? If you, Desmond and Richard will follow me, I have a map in my study. We will mark out all possible routes to London, and thereby save ourselves considerable time."

"I will go, too," the Comte de Lumfere volunteered, but Percy shook his head.

"Thank you, but no. Your good wife is considerably distressed. She should not be denied the comfort of your company. I will ring for a maid to show you to your rooms. Try and rest—and do not fear. Your daughter will be back with us, where she belongs, come morning."

Forcing his creaking joints to move, Percy left Jeannette's family behind and followed his friends into the hall, closing the door with a soft thud behind him.

Then he reached out to clutch Thomas's arm. "What took you so bloody long?" he snarled.

Chapter 4

Jeannette waited until the sailors had left the tavern's main room before creeping up the stairs. Silently traversing the long hall that branched off into a dozen bedrooms or more, she paused outside each portal to hear the sounds coming from within. Her hair had dried, but her clothes were still damp enough to make her shiver. She couldn't wait to rid herself of the wet, muddy garments. How she would filch Dade's tattered white breeches and striped shirt, or the clothes of another sailor, was quite another question.

In the last room on the left, she heard nothing but snoring and moved on. In the next, the movement of someone preparing for bed. Where were Molly and Dade?

A giggle two doors down answered Jeannette's question. Whether it was Molly or the maid who had accompanied the other seaman didn't matter.

She peered nervously behind her. No one was coming.

As she turned the latch and pushed, the door squealed on its hinges, making her fear a loud protest from those inside. But, as she'd hoped, the couple remained too preoccupied to notice. Heart ticking triple time, Jeannette slipped inside.

"Give *me* some blankets." It was a female voice—Molly's.

Trying to ignore what was going on in the bed only a few feet away, Jeannette scanned the room. The moonlight streaming in at the window lent just enough of a glow for her to see the outline of various shapes. Male and female garments littered the floor, but she couldn't tell Dade's from Molly's, so she snatched up the lot, including a pair of boots, and crept back toward the hall.

"That's it, my girl, there you go," Dade whispered as the sound of kissing, then giggling, came from the direction of the bed.

Jeannette's cheeks flushed hot. She had to get out of the room and find somewhere to change, somewhere she could take the time to feel each garment and determine between them. But where?

Molly began to moan, and Jeannette no longer cared. She slipped into the hall, closed the door and considered herself lucky to be away. Lovemaking wasn't anything like what she had pictured. It wasn't quick or pristine or polite. What she'd witnessed was intimate and personal . . . far *too* personal.

Shaking her head to clear it of the images that remained, Jeannette searched for a place to change. She couldn't go back to the common room. Neither could she strip in the alley. Some of the rooms might be vacant, but which ones?

The quiet settling of the inn emboldened her. She stole into the darkest corner of the hall and began to sort Dade's clothes from Molly's. She was likely to catch her death if she didn't make haste.

Once she had her own wet garments on the floor, she grasped the young tar's breeches and pulled them up over her hips. But before she could don his shirt and boots, she heard a tread on the stair. Panicked, she darted into the closest room. She'd hoped to find it empty or its occupant fast asleep, but the second she entered, the bed creaked and something sprang at her out of the darkness, slamming her to the ground.

"What are you doing sneaking about in the dark? Who are you?" the man who'd just tackled her demanded.

Jeannette couldn't speak. The air had been knocked from her lungs, but she recognized that voice. She was partially undressed beneath the lieutenant she'd seen downstairs, who was similarly without a shirt.

Of all rooms, she thought.

Treynor grasped her shoulders. "Molly? My, you are a lusty wench." His voice revealed irritation, impatience. "What are you doing creeping into my room? How did you lose Dade? Don't tell me he's finished with you already."

"He . . . he . . . passed out," Jeannette croaked with what little breath she could summon. Her safety depended upon this man not seeing her face or learning she was a stranger, but her accent could also give her away.

"You're freezing," he said on a sigh. "Did I hurt you?"

Grateful for the spirits she could smell on his breath, Jeannette shook her head. She could only hope his wits were dulled enough to conceal the more obvious differences between herself and the barmaid.

"Come on, then, if you're so eager," he said gruffly, rolling off her. "Perhaps I could use a diversion after all."

Rising, he reached down to help her up.

Jeannette's eyes cut to the door. She wanted to flee, but feared she wouldn't make the hall before the lieutenant caught her. Judging by his lithe movements, he could intercept her in a second if he tried. Yet she dared not protest or speak again because of her accent.

She allowed him to help her up and reluctantly followed when he pulled her to the bed.

"What? You have nothing to say?" He chuckled as Jeannette tried to jerk away, then turned and dropped back onto the bed, pulling her down on top of him.

The sensation caused by the renewed contact of their bodies made Jeannette gasp. His warm, sinewy flesh felt even better than she had imagined, watching him downstairs. She tried to ignore the strange yet evocative sensation of skin on skin—not at all easy the moment a much more private body part stirred to life against her leg.

"Don't be frightened," he said when she nearly bolted again. "You have nothing to do with my foul mood, and I think you're right. A few moments with your warm, generous body, and I will be good as new." His mouth slanted across hers, roughly insistent. Then, reining in whatever had prompted the harshness of his kiss, he rolled her onto her back and added, "Be calm. I won't hurt you."

Jeannette swallowed hard as he ran a finger along the line of her jaw.

He stopped at her chin, and she could taste the slight tang of his skin as he rubbed her bottom lip with his thumb. Struggling to control her fear and the flow of a strange emotion she couldn't name, she wondered if he could feel how hard her heart was slamming against her chest.

"You taste like honey," he said. "And your hair smells like rain." He buried his face in her neck, breathing deep while Jeannette lay frozen beneath him. The sensations assailing her body seemed to paralyze her mind.

"I may have underestimated your charms. You're cleaner than any barmaid I've ever met." He kissed the tip of her nose as his hands began to knead her back, slowly lowering to the curve of her hips. When he reached her bottom, Jeannette nearly screeched and jumped out of the bed. Only the hope that she'd have the opportunity to escape without incident, if she exercised patience, kept her where she was.

Treynor's hands wandered back up to cup her breasts as his mouth moved on hers once again. This time his kiss was deep, but not harsh. His lips moved over hers, gently compelling her to respond, and she found this coaxing technique highly effective. She began to feel as if she were on fire—as if something in her body had taken over that no longer accepted orders from her brain.

Who would have guessed a man could make a woman feel so . . . eager, Jeannette thought in surprise. Her father would surely abhor the thought of her being pawed by a sailor, even an officer, but she was almost glad to find she wasn't incapable of desire.

As Lieutenant Treynor pressed her lips apart and flicked her tongue with his own, letting her taste him as he tasted her, Jeannette's thoughts became fractured, disjointed. Her parents . . . she had to remember her parents. But the sweet, velvety softness of his mouth invaded her senses. Unresisting, she quivered at his touch.

"Are you still cold?" He'd misunderstood her reaction. After reaching back with one hand to throw a blanket over them both, he wrapped himself more tightly around her.

Oddly, Jeannette had no desire to break away. She could feel the ripple of muscle as he moved on top of her, feel his lean, hard stomach on her own as he nibbled her neck and then her ear.

"Let's get rid of these, shall we?" he mumbled, tugging at her breeches. "Why are you wearing them, anyway?"

Again, she didn't answer, and, fortunately, he didn't follow up on the question. He was too preoccupied with arousing her.

This is madness. It can't be happening. The lieutenant was no one to her, lowborn—but Jeannette's body didn't care about his station in life, especially when one hand slid down her breeches to cup her bare bottom and his tongue dipped into her ear.

Just a few more minutes. She nearly said the words aloud as the fingers of his other hand delved into her hair and his mouth began to travel down the sensitive skin of her throat.

If only she could pretend, for a moment, that this handsome stranger was her husband. Her arms ached to hold him, to caress his vibrant flesh until he fulfilled the strange new craving that clutched at her belly.

Tentatively putting her arms around his neck, she tested her power by pulling him back to her mouth.

"Nice," he said against her lips, and his hand closed over her breast, teasing the tip, fanning the longing he'd already sparked. She was being carried away on a tide of desire by a man she didn't know, a man she couldn't give herself to for a million reasons.

"I must have been crazy to turn you away," he whispered.

Don't listen. The warning seemed to echo in her head, somehow reminding her of her duty. Placing her palms on the broad expanse of his chest, she pushed in hopes of rolling him off. She had to escape the lieutenant's tongue and hands before it was too late. But her movements succeeded only in confusing him.

"What's wrong?" he asked, raising his head.

"Let me go."

Had he heard the French in her voice?

"Do you want your coin in advance?" he asked. "You'll get it. You have my word."

Thank God, he seemed oblivious to her accent. Or maybe her gruff whisper had masked it well enough. Regardless, she dared not speak again. He was drunk, or he might've realized she wasn't Molly, wasn't even English. And if St. Ives's men came searching for a French girl before dawn . . .

Get out! Now! She shoved at him again, but he resisted. Panicked, she resorted to the only thing she could do: she brought her knee up between his legs.

When he gasped, then doubled over, she flung herself out of the bed and dashed to the door, scooping up Dade's shirt and shoes as she went.

With the lieutenant writhing behind her, she slipped through the door, but she didn't get away before she heard his furious oath. "You teasing little bitch! I'll kill you for this!"

Treynor lay awake in the dark hours of early morning, the blankets thrown off his naked torso despite the chill air. His head still ached, but at least his testicles hadn't fallen off.

What a night, he thought wryly, cursing himself for trusting a woman, any woman. First he'd suffered through the encounter with his mother. Then the woman who'd appeared in his room nearly claimed his manhood.

A strange doxy, that one. Whoever it was, it wasn't Molly. Now that he'd finally sobered up, he realized that much. The body he'd held was too slim, too firm, too small. He had begun to realize that dimly, as her physical features became known to him in the dark room through touch alone. But by then, he hadn't cared. She'd come to him and awakened a raging desire, promised him a desperately needed release.

Bliss.

Until his groin had exploded in pain.

Once he could both breathe and move, he'd nearly torn the inn apart looking for her. He'd barged in on the real Molly, with Dade, had roused the other servants to question them and had awakened most of the inn's sleeping patrons—until the owner had insisted he stop or be thrown out.

Only then had he returned to his own bed, wondering what he would have done with his mystery woman even if he'd found her. She was the focus of his fury, but she was the least of his problems. The greater injury had been caused earlier, by his mother. But whether his mother was telling the truth or simply twisting the knife she'd buried in his back long ago, he could not let the knowledge of his father cause him to lose sight of his goal. He'd come too far, worked too hard. He would one day captain his own frigate, and he'd do it without benefit of money or connection. He'd beat the odds stacked against him in favor of men like Lieutenant Cunnington, whose titled father had exerted great influence on behalf of his son, and climb the ladder on his own.

Ability would be enough. It had to be.

But he'd still like to throttle the woman who'd kneed him in the goods.

Chapter 5

Something cold and wet awakened Jeannette just before dawn. She huddled deeper into what she imagined to be her bed until the smell of urine, rising from the gutter at her feet, reminded her that she was far from home. Then movement and a high-pitched whine made her gasp.

She sat up. A small black dog with curly hair nosed about the refuse surrounding her, apparently hoping for something to eat more appetizing than rotting vegetable peels and animal droppings. But Jeannette doubted it'd find much for breakfast here, at least anything that didn't stink.

"Hungry, are you?" she asked with a yawn. Her own stomach growled at the thought of food, but the filthy alley behind The Stag made her wrinkle her nose in disgust.

At her words, the dog cowered away, then ventured closer, sniffing at the oversize boots on her feet.

"I won't hurt you," she coaxed. "Come here." Reaching out to pet its shaggy coat, Jeannette wondered about the time. After her unnerving episode with Lieutenant Treynor, she had dressed and hidden in the alley, in case he came searching for her. But no one had disturbed the miserable hours that followed.

Jeannette grimaced. Dade's clothes were stiff with seawater and old sweat. And she was so cold! In the panic of her escape, she hadn't thought to steal a more substantial coat than Dade's threadbare jacket, though she knew several better ones hung, temptingly close, on the rack inside the inn.

The dog wagged its tail as Jeannette ran her hand slowly down its back. "Poor thing, you're nothing but bones."

She stood on cramped legs and wrapped her arms around herself to ward off the chill. She had to do something about her hair. It hardly looked boyish hanging down her back almost to her waist.

The kitchen of The Stag backed up to the alley, but it had been closed and locked by the time Jeannette sought refuge among the weeds and garbage that thrived in the narrow, muddy roadway. Now the door stood open, teasing her and the hungry dog with the smell of frying bacon.

Mouth watering, Jeannette crept closer. That the black dog watched with its tail between its legs and didn't venture to follow gave her no confidence, but she had to do *something*.

Hugging the inn's outer wall, she peered in the opening. A short man with a thick neck was cracking eggs into a skillet, humming to himself as he worked. Next to him, on a long deal table covered with flour, stood a butcher's block of wood from which protruded the handles of several knives.

Scissors would have been preferable, but Jeannette dared not take the time to search for something she wasn't likely to find, at least very close at hand. Stealing a knife out from under the nose of The Stag's cook would be challenging enough.

Selecting a stone from the muddy ooze created by numerous feet tramping in and out the back door, Jeannette threw the pebble inside, down the hall leading to the front of the tavern.

"Damn dog, I'll kill ye one day," the inn's chef muttered, and thundered after the noise as though he meant it.

Jeannette darted inside, grabbed a knife and hurried back to hide behind the pile of refuse where she'd spent the night. She felt as if the whole world could hear her heart beating at its frantic pace. Footsteps sounded from within, then the cook stomped into the alley, still cursing the dog, which wisely kept itself at a safe distance.

"One of these days, ye'll go in me soup!" he promised, stooping to seize a rock and throw it. The dog whined and skittered away and the man returned to the food cooking in the kitchen.

When he was gone, Jeannette took a deep breath and eyed the knife she'd managed to steal. Eyes shut, she grabbed a tuft of hair in one hand and began to whack at it with the other. Unfortunately, she had no time to take special care. She'd stayed close to The Stag so she could follow the sailors when they left. Now she feared she'd miss them if she didn't hurry.

Trying not to think about the shiny black hair that fell about her, Jeannette kept at her task. *It will grow back,* she chanted, over and over. But those words hardly consoled her when she stopped to run a hand over the short, jagged locks that remained.

Ignoring the remorse that suddenly engulfed her, she finished the job and stuck the knife into the mud at her side. Then she covered her shorn head with Dade's cap, wondering what kind of a sailor she made. She knew she must look like a ragamuffin at best. But could she pass for an unkempt boy of thirteen or fourteen?

The sailor's baggy clothes hung on her thin frame. Once she'd strapped her bosom down with strips of cloth torn from her ragged skirt, she felt more confident. Especially after she rubbed dirt on her face to hide the softness of her cheeks and on Dade's clothes to make them less recognizable. Unfortunately, nothing could be done to disguise her eyes. Their unusual violet color and the thick black lashes that framed them were anything but masculine.

She could only hope that no one would look too closely. And why would they? England was at war. With press gangs snatching any seaworthy man they could find, and the government emptying its jails into its ships, the navy would have little reason to question who or what she was. Nor would they want to. She had a pulse, and she was willing to go to sea and serve His Majesty, the king.

Voices rose, coming from the street. The dog, now ambling about the garbage at her feet, froze and cocked its head to listen. Jeannette did the same. The tars . . .

Fog swirled in from the sea, concealing the street that ran along the harbor. She moved toward it, anyway, squinting through the mist, but as she rounded the corner, she stopped in her tracks. Seven or eight men were clustered outside the entrance to The Stag, and they were, as she'd guessed, definitely sailors.

The unmistakable voice of Lieutenant Treynor floated on the air as Jeannette listened. "Where's Dade?"

"Still in Molly's arms. The idiot claims he wants to marry her," someone said with a chuckle.

"I'll have his hide," Treynor snapped. "If I have to drag him from his bed, he'll wish he'd never met the wench."

Jeannette winced at the guilty memory of her final moment with Treynor. She didn't wonder at the lieutenant's sour mood.

"Forgiveness is a great virtue, sir. We need every able-bodied sailor we have," the same man pointed out.

The dog, which had followed her, barked and ran into the street, causing the sailors to glance up. They saw her, but the fog and darkness kept her from full view.

Now or never. Summoning her courage, she stepped forward. "I would like to sign on, *s'il vous plaît.*" She considered the dog. With such an unfriendly cook at The Stag, she didn't see how the little stray could last much longer. "Me and my dog."

A cross expression settled on Treynor's face as he left the group to stride toward her. "You look young."

"I am thirteen."

"But you are French, and French is not an easy thing to be in His Majesty's navy at the moment."

"I am a royalist, *m'sieu,* and I will make as good a tar as any of you."

Treynor looked over his shoulder to the others, who watched them curiously, and lowered his voice. "You are eager, I will give you that. But have you ever even been to sea?"

He took her silence for a reply.

"Go back to your family, lad, until you're older and stronger. By my own blood, you look as though a good gale would blow you into the sea."

Jeannette lifted her chin. Everyone knew His Majesty's navy was hard-pressed around the globe. What with Vice-Admiral Sir John Jervis trying to capture the French colonies in the West Indies, Admiral Lord Hood and his squadron in the Mediterranean hoping to seize Toulon, and the French blockade intercepting ships carrying grain to the revolutionaries, frigate captains could hardly keep a crew. Her father spoke of it often. In the face of such need, she hadn't expected Lieutenant Treynor to have a conscience about using a boy to do a man's work. The possibility of refusal frightened her.

"I have no family," she said. "The ship provides food and drink, does it not? That is more than I have here." She kept her eyes lowered, afraid he might recognize her somehow, even though he'd never glimpsed her in the light.

"Take him on, Trey," one of the men called, turning away from the innkeeper who had just emerged from the building. "Dade's run off."

"What?" Lieutenant Treynor swung around as though tempted to start a brawl.

"You heard me. He's gone."

"Bloody hell!"

Treynor's curse caused the men to clear their throats and shuffle their feet. "The rest of us are here," someone said.

"I'm not going back without Dade," Treynor vowed. "Spread out and look for him." But, cursing again, he promptly reversed his order. "No, Bill and Luke, you go. The captain is expecting his beef. The rest of us will see it aboard. If you have no luck and we've the time, I'll come back later and see what I can find." His gaze rested on Jeannette. "What is your name?"

Jeannette began to stutter before her mind could lay hold of the name she had decided to use. "J-J-Jean. Jean Vicard."

"Where's your dunnage?"

"I-I-I have none, sir."

He looked down at the scrawny mongrel at her ankles. "Can that dog catch rats?"

"Of course," she answered swiftly. She would teach it how if she had to catch a few herself.

"Then you can bring him," he said. "We sail on the outgoing tide if the wind is favorable."

Jeannette only half heard him. A simple black carriage had emerged from the fog a few yards away. It stopped on the other side of the street, and a tall, gangly man descended. He ducked into one establishment after another until fear prickled the back of Jeannette's neck.

Was he looking for her? She bit her lip as something began to nag at her memory. She had seen him somewhere before—perhaps, she thought with apprehension, at her own wedding.

Jeannette watched as he made his way down the street, finally crossing to The Stag. He was probably asking about her even now, she thought.

Her identity would not remain a secret for long if the inquisitive stranger had met her as the baron's intended.

Treynor and the others headed to the wharves. Not wanting to be left behind, Jeannette scooped up the dog and followed, but once they reached the dock they had to wait. The frigate rode at anchor almost half a mile out of the harbor, while skiffs and other small craft came and went—all spoken for.

Jeannette struggled to keep watch on the entrance to The Stag, but the wives, well-wishers, ragged children and vendors mobbing the dock often obstructed her view. She put the dog down and fidgeted nervously, glancing seaward to survey the huge ship that was to carry her to London. What was taking so long?

The delay wasn't caused by any lack of skiffs, she saw. Evidently, even fishing boats were converted into ferries when a frigate docked. Unfortunately, nearly all the smaller craft were at the ship, waiting to bring the many women crowding its decks back to shore.

The sun progressed in its daily ascent, burning away the fog and making Jeannette feel all the more conspicuous for being viewed in full daylight. She folded her arms across her body and tried to keep from tapping her toe, hoping to appear as at ease as those around her.

Please don't let me be caught now, she thought while fighting the urge to look over her shoulder. But the skiff owners seemed determined to thwart her. They refused to shove off until they had filled their crafts and collected the usual fare from each passenger.

Jeannette wished Lieutenant Treynor had the power to speed their departure, but there was nothing he could do. Seemingly as impatient as she was, he paced in front of their small group, motioning to those at sea until finally a boat headed back toward the dock. It was overloaded and sailing so low that water sloshed over the sides, but the women aboard didn't care. They laughed and shouted and waved at those they left behind.

The going was slow. Twice the small vessel nearly capsized: once when a woman stood and bent over, lifting her skirts to the lot of cheering men on the frigate behind her, and once again when they all turned to wave and chant a farewell.

The prostitutes who serviced His Majesty's Royal Navy were a motley lot. Buxom wenches jostled against thin ones; the middle-aged vied with the young. Some were barely twelve if they were a day. With filthy, torn dresses and faces more heavily painted than that of any actress, they made Jeannette sad, even though their bawdy talk and laughter told her that many of them were drunk.

The small boat bumped against the wharf and was made fast. Then the chattering women climbed out. The sailors who were with Jeannette patted a round rump here or there, seemingly pleased with what they saw. But, in Jeannette's opinion, the prostitutes looked no better up close. One woman, who appeared a good bit older, though not quite so bedraggled as the rest, winked at Lieutenant Treynor and managed to brush up against him as she passed.

"In a 'urry, sir?" she asked.

Even a couple of paces behind, Jeannette could smell cheap brandy on her breath and clothes. But it was preferable to the stench it covered up, she decided, catching a whiff of unwashed skin and heaven knew what else.

Treynor raised his hand to wave her away, then thought better of it. Finding a coin, he flipped it to her before bending to hold the lighter while the others climbed in.

"My place isn't far," she said, a hopeful gleam in her eye. "A man 'andsome as yerself deserves somethin' for 'is money."

"Some other time."

The woman began to saunter up the dock. "Send for Patricia when yer in, love!" she called back.

With a noncommittal smile, Treynor stepped back so Jeannette could get into the boat. She handed the little dog to one of the oarsmen, but before she could climb inside herself, the man who had entered the tavern reappeared.

He stood on the pier at her elbow.

Chapter 6

The man stepped forward. Jeannette noted his odd attire— knit pantaloons and red silk waistcoat, which emphasized his narrow shoulders and ponderous hips. He did not deign to tip his tall hat, but cocked his head.

"I am Ralston Moore, solicitor for Lord Percival Borden, the Baron St. Ives," he told Treynor.

His soft, insinuating tone curdled the blood in Jeannette's veins.

"I am looking for a young woman who disappeared from Hawthorne House late last night. Perhaps you have seen her."

Jeannette couldn't help it. She caught her breath and bit her lip, waiting for the moment Ralston Moore would turn his attention on her.

Treynor glanced up. "Who is she?"

"The baron's new wife. The barkeep at The Stag thought he saw an unfamiliar woman by the hearth last night. He said you men were there at the time."

A fresh jolt of panic shot through Jeannette when one of Treynor's fellow officers spoke up.

"Treynor saw someone, too, a certain woman he took to his bed last night. He says she had the body of a goddess. Unfortunately, she also had the makings of a good pugilist."

The others burst into laughter, and Jeannette let her breath go. They were teasing Treynor; they had no real information to give.

Treynor scowled at them, but the solicitor cut off whatever he was about to say.

"I am not searching for a harlot." Peeved that the sailors had failed to take him more seriously, Moore sniffed. "She is gently born and bred!"

Treynor nodded at another lighter filled with prostitutes. "Then you are looking in the wrong place. They call this Damnation Alley for a reason." He stepped into the boat as a passing wave made it rock and had to fight to keep his balance. The boat tipped wildly and Jeannette nearly went overboard. Reaching back, he grabbed her by the collar and pulled her down next to him.

The hard muscles of his thigh rubbed against her leg as she landed with a plop on the timbers of the stern sheets, but the solicitor scarcely looked at her.

"Still, I must search. The baron will not rest until he finds her. Should you have any information that could lead to her eventual recovery, please contact me." Moore handed Treynor his calling card.

Treynor glanced at it, shoved it in his pocket and signaled the oarsmen. One rose and hauled on the line to pull the boat close to the dock and cast off.

"The baron is offering a hefty reward," Moore added, calling this information out over the slap of oars.

Jeannette turned her face to the sea. So St. Ives was offering a reward. She had expected him to go to great lengths. It looked as though he wasn't going to disappoint her. But none of that mattered. She would be in London soon. With Lord Darby's help, certainly she could find a way to avoid St. Ives for good.

If only for a quick, uneventful voyage.

Twenty minutes later, Jeannette looked up to see the ship rising from the water. Much larger than it had appeared on shore, it looked to have eyes all around. As they drew closer, Jeannette realized they were portholes for the long barrels of cannons.

Until that moment, she hadn't really thought of the *Tempest* as a fighting machine. Now the full realization hit her. She was about to board a ship that had been purpose-built for battle. Men fought upon her decks, were wounded and maimed. Some suffered terrible deaths. The ship could be blown to bits, burst into flame or sink into a watery grave.

But not before they reached London, she reminded herself.

Gazing worriedly over her shoulder, she could just see Mr. Moore on the pier, his back to her, stopping passersby. She'd slipped right past him and would soon be safe with Lord Darby. Her family would, no doubt, join her there soon.

If St. Ives only knew how close he'd come . . .

Too close, Jeannette decided, but she was free. She had only to bide her time. With a silent and very mocking good-bye to Moore, she faced front again.

"The *Tempest* was built by your countrymen."

Jeannette started at Treynor's voice and turned to see him watching her. "Oh?"

"Yes, captured by the English *Flora* in 1780." The wind ruffled the lieutenant's thick sandy hair as he spoke, and his eyes reflected the blue water surrounding them. He made a pleasant sight, but she forced her attention to the frigate. As they closed the distance, it loomed nearly straight up out of the water.

"C'est très grand."

"Not as big as some. She's fair sized at almost one thousand tons, but she carries only fifty guns." He pointed to the portholes Jeannette had noticed earlier and continued with unmistakable pride, "Thirty-six long twelve-pound cannons on the main deck, twelve twenty-four-pound carronades on the quarterdeck and forecastle and two long-sixes in the bows, along with a crew of more than five hundred men."

They were so close Jeannette could nearly reach out and touch the top of the greenish copper plating that covered the lower portion of the *Tempest*'s hull.

"Why is the bottom covered with metal?" she asked.

"To keep worms from burrowing holes into the wood."

Above the copper, a wide black band separated the gun deck from the others. Above the gun deck sat the main deck, cradled between the raised forecastle at the bow and the quarterdeck at the stern.

Jeannette shaded her eyes. Though she could see only their tips, three slender masts rose into the sky, looking like giant needles threaded with rope.

"The one in the bow is called the foremast," Treynor explained, following her gaze. "The one in the middle is the mainmast, and the one in the stern is the mizzenmast. The large, horizontal poles that cross them are called yards and bear the sails, but because we're in port, the sails are lashed down."

"You will see them unfurled soon enough when we set sail," one of the officers she'd seen at The Stag volunteered.

The skiff bumped another small boat, and Lieutenant Treynor and the others turned their attention to jostling for position at one of several ropes that dangled into the water. While they worked, choppy waves buffeted their small vessel and the wind whipped at Jeannette's clothing. She was going to freeze without a better coat.

"Frenchy?" Treynor was waiting for her.

Jeannette hesitated as she watched sailors use the ropes to walk nimbly up the sides of the ship. How would she manage with a dog? She wasn't strong enough to haul herself up, even without a squirming bundle under one arm.

His mouth quirked with impatience, the lieutenant laughed. "Put your dog down. I'll bring it."

She exchanged the dog for the rope he handed her and began lifting her own weight, only to feel his hands on her bottom as he shoved her halfway up the ship's side.

Once Jeannette gained her footing, she copied the others and struggled the rest of the way on her own, eventually heaving herself over the gunwale.

To her embarrassment, Lieutenant Treynor easily carried her dog, pinned between his arm and body, up behind her. When they were both on board, he handed the animal back to her. "What's your dog's name?" he asked, scratching behind its furry ears.

Jeannette's mind froze. "Name?"

"Yes, surely it has one. You seem so devoted to it." The lieutenant smiled at her, waiting.

"B-b-bull." She couldn't think of anything better.

Eager to be set down, the dog twisted and turned in her arms, revealing her belly.

Treynor glanced at it, then gave Jeannette a quizzical look. "Bull? Did you know she's female?"

"*Oui* . . . ah . . ." Jeannette tried to force her sluggish brain to provide some good reason her dog would be named Bull, female or no, but her wits had completely deserted her.

Fortunately, a heavyset man in an officer's uniform called for Treynor, and he turned, saving her from whatever inanity hovered on her lips.

The other man drew the lieutenant away, and Jeannette promptly lost herself in the crush of bodies that surrounded her.

"Bull?" she repeated, rolling her eyes. Something about the lieutenant turned her into a fool, and Jeannette felt fairly certain she could guess what it was. The memory of those few minutes in his bed came to mind every time she looked at him, and sometimes for less reason than that. Knowing how he behaved in such intimate circumstances, how his body felt against hers, how he smelled like soap and wool and man made her weak in the knees. Having held him almost naked in her arms made it too easy to undress him again in her mind.

The heat of a blush crept up Jeannette's neck, and she squeezed her eyes shut, wishing she could shut off her thoughts as easily as her sight.

Forcing herself to forget the lieutenant, she lowered the dog to the deck and searched for something to keep the animal from running off.

When she found a bit of rope, she improvised as best she could. "Be good," she said as the dog strained at the new leash. Then she looked around in earnest, this time concentrating on what she saw—which was purposeful action and chaos all at once. Sailors prepared the frigate to set sail. Their wives garnered a parting gift or hug against an uncertain future. And bumboat men and women sold merchandise to the crew.

The bumboat people fascinated Jeannette. From temporary stalls, they hawked their wares, just as they would in a marketplace on land. According to their bleating voices, they sold, on credit until payday, fresh fruit, clothes, trinkets and any other items that a sailor might fancy.

Ragamuffin children darted through the melee, along with numerous dogs, cats, parrots and other pets.

She might be safe from Lord St. Ives, but what would she face here? The hundreds of ropes that controlled the sails and supported the yardarms looked extremely complex . . .

But she would never have to learn them. She wouldn't be around long enough.

The thought of London cheered her as she watched barefooted sailors check the rigging high above.

"Vicard!"

Lieutenant Treynor had to call her three times before she realized he was speaking to her. Recognizing her blunder, she finally turned—but knew she'd never survive in this new world if she couldn't keep her own name, and her dog's, straight.

"Come along, Bull." She started forward, but wasn't particularly eager to meet the square, ruddy captain who'd been conversing with Treynor and a handful of other officers for several minutes already.

"Yes, sir?"

Treynor waved her to his side. Not wanting to get close enough to him to rouse any more thoughts of The Stag, she reluctantly obeyed.

"You need to accompany Captain Cruikshank to his cabin so his clerk can enter you in the muster book. Otherwise, you'll not get paid," he told her.

With all the news of the war, Jeannette had some understanding of the subject. Boys received a pittance, if that.

"Oui, monsieur." Pay was the least of her worries. She wouldn't be part of the navy long enough to collect it.

"Has the lad any experience?" The captain turned bloodshot, watery eyes upon her.

Another officer, who wore his impeccable uniform like a badge of honor, reached out to grab her hands. He turned her palms up and rubbed the soft flesh with his thumbs. "Not a callus in sight. With such delicate hands, I would say he has not done a stitch of work in his life. Isn't that just like the lazy French?"

Jeannette was glad she'd scrubbed dirt onto her face, for it had left plenty beneath her nails as well. She refrained from making a response to the officer's demeaning comment while hoping that the others wouldn't look too closely.

The captain waved off the other man. "It takes no calluses to be a bosun's servant, Mr. Cunnington. Those will come with the job. And a French lad can learn as easily as an English one."

"I didn't know a frog could do anything quite as well as an Englishman." Cunnington and another man laughed, but the captain cut them a glare that wiped the smiles from their faces.

"Regardless, the bosun needs a lad, and this one will do."

The officer named Cunnington eyed her again. "Actually, I have been in need of a steward for some time now. I could use the boy myself, Captain, if you could see your way clear to indulge me."

A prickle of fear skipped down Jeannette's spine. She already knew two or three days spent in the company of this man would be too many.

Fortunately Treynor spoke up. "Too late, Lieutenant Cunnington."

The captain hesitated, then affirmed his agreement with a nod.

"But I hardly think Hawker deserves more consideration than I." Indignation oozed through Cunnington's voice and his gaze lingered on Treynor before returning to the captain.

Treynor tensed. It was a subtle change in his demeanor, but one Jeannette caught right away—along with the gleam of extreme dislike in his eyes. "My apologies, Lieutenant Cunnington. Perhaps next time I go ashore I will be lucky enough to find you a good lad, a good English lad, if you can't manage to do that for yourself."

"You are pleased about this, are you not, Mr. Treynor?" Cunnington said.

The captain scowled. "We will have none of that, Mr. Cunnington. I have promised a servant to Mr. Hawker, and he shall have this boy."

Cunnington's lips thinned and his nostrils flared, but he did not speak again until the captain motioned to the confusion surrounding them.

"Get these people off this ship, Mr. Cunnington."

"Aye, aye sir. I am working on it as we speak."

Cruikshank stared at Cunnington for a moment, as if weighing his arrogant tone against his actual words. "That will do." Motioning to Jeannette, he lumbered toward the quarterdeck where she assumed they'd find his cabin.

Grateful for Treynor's reassuring presence at her side, Jeannette followed. As uncomfortable as the memory of their time together made her, he was the only thing remotely familiar in this strange world. Fleetingly she wondered what the lieutenant would do if he discovered her to be the wench who had left him rolling in agony.

With a sideways glance at his tall, muscular frame, she hoped he would never find out.

"Mr. Cunnington is first lieutenant and my second-in-command, Mr. Treynor," the captain said as they walked, with Bull still fighting his rope leash.

"I am aware of his rank, sir," Treynor replied, his hands behind his back.

"Then perhaps you have forgotten your own."

"No, sir."

Captain Cruikshank stopped and turned to face him. "Let me be more direct: Mr. Cunnington doesn't like you."

Treynor's eyebrows rose. "Does Cunnington like anyone, sir? With his excessive fondness for discipline, I sometimes wonder if we should fear mutiny more than the French."

The captain shook his head. "The two of you are very different. I know that. Do you think I cannot see how the men admire you? You are one of them. You rose to your present rank from a mere cabin boy. They would follow you anywhere."

"Thank you, sir."

"That's not all." He glanced in the direction of his first lieutenant. "Devil take him, Cunnington will advance to captain someday because of who his father is, regardless of his record, while you have less chance. That is how the system works, and there isn't a bloody thing any of us can do about it."

His weathered face lost in concentration, Cruikshank looked at Jeannette, but she could tell he wasn't really seeing her. He was thinking, selecting his next words carefully. "He is your superior," he said at last. "I will not intercede again."

A muscle twitched in Treynor's cheek, the only outward sign of emotion Jeannette could detect. He nodded once. "Yes, sir. I understand."

"Good. Wait here. When my clerk is done, you may bring the lad to the bosun."

Mr. Hawker looked much younger than his wife. Jeannette studied him from beneath her lashes, wondering what it was, exactly, that had drawn the two of them together.

Lieutenant Treynor, who was still with her, greeted them both before taking a seat in their small cabin on the orlop deck, which was one level above the hold, or so he'd said when he brought her here. "This fine, strong lad is Jean Vicard," he said. "Captain Cruikshank has agreed to let him be your new servant. And this is his dog"—he shot a glance and a half smile at Jeannette—"Bull."

Jeannette greeted the Hawkers in the deepest voice she could summon, and tried to look taller.

The stocky bosun was balding, but his thick reddish eyebrows and muttonchop sideburns gave him the appearance of a hairy man. "Strong, ye say?" he scoffed, reading the lieutenant's grin the same way

Jeannette had. "A weaklin's better'n nothin', I suppose. And 'avin' another dog might be nice. Rusty died last spring." The bosun scratched his hairless head. "But the wife 'ere looks a mite stronger'n yon lad."

Jeannette nearly burst into laughter. Mrs. Hawker stood behind her husband, a great hulk of a woman with shoulders almost as broad as Treynor's.

A kindred thought must have occurred to the lieutenant because he cleared his throat as if to conceal a chuckle. "He is young yet. He will grow."

Mrs. Hawker moved forward and poked Jeannette in the ribs as though looking for a good piece of meat. "Skin an' bones," she concurred.

Jeannette stuck her chin out, trying to look belligerent. "I am strong enough, *monsieur, madame.*"

"Ye'll do," the bosun replied with a shrug.

"We thank ye kindly, Lieutenant." Turning to the chest behind her, Mrs. Hawker withdrew two wrinkle-free shirts. "I finished yer laundry. They're clean an' pressed to perfection, that they are."

"Thank you." As Treynor reached into the pocket of his knee breeches to hand the older woman a few coins, Jeannette couldn't help admiring the long lines of his legs.

"When do we sail?" Mr. Hawker asked.

"I can't say for sure. The captain was just telling Lieutenant Cunnington and me that he's received orders to wait until tomorrow. There may be a change of plans."

A change of plans? Jeannette's breath caught. Certainly that did not bode well.

"We will see London a day later, then," Hawker said.

"Evidently." Treynor turned to Jeannette. "You will be all right here, Frenchy." He flashed her a ready smile. "If you need anything, I am not hard to find."

"Merci beaucoup, m'sieu," she murmured. "You have been most kind."

Jeannette quelled the urge to beg him not to leave her as he strode through the door and closed it behind him. As Jean Vicard, she'd experienced a very likeable side to the lieutenant. Gone was the cool, unyielding man she had seen in the tavern with the serving wenches, the one she'd met before passion had transformed his reserve into something else entirely. Now that he thought her a boy, he treated her with nothing but frank kindness.

She hoped the Hawkers would do the same.

"Are you listening to me, lad?"

Jeannette looked into Mrs. Hawker's narrowed eyes and swallowed. For more than an hour, the woman had been drilling her with information and instructions, most of which Jeannette had been unable to absorb. Her breasts ached in their bindings to the point of distraction; she longed to tear the strips of cloth from her chest. How would she survive another two days of such misery? She must have been mad to think she could play the part of a boy for so long. But, of course, she hadn't known their trip would be postponed.

"Where will I sleep?" she asked, and received a scowl for the interruption.

"Mr. 'Awker will sling yer 'ammock over there." She pointed to a corner of the small room.

"You mean I will stay in here with the two of you?" Jeannette sputtered. For *three* days?

Mrs. Hawker shook her head and chuckled, revealing a scant allotment of teeth. "Aye. Did ye think the captain might give ye 'is cabin?"

Jeannette's gaze circled the room, noting the small, confined space that contained the Hawkers' hammocks, a shabby wardrobe, a cumbersome sea trunk and the small desk where the bosun sat, absorbed in a ledger. A chamber pot sat at the base of a washstand, further proof of the complete lack of privacy in the cabin.

Panic plucked at Jeannette's nerves. She'd never be able to remove her bindings. She'd be under the Hawkers' watchful gaze every minute until they reached London.

Mrs. Hawker cleared her throat, her voice growing sharper. "Are ye listening, lad? I said yer not exactly a servant. Yer more like an apprentice, of sorts."

"Oui." Jeannette nodded to placate the woman. Somehow she'd assumed she'd have her own small quarters in a dark nook or cranny. In all honesty, she hadn't thought beyond the immediate and desperate need to reach London. Had she been able to imagine life onboard the frigate, she might have realized the folly of her plan.

Mrs. Hawker pinched her arm. "Did you 'ear me, lad?"

Jeannette flinched, and Bull growled softly at her feet. "Y-yes!"

"Then what, exactly, did I say?" The robust woman propped her hands on her hips, waiting for Jeannette's response, and easily glaring the dog to silence.

So much for loyalty, Jeannette thought, glaring at Bull herself.

She searched her recent memory for an answer. "You said your husband is a petty officer and one of the best seamen," she began, shooting a glance at the bosun, who didn't seem to be paying them any attention. "His responsibilities include inspecting the ship's sails and rigging every morning and . . . and reporting their state to the officer of the watch."

She almost smiled when she managed to recount this much, but the bosun's wife simply raised an eyebrow, wanting more.

"If new ropes or . . . or other repairs are needed," Jeannette fumbled on, "he informs the first lieutenant. And the bosun is also in charge of . . ." She racked her brain but couldn't remember anything else. " . . . of repairs," she finished lamely.

Mrs. Hawker sighed in exasperation and held out a small, silver pipe. "What about this?"

"Oh! He uses that to issue his orders."

"Right. An' 'e's in charge of all deck activities, like raisin' and droppin' anchor. What else?"

Jeannette barely heard the question. She had made a grave mistake by joining the navy. As cramped as their quarters were, the Hawkers would find her out in no time. An uproar would break out at the discovery of a woman dressed as a boy, and the *Tempest*'s captain would have her escorted to Plymouth. There, St. Ives's solicitor would return her to the baron, if Treynor or another of the men didn't take her to Hawthorne House and collect the promised reward first.

She should have struck out for London on foot. No one would have guessed a French boy begging a ride to the capitol to be the Baroness St. Ives. Certainly such a journey was less risky than shipboard life.

"Lad?" Mrs. Hawker prompted.

Before Jeannette could respond, the bosun frowned at them. "'Is name's Jean."

"I don't care what 'is name is. 'E'd better listen to what I'm tellin' 'im, or 'e'll wish 'e 'ad. Bloody arrogant French." She turned to her husband. "I don't know 'ow ye're goin' to teach someone who won't pay attention. Maybe 'e's daft."

"We 'aven't even sailed yet, Geraldine. Give the lad a chance to get 'is legs afore ye start 'arpin' at 'im. There's nothin' to replace experience. 'E'll learn, right enough."

Sensing an opportunity to beg leave of the cabin, Jeannette cleared her throat. "Speaking of sea legs, I have never been on a frigate before. Do you suppose I could take a turn around the ship?" She appealed to the bosun, knowing better than to ask Mrs. Hawker. His rotund wife was irritated enough to keep Jeannette under her thumb indefinitely.

"There's no need to go gettin' in the way—" the woman began, but her husband interrupted without the slightest acknowledgment of her words.

"There's a good idea," he said to Jeannette. "Off with ye."

Jeannette smiled. *"Merci, m'sieu."*

Passing immediately through the door, she planned to "find" a skiff. She had to get off the frigate, and she had to do it while there was still enough confusion to cloak the departure of a young boy.

Jeannette wandered about the upper deck with Bull at her heels, trying to devise a plan. To her untrained eye, it looked like mass confusion reigned, which could only help her. Amid so many, she felt anonymous.

Those in charge were easy to identify because of their immaculate uniforms. Fortunately, they were absorbed in their work. Even Lieutenant Cunnington, who stood in the midst of the fray, seemed preoccupied with giving instructions.

The bumboat men and women were still plentiful, although the prostitutes, or at least the more obvious ones, were nearly all gone. Jeannette didn't see Lieutenant Treynor, but with so large a crew, chances were small that he would stumble upon her at the wrong moment.

She had nothing to worry about. She hoped.

Lingering along the gunwales, Jeannette watched skiffs and other small craft load up and shove off. Suppose she climbed down and dropped into one?

She could pay the fare.

Her hand dipped into the pocket of her stolen breeches to feel the few shillings Dade had stored there. How much would it cost? If she managed to return to shore, she'd soon need coin to purchase food; she was hungry already.

She whistled to coax her dog to cooperate with his leash and moved back amid the vendors.

"Watch yourself!" A small man with a peg leg shooed her out of his way as he began to pack up his stall.

Jeannette watched him for a few moments before realizing that she'd seen him when she first came on board, selling liquor to a seaman.

She glanced around to be sure there were no officers in the immediate vicinity. "Can I help, *m'sieu*?" she asked, keeping her voice low.

He eyed her dubiously before turning back to his work. "Out of the kindness of your heart, I suppose?"

"No. But I do not ask for money."

His head snapped up. "Then what? A draught of grog? You know selling liquor is against regulations. I have none."

"You have none *left*, perhaps. I saw you with a pig's bladder earlier."

Sweat rolled down the sides of his face as he hefted a crate to the ground. "If it's a drink you're after, I could possibly arrange it, if you've got the coin."

"I want neither rum nor gin, and I am not out to cause you any trouble." She scanned the area again and lowered her voice still further. "I simply want you to take me with you. For my part, I'll help carry and load everything."

"You're asking me to help you desert?" A half smile twisted his lips as he shrugged. "Suit yourself. It's your bloody backside you're riskin'."

He was alluding to being flogged, of course. Tales of flogging in the navy were notorious. But she wasn't too worried. She'd joined up only a few hours ago. She'd simply unjoin and go on her way.

"Fair enough," she agreed.

Together they loaded several more crates, using old clothes to conceal the now empty bladders. While Jeannette dismantled the stall, her new benefactor went to coordinate their departure with a boatman.

Finished before he could return, she sat on top of the last crate until she heard the tap of his peg leg and saw his dirty blue coat. Then she hopped up.

"Let's get these to the side," he said, motioning to the crates.

They traipsed back and forth across the deck and used a rope and pulley to lower the merchandise into a waiting boat. Then the man waved Jeannette ahead of him. "After you."

Jeannette wanted to snatch up her little dog, but knew she'd fall into the ocean if she tried to scale the rope without full use of both arms. Reluctantly, she dropped the leash and left Bull behind in hopes the bosun would take good care of him. Then, without so much as a backward glance, she scrambled over the side, vowing she'd never come so close to one of His Majesty's vile-smelling frigates again.

The little boat shifted as she released the rope and took a seat. She looked up, expecting to see the bumboat man lowering himself down, but no one was coming.

Her dog yapped from somewhere far above.

Lifting her gaze even higher, she spotted her benefactor peering over the gunwale.

Nausea washed over her when she recognized the person standing at his side.

"Aren't you forgetting something, Jean Vicard?" Lieutenant Cunnington called down. He was holding her dog in his arms.

Chapter 7

Jeannette's stomach convulsed as the oarsman beside her grinned, revealing a handful of yellow, rotting teeth. The air seemed suddenly colder, saltier; the water that swirled between the frigate and the small brown boat, darker.

She glanced at the dock where she had been so eager to come out only a few hours before. Land had seemed close when she thought she was going back. Now it looked miles away.

Lieutenant Cunnington jiggled the rope. "Well, Vicard? Are you coming?"

His light brown hair was neatly combed and held back in a short queue. His face, though rather long, was otherwise unremarkable, except that his skin looked a good deal paler than the average seaman's. She found nothing objectionable in his appearance, but his calm, almost pleased expression unnerved her.

Forcing herself to move on rubbery legs, she took hold of the rope and began to struggle through the climb.

The moment she reached the top, her dog jumped out of the lieutenant's arms and began to wag its tail and bark. But Bull's warm reception contrasted sharply with Cunnington's icy glare.

"I warned the lad what running away might cost him." The bumboat man's peg leg thumped on the wooden deck as he crowded closer. "There is no need to wrestle with your conscience on that point, Lieutenant."

Abruptly, Cunnington stepped aside and dusted his sleeve where the man had brushed against him. "You have no more business here, Will.

64

Pack up your bladders and go, or next time I will not turn the same blind eye to your gin-selling."

Will blinked. "Aye, sir. Immediately, sir," he said and scraped away.

The lieutenant turned his attention on Jeannette. "Wait until the captain learns of this. You know what will happen, don't you? I can hardly think of anything less pleasant than seeing someone take a whip to virgin skin. The scars last a lifetime, you know."

His body language indicated eagerness, not regret. Jeannette swallowed hard. "Please . . . I-I made a mistake joining up. You said it yourself, I am not cut out for this type of work."

His eyebrows rose over eyes that held less warmth than the sea. "That is no longer your decision, young Vicard. It is my job to teach you what it means to serve in His Majesty's navy. And that means I will ask the captain to order a full dozen stripes for you."

"But . . . I am sorry," she protested. "Surely you can forgive this one indiscretion—"

"I am afraid this lesson is best learned early on. It is my solemn duty to report it to the captain."

"Please, *m'sieu*—"

"You give me no reason to show mercy. I despise the French. All frogs are cowards."

Forgetting her fear, Jeannette bridled. Who was this man to feel so superior and act with such cruelty? She wanted to spit in his face. "And you are so courageous, *m'sieu*? A brave man does not order the flogging of a boy," she bit out. But she regretted her hasty words when his hand clamped down hard on her arm.

"Evidently you know little about the navy." Cunnington's breath bathed her face. "The whip will teach you readily enough. The bosun's mate wields it with uncommon skill. I daresay you will keep a civil tongue in your head and stay where you belong in future. So will everyone else when I am finished making an example of you."

They were drawing more than a few curious stares. Jeannette glanced at the seamen around her in silent appeal, but they remained impassive.

No one would risk worse punishment of his own by interfering. "Let me go," she said, trying to wriggle away.

Cunnington tightened his grip and dragged her toward the captain's cabin. Bull snarled, but he gave the dog a kick that sent it howling.

"Do not hurt her!" Jeannette cried as her dog cowered several feet away, creeping forward and then back with its tail between its legs.

"Your mongrel is the least of your worries, Vicard," he promised.

A flogging. Even if it didn't proceed to actual blows, she couldn't withstand the kind of scrutiny that would result from disciplinary action. And being found out frightened her more than the cat-o'-nine. Captain Cruikshank would realize the truth. Then, as soon as Treynor and the others put her appearance on the ship together with what they had learned from the baron's solicitor, he'd return her to St. Ives.

Think, she ordered herself.

Lifting her chin, Jeannette stopped fighting for her freedom. "I can walk on my own, *m'sieu*, if you please."

Cunnington didn't release her, but her cooperation caused him to relax his grip. They strode past the mainmast, then Jeannette jerked away and plunged into the milling crowd.

She heard Cunnington curse as she darted between bodies that reeked of perspiration and unwashed clothing. Dodging coils of rope, the last of the bumboat stalls and crates and several of the goats that roamed freely on deck, she charged forward, where the crowd was thicker. With any luck, she could disappear from sight.

Depending on the weather, London might be less than a two-day trip by sea. Two days was not so long to stow away on a frigate.

"Stop that lad! Grab him!" Cunnington shouted as the startled cries of those he shoved out of his way resounded behind her.

Jeannette's blood turned to fire, heating her body until sweat ran freely. She was losing him. Her nimble feet and small size gave her the advantage, and she was using both to weave in and out, widening the distance between them. The sound of his voice grew faint, blending with the general tumult and giving her hope—until her foot landed in something soft and wet and slid out from beneath her.

The stench of dung rose to Jeannette's nostrils as she landed hard on her backside.

The jolt befuddled her brain. She shook her head to clear it and tried to scramble to her feet, but a wall of people cut her off, finally moved to action by the lieutenant's cries.

Cunnington came to stand over her, his nostrils flaring. The chase had loosened his queue, but he smoothed his hair back into place and brushed off his uniform. "You will pay for that," he growled.

She stared up at him with all the defiance she could muster. She cursed him in French, but she had little doubt that he understood.

He lowered his voice to a promising whisper. "You will take your lashes like a man, little frog, tied over a barrel, nice and tight. The bosun's mate knows how."

Jeannette almost blurted that she wasn't a man and would take no lashes at all, but she managed to hold her tongue. Surely the captain would come and put a stop to this madness. Cruikshank had seemed both fair and kind.

Carefully avoiding any contact with the dung in which she'd landed, Cunnington pulled Jeannette to her feet and began dragging her to the closest grate. But Bosun Hawker stepped out from among the crowd and placed a hand on her arm, forcing Cunnington to stop long enough to address him.

"What's 'appened? What's the boy done?"

The lieutenant's eyelids lowered halfway in a look of haughty contempt. "He tried to desert."

"I don't understand—"

"Then I will state it simply, Bosun Hawker. Evidently you care less for your new servant than I was led to believe, or you would have done your duty and stopped this piece of French scum from running off in the first place."

Cunnington glanced meaningfully at the hold Hawker had on Jeannette's arm. The bosun released her, but kept pace with them despite the buffeting crowd.

"'E wanted to come aboard," he pointed out. "Why would I feel the need to watch such a one?"

Cunnington relinquished Jeannette into the hands of a brawny, stubble-faced sailor. "Nonetheless, he cannot disappear whenever he likes. He is in His Majesty's service now."

"But—" The bosun looked at Jeannette, and the pity in his eyes made her yearn for the relative safety of his cabin. "Mrs. Hawker was a mite hard on ye, lad, but she meant ye no 'arm. What led ye to the devil's mischief?"

Jeannette could only shake her head as the crowd closed around her like a fist. She couldn't explain; there was no time, anyway.

"Make his lash, Hawker. If you want to help. I am going to speak to the captain."

Mention of the lash caused panic to rise in Jeannette's throat like bile. Surely the captain would not approve. "Please! I am not who you think—"

Her captor's thick fingers jerked her so hard her teeth clacked together. "Enough. Ye want more trouble? Do ye?"

They weren't listening. The crowd was too loud, Cunnington's hurry too great. As the first lieutenant turned away, she opened her mouth to—

"What is going on here?"

Her scream still stuck in her throat, Jeannette almost fell as she was released. Then the crowd parted, and Lieutenant Treynor came to stand at the forefront, a flush to his face revealing some strong emotion simmering beneath his calm demeanor.

"Do I understand this correctly, Lieutenant Cunnington?" He caught the first lieutenant before he could leave. "Do you mean to have this boy flogged before we so much as leave port?"

Lieutenant Cunnington's lips lifted in a snarl. "Do not interfere."

Jeannette felt Treynor's blue eyes flick over her and blinked hard to hold back the tears that threatened. Could he help her? *Would* he?

Treynor lowered his voice so that only those closest to them could hear. "Is this really necessary? I think the boy has learned his lesson."

Jeannette saw the same tic in Treynor's cheek she had witnessed earlier, when he and the captain spoke of Cunnington, and felt the deep-seated enmity between the two men.

"Everyone knows there is no discipline in the navy without the lash," Cunnington replied. "I think it is time to remind the entire crew."

"What have we here?"

The crowd shifted again. This time Captain Cruikshank emerged, his white eyebrows drawn into a single, furry line. "Cunnington, what are you about?"

Cunnington's attention shifted reluctantly from Treynor to the captain. "I witnessed this boy trying to flee, sir. At a time when we need every able body we can get, I feel it imperative that he be brought to quick justice. The appropriate punishment is outlined in the Articles of War—"

"I know the Articles, Mr. Cunnington," the captain said.

"This is a young boy, only thirteen," Treynor chimed in, appealing to the captain now, too. "And he is new to the navy. With that in mind, surely there must be some other more fitting punishment."

"This from a man who takes a party to shore and comes back with less than the number he started with," Cunnington added derisively.

The captain raised a hand to silence them both, but Jeannette could tell by his expression that he'd already decided against Treynor. Whether her fate had been determined more by Cruikshank's desire to prove his point—that he would not interfere between his lieutenants again—or by the appropriateness of her punishment, she didn't know.

"After Dade's disappearance, I think it time to remind the men of the consequences of such actions," he said. "We cannot have them running off every time we put in." To Treynor, and loud enough for the others, he added, "Discipline is inherent in the smooth functioning of any ship. Vicard might be a boy, but the rules apply to all."

"Twelve lashes, then?" Cunnington asked.

"Ten," the captain replied. "And for God's sake, use some discretion."

"Indeed, Captain." Cunnington gave Treynor a gloating smile. "Let's clear the deck."

"Captain," Treynor said, but they both moved away as he spoke and Jeannette could no longer hear what was said. The captain shook his head, listened some more, shook his head a second time. As they disappeared from view, the deck erupted once again in chaos.

An hour crawled by and not a soul dared talk to her. Following that initial eruption of energy, a strange hush had fallen over the ship. Jeannette needed nothing to bind her in place—her fear was more than enough—but the burly sailor stayed with her. Every once in a while, she shot him a glance. Could she survive a lashing without giving away her gender? She didn't see how . . .

"I have prevailed." Carrying a baize bag, Cunnington returned with another sailor. "Meet the bosun's mate. He will deliver your punishment. But because of your young age, we shall use a light cat. And I just happen to have one."

The bosun's mate hesitated when Cunnington shoved the bag holding the whip at him.

"Do as I say!" Cunnington snapped. "Or you will be next. This is the captain's order."

"Aye, sir." The mate glanced at Jeannette with sorrow in his eyes, but took the whip.

"That's it," Cunnington said in approval, then chucked Jeannette under the chin. "You will be fine. Only ten lashes. 'Tis nothing."

Fighting tears, Jeannette looked around for Treynor. He'd joined the group, but he wasn't saying or doing anything to help her. She couldn't even tell what he was thinking. His expression was an inscrutable mask.

Cunnington tossed him a gloating smile. "Lieutenant, you may record the proceedings and read the relevant section of law aloud for the edification of all. Bosun"—he turned to single Hawker out of the crowd that was forming—"pipe the men to the deck and maintain order. The rules must be observed."

Jeannette heard a small, fearful sound and realized it was her own voice. She tried to shrink away, but it did her no good. The burly sailor had too tight a hold.

"Remove his breeches," Cunnington said.

God, no! She turned beseeching eyes on Treynor. "Sir?"

The man grabbed hold of her trousers, but he didn't get any further than that before the second lieutenant stepped forward. He didn't drag her away from the man who held her tight, as Jeannette wished, but Cunnington didn't appreciate the interruption even still.

"What are you doing?" he asked.

Treynor began unbuttoning his own coat. "Dade's disappearance was my fault, not the lad's," he said, his words terse, his movements quick and decided. "I will take the lashes."

Cunnington's jaw sagged. He turned to the captain, who was just now lumbering up from behind, as did everyone within hearing distance.

"I suggest you let the boy take his due," Cruikshank said. "You will have twice as many if you don't." Resolute, he squinted at Treynor, waiting for his response. Despite his words, Jeannette could tell the captain hoped the lieutenant would listen and back down.

But if Treynor understood Cruikshank's wishes, he did not heed them. Instead, he untied his stock and removed it along with his shirt before stepping up to the grate. "Then I will have twice as many," he said.

Cruikshank shook his head. "You are a stubborn man, Lieutenant Treynor, but so am I." With a nod to Cunnington, he turned and left.

A satisfied smile spread over Cunnington's face as he motioned to the bosun's mate to do what was needed.

A gasp went through those who watched as Cunnington sent someone to his cabin for a sturdier cat-o'-nine, one intended for a man, not a boy. Meanwhile, the bosun's mate tied Treynor to the grate.

"No!" Jeannette had been as quickly forgotten as she was released—but she had to speak up before it was too late. "You cannot flog him!"

Treynor looked heavenward. His broad back already showed an abundance of scars—previous lashings, swordfights. It looked as though he'd even taken a ball. Jeannette had no doubt he knew what to expect. His muscles bulged beneath his skin, rigid with tension, and he clenched his teeth.

"Listen to me! Please!" Lunging forward, she grasped the bosun's mate before he could finish securing the lieutenant. "I can stop this if only—"

Cunnington yanked her away. "You can stop nothing. Stand aside, or I will ask the captain to double his lashes."

Treynor scowled back at her and before she could utter another syllable, a rough hand clamped down over her mouth. Twisting, she tried to pry it away, but whoever held her pulled her back through the crowd.

"Will ye get 'im double, ye little fool?" Mrs. Hawker snarled.

Jeannette continued to squirm, trying to fight off the much heavier and stronger bosun's wife. She had to gain sufficient air to cry out the truth. She had to stop the beating before it began. Except she couldn't so much as breathe. Kicking and flailing, she fought madly as the courier returned with the whip. Then the sound of the rope thongs cracked on the air and Jeannette froze, waiting in agony for Lieutenant Treynor to cry out. But the only sound she heard was the cat singing through air again, striking flesh.

Bosun Hawker came to assist his wife. Between the two of them, Jeannette could no longer move or speak. They held her still, ignoring the tears that coursed down her cheeks.

Treynor's sandy-colored head fell lower with each bite of the whip. Finally, it dipped below the height of the silent crowd, and she could see him no more.

"Look at that," Mrs. Hawker whispered to her husband.

Jeannette cringed inside.

"I told ye this lad was up to no good, but ye 'ad to let 'im go."

The bosun didn't respond, at least to his wife. He stood, still restraining Jeannette and shaking his head in apparent disgust. "I 'ope you're 'appy, lad," he said at last. "That's a fine man ye earned a beatin'." With a nod to Mrs. Hawker, they dragged her below.

His back was on fire. Lieutenant Treynor lay on his side in his dark cabin nearly eight hours after his whipping, trying to ignore the pain by counting the number of years it had been since his last personal encounter with the whip. As a boy one year older than the slight Jean Vicard, he had been sailing under Captain Edward Hamilton, a man known for his brutality.

A man not unlike Lieutenant Cunnington. Treynor's muscles tensed as his mind's eye conjured his superior officer's face. The first lieutenant was a cruel man, and the money and connections that provided him his rank gave him the opportunity to abuse others without reproach.

With a groan, Treynor shifted in his hammock. Twenty lashes was mild punishment compared with the eighty to one hundred most men received. Those who were flogged around the fleet received as many as three hundred, but they usually died.

Still, twenty lashes left an impression. The trick was to give the pain no audience.

A knock at the door made Treynor frown. Who might want him at this time of night and in his current state? The doctor had already rubbed salve on his back. The cook had brought him a bowl of broth for his supper. He wasn't due on deck until morning . . .

"Come in." Momentarily distracted by the promise of a visitor, he would have rolled onto his back had his wounds not prevented the slight movement of raising his head.

A large woman entered, judging by the outline of her bulk. Mrs. Hawker, he realized, blinking against the light that poured into the room from a lamp in the corridor. Only she wasn't alone. She had a boy in tow—Jean Vicard, by Treynor's guess.

"Mrs. Hawker? What—"

The bosun's wife plunged them into darkness by shutting the door behind her. "I hate ter disturb ye," she whispered. "But Mr. Hawker sent me."

In all of his and the Hawkers' acquaintance, never had Treynor known the bosun to send his wife anywhere. She acted only on her own initiative, but she was generally levelheaded, if forthright to a fault. He knew if she stood in his cabin in the middle of the night, she had good reason to be there.

"What is it?"

"Ye might want ter light a lamp." She proffered a small stick of punk, glowing at the tip.

Treynor was as surprised by this request as he was by her unexpected appearance. For what would they need a lamp? Was it truly necessary to make him move?

Biting back a groan, he stood. "You do it," he growled.

"What's going on?" he asked as soon as the lamp's wick caught.

"This." Mrs. Hawker turned flinty eyes on Jean Vicard. "Tell 'im."

The boy glanced at the bosun's wife, then at the floor.

Giving a snort of impatience, Mrs. Hawker reached out and grabbed hold of Vicard's shirt. Treynor heard the fabric tear right before he saw a pair of tightly bound breasts, their soft white flesh swelling above bands that looked tight enough to asphyxiate.

His jaw dropped. The woman—for it was definitely a woman, though she was young, perhaps eighteen—gasped and tried to shield herself from his view.

"Bloody hell!" He stared, swallowed, then glanced back to Mrs. Hawker for some sort of explanation.

The bosun's wife nodded smugly. "Name's Jeannette. She told me just as the mate finished with ye. Couldn't stomach the violence of it. Never seen the likes, I expect."

The young woman hung her head in shame.

"I would 'ave brought 'er right away, but she insisted on cleanin' up first. An' the way she smelled, I had ter agree. Then I began to wonder if it wouldn't be better ter wait until dark. I mean, ye brought 'er aboard an' all. I'd 'ate ter see what Cunnington would try to make of it . . ."

Refusing to gawk any longer, even though he was surely tempted to do so, Treynor clamped his teeth together. Jean Vicard was feminine in the extreme. He'd noticed before, but he'd never suspected . . . damn! The truth now crystallized with amazing rapidity. How could he have been so easily duped?

He knocked her hat to the floor with one hand and grabbed her with the other, dragging her closer to the light. Jagged locks of thick black hair stuck out in an unruly mess above a fine-boned, delicately sculpted face with arched eyebrows, a small nose and a rather sharp chin. A blind man could have seen what he'd missed. Not only was this a woman, she was a beautiful one.

"Hell!" His movements had caused the pain of his stripes to crescendo like some great symphony. He never should have brought Jean Vicard aboard. Had he paid more attention, had the others not been standing within earshot, had Dade not disappeared . . .

"Why?" he demanded.

"She won't say—" Mrs. Hawker started, but Treynor put up a hand to silence her. He needed answers, but the bosun's wife was not the one who could best provide them.

"You can go back and get some sleep, Mrs. Hawker. I will handle this from here. She will tell me what I want to know if I have to beat it out of her."

"But you're in no condition—"

"Which is fortunate for her."

The bosun's wife nodded. "Yes, sir. I am sorry ter disturb ye. I didn't know what else to do—"

Treynor softened his voice. "You did the right thing. Thank you. And please, don't tell anyone about this until I have made a decision."

"Aye, sir. Ye've been right good ter me and Mr. Hawker. I'll leave the matter up to ye an' not speak a word of it to anyone. Not a word."

"Very well." Treynor held himself rigid until after she left. Then he moved to the only chair in his crowded cabin and carefully sat down. The change in position did little to relieve his misery.

"So. Do you volunteer the information, or must I drag it out of you?" he asked. "I should think, after everything you have put me through today, that you would cooperate to that extent."

He studied the abject girl before him. There was something vaguely familiar about her. Had he met Jeannette before? What could have motivated her to dress like a boy?

Suddenly, her petite size, and the fact that she was wearing trousers, connected with a memory—a very vivid and recent memory.

He sprang to his feet. "Dear God! You're the woman! The one in my bed!"

She backed up until she bumped against the far wall. "No. I do not know what you are talking about." A blush stained her cheeks, revealing her words for the lie that they were.

"Let me refresh your memory," he said. "We were nearly naked, the two of us. In my bed. You were warm and responsive"—he advanced upon her—"as eager as any barmaid I have ever met, until you had me so full of lust I would have done anything for the pleasure of five more minutes with your glorious body. Then you—"

"Enough." She clapped her hands over her ears—an infantile gesture, but proof in itself.

"You don't deny it?"

"No."

"Then why?"

"Why what?"

"Why are you wearing these clothes? Why did you come to my room last night and damn near do me in? Why did you join His Majesty's navy and then try to desert, managing to get me flogged in the process?"

Treynor realized that he was almost shouting and struggled to keep his voice down. "I will have those answers, for a start."

She bit her lip and did what she could to avoid his gaze. "I had to steal Dade's clothes to join the navy. Appearing in your room was an accident that I could remedy only by"—her voice faltered—"by the action I took."

"You could have said something."

"I was frightened. I did not know what you would do."

He glowered at her. "And you are here now because . . ."

Her words started slow, then came in a rush. "I lost my post as a governess and had no other way to provide for myself."

"Like hell!" Treynor pounded his desk, then winced at the pain it caused him. "That man on the docks was looking for you. That is why you couldn't say anything last night. You didn't want me to know who you were."

Her eyes widened. "No!"

"You have to be the baron's wife. There is no other explanation for all of this. Had your husband's solicitor mentioned that the woman he sought was French, perhaps I would have realized sooner that you were no boy." He scrubbed his face with his hand. "But I stupidly fell for your ruse, to the point of taking twenty stripes. You must be very proud of yourself. Perhaps you should take up the stage instead of navy life."

"Please stop shouting. Others will hear." She squared her shoulders and lowered her voice. "You volunteered for the flogging. I did not mean for it to happen, to either of us."

"You did nothing to stop it." Treynor grabbed her by both arms, noting with satisfaction the fear that flickered behind her eyes, fear she struggled to mask as she glared up at him.

"Do not touch me! You are going too far."

"Whatever I do will be less than what you deserve. Did you ever stop to think how your actions might affect those around you—like me, for instance?"

"You were the last person on my mind."

"That, I believe. You are not the first lady I have met who could not see beyond her own wants and desires."

"I couldn't say anything—"

"Because you were too busy trying to escape your new husband, who happens to be a friend of my own mother's."

Jeannette reached up to remove his hand from her arm. Her fingers were as cold as ice, but her voice remained surprisingly steady. "You know him?"

"I know of him."

"He is not what he appears."

"Many people aren't. You have proven that quite nicely." The light scent of soap on her skin brought back the feel of her, nearly naked, in his arms, and with that came the memory of her painful blow to his groin and a fresh desire for revenge. He smiled. His mystery woman hadn't escaped him after all; he would take great pleasure in making her pay. "Take off Dade's clothes. The ripped shirt—the trousers—everything."

"What?" Her bottom lip quivered but he saw no tears.

"You heard me."

"But I . . . I have nothing on beneath them."

Treynor's grin widened. "I know."

"I will not let you force yourself on me." She spoke imperiously but with a slight tremble to her voice.

He laughed. "I am interested in a more subtle form of revenge. And the thought of getting some sleep appeals to me. If you do not have any clothes, you cannot go anywhere."

She squeezed her arms more tightly over her chest, a protective gesture that did little to soften Treynor's heart. This woman could have stopped him from being beaten had she only revealed herself soon enough.

"If you do not want to cooperate, I will help you." After pulling his dirk from its scabbard on his desk, he sliced the fabric of Dade's shirt in half in a completely new place than the one Jeannette held closed already.

She screamed and tried to whirl away, but he tossed the dirk on the floor before she could cut herself on it and shoved her up against the wall.

"You little idiot. You will bring the captain down on us if you are not careful, and I am not sure I want that just yet. Give me Dade's clothes and be done with it."

The sting of her nails across his chest made Treynor begin to strip her in earnest. He ripped off Dade's shirt. "This is for the knee to my groin," he told her as he tore the shirt into strips. "And this"—he grinned as he pulled the baggy breeches down over her hips—"is for my stripes."

"You fool! Now what will I do?" Her chest heaved above the white bands that bound her breasts, as if she couldn't draw a deep breath.

"We are not finished yet, my sweet." He retrieved his dirk. "Hold still."

Covering her head with her arms, she hunched into her shoulders as though she expected him to slit her throat. When he simply cut away the strips of fabric she'd knotted around her chest, Jeannette used her hands to shield herself. But Treynor wasn't about to let her hide or huddle in a corner. Her wrists clamped tightly in one of his hands, he hauled her forward, though the effort agonized him, and tied her to the brass handles of his sea trunk, using the same strips of fabric he'd just cut off her.

"I cannot believe I felt badly about seeing you flogged," she seethed when he stood back to admire his handiwork. "I hope your back pains you greatly."

Treynor's eyes traveled the length of her firm, supple body. He had to admit he'd seen few women more beautiful. She had round, full breasts despite her small size—making him marvel that she'd been able to pull off the boy masquerade at all—a flat belly, and slender limbs.

The sudden tightening in his groin annoyed him. "That ought to keep me safe from your mischief for a while."

She glared at him. "You will be sorry. My father is the Comte de Lumfcrc. He will not allow you to get away with this!"

Treynor chuckled and fixed his gaze on her chest. "You and your father should be grateful."

"Grateful?" she repeated incredulously.

"You are getting off easily. If I wanted to, I could take what you so foolishly promised me at The Stag." He ran a finger over her collarbone. "What would your father think of that?"

She shrugged his hand away, but Treynor marked the goose pimples that dotted her flesh. "He would see you hanged."

He swiped at some blood that had seeped through his bandages to trickle down his lower back. "Lucky for both of us that I am in no condition to tumble you about my hammock."

Giving her a mocking bow, he headed to bed, although he doubted he could sleep. His back pained him, but what bothered him more was that he was perfectly capable of finishing what they had begun at The Stag.

And, count's daughter or no, he still wanted to.

Chapter 8

Under her breath, Jeannette called Treynor every name she could imagine and wished she knew a few worse ones to use. She didn't care that a lady never spoke in such a way. Never had she felt more desperate, more humiliated or more vulnerable.

She sat on the cold, hard floor, hugging her knees to her chest, and rocked back and forth to keep herself from crying. Much to her relief, the lieutenant had locked the door, blown out the light and was settling into his hammock. She was rid of him for the moment, but morning would come, and she'd still be naked and tied to his blasted trunk.

"I hope you bleed to death in your sleep," she mumbled, only half expecting a response.

He laughed. "I doubt you want that. The men who would find you in such a compromising position would not treat you half so well as I have. Do you think most sailors would care if you are a baron's wife or a count's daughter when the promise of your sweet flesh awaits them?"

Jeannette shuddered at the thought of what might happen should she be discovered. Most of the men on the ship hadn't had a bath in months. Then there was Cunnington, of course. His manner and dress bespoke a man of gentle birth, someone, perhaps, of her own class. But she knew Lieutenant Cunnington was no gentleman at heart.

"What are you going to do with me in the morning?" she asked.

"Don't know. Probably take you to the captain."

Jeannette's heart sank. "But he will have me escorted back to Plymouth, to the baron."

"Exactly."

"I will not go."

"May I remind you that you are sitting naked on my floor? You are in no position to tell me what you will or will not do."

At first Jeannette didn't respond. When she did, she made her words as beseeching as possible. "You have had your revenge, no? If it makes you feel any better"—she fought the slight wobble in her voice—"I am terribly sorry. Do you hear? I had no intention of getting you flogged, or of having such an . . . intimate encounter at the tavern."

Treynor sighed. "Evidently you have no idea what it feels like to be flogged if you think a pretty apology is enough. Can we please get some sleep?"

"Will you leave me at the dock and say nothing of my identity at least?"

"I cannot. The flogging drew too much attention to you. I will need to gain the captain's sanction before I take you home, which means revealing why you must go back."

"No!"

When the lieutenant's voice grew louder, Jeannette guessed he had turned to face her. "Yes. The moment news of your femininity gets out, Cunnington, at the very least, will not rest until he knows who you are and why you were here. Like my mother, his parents are friends of your husband's, so I doubt he will give you much sympathy."

"I will be gone by the time they figure everything out."

"You might be gone, but I won't. I am the first person Cunnington would suspect of helping you, since I stepped in on your behalf once already. And I will not have your husband call in favors to strip me of my post."

Jeannette squeezed her eyes closed. She wouldn't cry. She wouldn't . . .

One rebellious tear fell.

"Have I answered all your questions?" he asked. "Can we go to sleep now?"

Jeannette didn't respond. She swiped at her cheek, vowing to get even with Lieutenant Treynor. She'd not go back to St. Ives, even if she had to gnaw through the bands on her wrists with her teeth.

The room fell silent, except for the creaking of the ship, which soon worked better than a lullaby on Jeannette's weary body. Well into her second sleepless night, she felt exhaustion pressing down on her like an invisible hand. Arms sagging, eyelids growing heavy, she caught her head several times when it threatened to fall from its precarious perch on her knees. Then she heard Treynor get up and her spine went rigid as he rustled about. What was he doing?

After a moment, he came close and she tensed further, but she had nothing to fear. He was only draping a blanket around her shoulders.

Jeannette didn't speak as he walked away. She hoped he'd think her asleep. When she dared move, she pulled the blanket as tight as she could with the slack he'd allowed her, and felt an almost overwhelming sense of relief for the chance to cover her nakedness. The blanket he'd given her still held the warmth of his body and did much to relieve the chill in the drafty room.

"Was your marriage arranged?" he asked out of the darkness.

"Do you think I would choose a man older than my father?" Jeannette replied, burying her face in the blanket and trying to ignore the subtle scent that clung to it—Treynor's scent—as she warmed her nose.

"The Baron St. Ives is rich and powerful. He has an impressive pedigree. Isn't that what a woman wants?"

Now that the rain had stopped, moonlight filtered through the circle of a single porthole. Jeannette squinted at the lieutenant even though she could see little more than the hazy silhouette of his body and the quilt he'd kicked to the bottom of the hammock.

"Oui," she responded on a sigh. "We are all shallow, uncaring creatures."

When Treynor spoke again, it was on an entirely different subject. "Aren't you going to thank me for cutting those bands away? Or have you too much pride to take it as the kindness it was meant to be?"

Jeannette pressed her forearms to her breasts. They still ached. Her body could not have withstood the pressure of the bindings much longer. "How did you know?"

He chuckled. "I am intimately familiar with certain parts of a woman's anatomy—and yours in particular, remember?"

She cursed herself for being stupid enough to ask. "You could not have been thinking honorable thoughts to have realized it."

"I never said I was thinking honorable thoughts."

"You are no gentleman, *monsieur*."

"I won't argue with you there. If it makes you feel any better, you are not the only one who thinks so."

Jeannette didn't know how long it was before Treynor's breathing evened out, but she guessed, with his back in the condition it was, he could not be sleeping soundly. The deep cuts crisscrossing his flesh still oozed blood. She winced to imagine how it must have felt to be Cunnington's pawn, and had to admit that Treynor was right to hate her. But she had too much at stake to allow him to take her to the captain. She had to escape, and long before morning.

Using her feet as leverage, she yanked against her bonds, hoping they'd give way, but the fabric cut into her wrists without loosening. She bit her lip against the pain and started to work the knots, quickly growing too nervous to take the time to do it right. In just a few hours, the entire ship would know about her, and she'd have no chance of reaching London.

Not that she had much of a chance now. Gasping from her efforts, she leaned her forehead on the wood, trying to think of another way. Perhaps she could find something on the desk to help her. She'd already tried searching for the lieutenant's dirk and hadn't been able to find it.

The trunk was heavy, but she managed to drag it by inches. The scraping sound seemed to reverberate through the cabin, but there was nothing she could do about it. The creaking of the ship's timbers was nearly loud enough to mask it. It certainly seemed as if he were oblivious—until he grunted. Then she froze.

The blanket he had given her was somewhere on the floor behind her. She'd been unable to hang on to it and drag the trunk at the same time. She had only the darkness to cloak her—and felt the scantiness of that covering all too poignantly.

Had she awakened him? She thought so. But then his breathing grew steady again. He seemed to be dreaming, or reacting to the wounds on his back. She had no idea what the lieutenant would do if he caught her, but she'd seen enough to know he had a temper.

Sweat rolled down Jeannette's back as she pressed on and, eventually, she reached her goal. The light filtering in from beneath the door and through that one porthole coaxed her to wrench free, find something to wear and slip out into the hallway. Stowaways were common enough in the navy. Perhaps she could hide until they reached London. It was a chance, however small. If she did nothing, she'd be returned to St. Ives at dawn.

Rising to her knees, she pulled as far from the trunk as her bonds would allow so she could examine what Treynor had on his desk. His dirk had to be somewhere. He'd used it to remove the bindings. But precisely where had he put it?

Papers and shadowy objects covered that horizontal space. Jeannette squinted, wishing for more light, and tried to get closer. Finally, she rolled onto her back and used her feet to scoop all she could reach onto the floor, turning her face away when an avalanche of paper and other articles came showering down on top of her.

The noise seemed earth-shattering, but Treynor didn't stir, so Jeannette struggled into a crouched position and studied the objects on the floor. A quill pen—thank God she hadn't knocked herself senseless with its heavy holder or splattered herself with ink—a few coins, maps, various papers, letters . . . and a letter opener!

Dragging the trunk a few inches closer, Jeannette retrieved the sharp instrument with her teeth, put it into her right hand and stabbed at the fabric, ignoring the pain such an unnatural position caused her wrists.

After what seemed like forever, she cut far enough into the fabric that she could tear the rest away, and finally, *finally*, she was free.

Now to get out of the room before Treynor awoke. She started working the latch on the trunk so she could steal a shirt to go with Dade's breeches when footsteps thundered down the hall outside, and a heavy fist, judging from the racket it made, thudded on the cabin door.

"Lieutenant!"

Jeannette stifled a squeal and ducked beneath the desk.

Treynor shot up and lunged toward the sound. "What is it?" he asked, his voice muddled by sleep as he unlocked the door and peered out through a narrow crack.

"The captain wants you in his cabin right away, sir."

With a groan, Treynor scrubbed the sleep from his face. "What's going on?"

Jeannette's pulse raced as they talked. What now? As soon as his visitor left, he'd turn and see the trunk out of its place and realize she was free.

She'd never escape without a weapon. Her eyes and hands sought Treynor's jacket, slung over the chair in front of her. She felt its heavy wool, the thick gold braid, the round brass buttons and the leather strap beneath it before her fingers located his pistol.

The heaviness of the gun felt foreign in her hands—cold, alien, frightening—but she had to do something.

Careful to stay out of the line of sight of the person who'd come to fetch him, she crept out from beneath the desk and slid around behind Treynor. Gripping the pistol by its iron muzzle, she rose silently, lifting it above her head with both hands. Timing would be everything . . .

The stranger finished telling Treynor he had no idea why the captain wanted to see him. Then Treynor shut the door and she brought the gun down with all her strength, aiming for his crown.

Jeannette expected the lieutenant to crumble at her feet. She didn't anticipate the lightning-quick move that caused the blow to glance off his shoulder.

"What the devil!" He spun and slammed her back against the desk, seeking control of the weapon.

Jeannette clung to the muzzle with all the tenacity she could muster. If Treynor gained possession of the gun, she'd have nothing to stop him from doing whatever he pleased.

The lieutenant was bigger and stronger by far, but she'd taken him by surprise. For a moment, Jeannette thought that small advantage might be enough to preserve her weapon, but then he twisted, gained a better grip and together they crashed to the floor.

Fortunately the lieutenant took the brunt of the fall. Jeannette knew by the curse he muttered how badly it had cost him and felt a fleeting concern for the wounds on his back. Surely they'd start bleeding again. But she couldn't give up the fight. If he'd been angry before, he'd show her no mercy now.

"What are you trying to do? Kill me?" He rolled on top of her and pinned her hands above her head.

Jeannette still grasped the pistol, but the pistol did her little good while he held her wrists in the vise of his hands.

He was stretched out on top of her, so damnably heavy she could scarcely move. Laboring to suck some air into her lungs, she gasped, "If I had wanted to kill you, I would have shot you dead."

He shook his head in disbelief. "Your husband should be glad to be rid of you. You're too wild to make anyone a good wife."

"I won't go back!" Infinitely aware of her nakedness, Jeannette began to squirm again. She managed to raise a knee halfway to the lieutenant's groin, but he shifted before she could reach her intended target.

"Oh, no you don't! Not again!" He squeezed her sore wrists until tears trickled from the corners of her eyes. Then he shook her hands, banging the gun on the floor like a hammer, but she gritted her teeth and held fast.

"Let go, you little hellion." Finally, he wrenched the gun from her grasp and slid it away from her. "What in the name of God is wrong with you?" he demanded, straddling her middle and keeping her arms pinned above her head.

Jeannette blinked several times, trying to still the quiver of her chin. He was too heavy, her hands hurt and now she had nothing to stop him from returning her to St. Ives, who would no doubt exact a costly revenge for her escape.

"Don't start crying, dammit. I'm not so easily swayed."

The mere mention of tears weakened the tenuous grasp Jeannette had on her emotions. The more she tried to hold back, the greater her need to cry. Fat teardrops blurred her vision and dampened her temples as they rolled back into her hair.

"Get off me. There is nothing I can do to you now."

"No? Well, there is still plenty I would like to do to you. A good spanking would not be undeserved, I think. You might tweak your husband's nose and get away with it, but your little escapades have cost me a pound of flesh in the most literal sense. Tell me, how merciful should I be?"

"I expect no mercy from a lowborn sailor, and neither will I ask for it."

His grip tightened. "Feeling superior, are we?"

Jeannette detected a harder edge to his voice than she'd heard him use before and couldn't help needling him further. She was so angry and miserable and desperate. "You are a pig."

"If I am to be classed with swine, perhaps I shall act the part. We sailors are a rough lot, forever hungering for a woman after going weeks, even months, without the comforts of the flesh. And I am no different."

The sparkle in his eye made Jeannette wonder what she had provoked in him.

"Except that I am more familiar with your kind than you might think," he continued, "titled ladies who are all show and manners on the surface while holding their virginity like a prize to be awarded to the highest bidder."

Jeannette stiffened at his cutting words. "How dare you—"

"No, how foolish of you, my pretty friend, to risk yourself by coming among such men. Or were you hoping for something a little more stirring than polite?" He bent his head and claimed her lips in a harsh, demanding kiss.

She squirmed and tried to twist away, but he held her fast, forcing her to capitulate, dominating her will as effectively as her body.

"What's the matter?" he murmured against her mouth. "You didn't seem to mind at The Stag."

Jeannette felt the warmth of his breath on her face and longed to inhale it in spite of his hateful words. She didn't know when she quit fighting him, or when Treynor let go of her wrists, but every sense brimmed with his sinewy flesh and the musky smell of his body.

Letting her arms circle his neck, she returned his kiss with all the feverish intensity that swelled within her. She wanted something from him she couldn't quite understand, and needed to vent her own anger and passion as freely as he had.

His hand grasped her breast almost painfully, that single action more erotic than anything Jeannette had ever imagined as his tongue invaded her mouth.

Frustrated by something she could not name, Jeannette tried to push him away, but he was too strong and too angry. Her efforts had no effect—until she sank her teeth deep in his lip. Then Treynor recoiled, breathing hard.

"I have to go," he said tersely, wiping blood from the corner of his mouth with the back of his hand.

The tattered strips of fabric lay on the floor. Recovering them, he tied Jeannette to his trunk again. "That ought to keep you here until I get back." He tested the knots to be sure they'd hold, then gazed down at her with an unfathomable expression. Finally, he took the letter opener, dirk and pistol, dressed, and left, slamming the door behind him.

Treynor stalked down the corridor, tasting the blood on his lip and chafing from the feel of his heavy uniform on his lacerated back—all thanks to the she-devil in his cabin. But his stripes didn't bother him half so much as what had transpired in the past ten minutes. He'd never forced his attentions on a woman before; he'd never even wanted to. Jeannette drove him wild.

How could a slip of a girl with chopped-off hair and sailor's garb inadvertently trigger such desire? She was rich and spoiled—a lady of his mother's ilk and French to boot. The pretentiousness, the haughtiness, the lies: he despised it all.

A muscle began to twitch in his cheek as Treynor tried to distance himself from the pain associated with any reminder of his mother. Captain Cruikshank wanted him. He had to keep his eye on his duty if he were ever to prove to himself that he needed nothing, and wanted even less, from Lady Bedford.

As he emerged on deck, Treynor felt the sprinkle of a light rain on his face. The sea was calm, a steady wind rocked the ship as gently as a cradle, and only a few lamps competed with the stars that glimmered through the thin clouds overhead. Such mellow weather was rare this time of year and offered hope that the morning would be clear and bright: a perfect day to set sail.

"Evening, Lieutenant."

Treynor nodded as one of the ship's carpenters saluted.

He needn't worry about Jeannette, he thought, moving on. He'd return her in a matter of hours, possibly search for Dade, since the party he had sent out for him earlier hadn't been able to find him, then be on his way. The hope of prize money should they capture a French or other merchant ship would keep him occupied until he eventually achieved his long-coveted promotion to the rank of post-captain. His career had always been enough before.

Cruikshank glanced up when Treynor entered the cabin. Along with Cunnington, two other lieutenants and a couple of midshipmen, the captain sat at a table in the center of the room. Two cannons, a rolltop desk, several cushioned bench seats with plenty of storage beneath and a hammock filled the rest of the space. The rear of the ship rarely came under fire, so this cabin had windows as well, to give the captain a good view and to let in as much natural light as possible, although dawn had not yet arrived.

"Lieutenant Treynor." Cruikshank hefted himself to his feet, clasped his hands behind his back and began to pace between the two cannons on opposite sides of his cabin.

"Captain, sir." Treynor saluted and nodded to the others.

Toddy Pratt and Richard Knuthson, the third and fourth lieutenants, along with the midshipmen, greeted him, making an effort to treat him as though the flogging had never occurred. Cunnington, on the other hand, relished the memory. The first lieutenant sat erect, watching him with a hawk's eye, so well groomed there was no way to tell he'd been summoned from his bed in the middle of the night.

Fleetingly, Treynor considered his own appearance. No doubt he looked like he'd been dragged behind a horse. He certainly felt like it.

"You sent for me?" he asked, curious as to the significance of this late-night gathering.

The captain pivoted to face him, pursing his lips until the lines around his mouth deepened into grooves. He motioned toward the table, where Treynor spied a folded piece of foolscap. "A courier has delivered a letter via boat. It is from the Baron St. Ives."

Treynor took this information in, but kept his expression impassive.

"Mayhap you are familiar with the name," the captain continued. "His estate is not far from Plymouth."

"I am sure the lieutenant would have no opportunity to associate with a nobleman," Cunnington interjected.

Pratt and Knuthson and the midshipmen looked slightly uncomfortable as Cruikshank sent his first lieutenant an irritated glance. "St. Ives is a Tory. The government being what it is today, he wields significant power in Parliament and, hence, the navy."

"I know of him," Treynor admitted. Although the captain had just presented him with the perfect opportunity to divulge Jeannette's identity, Cunnington's manner, as always, incited Treynor's temper. He wanted to hear the captain out before he did anything. "The baron married last night, I hear," he added, smiling at Cunnington as he took the seat opposite him. "My mother was in attendance."

"Maybe your father was there, too," Cunnington said. "But who can say? Even you don't know who he is."

"That's enough," Cruikshank barked. "It seems that his young wife disappeared after the wedding feast. Lord St. Ives has traced her movements to Plymouth, and because we were slated to put in at London, where she has family or friends or somesuch, he thinks she might have boarded the *Tempest*."

"A baroness stowed away on a frigate?" Lieutenant Pratt exclaimed.

"Ludicrous," Cunnington said and the midshipmen seemed to agree.

"She must be insane to run away in the first place," Cruikshank countered. "When her husband gets hold of her, no doubt she will have the devil to pay. But here is my dilemma: we have received new orders. We no longer need to pick up that diplomat in London. It seems the *Phoenix* can take him in our stead."

"Which means what?" Pratt asked. "We head straight out to sea?"

"Aye." The captain took up a pipe from his bureau and added tobacco from a pouch in his pocket. Although smoking was banned as a fire hazard, no one was going to remind Cruikshank of that. "Admiral MacBride wants us to join the Western Squadron south of Brest. There is an American convoy on its way to France, and the blockade is stretching thin."

"A blockade that extends all the way from the North Sea into the Bay of Biscay needs every ship it can get," Treynor said. "But what of the baron?"

"He wants us to allow his men access to the ship come morning to search for her. But I do not take kindly to the thought, I will tell you. We must stop that grain convoy. And if we are forced to wait here, we will probably miss it."

"Our duty to king and country is far more important than a baron's silly wife," one of the midshipmen agreed.

"Indeed." The captain stroked his chin.

"Does he think the war will wait until he solves his domestic problems?" Pratt asked.

"The war might not wait for the Baron St. Ives, but we had better," Cunnington said.

The captain shook his head. "I have no sympathy for a man who cannot keep track of his wife for one full day."

"While we were in town yesterday, I heard he was to marry a woman less than half his age," Knuthson said. "He's probably furious that she robbed him of his wedding night."

"He has every right to drag her back, kicking and screaming," Cunnington pointed out. "Legally, she belongs to him."

Cruikshank drained the glass of brandy that awaited him on the sideboard. "True. So do we stay?"

"I say yes." Cunnington flicked a speck of lint off his uniform. "If she is here and we do not allow the baron his search, then we have made a powerful enemy."

Every time Cunnington spoke, Treynor found his support shifting more firmly in Jeannette's favor. But he was already naturally inclined to sympathize with the underdog, especially when it sounded as though the Baron St. Ives expected the world to stop spinning if he only asked. "What if we formed our own search party?" he asked. "The tide should be in our favor for seven hours. We could spend a short time looking and then, if the wind holds and we don't find the lady, we set sail as scheduled."

"That just might mollify the baron without causing us any delay," Pratt said.

Cruikshank nodded slowly. "Perhaps that is best."

"Or I could search for her myself," Treynor said. "I am not up to much else in my current condition."

When Cunnington smiled at the reference to his stripes, Treynor smiled, too, but only on the inside. With any luck, he'd just distracted the first lieutenant from what he really hoped to accomplish—and that was to obtain the search detail. He wasn't completely sure he would keep Jeannette's secret in the long term, but he found he wasn't quite ready to reveal her, either.

Cruikshank lit his pipe before sitting heavily in his chair. "Why don't the seven of you see what you can find? If we discover any evidence to indicate the baroness might have joined us, we will go from there. If not, we are clear to sail. But we haven't much time, so you had better be quick about it."

"Aye, aye, sir." Lieutenant Cunnington stood, saluted and moved toward the door. Knuthson, Pratt and the midshipmen did the same.

"Is there something else?" Cruikshank asked Treynor when he made no move to follow them.

Treynor hesitated. He didn't want to get more involved in Jeannette's problems than he already was, but the thought of her with a man like the baron bothered him. St. Ives was ancient; he'd dabbled in politics far longer than Treynor had been alive. Marriage to such a man seemed like a travesty, considering Jeannette's youth and vivacity.

"What if the baron's wife *is* here, and she doesn't want to go back?" he asked.

"We have no choice but to return her," Cruikshank replied. "You heard Cunnington. She belongs to St. Ives, just as surely as his house and his lands belong to him."

"We could put her off the ship discreetly."

"Why, when we could collect the reward?" Cunnington had paused at the door.

"What about Dade?" Treynor asked, stalling for time to think.

Cruikshank scowled. "If we took the time to search for every man who ran off, we would never leave England. Forget about Dade. Sometimes you take your duty too seriously, Lieutenant, if that's possible. Is there anything else?" A look of impatience etched itself into the creases of the captain's face. Treynor glanced over his shoulder to see that Cunnington still watched him, as well.

"No, sir. I will start looking immediately."

Silently calling himself a fool, Treynor's tongue played with the small cut Jeannette's teeth had left in his lip as he brushed past the first lieutenant. He was making a mistake, but for some reason he couldn't give her away. Not yet.

Before returning to his cabin, Treynor visited the bosun and his wife to ask Mrs. Hawker to keep her silence and to alter a set of clothes to fit Jeannette. Then he headed back, wondering at the reception he'd receive when he told the baron's wife she'd be a passenger on the *Tempest* for a while longer.

He smiled to think of Cunnington searching for the very woman who was safely ensconced in his cabin, but that smile froze on his face when he opened the door. The cloth strips he'd used to tie Jeannette up were once again piled on the floor.

She was gone.

Chapter 9

Hunching her shoulders and keeping her head down, Jeannette hurried along the companionway. There'd been no time to bind her breasts, and she was only too aware of her bosom bouncing as she walked.

Fortunately Treynor's shirt was even baggier than Dade's. Despite having rolled the sleeves back several times, the cuffs fell to the tips of her fingers. But at least the lieutenant had had plain clothes in his trunk.

The predawn light was dim below the gun deck, despite the open gunport. Only a few whale-oil lamps illuminated several sailors as they began the daily ritual of scrubbing the decks. Immersed in their work, they scarcely glanced up when she passed.

Jeannette was grateful for their preoccupation and this bit of housekeeping. Maybe it would alleviate some of the more pungent smells. Except that the constant washing never allowed the lower decks to dry, despite the use of portable stoves.

Her stomach growled as she went below and wearily searched for some place to hide. She'd been loath to venture into the unfamiliar ship amid five hundred strangers, but Treynor had left her no choice. She couldn't sit and wait in his cabin, tied to his trunk like a cow, until the captain sent her back to St. Ives. She had to reach London and have her marriage annulled. And the only way she was going to do that was by disappearing until they reached port.

An increase in activity, evidenced by the tramping of numerous feet and the hum of voices, sent fear prickling down Jeannette's spine. Treynor had to have told the captain about her by now. Were they searching for her? Would they postpone their departure on her account?

Surely a runaway wife was insignificant when compared to the mission of a frigate, especially during war.

But her husband was a very powerful man . . .

She turned a corner and discovered the steward's store. A glimpse at the shelves and floor revealed marked barrels of dried peas, hardtack and slabs of salt pork and preserved beef. A man with his back to her took stock of these commodities while Jeannette stared with longing at stacked rounds of cheese and fresh bread, dainties reserved for the officers. She would have traded a fortune in gold for just one slice of cheese or even a crust of bread. But, afraid of drawing the man's attention, she forced herself to move on.

Not far from the steward's larder, she eased past several carpenters storing their planking and fittings. Staying in the shadows, she hoped to go unnoticed amid the constant motion around her.

A few minutes later, grunting sounds drew her attention to a manger filled with pigs. Two men stood on the far side of the pen, pouring slop into a trough. They were nearly finished—soon they would leave.

Making it a good place to hide.

She hung back until the men took their buckets and left, then sallied forth. Certainly on their first day out of port the animals would require little attention. And this early in the voyage the pens were relatively clean.

Or so she hoped.

After scrambling over the wall, she burrowed beneath the straw along the edge farthest from the trough and cradled her head in her arms. By turning her face into the fabric of Treynor's shirt, she did what she could to block out the stench and tried not to think about the manure the straw was meant to sweeten.

The hogs grunted as they ate. They were sure to smell her and come rooting around her hiding place, perhaps even step on her. But for the moment she was alone, and even the fear of being trampled by pigs couldn't keep her from falling asleep.

Treynor was furious, at himself and Jeannette. He'd taken a risk to help her, and she'd ruined their odds by disappearing from his cabin. Now Cunnington or any of the others could find her as easily as he could.

Perhaps he had one small advantage: they were looking for a woman.

He headed around the carpenter's walk, hoping Jeannette had somehow managed to hide herself in the narrow passageway just below the waterline. Used mostly by the carpenters to check for leaks, it was deserted now, which would make getting her back to his cabin easier. But what were the chances of finding her in the first place he looked?

None, evidently. There was no trace of her.

Treynor completed his search and headed out, startled to see Cunnington blocking his way.

"No fair maidens?" the first lieutenant asked, evidently coming to inspect the carpenter's walk himself.

Treynor shook his head, now glad he hadn't found Jeannette. Towing Jean Vicard behind him might have looked curious. Treynor wanted nothing to connect Jeannette with Vicard, for once such a thought passed through Cunnington's head, the truth would be obvious. "Not yet."

"Have you checked the hold?"

"Aye, briefly." He lied to discourage the first lieutenant from taking any interest in the belly of the ship, just in case. "I doubt a baroness could survive the smell of the place."

A flicker of distaste passed over Cunnington's features before his face twisted into a taunting jeer. "Did you descend to the bilge?"

"Of course."

"I admire your strength. Your back cannot have healed so soon."

Treynor smiled. "My injuries are nothing to concern yourself with. A woman could have caused more damage," he replied and walked away.

"Lieutenant Treynor!" Mrs. Hawker called after him, hustling down the companionway to meet him.

From behind, Cunnington hissed something about Treynor's low birth. Treynor heard the word "bastard" but, refusing to let Cunnington bait him, he focused on the bosun's wife. "What is it?"

She waited until Cunnington had stalked away before speaking, then glanced around as though she were still afraid they would be overheard. "I 'ave the clothes ye need."

"Thank you. Put them in my cabin, please."

He turned to continue his search, but stopped when he felt her hand on his arm. "I 'ope ye know what yer doin', sir. When ye came to my cabin ter ask for the clothes, ye said nothin' about the lass bein' a baron's wife."

With the number of officers searching the ship, Treynor wasn't surprised Mrs. Hawker had already learned Jeannette's true identity. Nothing escaped the bosun—and the minute Mr. Hawker knew something, Mrs. Hawker knew it better.

"Makes no difference."

"Aye, it does! Now that the captain an' Cunnington know about 'er, you 'ave to give 'er up."

"Why?"

"Because ye can't 'ide her forever. Think what it would do to yer career if ye was to be caught doin' what yer doin'! Cunnington would finally 'ave a serious complaint against ye!"

Treynor had long known that Mrs. Hawker felt motherly toward him, but he didn't have time to be waylaid now. "I am not planning to hide her forever. Soon the *Tempest* will be too far from Plymouth to turn back, even if the captain realizes she's on board. That could buy her a month, maybe more, depending on the war. She might even be able to get off at another port."

Mrs. Hawker propped fisted hands on her hips. "An' if yer caught?"

"We only need a few days. We can manage that easily enough, but not if Knuthson or Cunnington or someone else gets to her before I do."

Lines appeared in Mrs. Hawker's forehead. "It makes no sense for ye ter take the risk."

And Treynor couldn't explain it. He had a weakness for a pretty face, that was all. He knew he should wash his hands of her, put an end to the trouble she'd caused him. But he hated to send her back to a man who would crush her fiery spirit.

"For some reason, she's afraid of the baron."

"And ye feel obliged to play the gallant?" The older woman regarded him shrewdly. "But it's none of yer affair."

"It is now."

Mrs. Hawker heaved a sigh and released him. "Most stowaways try ter get as far below as possible," she said grudgingly.

"I shall begin at the front hold," he said, but he doubted the delicate Jeannette would go below—or stay there if she found it. Everything drained into the ballast. On some French vessels, dead men were buried there. Even without human decay, the ballast reeked, awash in bilge. Although the *Tempest* had been fumigated while they were in port, the fumes caused by sprinkling vinegar and brimstone over braziers of hot coals often made one sicker than the original stench.

But the baroness had to be somewhere. Could be anywhere. Which meant he had to look everywhere.

With a conspiratorial wink at the bosun's wife, he hurried away, shifting in his jacket to keep his shirt from sticking to his back. Part of him was stubborn enough to let Jeannette face the consequences of her actions alone, as Mrs. Hawker evidently thought he should, but another part—a stronger part—urged him to continue looking.

The beat of a sea chantey rose like the pounding of distant drums. All hands were gathered around the capstan, hauling in the anchor so they could set sail. The chanteyman's verses changed according to his whim, often making good-natured fun of the officers. Treynor smiled to himself when the men joined in for the chorus. He wondered whether his fellow officers would now give up the search and if Knuthson and Pratt had found anything.

Ignoring the lure of the song that beckoned him back to his duty, he headed to a narrow room at the heart of the ship where the spare sails were folded and piled high. But a thorough search of the area left Treynor as empty-handed and even more irritable than before. When he got hold of Jeannette, he'd turn her over his knee and warm her backside as she deserved.

The anchor cable was stored next door to the sails—another good hiding place if they were at sea. For now, Treynor doubted Jeannette would go where men would be coiling the wet, heavy hemp cable on the slatted floor. So he passed the cable room and headed to the gangway that would take him down to the hold.

Before long, Lieutenant Cunnington would surely give up the search to supervise the deck, he thought. The bosun's mate would pipe, "All hands, up hammocks," at promptly seven thirty, and the rest of the crew would go topside. After they stowed the last of the hammocks, the captain would appear at eight bells. Then Bosun Hawker would pipe breakfast for the crew, after which they'd return to their duty as the new watch came up, bringing bags and chests with them from the lower decks to allow for cleaning.

They'd not get much farther into the day before Cunnington or someone else missed Jean Vicard. The "boy" had to make an appearance on deck today, and possibly tomorrow as well. Then the truth could be discovered.

As the baron's wife, Jeannette would be protected from the rank and file. Cunnington would look the fool and repent having tried to flog her, Cruikshank would treat her like a highly favored guest, despite the inconvenience, and Treynor's own career would no longer hang in the balance.

Until then, however, anything could happen.

The straw made Jeannette itch miserably. She burrowed deeper, trying to fall asleep again, but the scratchy manger and her complaining stomach allowed her no respite. Somehow, she had to find something to eat and drink.

Shifting carefully, she listened for voices or footfalls before poking her head out of her hiding place.

The sun was up. Its rays poured into the ship's portholes, bright enough to float dust motes. The pigs had settled beside the trough, but her movements gained their attention. One stood on its short legs and grunted, then came to investigate.

Jeannette wasn't particularly fearful of animals, but coming eye to eye with a pig made her nervous. She nearly burst from her hiding place—but the sound of someone approaching made her sink back into the shelter of the straw.

The pig came closer, rooting around her head and sniffing the air. Hungry for more slop, no doubt. Or her. She bit back a scream as its snout wet her cheek.

Queasy, she tried to twist away without making any noise.

The footfalls passed and receded without pause. Cautiously easing out of her hiding place, she sent the pig scurrying.

Bits of straw clung to her hair, Treynor's shirt and Dade's breeches. She brushed herself off, climbed over the wall and headed in the direction of the steward's cabin. She knew nowhere else to find food. According to Mrs. Hawker, the men ate in small groups, each taking a turn to be mess cook. But she dared not go among them.

The steward's cabin was locked. Jeannette shoved against the door to see if it would give way.

Unfortunately, her puny efforts netted nothing more than a thump loud enough to wake the dead and a possible bruise on her hip.

Voices rang down the corridor, causing her to jump into the shadow of an adjoining hallway as some sailors trudged past. When they were gone, she tried forcing the steward's door again, but to no avail. She was just about to give up when she caught sight of a dead fish lying across a sack of biscuits not far away.

Bread of sorts. Probably old bread, but old bread was better than nothing.

Blessing the hand of providence and being careful to avoid the carcass of the fish, she stuffed her pockets with the hard, round disks and hurried off to find a place where she could enjoy them.

After descending another deck, she found herself in an arsenal among containers of priming-irons, wads, shot and various pieces of hardware used in the rigging and sails. Too bad she hadn't found the reserves of beef, pork and other food—although how she'd get into such barrels she didn't know.

A couple of sailors worked in the dark, cavernous hold, hammering wedges between barrels to keep them from rolling.

Jeannette hovered just outside the light shed by their lantern. Their presence gave her a modicum of peace. This would have been a frightening place to be alone.

Several crates were stacked nearby. She climbed up and set about eating.

Her stomach rebelled at the taste; she'd never tried the likes of the hard old biscuits before. But they were food. Determined not to starve, she chewed and swallowed—and nearly screamed when someone at her elbow murmured, "Do ye 'ave any more?"

"What?" Jeannette whispered, turning toward the voice that had come out of the darkness. "Who are you?"

"Don't matter, does it? I'm 'idin' down 'ere, same as ye. Only I'm 'ungry. I could 'ave sworn ye were eatin' somethin' a minute ago."

Judging from the voice, it was a woman. "I have got a little bread."

Whoever it was moved beside her. Then a distinctive odor filled Jeannette's nostrils—a combination of sweat, dirt and cheap perfume. She recognized the stench as one she had smelled on the docks at Plymouth. Was this woman a prostitute?

A hand reached out and touched her, and Jeannette steeled herself against pulling away from the faceless stranger. Whoever it was was hungry. She handed over what remained of her supper as the sailors finished their work and moved away.

When their light was gone, the blackness became complete. Jeannette imagined herself as Jonah, lost inside the whale. She hugged her knees to her chest, wondering if she could tolerate the cold, damp darkness.

"Where'd ye find these?" her new friend asked. "I wish I 'ad a dozen, at least."

Jeannette grimaced, thinking she'd rather go hungry than eat another. "They were in a sack next to the steward's room, with a dead fish on top. I am sure there are more, if you want them."

A low chuckle sounded. "I thought I tasted bargemen."

"Bargemen?" Jeannette echoed.

"Aye. Ye know, little white worms. Surely ye've seen 'em."

Jeannette's stomach lurched. She fought to keep her supper down, but the thought of "bargemen" was too much for her.

The person at her elbow pulled her away from the mess and led her to some barrels farther back. "That smells worse than the damn bilge," she complained.

Jeannette said nothing. She sat beside her new companion, utterly miserable.

The thought of Henri and her parents caused a sharp pang of loneliness. Two days, she reminded herself. She only had to survive on the frigate for two more days. "How did you know?" she asked. "About the . . . maggots, I mean. Can you really taste them?"

"When I concentrate I can. But it's the fish what was the clue. Ye said yerself ye found a fish on top of the sack. It's supposed to draw 'em out, though if the steward's left the whole lot for anyone to take, 'e's not much concerned with savin' 'em, eh?"

"I don't suppose so." Jeannette shivered. In an effort to block the maggots from her mind, she said, "It's so cold down here."

"Aye. And dreadful damp. But ye get used to it."

Jeannette felt an arm go around her as the stranger briskly rubbed her limbs. She didn't know who this woman was, or what she looked like, but she didn't move away. She was far too desperate for any crumb of human kindness.

"That oughter 'elp, oi? Now . . . what's this? Yer soft as a—" The woman's hand encountered the swell of one breast, then dropped away before Jeannette could react. "I thought ye were a lad. Ye're a woman?"

"Yes."

"Then why are ye wearin' trousers?"

"For the same reason you are hiding in this hellhole."

"Ye got a lover on board?"

Jeannette thought fleetingly of Treynor. Why, she couldn't say, didn't want to contemplate. "No. You?"

"Yeah. 'E's gonna marry me when the war's over."

"Doesn't he bring you any food?"

"When 'e can. We're just out of port, so for now, I've got to lay low."

"I see."

Silence fell between them. They were two of a kind, in some ways. "Do you stay down here all the time?"

"For the most part. This is as good a place as any. The men work 'ere once in a while. They 'ave to make the stores secure in case of bad weather or battle. But the smell from below keeps everyone away, if they 'ave a choice."

"What's your name?"

"Amelia."

Jeannette gave her name in turn and listened as Amelia boasted about the many virtues of her beau. He was a regular seaman, she said, but she was as proud of him as most women would be to catch an officer.

"What's his name?" Jeannette asked.

Amelia paused. "That I'll not say. I don't know ye, after all. An' I'll not do anythin' what could bring 'im a floggin'."

Jeannette didn't press her. Considering the circumstances, she had no desire to become embroiled in someone else's intimate affairs.

Still, they sat huddled together as if they'd known each other for years.

"Do you like life at sea?" Jeannette asked.

"Aye. It keeps food in me belly, for the most part."

Jeannette pictured a gap-toothed smile. None of the prostitutes she'd seen on the pier had possessed all of their teeth. "Not today, evidently."

"I'll live till tomorrow. My man will bring me a bite or two. He'll be wantin' somethin' 'imself by then."

Jeannette thought of Treynor—the memory of his smooth skin, the latent strength of his well-muscled body, the tingle of his lips moving against hers. They were all sensations connected with desire, a desire she would never feel again if she couldn't free herself from her hateful marriage.

The ship rocked to the side, knocking Jeannette against her new companion. When she encountered a hard, well-rounded belly, she pulled away as quickly as she could gain her balance.

"Don't worry, ye didn't 'urt me," Amelia said.

Jeannette didn't know how to respond. That Amelia was pregnant was obvious. That she would stow away on a frigate while in such a condition was alarming. "When do you expect your baby?" she asked, hoping that what felt like a melon-size middle wasn't quite melon-size at all.

"In another month. P'raps two."

Jeannette's nails curled into her palm. Two of her mother's four babies had not survived their first year, and Maman had hinted about the pains of childbirth when she deemed her daughter old enough to know such things. Jeannette could not imagine braving such an ordeal at sea.

What if the baby came early? And why didn't Amelia know with more certainty when the baby was due to arrive? A month was a long time. It could mean the difference of being in port.

Of course, considering the woman's probable profession . . .

"Does your, um, man know?"

"'Ow could 'e miss it?" She laughed. "'E wants a brat of 'is own. 'E's goin' ter marry me after the war."

She'd said that already. Doubt nipped at Jeannette, but she hoped, for Amelia's sake, that her beau was truly as devoted as she said. That he'd not brought her anything to eat while she was in such a delicate condition certainly gave Jeannette reason to wonder.

"I am sure he will." She hoped she sounded more convinced than she felt.

"Shhhh!" Amelia stiffened next to her. "We must 'ide," she whispered and scrambled away.

Dumbfounded, Jeannette blinked after her until she heard what Amelia had already detected. Someone was coming. Boots ground on the wood floor, then a light appeared.

Ducking behind the barrel on which she'd sat, Jeannette crouched in the darkness. Whoever it was was alone, but it took only one man to drag her back to the main deck.

"Jean, are you down here?"

The rich timbre of Lieutenant Treynor's voice echoed against the walls, causing Jeannette's heart to pound.

"Jean?"

Hunching lower, Jeannette held perfectly still. It would be next to impossible to find her amid the barrels. The halo of Treynor's light extended only so far; she could circle around him indefinitely. Unless he went back up and brought others to canvass the hold with him, she was safe if she could only move quietly enough. The steady creaking of the ship would help.

"Jean, if you're down here, you must come to me immediately. We have left port. We are not going back."

Was he lying? He called her by her boy name, but she would be a fool to let him trick her so easily.

"There are others who are looking for you. It would be wise to let me help you." Treynor walked to the other side of the room, flushing Amelia out of whatever hiding place she'd chosen. She voiced a short cry of pain as she stumbled over something in her rush to avoid him.

The light bobbed as Treynor weaved between the barrels, homing in on the sound. With Amelia so far along in pregnancy, Jeannette knew her movements would be slow and awkward. Chances were good that Treynor would catch her. Jeannette didn't know exactly what that would mean, but she knew by Amelia's reaction that she was afraid.

Jeannette didn't want to get her in any trouble. She thumped the barrel next to her, hoping to draw the lieutenant away, and he stopped and cocked his head.

"So you want a game of chase, do you?" he said.

The subtle threat in his voice made Jeannette swallow hard as she ducked behind a hogshead and waited. Only this time, the light didn't move. When she braved a peek over the rounded slats of her hiding place, she spied Treynor's lantern sitting alone on the floor. The lieutenant was nowhere to be seen. He'd relinquished the one thing that gave him away and was pursuing her stealthily.

She held her breath again, straining to hear his movements. Was the rustling she detected the lieutenant or Amelia?

Afraid to move for fear she'd run straight into him, she crouched down and kept still. She hoped Amelia would do the same. But when a rat scampered over her hand, Jeannette squealed and fell back.

Footsteps pounded in her direction. She scrambled away, scaled a stack of crates and tried to see Treynor come at her through the dark. But outside the edge of the light, shadows and darker shadows created the illusion of the lieutenant to her right, then to her left. The noise of his movement was gone; she could hear nothing until he laughed behind her.

"Are you afraid, my sweet?"

He sounded close enough to grab her by the shirt. Jeannette jumped to the floor and tried to run, but she careened into something angled that nearly sent her sprawling. Crying out before she could stifle the sound, she teetered on her feet as a moment of dizziness combined with the darkness to disorient her. Terrified to move, yet unable to stay where she was because of Treynor's predatory closeness, she began to turn in circles.

Then he was there, directly behind her. His hand snaked around her, inadvertently catching her breast as he slammed her back against his chest.

Chapter 10

As soon as Treynor realized what part of Jeannette's anatomy he'd laid hold of, he wondered again how he could ever have thought her a boy. Her bosom was full, especially for her small size, and the weight of it in his palm threatened to change his anger into something else entirely. For the briefest moment, he felt the impulse to turn her in his arms. Instead, he shifted his hold to preserve her modesty, then cursed himself for trying to be the noble gallant when she thanked him with a hearty kick in the shins.

"Let me go!"

"The game's over," he told her, crushing her resistance. He didn't care about being noble or gallant, he told himself. If Jeannette wasn't careful, he'd coax her into satisfying the hunger she inspired in him.

Remembering how her body had once quivered like the string of a violin at his touch, he felt his pulse quicken. She wouldn't be hard to press beyond denial. Here. Now. Seek his revenge in the only kind of pleasure a woman could give him.

But he'd never had a highborn lady and refused to risk his career—at least any more than he'd already done—on this one.

Taking hold of one wrist, he pulled her after him. This time she didn't resist. She followed so meekly he couldn't help casting a glance at her face as he retrieved the lamp.

"Were you lying when you said we wouldn't turn back?" she asked.

"I didn't tell the captain about you."

"Why?"

Treynor searched for an answer. How could he explain his actions to her when he scarcely understood them himself? "You're along for the ride," he said simply, wiping away a trickle of blood where she'd gouged her temple.

"I am?"

"You are. But from now on, you shall play by my rules."

When they reached Treynor's cabin, he opened a package wrapped in brown paper that was sitting on his desk and shoved it at her. "Mrs. Hawker has sent you something to wear—something that might actually fit," he added, eyeing her dishabille.

Jeannette's stay in the manger and the hold had made her filthy. She longed for a bath, couldn't wait to peel her boy's clothes off her body.

She eyed the man who had taken the lash for her and wondered why he hadn't revealed her identity to the captain as he'd promised he would. He had no reason to help her, unless he expected something in return, something she wasn't willing to give.

She shook out the fresh pants and boy's shirt he tossed in her lap. They were crudely made but nearly small enough to fit, and they were surprisingly soft, as though they'd been washed in fresh water. "Whose were these?"

He cocked his head to a jaunty angle. "You weren't so concerned with ownership when you took Dade's clothes or mine. Just put them on. You're going out on deck."

Jeannette pictured Lieutenant Cunnington and Captain Cruikshank pacing above them and felt reluctant to return to their presence. "Why?"

"Because I said so." He picked up the strips of cloth that had once been Dade's shirt and began to make better bindings. "First, conceal your breasts. Right now, any man with eyes in his head can see you're no boy."

"Why are you helping me?"

He didn't respond.

"Lieutenant?"

"Maybe I don't like your husband." He shrugged, but then a smile deepened the cleft in his chin. "Or perhaps I simply enjoy your company."

"I'd hate to see how you'd treat a woman whose company you do not enjoy," she said. "First you strip me of my clothes, then you tie me to your trunk to wait out the night."

His grin grew more meaningful. "I usually tie up only those who ask me nicely. Women who can't kiss me without drawing blood or striking me in my more vulnerable parts generally don't fare so well."

Jeannette rolled her eyes. "I see you have a healthy opinion of yourself, Lieutenant Treynor. A gentleman would never speak the way you do—"

"I think we have established that I am no gentleman, which brings me to my next point. If you want my help, you had better be prepared to compensate me." He moved toward her, a purposeful glint in his midnight-blue eyes.

Jeannette swallowed hard. So there was a price. She'd thought so. "I will not be your paramour—"

"Not what I had in mind, I assure you. You don't appeal to me beyond your ability to wash and mend." He chuckled as he pulled a basket of dirty clothes out of the wardrobe. "All my laundry will become your responsibility. And I will expect you to attend me at my bath when I require it."

Jeannette blinked in surprise. He wanted her to be his maid? His personal servant? She felt her spine stiffen. No matter how desperate her circumstances were, her pride rebelled at allowing this particular man to exploit her weakness.

"You will enjoy making a count's daughter fetch and stitch and do your bidding, won't you?" she said.

"I can't think of anything I would enjoy more . . . except having that same count's daughter perform"—he grinned—"other, more personal, services."

"I thought I didn't appeal to you."

"Perhaps you could convince me that I am wrong."

Jeannette felt a flush rise to her cheeks. "I doubt that's an argument I will ever make."

"Don't speak too soon," he said with a chuckle. "I certainly wouldn't want pride to stand in your way." His gaze roved over her. "So, are you willing to accept my terms of employment?"

"Do I have any other choice?"

"Not if you want to stay on board."

"Do I have your word that you won't ever force me to satisfy your sexual appetites?"

He gave her a disbelieving look. "Certainly. You have my word, madame," he said with a bow.

She lifted her chin. "Then you have yourself a servant."

"Wonderful. Now, put on these bindings and change. We're going topside."

Jeannette glanced at the strips of fabric he threw at her feet. "There is only one more thing," she said. "I will be your personal servant as long as I don't have to wear those miserable things, and only if you allow me to remain in the privacy of your cabin."

He whirled to face her. "You are hardly in a position to dictate terms, *my lady*. Now get dressed."

"I am not going out on deck." Unable to abandon her pride completely, Jeannette glared at him. "The captain is there and that Cunnington fellow, and . . ."

Her words died as his eyes narrowed. "If I may . . . what exactly do you want me to call you, anyway?"

Jeannette thought for a moment before settling on the name most likely to irritate him. "Baroness," she replied with as much disdain as she could muster.

"Oh, baroness, is it?" Treynor walked around her, circling like a hawk.

She squared her shoulders. "That is correct."

He stopped only inches in front of her face. "First you want to hide from your husband. Then you want to hide behind him. I think you need to decide how you want to play this game." He braced himself against the wall, one arm over her shoulder. "After you leave me writhing in my bed, and get me flayed alive, I still come to your rescue. I'd say you owe me your utmost cooperation, Baroness St. Ives, which means we are going topside."

Jeannette began to slide away, but he gripped her arm and held her where she was while bending to retrieve the strips of cloth he'd dropped on the floor. "Put these on, or I will put them on you myself. Is that clear?"

She tried to jerk out of his grasp. "You are hurting me."

His eyes dipped to her bustline. "Conceal your curves or the sailors on this ship will eat you for supper. Then you will know what it means to be hurt by a man."

"I am a baroness. They would not dare."

"Do you think they would believe anything you said?" He let go of her.

"Every sailor cannot be as lecherous as you say." She toyed with the fraying sections of fabric in her hands to conceal her doubt. That many sailors had been taken directly from prison, or been pressed, was a well-known fact and made her less than sure of her hastily uttered statement.

"And what about the reward?" she continued. "As soon as I tell them there is a purse of gold offered for my safe return, I doubt they would dare touch me. Do you think my husband would pay anything after I have been pawed by men like you?" She'd said it to prop up her crumbling bravado, but she regretted her words the instant she saw their effect.

"I am afraid you misunderstand." He moved even closer, leaning down until his nose nearly touched hers. "You wouldn't be pawed by men like me. You would be used by sailors. Filthy men. Crawling with lice."

Jeannette tried to wiggle away, but he stopped her. "They would ride you long and hard, and they would take turns doing it." His eyes swept over her, feeling every bit as personal as his touch. "Besides, if I remember correctly, the night we first met, I heard not a single protest to my pawing."

Jeannette's hand came up to push him away, but he caught her wrist. Taking hold of her chin with his other hand, he tilted it up until she could look nowhere but into his eyes, eyes that were as velvety blue as a moonlit night.

"Most of my men care for little besides their daily ration of rum and tobacco, living to see another battle and taking their pleasure with a woman—any woman. The promise of reward at some undetermined point in the future would not deter them while the pleasure of your flesh awaits."

He was right. Jeannette knew it and feared nothing more, except perhaps the pounding of her heart whenever Treynor touched her—and the knowledge that she wanted him to go on touching her. "You are the only man I have ever known who speaks so vulgarly to a lady." It was a weak defense, but playing the injured aristocrat was the only card she had.

"You mean I am the only man you have ever met who is unwilling to put up with the silly pretenses of you and others like you." Treynor laughed as he put her away from him. "At least you know to keep your distance. I promise to hold my appetites in check so long as you cooperate with my every command."

Jeannette threw back her shoulders. In the past twenty-four hours, she had gone hungry and cold, felt abandoned and thrown up maggots. Before that, she had lost her homeland, left her parents and broken her vows. She was afloat on the sea with more than five hundred men and not a single friend among them, but she still had her dignity. "I will not bow and scrape, not for you or anyone," she said and threw the strips of cloth in his face.

"Then you will accept the consequences." Grabbing her by the waist, he began to haul her over to a chair. "Evidently, I saved you from a flogging that might have done you some good."

She twisted and turned, trying to rake her nails across his face or grab a tuft of his thick hair. She wanted, needed, to find a release for her misery, but he held her fast.

"Damn hellcat," he cursed, taking the seat next to his cluttered desk and turning her over his knee.

"Don't you dare strike me!"

His hand landed on her backside with a resounding thwack. The power behind the blow stunned Jeannette. She tried to twist around, but couldn't escape his iron grip.

"Oh," she cried in outrage. "Stop this instant! Stop!"

Thwack.

Tears sprang to her eyes, but she gritted her teeth and blinked them back. She would not give Treynor the pleasure of seeing how much he hurt her, no matter how hard he spanked her.

"Have you lost your mind? Unhand me!"

Thwack.

She clutched at his shirt, every blow stinging more than the one before. Soon, she had no more energy with which to fight him.

He didn't stop until she lay without moving, focusing all her will-power on enduring the ordeal without succumbing to tears or breaking down and begging him to stop. She couldn't escape; trying only made the spanking last longer.

When he finally set her from him, she moved as far away as the narrow room would allow and glared her hatred. To think she had actually admired this man! "You had better take more care with your pistol in the future, Lieutenant," she said, fighting to keep her lip from trembling. "Because if I ever come by it, I will not use the wrong end of it again."

He stared at her for a moment, but he seemed almost crestfallen, more disgusted by his own behavior than triumphant. "I am no better than Cayle."

"Who is Cayle?"

"Never mind." With a rattled sigh, he jammed a hand through his hair. "I consider myself forewarned. Now conceal your breasts and put on those clothes."

"Why must I be Jean Vicard again?" Jeannette grumbled once she was completely dressed.

Treynor adjusted the hat on her head to hang lower over her brow and wiped a smudge from her cheek. "Because, after yesterday's flogging, the new boy who caused such an uproar will be missed if he doesn't appear."

"So? They won't be able to find him. What can they do?"

"Plenty, if they decide on it. In any case, I can't leave you to run about the ship and try to hide on your own. Anything could happen to you. And I will not risk leaving you in my cabin for Cunnington or one of the other lieutenants, or even Cruikshank, to discover. If Jean Vicard doesn't mysteriously disappear, the next few days will pass without footnote—"

"Next few days! But it cannot take so long to reach London."

"We are not going to London."

Jeannette felt her knees wobble. "What? What do you mean?"

"We have received new orders. We are joining the blockade. We could be at sea for months."

"Tell me it isn't true! You are teasing me, getting back at me for the flogging—"

"No." Treynor studied her closely. "But it's not too late. You can go back, if you want. But you must tell me now."

"Go back? To St. Ives?"

He nodded.

She felt behind her for the chair. "I can't."

"Why not?"

Forgetting the sting of her spanking along with her bruised pride, Jeannette sank down and buried her face in her hands. What to do? She was aboard a frigate that was part of the war effort against the revolutionaries of France, and she could be here indefinitely.

Peeking out from behind her hands, she whispered, "I cannot be Jean Vicard for long. The bindings hurt too badly, and with the lack of privacy aboard ship, sooner or later I will be found out."

"Eventually, but I plan to give you away. Once the captain knows of your presence, he will look after you until we reach the next port."

What had seemed like a brilliant plan only a day or so earlier—to escape to London on a frigate—now seemed like utter foolishness. What had she done? Her family would think something terrible had happened to her. "What might the next port be and when will we reach it?"

"That depends. I cannot say with certainty."

"And the Hawkers? Will they go along with this?"

"They will keep our secret, yes."

"So I will be your servant—"

"Until I pretend to find out something that tells me you are female, at which time I will go to the captain."

"And he won't turn back?"

"Not if we are well underway."

Jeannette regarded the lieutenant warily. "Where will I sleep until then?"

He grinned as he eyed his hammock. "I am not completely heartless. You can sleep with me if you wish."

Jeannette groaned. "It seems as though you have thought of everything, Lieutenant."

He bowed. "Ever glad to help a lady in distress."

"Except for one thing. I am not your doxy and never will be. I shall sleep on the floor."

Treynor laughed and motioned her through the door. "Suit yourself."

Jeannette followed Treynor past a line of doors to various cabins—those of the other lieutenants, she guessed—to the companionway and out onto the main deck. Now that he knew her true identity, she felt doubly conspicuous and worried that others would recognize her for the woman she was, if not the baroness who had escaped from Hawthorne House. But the men continued with their work, seemingly oblivious to her presence, and she let go of her fear long enough to enjoy the sea-tossed roll of the deck.

Huge, rectangular sails billowed out above her head, cracking loudly in the same strong breeze that sent an icy spray up over the bow and made Jeannette's face tingle.

Treynor turned. She guessed her excitement showed on her face when he gave her a genuine smile instead of one of his taunting grins. "There is nothing like it, is there?"

"Nothing," she agreed. The horizon seemed endless. In every direction, water. That their lives depended upon so little amid the immensity that surrounded them was frightening.

A strong voice rose on the air behind her. "Steady as she goes."

Others shouted the same words in a relay toward the bow. That everyone worked in such a cooperative manner awed Jeannette. It resulted in a smoothly running frigate despite the complexities and difficulties involved.

She studied the plethora of ropes that crisscrossed above her head. At first they appeared to be little more than a mass of tangles, but a closer look revealed how carefully they were organized. The lines that controlled the position of the sails were tied around belaying pins, which passed through holes in the rail behind the mainmast. Pulling out the pin would instantly release the entire line, enabling the frigate to change the position of her sails quickly and easily.

A man in a spotless blue coat, like Treynor's, made his way toward them. Jeannette didn't recognize the officer, but she had no desire to draw attention to herself by hanging about Treynor's coattails. No doubt he had work to do—and she had a small problem herself.

"Jean, please gather eggs for the cook and take them down to the galley." Treynor's eyes rested on the man coming toward them as he spoke. Jeannette knew he wanted her gone, but she had no idea where to find the chickens, the eggs or the galley.

"Where?" she whispered.

He nodded toward two boats tied to the deck just ahead, covered with canvas to keep out the rain.

As Jeannette drew close to them, she could hear the clucking of chickens. She looked for something to put the eggs in and found a wicker basket hung to one side. Pulling the handle over her arm, she peeled back the canvas cover to reach tentatively into the warm straw, nervous despite the simplicity of her task. This was servant's work. She had no idea how anyone gathered eggs.

Her efforts met with a squawk and a fluster that caused her to withdraw her hand several times, but she persevered until she realized she was wasting her time. The nests were empty.

She pretended to be busy until the man conversing with Treynor left. Then she said a silent prayer of thanks as she could wait no longer to find a privy.

Approaching the lieutenant from behind, she said, "Lieutenant Treynor, I need to . . . I need to . . . you know . . ."

Treynor twisted around, a familiar, wry grin on his lips. "You need to what?"

"To use the necessary," she whispered angrily. "Where do I go?"

"Most of the men use a bucket and pitch it over the side." He laughed at her horrified expression; she would be discovered if she had to rely on such a practice.

"There are private lavatories for the officers farther aft," he continued. "But stay out of those. Use the heads in the bows, one deck below. The roundhouse offers the privacy you desire, but be careful even there. It is for junior officers."

She nodded, hoping she would know a roundhouse when she saw it, or the heads, for that matter, and set off.

The eyes of those she passed slipped to her occasionally. Were they wondering if Treynor had exacted any retribution from her for his flogging? Or were they thinking that she looked more like a girl?

Except for the officer's lavatories Treynor had mentioned, there were only six heads for the entire crew, assuming what she saw was all they had. The walls of this part of the ship were ornately painted in blue and gold with cornices and other decorative woodwork, and a female figurehead thrust proudly out over the water at the bow. Unfortunately, the heads were located out in the open where a gale or wave could carry their users overboard.

No wonder most men used a bucket.

Jeannette came to an abrupt halt as a sailor on the far end, whom she hadn't noticed before, stood and pulled up his breeches.

So that's what it looks like. She tried not to appear as startled as she felt. Somehow she'd imagined the male anatomy to be more . . . she wasn't sure exactly. More threatening than droopy, perhaps.

Quickly averting her gaze, she tried not to show her embarrassment. But it was difficult to reconcile the shriveled, rather unattractive bit of flesh with what she remembered about Treynor.

The stranger belched and adjusted his privates as Jeannette began to recognize some of the smells she'd noticed while in the hold and so close to the bilge. The slatted floor on which she stood allowed whatever went into the raised wooden seats to drain into the bottom of the ship.

She shuddered and glanced around, searching for the roundhouse. Treynor had said it would offer her a modicum of privacy. She wanted to finish her business and be away before being treated to another view of a man's penis.

With a nod, the sailor left. She shook her head to rid her mind of what she had just seen, then spotted a round cubicle. Evidently the roundhouse was aptly named. What else could it be?

As she knocked gingerly on the door, Jeannette prayed she'd find it empty. Treynor had said the roundhouse served junior officers; she would be upbraided for using it.

When no sound issued from within, she tried the knob and swung the door open to find two seats inside. Both, to Jeannette's profound relief, were currently vacant, but the door had no lock. She stood inside, listening for approaching footsteps, too afraid to make her move until necessity forced her to act.

As soon as Jeannette fastened her breeches again, the door flew open and a young, stocky man with raven hair and a pockmarked face blinked at her.

"What's this? Our little froggy?" he cried. "Get the hell out of here before you get the lashes you deserved yesterday."

Jeannette ducked her head, hoping to appear as cowed as possible. *"Oui, m'sieu."*

"French pig," he muttered, cuffing her as she passed.

He delivered the blow out of irritation, not true anger, but it clipped Jeannette on the chin just hard enough to upset her balance. She knocked into the door, then staggered back, falling into him.

Snarling a curse, he kicked her leg.

Tears sprang to Jeannette's eyes as pain exploded just below her knee. *"Excusez-moi."* She groaned the words, trying to forestall his fist, which drew back to strike her while she was down.

"Next time you'll know your place, by God," he swore, and Jeannette cringed as his fist hit her square in the stomach.

The blow made her nauseous. She rolled into a ball and didn't move or speak again. Her accent provoked him more than finding her in the roundhouse, where she didn't belong. Vaguely, she wondered how many times he'd hit her before exhausting his desire to hurt.

She covered her head to protect her face, but he didn't strike again. With a harsh laugh, he shoved her out of his way with one foot. Then he dropped his pants and sat down to relieve himself.

Jeannette heard him above the buzzing in her head. He seemed to take forever.

"That'll teach ye." He fastened his pants and straightened his jacket before he strode out, leaving the door hanging ajar.

Gulping the fresh air that came in puffs as the door flapped with the movement of the ship, she tried to drag herself toward the opening. She didn't think the petty officer had caused any major damage. It was more of a combination—pain, lack of food and too little sleep—that left her unable to stand.

The pain and dizziness would pass, she assured herself. But the world outside the roundhouse suddenly seemed so hostile and foreign that she let herself curl back into a ball. She would move in a few minutes. She just needed to rest.

How odd that the smell didn't bother her anymore . . .

Chapter 11

Treynor's eyes flicked once again over the deck, searching for Jeannette. She should be back by now. Had she gotten lost?

He forced himself to wait a few more minutes, hoping she'd appear. Following after her might draw unwanted attention. Cunnington watched everything he did, always looking for the slightest indiscretion.

He sauntered to the stern where the log line was being towed in the water behind them. The ship's master counted while sand ran out of the log glass. He compared the time passed to the number of knots released, calculated the ship's speed in nautical miles per hour, then recorded it in his daily logbook. It was all routine, and Treynor paid little attention. His mind was on Jeannette.

Succumbing to the worry that gnawed at his gut, he pivoted and found the hatch. Something had to have happened. Had she defied him again? Stolen back below? Certainly she wasn't that foolish. She *was* stubborn, though. He'd expected her to cry, or show weakness in some way, when he'd spanked her. But she hadn't. Perhaps this was part of her revenge.

Two seamen were using the heads when Treynor stepped through the door. As soon as they finished, they saluted, turning their palms toward their faces to hide the black tar stains on their hands. If they were surprised to see him, they didn't show it. Officers generally preferred the lavatories, but sometimes convenience dictated a visit to the heads.

Treynor waited until the men left before moving to one of the two roundhouses located on either side of him. The first he found to be empty. For a moment, he thought the second one was, too. But then he heard a moan.

His breath caught as his eyes adjusted to the dim interior and he saw Jeannette crouched against the wall. "What the—"

She sagged to the floor. "I was afraid . . . you were him."

"What happened?" he asked, kneeling beside her.

"It seems that some of your friends take"—she swallowed—"more of a proprietary interest in the roundhouse than you thought." She tried to chuckle but groaned instead.

"Who did this?" He ran his fingers through her thick, dark hair and over her scalp, finding a small knot just above her temple near the cut she'd sustained in the hold, but no fresh blood. And she seemed to have no broken bones.

"I was not in a position to ask his name."

Her eyes slid shut, and Treynor cursed himself for letting this happen. If he had told the captain about her as he was obliged to do, she would be safely back with her husband by now.

Gently lifting her into his arms, he said, "Don't worry, you're going to be all right."

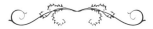

Jeannette snuggled deeper into the soft quilts that covered her, dreaming of her childhood. Her mother rocked her and sang softly. The sun streamed in through the window, warming her face. She was full and content. Until the chair seemed to dip, sending her sprawling. Then she jerked awake.

"How do you feel?"

Lieutenant Treynor sat beside her, his lower jaw shadowed with stubble. His shirt was off, revealing a light matting of hair that swirled over a dark, muscular chest, contrasting the white dressings that covered the healing wounds of the lash. The sun in her dream was a lamp on the desk not far away, and her mother's rocking chair, the lieutenant's hammock, which swung back and forth with the movements of the frigate.

"Have I been asleep long?" She squinted against the pounding of her head.

Treynor retrieved a bowl from the desk. "All day and most of the night. You started to stir an hour or so ago, so I had Cook prepare something for you to eat. Here, get this down."

He offered her a bite of a thick, gelatinous substance that tasted like meat.

"What is it?"

"Portable soup. It's made by boiling down broth so it's easier to transport."

She nodded, letting him spoon several bites into her mouth before realizing she was naked beneath the covers of his bed. Pulling the blankets up to her chin, she turned accusing eyes on him. "Where are my clothes?"

"They were filthy. I wasn't about to put you in my bed with them on."

"You could have given me others!"

"I still would have had to remove the ones you wore." He challenged her with a look.

"You were eager for just such an opportunity."

"I cannot deny I enjoyed it." His smile slanted toward the wicked. "But I prefer my women to be a bit more responsive when I touch them."

Jeannette felt a blush rise from her neck. "You touched me?"

He chuckled. "It would have been difficult to undress and bathe you without doing so."

"You bathed me?" She saw no tub.

An enigmatic smile curved his lips as he picked up a damp cloth and waved it at her.

"Did you touch me more than you had to?"

He leaned closer, his long fingers playing with her hair. "Unfortunately, I was too worried to take advantage of the situation."

"I don't believe you." Jeannette knocked his hand away, and he laughed.

"Then I can't put your mind at ease. So finish eating, like a good girl."

"I am not a girl."

"How well I know."

"What do you mean by that?"

He pressed a hand to his chest in a gesture of innocence, the movement drawing Jeannette's gaze back to the smooth skin that covered the bulging sinew. She'd been trying not to notice the way the light played against the firm contours of his body, but her eyes had flicked over him repeatedly. "Can't I make a simple statement?" he asked.

"Nothing is simple with you." She shifted, trying to get more comfortable by telling herself that the rapid pace of her heart had nothing to do with the sight of Treynor, half-clad, only an arm's distance away. She remembered the feel of his hands on her body so vividly only because she had never experienced anything like it before.

"You are wrong about that." He picked up her hand and kissed the tip of each finger. "With me, some things are as simple as they get."

Treynor's lips were warm and soft. He made Jeannette gasp when he took her thumb into his mouth and tickled the sensitive pad with his tongue.

She pulled away. "Don't do that."

"Why? You like it."

She gave him a look of impatience. "How do you know?"

"It's obvious."

"And do you think I liked the spanking, too?" She struggled to sit up. "Here, give me that. I can feed myself."

Treynor's eyes went to her cleavage but he made no move to restrain her until she reached for the spoon. Then he batted her hand away. "Tell me what happened at the roundhouse," he said, sobering.

Jeannette explained briefly. She didn't want to remember the incident. Her head throbbed, and her stomach still felt tender where she'd been hit.

Treynor's jaw tightened as she related the experience. "Sounds like John Grover. I will see to him."

Jeannette wondered exactly what he meant by that, but she didn't question him. He might feel the need to protect her from others, but who was going to protect her from him?

Seemingly preoccupied, he fed her in silence. When she had finished the entire bowl, he set it aside.

"Why did you marry the baron?" he asked suddenly, focusing his blue eyes on her face.

"I had no choice," she replied.

"You made one when you ran away."

She blanched. "I don't want to talk about it."

"I do."

Jeannette drew the blankets more tightly around her. "My family needed the benefit of whatever alliance I could make. And the baron didn't mind that I had a mere pittance of a dowry."

A look of contempt claimed his features. "So I was right. Your parents sold you to the highest bidder."

"Do not judge them too harshly," Jeannette said with a grimace. "My family has been through more than you can ever imagine."

He seemed unconvinced of the necessity of their actions.

"As you well know, the French are not particularly popular in England at present," she went on. "I could not expect to catch one of London's most eligible bachelors."

"No, but someone within a decade of your own age might not have been asking too much. Your parents should not have given their consent." He stood and prowled around the cabin. "Damned aristocrats think everything revolves around blood and money."

"Why do you hate us?" she demanded. "You lead a good life. You have the things you need." She waved her hand at the expensive furnishings in his cabin. "Most of the women in England would consider themselves lucky to be on your arm."

He gave her a bitter smile. "But not someone like you. A noble-woman would never settle for a bastard."

Jeannette stared at him without speaking. She hadn't realized he was illegitimate. What could she say? He was right.

He chuckled. "Never mind. I have no plans to marry, noblewoman or not."

"You have made that clear. But if you ever change your mind, you might want to let me teach you how to treat a lady."

Ignoring her remark, Treynor watched her with hooded eyes. "If you wanted the marriage so badly, why did you run from your new husband?"

She stared at the tiny stitches on Treynor's quilt. "He had a rather creative plan for obtaining an heir."

His eyes narrowed. "What do you mean?"

"Nothing." Jeannette waved his question away. "Only that I won't go back, ever."

Treynor sighed. "It's late. You had better get more sleep." Retrieving the shirt he'd slung over the back of the chair, he winced as he shrugged into it.

"Where are you going?" she asked.

"I am the officer of the next watch."

"What time is it?"

"Nearly four in the morning."

A knock on the door made Jeannette cower beneath the covers, but Treynor cried, "I'm on my way," without bothering to answer it.

"That was the quartermaster," he explained. "There is more food here, if you get hungry." He nodded toward a tray covered by a linen napkin. "Lock the door behind me and whatever you do, don't go anywhere."

"Wait," she said.

Treynor turned back when he reached the door.

"What happened to my dog?"

"You mean Bull?" he said. "The Hawkers have her, and even she's happy that they've changed her name to Bonnie. Is it really your dog?"

Jeannette shrugged. "I found her."

"Do you want her back?"

"Not if the Hawkers are taking good care of her."

"They are good people. I am sure she's fine," Treynor said and left.

Wondering if he'd had any sleep beyond an occasional doze at her bedside, Jeannette locked the door behind him, blew out the lamp and climbed back into his hammock.

"All hands!" The bosun's voice rang down the companionway. "Larboard watch, ahoy. Rouse out there, you sleepers. Hey! Out or down here."

With her stomach full for the first time in two days, Jeannette's eyes grew heavy again. The warm bedding smelled of Treynor, and his hammock swung as steadily as a pendulum, lulling her to sleep. She had all but succumbed to its blessed oblivion when she heard the doorknob rattle.

Sitting up, she tried to see through the darkness. How much time had passed since Treynor left? Could he be returning? Did he need something?

She managed to wrap the blankets around her naked body and climb out of the hammock, which, encumbered as she was, proved no easy feat. Then she padded to the door, expecting the lieutenant's voice to tell her to open it.

A soft knock came instead. "Jean Vicard? You in there, froggy?"

Cunnington! Jeannette jumped back as though burned.

"You might have escaped without a scratch the other day, but I am willing to bet it is just a matter of time before you earn another whipping." His voice was laced with the promise of violence. "And I shall watch with pleasure."

Jeannette bit her tongue against a stinging rejoinder. Cunnington hated her enough already. The last thing she needed was to provoke him to act on his words. "I will see to my duty in future, *m'sieu*."

His laugh sounded like a high whine through the door. "I will keep my eye on you, just to be sure."

The knob rattled again. "Do you hear me, froggy bastard?"

Afraid he'd keep banging or force his way in if she didn't, Jeannette responded. *"Oui."*

Silence fell, then she heard the tread of boots on the wood planking as he moved away. But she couldn't relax after that. She lit a lamp and began to search for her clothes. Being naked left her feeling especially vulnerable, not only to Cunnington, should he demand she open up to him, but to Treynor when he returned.

Her breeches and shirt were in a heap against the wall. Jeannette donned them before taking a seat on the floor in the corner. She didn't want to soil Treynor's linens with her dirty clothes any more than he wanted her to.

Hugging her knees to her chest, she waited several minutes before creeping across the room. She wanted to make sure Cunnington had truly left, but even after pressing her cheek to the floor she couldn't see anything through the narrow crack beneath the door. For all she knew, he hovered about the corridor, waiting for her to peek outside.

She returned to where she had been sitting and tried to doze off, but the itchy stiffness of her clothes prevented her. Preoccupied with thoughts of Cunnington, she fidgeted for an interminable time. But eventually she remembered Amelia, the woman she had met in the hold. Had Amelia's beau brought her something to eat? Was she warm enough?

Treynor had left food for her, which provided an opportunity. Each watch lasted four hours. She didn't know how much of that time remained, but she hoped it would be enough to visit Amelia. It seemed unlikely that whoever had impregnated her was taking good care of her.

After strapping down her breasts so she could venture from the cabin, she wrapped some bread and cheese and a few slices of cold meat in the napkin that had covered the food and placed the small bundle under her hat. Then she stole the wool blanket from on top of the lieutenant's feather comforter and rolled it up, tucking it beneath her arm.

Despite a firm belief that Cunnington had returned to his own cabin, Jeannette's fingers shook as she unlocked the door. She waited several seconds before swinging it open, half expecting a hand on the opposite side to force it the rest of the way.

When she finally stuck her head out, she found the corridor empty.

Taking a small lamp, she sallied forth before she could lose her nerve and headed to the companionway that would lead to the lower decks.

Almost directly below the lieutenant's cabin, she stumbled upon the galley. The ship's cook was there, a one-legged, balding man with long sideburns. He had already lit the range and was busy preparing what looked to be an oatmeal gruel for breakfast.

"Morning," Jeannette murmured as she passed.

He nodded, and she hurried on.

The decks were being scrubbed again, with sand and holystone, then mop and bucket. Other men polished brass fittings until they gleamed in the predawn light that was just beginning to filter through the portholes.

She descended another steep flight of stairs lined with cannonballs set into wooden planks and found several locked rooms, which she guessed were gunpowder stores, maybe even a handling chamber or two.

In the very cradle of the ship's hull, the hold was cool, damp and pitch-black beyond the circle of Jeannette's light. No seamen hefted barrels through the door and up the stairs. Neither did any voices break the silence until Jeannette raised her own in a whisper.

"Amelia? Are you here?"

Nothing. Only creaking timbers and an occasional scratching broke the tomblike stillness. This last noise caused the hair on Jeannette's arms to stand on end despite her efforts to ignore it. Rats. From the sound of their movements, they hovered just beyond the ring of her light, but she tried to convince herself that only her fear made them seem so bold.

Wrinkling her nose against the noxious air, she lifted her lantern high and called louder. "Amelia! It is me, Jeannette."

The halo of her lamp revealed only barrels and crates. The outer reaches of the hold were draped in blackness; waves outside brushed against the hull, seeming to order all within not to break the silence.

Shhh . . . shhh . . . shhh . . .

Jeannette opened her mouth to call again when an angry voice finally snapped, "Go away!"

"Amelia?" She paused, unable to remember with any certainty the sound of her friend's voice. "Is it you?"

"Aye, 'tis me. Who'd ye expect? But I don't need the likes of ye thunderin' about down 'ere, callin' after me. Ye'll cause me nothin' but grief, that ye will. Ye almost got me caught last time."

"I have brought something for you to eat." Gingerly, because of her sore stomach and aching head, Jeannette walked closer to the voice. "Are you hungry?"

Momentary silence answered her, as if Amelia's hunger warred with her desire to be left alone.

"A bit," she admitted at last.

"Hasn't anyone brought you some food?"

Another silence, then, "Ye can take yer grub an' go. My man will be 'ere any minute. 'E's just busy, ye know. 'Tis 'ard ter get away."

So the situation was as she'd feared . . . "Come and eat. I got the food from Lieutenant Treynor's cabin, so it's fresh. And there is meat."

"Why don't ye eat it yerself then?"

It wasn't difficult to hear her skepticism. "I am full."

Amelia crept out from a narrow alley between the ship's stores and entered the light, giving Jeannette her first glimpse of the pregnant stowaway. Her heart-shaped face was plain, but not wholly unattractive, and she certainly wasn't as old as Jeannette had hoped—probably no more than fifteen. She possessed a rather pointy chin; a quick, furtive gaze; and long, stringy dark hair that fell down her back, matted with the same dirt and grime that stained her dress. As for the pregnancy, her stomach was every bit as swollen as Jeannette had feared.

Amelia squinted against the lamp's brightness as Jeannette retrieved the food from under her hat and placed it in the girl's outstretched hands.

"What's the lieutenant to ye?" she asked, swallowing an entire mouthful almost before she had begun to chew.

"The lieutenant?"

"The man what came after ye. Ye daft?" She stopped eating long enough to shoot Jeannette an irritated glance.

"He is nothing to me, of course. He is an officer—"

"I know *who* 'e is. What I can't figure is where ye fit in." Her gaze slid over Jeannette's boy's clothing.

"I do not fit in," Jeannette admitted. "I stole aboard like you, which is why I am wearing these clothes."

"Then 'ow'd the lieutenant find out about ye? An' if 'e caught ye—which I saw that 'e did—what ye doin' runnin' about an' carryin' off 'is food?"

Jeannette almost explained that the food she'd brought had been given to her, not stolen, except that she had, indeed, taken the blanket. "I brought something to keep you warm," she said, ignoring the question.

"Ye'll get yerself flogged, woman or no." Amelia glanced askance at the covering Jeannette held out. "The navy don't take kindly ter thieves."

Jeannette's gazed move to Amelia's swollen belly. "At the moment, you need it more than the lieutenant. Here."

Amelia shook her head. "Oh no, ye don't. I'll not be caught with an officer's blanket."

"Take it." Jeannette wondered how a child born to this stubborn girl would ever survive. "You can always tell them you found it."

Amelia made a noise of incredulity. "They'd never believe me!"

"Then say I gave it to you. I will not deny it."

"An' why would ye do that for me?"

Jeannette sat the blanket on the closest barrel. "Not for you. For the baby. How is it, by the way?"

She shrugged. "It's still there."

"You have been feeling well then?"

"Better now." She cracked a smile. "Thanks for the food. I'm sorry I was . . . well, ye know . . ."

"I understand. Have you had anything to drink?"

"Aye. There's a leaky barrel. Rum," she announced as if it were liquid gold.

"Why not come out of here?" Jeannette asked. "This dank place cannot be good for you. The smell alone would kill me. And what about the rats?"

"They don't bother ye so long as ye can move." The suspicious look returned to Amelia's face. "Who are ye, anyway?"

"I told you. I am no different than you—"

"Oh, yer different all right, with yer fancy French accent and fine speech. But I'm not one ter nose in what don't concern me. An' if ye really want ter 'elp me, ye'll keep yer bloody trap shut an' not come back 'ere."

But how could she? "What about your baby?"

"My baby is just that—*my* baby! Ye worry about yerself before ye get us both in trouble."

Jeannette silently cursed the sailor who had gotten Amelia with child and then, by all indications, abandoned her. "Can I give your man a message for you?" she asked, hoping to deliver him a good tongue-lashing as well. "If you will give me his name, I could—"

"No!" The protective note in Amelia's voice warned Jeannette not to press the issue. She'd only undermine Amelia's trust and ultimately get nowhere.

"All right. I am staying in Lieutenant Treynor's cabin for the next couple of days if . . . if you need anything. Otherwise—"

"Are ye Treynor's girl, then?" Wistful admiration overrode Amelia's gruff manner. "That man's 'andsome as the devil, that 'e is."

Jeannette flushed. Treynor was virile enough to tempt the most virtuous maid, to say nothing of the hussies. Even she had to admit that. "No. He is . . . he is merely helping me a bit."

Amelia let out a soft snicker. "A man such as 'e likes to use what 'e's got in 'is breeches. If ye don't know that yet, ye'll be learnin' it soon enough."

"I'd better go." Unwilling to examine Treynor's motives in front of the other woman, or to even consider them herself, Jeannette stepped away.

A backward glance revealed Amelia draping Treynor's blanket around her shoulders. With that small reassurance, Jeannette let herself out of the dark hold, but voices on the landing near the companionway caused her to pause in the shadows. A knot of sailors huddled near a lantern that swung there. Fortunately, none of them wore an officer's uniform.

Ducking her head, she proceeded toward the stairs only to be yanked back by the collar and relieved of her lamp.

"'Ey, lookee 'ere!" The man who grasped her by the coat raised the light to her face. "This lad's the one what got Lieutenant Treynor flogged."

The dirt-streaked faces of the others turned her way, all except three who crouched near a lamp of their own, busy with something Jeannette couldn't quite see. At their feet lay several bottles of colored liquid and a rag.

"Wanted ter run off, did ye? Changed yer mind about a life of rum, buggery and the lash?"

An aging tar, wearing a greasy bandanna, ripped off a thick, yellow fingernail with his teeth and spat it on the floor. "'Is tender flesh 'as never seen the likes of the whip, I'll bet."

Having learned her lesson from that incident with the petty officer, Jeannette kept silent. These sailors hated anything or anyone French. She didn't want to give them further reason to bother with her.

"Did the lieutenant give ye the beatin' ye deserved?" It was the man who held her that spoke. "'Tis only right ye get somethin'. I've always taken me own stripes."

That he probably never had a choice left little room for pride, but Jeannette was not of a mind to point that out. She nodded, wincing against the pounding of her head and the fear that was making it difficult to breathe. The slightest provocation could cause them to take to their fists, as the petty officer had done.

The man holding the light glanced up. Without his curly, dark head in the way, Jeannette could see what they were doing. A bare-chested sailor was having his arm tattooed by a tall, gaunt-looking man.

"Jack, 'e's just a lad. Let 'im go," said the tattoo recipient.

"Go back ter admirin' Smedley's work there, Beaner. It's all in good sport. This snot-nosed French brat could use a lesson on 'ow to get along in the navy." He jammed his face in front of Jeannette's. "Ye see, lad, tattoos are manly things. They might 'urt some, but notice 'ow Beaner acts as though it merely tickles."

"He's even paying for the pleasure," Smedley pointed out with a self-satisfied grin.

"I'll not give ye a farthin' unless ye make this bloody ship into a man-of-war. Looks like a stoved-in skiff so far," Beaner said with a chuckle.

"You couldn't settle for hearts and anchors, like everyone else," the tattooer grumbled.

"Like ye said, I'm payin' for it. I should get what I like, eh?"

The light swayed as the men guffawed, evoking a curse from the one bent over Beaner's arm.

"Hold bloody still!"

"I got an idea." Jack pulled Jeannette closer to Smedley and Beaner. "A tattoo might 'elp rid this lad of 'is French cowardice. Make 'im a real sailor."

"Aye," one of his companions agreed. "Let's make 'im look like a gen-yoo-ine tar. Toughen 'im up."

Hoping to break Jack's grip and run up the stairs, Jeannette struggled in earnest. She doubted the sailors were interested enough to follow her very far. They'd been drinking—the water on the ship tasted so bad that most sailors consumed little liquid besides ale and as much rum as they could get their hands on. They were just having a bit of fun.

But she couldn't risk them having that fun at her expense.

"What do ye say, lad?" Jack took firmer hold of the front of her coat and lifted her off her feet with one brawny arm.

Jeannette cleared her throat. "I have no coin."

"Thomas Smedley's not a greedy man, eh, Smed?" Jack glanced at the artist.

Smedley cocked an eyebrow at them. "I might find it in my heart to do the wee lad a favor, should the rest of you make generous with your rum rations this evening."

The group's enthusiasm dimmed at the prospect of sharing their rum until Jack shored it up again. "We'll slake yer thirst well enough, eh, boys? What's a wee draught to us, after all?"

He pulled Jeannette closer, and her trepidation escalated. She couldn't allow them to mark her skin like a common sailor. And what part of her body would they choose to mar? Her boy's costume couldn't withstand much scrutiny, even by drunkards.

"Please." She twisted in her coat, trying to pry Jack's fingers away, but flailed helplessly, suspended in air. "I don't want a tattoo. I have work to do, no? You will get me another beating if I do not get on my way."

"Ye deserve a taste o' pain for the lieutenant's floggin'," Jack said, her coat still firmly in his grasp.

Thomas Smedley used an ink-stained rag to wipe the arm of his current patron. "What should I put on the boy? Beaner's done."

Beaner flexed so all could admire the improved frigate tattooed on his upper arm. Then he stood and moved out of the way.

"French bastard," someone volunteered.

The laughter swelled as another cried, "Son of a French whore."

"Bloody coward, is more like it," Smedley responded. "Set him down here, Jack."

The sight of the needle made Jeannette frantic. "No! *Mon Dieu,* let me go!" Managing to break Jack's hold, she tried to dash up the stairs, but one of his mates grabbed her arm and hauled her back.

Beaner counted out his coin and tossed it at Smedley.

"Mr. Beaner, please, do not let them do this," she pleaded, appealing to the one who had seemed most sympathetic to her.

Beaner seemed mildly surprised. "It's not so bad. I just paid good money for the privilege." Again, he displayed the result of Smedley's work, then gave her hat a friendly jerk. "Don't worry, lad, I'll make sure they don't give ye anythin' too vulgar." With that he turned to Smedley. "Put an anchor on 'is arm or some such."

"'E'll 'ave nothin' so plain," Jack argued. "Do a 'eart on his pecker. That'll give 'im somethin' to show the ladies."

Smedley scowled. "I'm not touching his pecker. What do you think I am, a bloody sodomite?"

Jack's face reddened. "All right. A naked lady, then, on 'is chest."

That Smedley rubbed his chin as though considering this latest proposition caused Jeannette to redouble her efforts. Regardless of the hands that held her back, she had to break free.

"Let me go, bloody swine." She cringed to hear herself, but she had to be Jean and not Jeannette to survive.

"Hold him fast," Smedley said.

Chapter 12

Jeannette cried out as four tar-blackened hands pinned her against the wall.

Smedley hunched over to examine the corked bottles that contained the colored inks and tapped his needle thoughtfully on the blue.

"So what's it going to be?" the others asked, their rum-soured breath bathing Jeannette's face as they crowded closer.

"Hold him steady, I said, or it won't look like anything at all," Smedley replied with more than a little self-importance.

"A naked woman," one man insisted.

Smedley shook his head. "I'm thinking an English flag might be nice, you know, to remind Frenchy here where his loyalties lie, just in case he ever wonders."

"Then make it as big as life," Jack said with a snicker. "So no one else can mistake 'is loyalties either. We'll be doin' 'im a bloody favor, makin' him one of our own."

"Aye," Smedley said. "But something as big as all that would take hours. And I'm working for free, remember? I'll do a small flag on his arm."

Gripped tight, Jeannette winced as the first prick of the needle drew a bright red drop of blood, which Smedley wiped away with his stained rag. The pain grew worse with each jab, but the tattoer worked quickly, only bothering to glance up when Jeannette's struggles caused him to miss his mark.

"He's wriggling," he snapped to the men restraining her. Then he bowed back over her tender flesh.

Staring at the bottles of ink that would soon permanently mark her body, Jeannette refused to lie meekly beneath their hands. She could not return to her parents with a tattoo on her arm, be it an English flag or a French one.

Booted feet moved on the deck above and Jeannette cried out; she could never gain her freedom on her own. "Help me! Please!"

A callused hand clamped over her mouth, but the sailor who silenced her was too late. Someone had heard, and they were coming. Jeannette's heart raced faster in hope, then skidded and bumped when she realized who had answered her plea.

Lieutenant Cunnington's heels tapped on each step as he descended the stairs. Dressed impeccably, as always, he stood tall, his cologne reaching Jeannette long before he came level with her.

When the others pulled back and saluted, Jeannette wanted to run. But she could not. She was encircled by half-drunken sailors, and Cunnington blocked her escape up the stairs. She could only attempt an awkward salute of her own.

"Having fun, lads?"

"Aye, Lieutenant. Didn't mean no harm, though." Smedley's glance flicked toward his mates.

The others averted their eyes.

"Beaner? Don't you have this watch?" the lieutenant asked.

"No, sir. I 'ave the next one."

"Which begins in a matter of minutes."

"Aye, sir."

"Carpenters have much to do in a day."

"Aye, sir."

"Perhaps you are not taking your work seriously enough. At this rate you will all miss muster."

Jeannette felt no relief at Cunnington's words. If he sent the sailors scurrying to their respective duties, she might avoid a tattoo, but she wasn't sure she'd be able to escape the first lieutenant. Would he manufacture a charge against her? Take his hatred out on her another way?

"I was just leavin' when the boys decided to rile this lad," Beaner explained. "I lingered ter watch."

There was a quiver in Beaner's voice. Jeannette could almost hear him wonder if he would soon find himself at the receiving end of the mate's whip.

"Indeed." The first lieutenant's gaze switched back to Jeannette. His glacial smile and the memory of his voice through Treynor's door made her wish she could sink into the deck.

She'd escaped his wrath once; she doubted she could do so again.

"Am I to understand the lad opposes such an initiation into your ranks?" He spoke to Beaner, but his eyes never left Jeannette.

"Aye, sir."

"There is nothing quite so annoying as a boy who resists those in authority. Wouldn't you say, Mr. Beaner?"

"Aye, sir."

Jeannette stared beyond Cunnington. How far would she get if she made a dash for it?

Her chances didn't look good . . .

"I was just going about my duty, *m'sieu*," she said. "Lieutenant Treynor is expecting me in his cabin. He will not be pleased if—"

"Do I care if Lieutenant Treynor is pleased?"

The others made no sound.

"I would not know, sir," Jeannette replied. "I am only trying to do as I have been told."

"So eager to please," Cunnington mused. "Where is the lad who tried to run away? Working for Lieutenant Treynor must suit you better than working for the Hawkers, eh?"

Jeannette wasn't sure how to respond. "Well enough, *m'sieu*."

"Well, now." The way he considered those around her caused the sailors to stir uncomfortably. "I doubt Lieutenant Treynor will miss a few minutes more of your time. Smedley here is quick with his needle, I hear."

The tattoo artist blinked, and the others shifted, their change in posture revealing both surprise and relief.

"I will hurry, sir," Smedley promised.

"Hurry to do what, Mr. Smedley?"

Treynor's voice descended from above. When Jeannette saw him coming down the stairs, she nearly collapsed in relief. The chiseled planes of his face were hard, his eyes alight with an inner glow. But she knew he wouldn't let them hurt her. At least she hoped he wouldn't.

"I heard my name," he explained when Cunnington scowled up at him. "Did you need me?"

"Hardly."

Only a slight flaring of Treynor's nostrils revealed his surprise, or his impatience, at finding her outside his cabin. "I thought you were polishing my boots, lad?"

Jeannette wondered if he had already been back to his room and had come looking for her, or whether he'd truly happened upon them as he made it appear.

Smedley, Beaner and the others looked uneasy in the face of yet another officer's anger. They eyed the companionway as if they'd lost all taste for tattooing the new French boy and desired only to flee the presence of their two senior officers.

Cunnington, however, seemed reluctant to let them change course. "You arrived at an opportune time. Your new servant's about to receive his first tattoo. Perhaps you would like to watch."

"Unfortunately, I have work to do." Treynor's voice was soft and even, not overtly disrespectful, yet ripe with censure. "As does Jean."

"When we are finished, Lieutenant." Cunnington stepped between them. "I see no harm in letting the men have some fun now and then, which, I believe, is something I have heard you say upon occasion."

Treynor bowed slightly. "Indeed, sir, but not at the expense of duty. If I am not mistaken, many of these men should be making ready to appear on deck for the next watch. Perhaps another time would be better for this?"

Cunnington's face beamed scarlet, making Jeannette fear Treynor had pushed him too far. She sent a worried glance to where he was standing a step or two above Cunnington, but he simply motioned for her to precede him up the companionway.

Reclaiming her lamp and straightening her clothes, Jeannette started to obey, but Cunnington raised a hand to bar her passage. "How dare you," he said to Treynor. "I am in charge here."

"I apologize if I have offended you, sir," Treynor said. "I merely meant to suggest a course of action more compatible with the orders I have received from the captain."

Cunnington's colorless lips pressed tightly to his teeth. "Which are?"

"To see to the smooth running of the ship, of course. It is still my watch, for the next few minutes. However, should you wish to discuss my actions or my orders"—his eyes darted pointedly to the men who watched—"it might be wise to do so in the privacy of my cabin. Or yours."

Reminded of the spectacle they were making in front of the others, Cunnington seemed to waver. He obviously wanted to pull rank on Treynor, but he didn't want to risk looking like a fool for playing out such a weak hand. The men should be about their work, not tormenting the newest lad on board. Treynor had the right of it, and from the look on Cunnington's face, he knew it.

Still, for a moment, Jeannette expected pride to push him beyond wisdom or care.

"Attend to your tasks," he said to the sailors. "Now. And if any of you are so much as a minute late for muster, you will pay with your hides."

Jeannette breathed a mental sigh of relief as Beaner, Jack and the others mumbled an "Aye, aye, sir," and scattered. She tried to circumvent the first lieutenant and disappear herself, but Cunnington caught her arm.

"Watch yourself, Jean Vicard." He regarded Treynor as though daring him to intervene, but Treynor said nothing. "Someday you will get what you deserve."

"A tattoo?" Jeannette asked innocently.

Treynor coughed into his hand, and Cunnington's eyes narrowed into slits. "A tattoo will be the least of your worries."

Struggling to keep a tight leash on his temper, Treynor led Jeannette up the companionway without speaking. He wanted to shake her until her teeth rattled, but he doubted it would teach her anything.

"What are we doing?" she asked when they passed his cabin without stopping.

He gave her a withering glare. "Keeping you out of trouble. Since you won't stay put, I have decided to keep track of you another way."

"Which means . . ."

"You will work—something I doubt you have tried in your short, pampered life."

"I was about to thank you for coming to my aid, but—"

"If you had listened to me, my interference would not have been necessary. What do you do, sit and plot ways to get one of us flogged? Or are you looking for another turn over my knee?"

"Certainly not—"

Treynor whirled to face her. "Then why didn't you do as you were told and stay in my cabin?"

Her eyebrows drew down over her startlingly pretty eyes. "I . . . I . . . had something to take care of."

They were almost out on deck in the cold winter air where one had to shout to be heard. The singsong voices of the crew rose to Treynor's ears, relaying messages from stern to bow and back again as the wind whined through the rigging far above, so much a part of his life he scarcely noticed it.

"Such as?"

She propped her hands on her hips. "I am not at liberty to say."

He studied her for a moment, waiting for her reasoning, knowing he probably wouldn't agree with it, anyway. "Suit yourself," he said when she glared back at him, her chin set at a defiant angle.

With a slight nod, he strode across the deck, pausing only long enough to tap the shoulder of a man who was busy hammering oakum into the cracks of the deck. "Teach this lad how to caulk and then put him to good use, Simon," he said, indicating Jeannette.

"Aye, aye, sir."

A stout man with a paunch that rolled well over his belt, Simon was a quiet sort who kept to his own business. Treynor had known him for years. The man didn't gamble or drink too much, and he religiously sent his wages home to his wife and children, something most sailors were not wont to do. Jeannette would be safe with him. Better yet, she'd be busy until dark and then too tired to cause him any more headaches.

Jeannette stayed next to Simon, but Treynor could feel her gaze trailing after him as he continued on to the wheel. He felt guilty for abandoning her to rub elbows with the crew. They were a crude lot, and hammering oakum was a tedious, grueling task. But she was the one who refused to listen, and he was determined to teach her a lesson.

The sooner she learned to obey him, the safer they both would be.

"That lad, Jean Vicard. Something isn't right about him." Lieutenant Cunnington stood with the captain at the helm, watching the boy clumsily wield a hammer as he pounded oakum into the deck.

Captain Cruikshank eyed him before looking out over the sailors moving about the forecastle. "Could the problem be that he is Treynor's servant and not yours, Mr. Cunnington?"

Cunnington hid the flare of anger sparked by the captain's pointed question. Keeping his voice neutral, he marked Treynor's presence across the deck, where the other lieutenant was talking to a marine sentry. "Vicard was supposed to go to Bosun Hawker, if I remember correctly."

The captain's bushy eyebrows rose. "Are you questioning my decision, Lieutenant?"

Cunnington squinted out to sea. "No, sir."

"Mr. Treynor earned the lad's services when he took his stripes. Hawker agreed."

"Yes, sir. But *why* did Mr. Treynor sacrifice himself for a French deserter?"

The captain chuckled. "After serving with Treynor for more than four years, you don't know? Vicard might be French, but he is only a boy, and Treynor is an unusual man. He refuses to patronize the rich and often sacrifices himself for the weak. As strange as that may seem to you, Treynor has done such things ever since I have known him."

"Perhaps being a bastard has taught him more empathy than is good for an officer."

"Some might fault him there." The captain clasped his hands behind his back and rocked up on the balls of his feet. "But it seems to work for him. The men go to great lengths to obey him. An officer could do worse."

Cunnington stiffened, wondering if the captain's words held hidden censure.

A glance at the older man's weathered face revealed nothing. Still, a fresh wave of hatred for Treynor washed over him. How could Cunnington, the son of a viscount, born to the nobility, distinguish himself in the shadow of such a paragon? The captain's voice never held the same respect for him as it did for Treynor.

"He seems to be particularly protective of his new servant. More so than the situation warrants," Cunnington pressed.

"How so, Mr. Cunnington? Treynor could have the lad in his cabin darning his socks, if he wanted. Yet it looks to me as though Vicard is helping with tasks that benefit us all. Is that not the lad there?"

"Aye."

The master approached, and the captain turned away to discuss their navigation plans. When finished, he looked back. "Are we done?"

Cunnington remembered how Treynor had interfered in the tattooing incident and taken his servant with him. But he hardly wanted to share the details of that encounter with the captain. Any recounting would paint Treynor as properly justified and mindful of his duty. Yet Cunnington sensed something more in the second lieutenant's behavior—a marked attention to Vicard that went so far as to interrupt the man's usual focus.

"I suppose," Cunnington said.

Cruikshank chuckled. "I suggest you spend your time on more worthy pursuits than pondering Mr. Treynor's actions. He is not the enemy, you know. I will be in my cabin," he said and lumbered away.

As Simon chastened the young Vicard, Cunnington wondered again what it was that bothered him about the French lad. Something in the way the boy moved. And there was a subtle difference in Treynor's manner when he approached his new servant . . .

Cunnington couldn't put a finger on it now.

But he would figure it out eventually.

Large blisters on Jeannette's hands made it impossible to grip the handle of the hammer with any real conviction. She'd been pounding oakum into the cracks of the deck for hours, breaking only long enough to eat a breakfast of what Simon called "burgoo." As far as Jeannette could tell, it was simply a concoction of poor oatmeal and bad ship's water, but she'd been hungry and eager for anything to fortify her strength.

She saw Lieutenant Treynor occasionally, walking past her with the captain, calling to the men aloft, or checking the ship's compass. His watch was over, but he didn't seem inclined to go below where she'd no longer be plagued by the sight of him.

Cunnington had met with the captain at six bells, or eleven o'clock, part of his daily routine from what Jeannette could gather from the taciturn Simon. The first lieutenant was so preoccupied, she doubted he'd take further notice of her for the morning. Had Treynor been less angry, he could have let her return to his cabin. Instead, she was bloodying her hands by trying to swing a hammer.

Remembering the spanking Treynor had given her made her resentment grow. He was such a contradiction. He behaved like a gentleman sometimes and a rake at others. He was hard and unyielding, yet he would take the stripes for a lad and help a runaway woman he didn't even like. Jeannette didn't know whether she wanted to slap him . . . or kiss him.

Slap him, she decided. His arrogance irked her.

"Don't give out on me." Simon watched her with a wary eye. "The bosun's mates will start ye right enough."

Jeannette had collapsed in an exhausted heap while Simon's hammer rang loudly in her ears. Renewing her efforts to help him with the caulking, before the bosun's mates lashed her with one of the short, hard ropes they carried for just that purpose, she cursed Treynor under her breath for his roughness with her, for abandoning her to Simon and for confusing everything she once thought she admired in a man.

"I hate him," she grumbled to herself.

"Who?" Simon asked, overhearing.

Jeannette hesitated. "Treynor," she admitted at last, enjoying the vitriolic bent of her own words.

"What ye got against the lieutenant, lad? 'E's not a bad bloke, far as officers go. 'E's done pretty well for himself."

Jeannette made no reply.

"And 'e's done right by you. A boy in yer position 'ought ter be grateful fer that," he went on. "The navy'll teach ye fast enough."

"So I hear." A blister burst, leaving raw skin exposed to the hammer's handle. Shaking the pain away, she tried using her left hand, but her awkward wielding of the tool only earned her another sharp look from Simon.

"I've known girls what can 'ammer better than the likes o' ye."

Jeannette was so cold, sore and tired that, in utter resignation, she almost told him she was a girl—and that his beloved and revered Lieutenant Treynor knew it. Rather than do that, she pulled her shirt-sleeve down to protect the sores as best she could and transferred the hammer to her right hand.

Many of the crew performed maintenance chores such as Simon's caulking. Some retarred the rigging, sewed worn-out sails or repaired a damaged cannon. Others worked in messes, preparing the main meal of the day to be served at noon.

Jeannette kept one eye on her work and one on the hatchway to the galley as the sour smell of cheese rose to her nostrils. She never dreamed she'd be so eager for such simple fare, but her stomach's growl gave evidence that the bad-tasting burgoo of breakfast had long since passed through her system.

Catching sight of the petty officer who'd beat her in the roundhouse, Jeannette ducked her head. She had no desire to gain his attention, but the sight of him carrying a bucket tied around his neck piqued her curiosity.

She studied him from beneath her lashes. "What is that man wearing around his neck?"

When Simon glanced up, she gestured to indicate who she meant.

"'Tis a spitkid."

"A spitkid?"

"Aye. Lieutenant Treynor caught 'im spittin' on the deck. Now 'e's target practice for the rest of us."

Jeannette couldn't resist the smile that spread across her chilled face. Because they couldn't smoke, most of the crew chewed tobacco. She had witnessed the telltale bulge in many a sailor's cheek and had viewed, with great disgust, the steady stream of brown juice they spat from between dried, cracked lips. It was a pleasure to imagine them trying to hit the petty officer's bucket and missing, as they often did.

Lieutenant Treynor stood at the wheel, deep in conversation with a fellow officer. Jeannette glanced covertly at his broad shoulders, noting how his uniform accentuated his lean hips and long legs. Was she the reason the petty officer wore the bucket? Had Treynor punished the man who'd harmed her?

Probably not, but if so, Treynor's retribution represented yet another contradiction. He hated her. Why would he bother to punish one of his crew for hurting her?

Just before noon, Jeannette watched the master and the master's mates measuring the angle of the sun as it reached its highest point off the horizon. Prodded by her many questions, Simon explained that they were calculating how far north or south the ship was by using quadrants, which also established the correct time.

A gangly youth changed the date and day of the week on the logboard, eight strokes clanged on the ship's bell and Bosun Hawker piped them to dinner.

Jeannette gladly relinquished her hammer as Lieutenant Treynor approached. Anticipating a tray of food to equal the one he had brought her the night before, she stood, even forced a smile to her lips, only to learn that he expected her to mess with Simon while he visited the wardroom to eat with the captain.

Remembering the eggs she'd tried to gather, the goats that roamed freely over the deck, and the pens of both cattle and pigs stabled below, all reserved upon slaughter for the captain and his officers, Jeannette jealously watched him disappear. Regular seamen's rations paled in comparison to the sumptuous fare that graced Cruikshank's table.

But there was nothing to be done to better her lot. Her disappearance from Treynor's cabin had angered him such that he offered her no reprieve. She had to descend to the mess, like the rest of the rank and file, and take a seat on one of the sea chests the men used as benches while eating.

As they began to serve the meal, Jeannette pictured Treynor enjoying his food while thinking with silent pleasure how he had made the Baroness St. Ives work like a common sailor. She vowed she'd get even. But it was difficult to stay angry with him when she saw the petty officer who'd struck her in the roundhouse attempting to eat while encumbered by his leather bucket.

Jeannette finished her salty beef and boiled peas just as a man with baggy clothes and a jagged scar across his cheek began to play a flute. She listened in a tired stupor until the others filed out, then she followed them to the main deck where she received her liquor ration from a barrel.

Although Jeannette doubted she'd require so much, she accepted the tankard the purser's mate shoved toward her. The ship's water tasted brackish already; she could hardly gag it down. And the beef had heightened her thirst. But Jeannette had never sampled anything stronger than wine.

The rum burned her stomach and warmed her body, boosting her flagging spirits. Grateful for this one moment of reprieve and relative enjoyment, she drank what was in her mug and returned for more.

Lulled by the lively notes of the flute that carried up from below and the first pleasant sensations she'd experienced since picking up that hammer, Jeannette drank far more than she had intended. She gave the last few swallows of her second tankard to one of the greedy fellows who had been hoping she'd do just that, then stumbled back to her detested task.

Simon was already at work, humming along with the notes of the flute. Jeannette added her voice to his as she plopped onto the deck and began pounding the fibers between the planks.

"This ship will be watertight thanks to us, no?" Her tongue slid and stumbled over the words as she tried to focus on Simon, who had suddenly grown fuzzy. Jeannette squinted to see his face more clearly, but could pinpoint only his bandanna, the one bright spot on his plain clothing.

He didn't answer.

She shrugged and swung her hammer with more abandon. Her hands didn't hurt so badly anymore, and she enjoyed greater warmth than at any moment since leaving Treynor's bed.

Treynor . . . Jeannette giggled at the thought of him. He knew how to taunt a woman, but he certainly knew how to please one, too. She remembered his arms around her at The Stag, the soft furring of his chest against her breasts . . .

She closed her eyes, then opened them again when she swooned and almost toppled over. The deck seemed to be shifting more than before. She could scarcely keep her balance even though she was sitting down.

What had changed?

When she glanced skyward, she saw nothing but blue—blue all around, which only increased her dizziness. The whole world seemed to be rocking. She felt as if she'd be swept away if she stood, but she couldn't find any handholds on the smoothly polished deck.

"Simon?" Jeannette studied the blurring shapes around her, but could not identify him. "Simon?"

"Be quiet, you're drunk." The voice didn't belong to Simon. The words were harshly uttered and carried a note of warning, but Jeannette recognized their warm timbre and smiled at the sensual memories that voice evoked.

"Lieutenant?" She blinked up at him, confirming his identity by the shiny brass on his uniform. "I am doin' a good job. Just ask Simon. I am doin' a good job, am I not, Simon?"

She slammed the hammer into the deck again, but she couldn't remember whether she'd stuffed a bit of oakum in the crack. She bent to better examine her work when long fingers removed the handle from her grasp.

"Ow," she complained at the jolt of pain it caused. "My blisters."

Treynor took her hand and ran his thumb over the skin of her palm. "I will take care of him, Simon," he said. "The lad's new and does not know any better."

"Aye, sir." Simon's voice floated to her as if from a far distance, right before Treynor's acrimonious whisper sounded in her ear. "Walk, damn it. I dare not carry you."

Jeannette laughed. "Do not be angry, *m'sieu*. You are far too handsome to be angry."

"Hush." Lifting her to her feet by one arm, he nearly dragged her along beside him as she tried to use her rubbery legs. Then, when they were out of eyesight of the others, he swept her into his arms and strode hastily to his cabin.

"You little fool," he whispered. "You will get yourself caught yet. And me with you."

Jeannette didn't care what he said. He was holding her. That was all that mattered because it kept her from spinning away. She was becoming sleepy, so sleepy that she could hardly keep her eyelids open. Wrapping her arms around his neck, she nuzzled her face into the hollow of his throat, breathing in the sharp, clean scent of him, the same scent she had recognized on his bedclothes.

"You smell good enough to eat," she announced.

He chuckled, his breath tickling her ear. "Are you admitting, my lady, that you are hungry for a man?"

Chapter 13

Jeannette began to wiggle in his arms as soon as they reached his cabin. "I must get these bindings off," she complained. "I cannot breathe."

As soon as Treynor deposited her in his hammock, she unbuttoned her shirt and began to worry the knots.

"Give me your knife. I cannot wait a moment longer."

"No." He brushed her hands aside. "Do not cut them. We will need them again." His fingers worked to loosen the bands until they fell away, rewarding him with a full view of her bosom. He couldn't help but smile at the glorious vision, his earlier consternation easily forgotten.

Jeannette didn't bother to cover herself. She rubbed the welts that marked her flesh, propriety and embarrassment lost in drink and her marked relief. "Ah, that feels better."

Treynor's gaze fell to the pulse above her delicate collarbone. The soft flesh between that bone and the swell of a woman's breast was his favorite part of the female anatomy.

He allowed his eyes to fall lower. Well, besides the breast itself, perhaps.

Following the direction of his gaze, Jeannette bit her lip and smiled uncertainly, but whether or not she blushed was hard to determine. Her face was already tinged with red from the rum.

"Do you want to touch me, Lieutenant?" she asked softly.

Treynor guessed his desires were as obvious as those of a dog who sits near the dinner table, wagging his tail and begging with his eyes. He cleared his throat and tried to turn away, but she reached out to stop him.

"Don't go." Her lovely eyes pleaded with him.

He raised his hand to her breast and felt his breath catch in his throat. He'd promised he'd not force her. Taking her while she was drunk was probably just as bad. He knew better than to stay, but the soft mound of flesh felt so good in his palm . . .

"I will be happy to oblige you in the morning, if you still desire my company." Hearing the thickness of his own voice, he forced his hand to let go of its prize while he still had the power to do so. "Before anything happens, I want to know you are in full agreement."

"I don't think I want to be a virgin when I meet my next decrepit husband." She giggled and went for his buttons. "Will that do?"

"What about your family?"

She couldn't seem to concentrate on anything other than ridding him of his clothes. "After stowing away on a frigate, my reputation will be ruined. Besides"—she paused long enough to wave a distracted hand—"my husband wanted to send his male friends and relatives to my bed. What is so wrong with me choosing the first one?"

"What?" Treynor stilled her hands and forced her to look up at him. "Is that why you ran away?"

She nodded and went back to his buttons.

"He told you this?"

"No. My brother overheard some men at the wedding placing wagers on whose seed would take in my belly." She frowned. "I think I even met some of the candidates."

"What about your parents? Would they not protect you?"

"What could they do? We are powerless, even pitied in this country. But . . . do we have to talk about this now?" Slipping her arms inside his shirt, she pressed her cheek to his chest.

They had to talk about something or he'd be swept away by the lust leaping and burning through his veins. "You're drunk," he said.

Jeannette lifted her head. "And you are beautiful!"

Warmed by a smile that was as frank as her words, he laughed. Dear God but she was a difficult woman to refuse. Despite his anger at her and the difficulties she'd caused him, there was something about Jeannette that would not let him forget her. "I think that's my line."

He took in her curly hair, her small, pert nose and sensuous mouth, then lowered his gaze to feast on her firm young breasts and narrow waist. He'd undressed her before. He knew what treasures lay beneath her clothes, but he never dreamed he'd be invited to sample them, touch them, taste them.

With a groan, he tried to pull away, but her fingers roved over his chest, turning his will to mush. Perhaps if he made love to her, finished what they'd started at The Stag, they'd both be satisfied. She'd stop invading his thoughts at the most inopportune moments, and he'd be able to concentrate on his work.

Bending, he took the tip of one breast into his mouth.

Jeannette started in surprise, then arched toward him. Her head fell back on his pillow and her eyes slid closed as he began to trail tiny kisses up her neck. She felt as greedy as he did; he could see it, sense it in the tension of her body.

But she was drunk. And she was young and probably untouched. As much as he wished to justify taking what he wanted by telling himself his lovemaking would give her a positive experience for her first time, he could not.

Letting go of her, Treynor raked a hand through his hair, but he didn't move far enough away that she couldn't guide his hands back to her body. Sweet torture, what was she doing to him? Was she trying to amuse herself by discovering how the other half lived? Or was she merely trying to prove that she could make him want her, take her and beg her for more when he was done?

Her skin was warm and smooth to his touch, her lips wet, parted. He longed to tear their clothes away and enter her warmth, to push past the barrier of her virginity and feel her close tightly around him. He wanted to carry her with him like the wind buffets a leaf, higher and higher until, together, they plunged off the tallest pinnacle to fall freely through space, suspending both time and reality until, eventually, they swirled gently back to earth.

But Jeannette was uninitiated in the ways of love. And he had been born on the wrong side of the blanket. She needed a nobleman and a wedding.

"Show me what it is like to make love with you," she said. "Let me feel you inside me before it is too late, and I am doomed to never know."

The enticement echoed in Treynor's ears, challenging everything he believed himself to be. "Perhaps another day," he managed, but it felt like he might burst if he didn't take her. "When you know your own mind."

"But I do," she protested. "This is exactly what I wanted the first night I met you."

He grimaced at the thought of how that night had gone and tried to move back. He wanted to slow the rapid pounding of his heart, but the temptation of her body shackled him to the bed.

"I did not mean to hurt you that night," she whispered.

"Then you know very little about the anatomy of a man."

"Show me." She touched his hardness through the fabric of his uniform, and he gasped at the sensation.

"I don't think you want to do that." He meant to move her hand away but ended up covering it with his own. "I may not be able to stop myself."

"Do not worry, I will stop you."

There wasn't a shred of commitment in her words, but they were enough to make Treynor teeter on the edge of indecision. The feeling of her naked breasts against his chest would be worth the cost of drawing closer to the flame—worth almost any cost.

He pulled her against him, marveling at the pleasure of such a simple thing.

Jeannette seemed to like the contact as much as he did. She gave him a sultry smile, wound her arms around his neck and turned her face up to receive his kiss.

Treynor took his time with her lips, then gently explored her small, straight teeth and velvety tongue.

She responded tentatively at first, until she grew confident in what she was doing. Then her lovemaking took on a wild abandon that stole his breath. When he felt her quiver against him, his hands moved to finish with their clothing. But this last barrier was all that stopped him from possessing her completely. Were he to remove it, he knew he'd be powerless against the animal inside him.

"Damn it!" he groaned.

"What?" She gazed up at him as if thoroughly confused as to why he might be unhappy.

Staring at Jeannette's wide eyes and her lips, swollen from his kisses, Treynor knew he couldn't win. His conscience wouldn't allow him to proceed; his need wouldn't allow him to stop.

Finally, he extricated himself from her arms and stepped away.

She blinked at him in surprise. "Where are you going?"

"Anywhere but here."

"You're not leaving . . ."

"Yes." He quickly buttoned his jacket. "But I must be the stupidest bastard in the world."

The war between his mind and his body was making him angrier by the minute. Why did his damned conscience have to intervene at a moment like this? At the very peak of sexual desire? How long had it been since he'd wanted a woman as badly as he wanted Jeannette?

Never came the answer. And that terrified him. *God,* he prayed, *not her. Anyone but her.*

Silently, he railed at himself and cursed Jeannette, too. But, considering the situation, only one thing could set his world right again—besides another fifteen minutes with the count's daughter.

He needed a good brawl.

Fortunately, he knew several members of the crew who'd be happy to oblige.

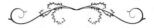

Helen crumpled the letter in one hand and tossed it into the wastepaper basket below the mahogany secretary where she sat in her study. She'd spent all evening composing the lines that had covered the perfumed sheet. Yet there seemed to be no good way to express what she had wanted, for many years now, to tell her son.

She stared out the second-story window near her desk at the moon-lit, snow-covered box hedges and Greek statues in the gardens below and thought back to their last interview at the cottage near Liskeard. Treynor had been livid with rage. She'd made him that way. But she'd only been striking out at herself. By behaving as he expected her to—by being what he thought she was—she ensured his continued rejection and no longer needed to fear it.

Dipping her quill into the inkwell, she pulled her gaze away from the glistening snow and shadowy, leafless trees to start again. She'd never spoken of Treynor's true father. His name wasn't recorded in any journal or previous letters—none that she hadn't destroyed. Even her husband, the marquess, did not know the truth.

She'd had a short affair with their stable master, but that had come at least a month after the pregnancy, as a purposeful cover. The marquess had not returned from the colonies as planned, and she'd been forced to do something.

When her husband finally did arrive, her condition was quite obvious. He was so embarrassed that she would take a servant into her bed, he'd hushed it up as carefully as she'd guarded her own secret, until no one knew, really, where Treynor had come from.

"Ah, 'ere ye are. Busy tormentin' yerself again, I see."

The voice of her housekeeper broke the silence. Surprised that Mrs. Peters was still up, Helen lifted her head. "It's late, Elizabeth. What are you doing looking over my shoulder?"

"I don't need to look over yer shoulder to know what you're doin'. It hasn't changed for years." Her jowls wagged as she shook her head. "Ye closet yerself away up 'ere an' write an' write as though ye might actually send a letter or two. But precious few make it out in the post. Writing them is just yer penance."

Helen sighed. "Perhaps someday I will send all the ones I haven't destroyed."

"Ye need to forget the past." The harsh expression on Elizabeth's round face softened with love and pity. "Ye've punished yerself long enough. It's been nearly thirty years."

The sting of tears burned behind Helen's eyes, but she'd become adept at keeping her composure. She knew her tears would never fall, not while she had a witness. "You may retire," she said, using her most imperious voice. "I can take care of myself from here."

But mere dismissal wasn't enough to get Elizabeth to leave her in peace, not this night. "M'lady, per'aps I should 'ave said these things before—"

"You didn't need to," Helen broke in. "I can always tell what you think."

"Then why not pay 'eed? I might be an old, fat crone, but no one knows ye better. No one's cared for ye longer."

"I know." Helen set her quill aside and pinched the bridge of her nose. Elizabeth had been her mother's housekeeper when Helen was just a girl—and her only comfort for years.

The housekeeper moved beside her, her hand, chafed from so many years of work, resting on Helen's arm. "One mistake didn't warrant another. That's why ye let the babe go. Are ye forgettin' ye had to provide yer 'usband with an 'eir an' protect 'im from all the waggin' tongues? Ye be'aved as befitted a marquess's wife an' ye gave no name to yer pain. Lord knows it wasn't an easy sacrifice." She paused as if waiting for a response, but Helen had nothing to say.

"An' what of the boy's father?" she went on. "Ye loved 'im." She frowned to stop Helen when she would have denied it. "But ye gave 'im up, too."

"He had a wife. What we did was wrong."

"Ye think I don't know that, m'lady? 'Twas a sad business all around, but whether ye can justify yer actions now or no, don't matter. 'Tis over and done with."

Wishing she could banish the regret as easily as Elizabeth relegated the whole incident to the past, Helen closed her eyes. "But you should see Treynor now," she whispered. "He is so handsome and tall, in command of himself and others, always the perfect gentleman."

"I can imagine, m'lady." Her voice filled with affection. "I knew there was somethin' special about 'im the first time I saw 'im."

Helen rubbed her eyes, eyes that were as tired as her heart. "Yet he carries the filthy label of bastard while the marquess's heir, my second son, is drinking and gambling his life away."

"'Tis a disappointment, to be sure," she pronounced.

"Tell me something, Elizabeth." Helen fiddled absently with the corner of a fresh sheet of paper. "How could one small indiscretion affect my whole life and the lives of so many others?"

"That's fate, m'lady. Ain't no explainin' it or understandin' it."

"You're right, of course."

"At least ye've been in contact with Mr. Treynor for the past several years, m'lady. Ye had to stand up to the marquess to do that. Give yerself credit."

Helen shook her head. "I deserve none. I should have stood up to him long ago. He has never cared about me. His only concern is for our two sons and daughter, and making his mistress and the children they have created happy."

"Now there's a woman I'd like ter see suffer the consequences of 'er actions." Elizabeth's lip curled as she crossed her arms over her considerable bosom. "She's waxin' bold, that one."

"At least my husband leaves me to live as I choose," Helen responded. "And I choose to reveal to Treynor, at last, the truth. He—" She broke off as her husband walked in without knocking.

"Ah. Thought I might find you here," he said.

Helen experienced a sharp pang of irritation. He had his own quarters and insisted on complete privacy, a courtesy he rarely returned. But she was determined to treat him civilly.

"Good evening, William."

Mrs. Peters—Elizabeth—slanted a knowing glance at her, said good night and bustled out. She always made herself scarce when the marquess appeared. She was too loyal to Helen for William to trust, and she had no interest in gaining his confidence.

"Milady. What keeps you busy on this cold night?"

She tapped her quill inside the inkwell so she could rid it of ink and set it aside. Out of habit, she also folded the letter to shield it from her husband's view, although she didn't care overmuch if he saw that it was addressed to Treynor. "I was just answering some correspondence."

"And what do you hear from Georgie?" He moved closer, until Helen could smell the scent of the expensive tobacco he smoked. "Is he well at Oxford?"

Georgie, their youngest son, was by far Helen's favorite, but she couldn't avoid the truth. "I have received no word this week. But I am comforted by that. It means he is not in some sort of scrape that requires extraordinary amounts of money to fix."

The marquess chuckled. "He will be a force to reckon with, our Georgie."

"If he ever grows up. Is there something you require, William?"

The marquess eyed her shrewdly. "Brooding over the stable master's brat again, are you? You spend all your evenings the same way. And it only serves to shorten your temper. A wife should not speak so to her husband."

If he only knew how constrained she had behaved thus far . . . "I prefer to think of it as getting to the point. You want something or you wouldn't be here. Supper is the only time we see each other anymore, besides social outings. You normally sleep in Exeter with . . . what's her name?"

"Clarissa." The clock in the hall outside struck the hour of midnight as he studied her. "You were the one who set the boundaries on our relationship, not I."

He referred, of course, to her infamous betrayal, but he'd dabbled with other women long before she'd become involved with Treynor's father. In his mind, there was a great difference between their taking of lovers, but Helen had never conceded that point and never would. She'd agreed to her marriage, and done her best to honor it. Except for how she had neglected Treynor, she had few regrets.

"I will not argue with you, William, if that's what you're looking for. It has been a war of words for years on end."

After setting her pen in its silver-and-marble holder, she put away the rest of her writing implements. She wouldn't get a letter off to Treynor tonight. She'd sit and compose until the wee hours of the morning, as she did so often, and never find the right words to convey her feelings. Words weren't enough to excuse what she had done.

"Clarissa is going to have another baby," her husband announced without warning.

Helen closed and locked her secretary, then deposited the key in the pocket of her silk dressing gown. So that was it. "Oh?"

She looked up to search his face, but there wasn't a single trace of sensitivity for what she might feel.

"I wish her well," she said. Barely twenty-five, her husband's mistress was still capable of bearing him many children. It wasn't as if his infidelity would become less obvious any time soon. "Now, if you will leave me in peace."

Instead of heading for the door, he fidgeted with the miniature portrait of Mary, their daughter, which sat on the table by the window. "You don't care?"

Helen shook her head. She felt ancient. "I ceased to care long ago."

When Jeannette awoke, she found herself swinging in the lieutenant's hammock, half-naked and burrowed deep into his feather tick. The sun's rays floated dust motes through the porthole above the bed, letting her know that night had long since passed.

With a groan, she squeezed her eyes shut and pressed a hand to her aching head. Her tongue felt thick, her mouth dry. And even with supreme effort, she couldn't stop the memories of her behavior the night before from tumbling back to her.

Fortunately the lieutenant wasn't in his cabin. She opened one eye and glanced around, grateful for that small blessing. Then she sat up and tried to get out of his bed.

The skin had peeled away from many of her blisters, leaving open sores. They made it difficult to dress. She managed as best she could, then looked around, hoping to find salve to ease the sting.

The lieutenant's cabin was rather spartan. Besides the hammock, a wardrobe and the large trunk Jeannette had ransacked when she'd stolen away that first night, only a desk and chair competed for the limited floor space.

She rolled back the desk's dark walnut cover to reveal multiple cubbyholes, none of which contained anything of medicinal value. A brass-and-marble inkstand and the letter opener she'd used before sat on a leather blotter. Various maps and a few coins were strewn about, and several letters were jammed into a slot. The corner of one revealed a woman's flowing script.

Curiosity tugged Jeannette's hand toward it. Treynor had never mentioned any of the details surrounding his personal life. She couldn't help but wonder who the letters were from.

She sifted through the pile, surprised to find that most were signed by the Marchioness of Bedford, an older woman she had met in London once, a year ago. How had someone so high in society come to write him—and so often?

Shooting a guilty glance toward the door, Jeannette played with the perfumed sheets. She wanted to read what the marchioness had written, but her conscience wouldn't allow her to invade Treynor's privacy any more than she already had.

She was about to stuff them back into their slot when the door banged open. Before it could slam shut, she dropped the correspondence like a handful of hot coals. But when she whirled to greet Lieutenant Treynor, she faced a sardonic glare. He'd seen what she held.

"Doing what women do best, my dear?" He shrugged out of his rumpled coat. A wince indicated injuries beyond the cut lip and purple bruise on one cheek she'd already noted.

"I wasn't reading them," she said, trying to appear composed. "I was looking for something to put on my hands."

"Of course. My mail looks a great deal like salve."

Jeannette grimaced as he hung his coat in the small wardrobe in the corner. "The letters caught my eye. That is all."

He offered her a halfhearted grin. "Fortunately, spying is only one of a woman's many talents."

"And you like the others even less."

He chuckled. "All except one."

"I am sure I could never guess what that might be."

"You already did—last night."

She studied him. How badly was he hurt? "Thank you for reminding me. I should have known you would gloat."

"You are just angry that you didn't get what you wanted. But I am willing to remedy the situation, should you feel so inclined." He sauntered closer, until she could smell the liquor on his breath.

"No, I do not feel so inclined," she responded with a glower. "Judging by the damage to your face, you have been doing what men do best."

"You do not know what I do best, my sweet."

"Drinking and brawling would be a good guess, no?"

"Aye, but such activities fall a good measure behind—"

Jeannette put up a hand to stop his words. "I do not want to discuss it."

His eyes ranged over her as he laughed. "May I say, then, that you look lovely this morning?"

Feeling anything but lovely, she moved cautiously away from him.

Her head seemed entirely too large for her body, and the blisters on her hands complained at the slightest movement.

"Remind me to thank you for saving my virtue," she said. "I seem to remember that I behaved like a common tavern doxy."

Treynor's gaze followed her. "There was nothing common about you. But I take great pride in having preserved your virtue. It was probably the most gallant thing I have ever done. And it cost me in more ways than one."

"So I see." She eyed his injuries once again.

He motioned toward the hammock. "By the way, we are short a blanket. You wouldn't happen to know where it went, would you?"

She swallowed hard. "No-o-o."

"You have no idea?"

His look of disbelief completely undermined her desire to lie. "Actually, I might."

"Let me guess. Down in the hold?"

She shook her head. "No, of course not."

Again, she met that sardonic gaze. "I was there, too, Jeannette. I heard the movement, know you could not have been in two places at once."

"But you have not gone back . . ."

"No. I am not sure I want to know who or what is down there."

She breathed a little easier. "Good. Then just rest assured that I put your blanket to good use."

He considered her answer as if he wanted to be harsh but honestly didn't care enough about the missing article. "Fine. So long as you are finished stealing from me."

The warning in his voice was unmistakable. "Yes."

"Good. Come here."

"Why?"

He pulled a tin from the pocket of his coat. "Because I brought something for your hands."

Jeannette inched closer. When she stood next to him, he turned her palms up and sighed at the sight of her blistered flesh.

"I see you are used to swinging a hammer." His words were sarcastic, but he surprised Jeannette by raising her hand to his mouth and gently kissing her palm.

Jeannette jerked away to avoid a repeat performance of last night's wanton behavior. What was it about this man? He taunted her, hated her, infuriated her, yet he made her pulse leap at his touch—at less, even the mere thought of his touch.

"That hurts," she complained, to hide the real reason she'd withdrawn. "And you knew I had no experience with such work."

"I had to do something to keep you out of trouble. Besides, I was merely perpetuating the lie you created when you enlisted in the first place. You signed on as a boy. Were you not planning to work?"

"I could have stayed in the hold until we reached London."

"A long stay since we are not going there anymore. And what of the rats?"

Jeannette couldn't stifle the shudder that made her a liar even as she spoke. "I would take a rat over a rake any day."

His sonorous laugh filled the cabin. "Truly, madam, I am wounded. I behaved most admirably last night, at no small discomfort to myself, and now you are calling me a rake."

"Are you denying it?"

"Not necessarily. But I must warn you that the long hours of the night have done little to cool my ardor." He pulled her to him and tried to kiss her, but Jeannette wiggled away. "I will not succumb to your charms again. I don't know what got into me last night."

Jeannette thought she saw a flash of disappointment in his eyes, but his voice remained light.

"Quite a bit of rum, if I had to guess."

"Of course. Or I never would have . . . you know."

"Are you saying you didn't enjoy our little encounter?"

His words dared her to contradict him, but the way he watched her seemed to indicate that he was looking for the truth.

"Maybe I didn't. Is that completely out of the realm of possibility, sir?" she asked, determined not to commit herself on the subject.

"No. Just directly at odds with what I observed myself."

"Is there a point to this, Lieutenant?"

"If you won't allow me to make up for what we missed last night, then no. Come back here and let me salve your hands."

"Do not trouble yourself. I can see to it." Jeannette took the jar, but regretted it when doing so freed his hands so that they could strip off his shirt. His torso was the most magnificent sight Jeannette had ever seen—golden, square shoulders, a well-toned chest and a lean, flat stomach.

"I have a surprise coming," he announced. "Something I believe you will relish."

"If you are planning to treat me to a view of the rest of you, don't bother." Jeannette scowled, trying to feign disinterest when she really hoped he'd do exactly that.

"My, you have a waspish tongue this morning."

Unable to wipe the glower from her face, she said, "Have some modesty, please."

"But I am a rake." He stopped disrobing after pulling off his boots, but his breeches fit snugly enough to outline his narrow hips and firm, well-rounded buttocks. The manly bulge that swelled in front left little to Jeannette's imagination, especially when linked with her vivid recollection of the night before.

Someone knocked and Jeannette climbed into the wardrobe where she could watch what went on through the crack in the door but couldn't be seen.

Treynor strode to the portal and motioned whoever waited outside to come in.

A lad not much beyond fourteen hauled a large empty barrel, which had been cut in half, across the floor. Other servants followed, carrying buckets of water to fill it.

When they were gone, Treynor shut and locked the door, and Jeannette stepped out, allowing herself a sigh of intense longing. "Is this your surprise?"

"It is."

"Is it seawater?"

"No. Sweet and fresh."

She knew those caskets were inaccessible to most. "Whom did you bribe?"

"Everyone," Treynor said simply.

"I must say you were right. I would do anything for a bath."

"Anything?" He cocked an eyebrow at her.

"*Almost* anything."

"Then a kiss should not be too much to ask. A kiss for first bathing rights."

A kiss? Dare she accept? No, he was too dangerous to her peace of mind. "I cannot."

"Then you don't want to go first badly enough." He clucked his tongue and pulled off his breeches, causing Jeannette to flush and turn her face to the wall. She focused on the letters she'd found, to keep her mind off what was going on behind her.

"I am curious," she said. "Who might the marchioness be to you?"

She heard Treynor step into the water, heard him moan as he folded his long legs and sank in. "I thought you weren't reading my letters."

Her fingers knotted in the tails of her shirt. "I didn't read them. I just . . . happened to see the return address."

"Hmmm."

"Are you going to tell me?"

"Does it matter?"

"No, I was only curious."

"Well, we can't have that."

She heard a smile in his voice. "So?"

"Would you believe she is my mother?"

Jeannette cast a surprised glance over her shoulder, then immediately turned back. "Really? The one who attended my wedding?"

"Yes, but don't get excited, sweet. I scarcely know her. You will gain no ties to the English aristocracy through me."

There was that arrogance again . . . "Must you make it all so . . . mercenary?"

"I am certainly not the one who made it that way."

"What about your father?" She changed the subject before they could argue.

"I know nothing about him."

The gruffness of Treynor's voice was a warning, but she persevered. She wanted to know who he was, what had shaped him, where he came from—for memory's sake, she told herself. Someday her adventure on the frigate would be over, and she would have to go back to living the life she once knew, which did not include the company of handsome lieutenants. As much as she hated to admit it, she would miss him.

"Who raised you?" she asked.

"I was pawned off, so to speak, to a farmer by the name of Cayle Abbott."

"Do you keep in contact with him?"

"No."

More bitterness. "You have no love for him."

Silence.

"Lieutenant?" For a moment, Jeannette thought he'd gone to sleep on her midconversation, but when she turned, she found him staring off into the distance, the muscles of his jaw clenched.

"No, I have no love for him," he said at last. "I was beaten. Often. He showed me no mercy. No kindness."

Jeannette remembered the scars on Treynor's back. "I'm sorry."

He met her gaze and opened his mouth to say something. Jeannette was sure it would be flippant, to mask the hurt in his eyes, but he wound up saying nothing at all. There was simply a moment when something passed between them, when her pain for his wounds somehow registered and he accepted her sympathy.

"How long were you there?" she asked when the silence stretched.

"I ran away at fourteen."

Fourteen? Had he suffered the whole of that time? Jeannette couldn't stomach the thought of it. "Those scars on your back, the old ones, they're not—"

His voice, when he broke in, was ragged. "A couple are burns. Cayle amused himself by touching a hot coal to my back more than once. And he thought it entertaining to beat me with a shovel. The rest are from his belt buckle, most likely. Ugly, aren't they?"

There was nothing ugly about Lieutenant Treynor except what had happened to him. Jeannette winced at the thought of a young boy being treated so cruelly. "And your mother didn't know?"

"I once sent word through a country parson, begging her to come and get me. She never did."

Tears filled Jeannette's eyes, but she struggled to blink them back. Treynor was a proud man. He wouldn't respond well to her pity. But at last she understood. She had been raised in luxury and, until the Revolution, had never heard an unkind word. She represented all he could have had but was denied by his mother. Or perhaps it was even simpler than that. Perhaps he viewed all women as uncaring creatures little different from the marchioness.

Treynor closed his eyes and leaned back in the tub, but he looked far from relaxed. Jeannette imagined he was remembering the past, and longed to make him forget.

After crossing to stand behind him, she rolled up her sleeves, retrieved the cake of soap and began to wash his back, careful not to scrape the scabs left over from his flogging.

At first, the soap stung the blisters on her hands, but the pain eased quickly.

He tensed as if he might refuse her ministrations, but gave himself over to the pleasure of her fingers when she left off with the washing and began to rub his shoulders where the skin was unmarred.

"What are you doing to me, Jeannette?" he murmured after several minutes.

He wasn't talking about her massage. Jeannette knew that instinctively. She smiled. The implacable lieutenant didn't know what to think of her.

"What *could* I do to you?" she said. "You are immune to women like me. You hate us, remember?"

"I wish to God I could hate you," he muttered, but moaned as her hands rubbed slower, more sensuously.

Jeannette closed her eyes, reveling in the solid feel of Treynor's body beneath her hands. Surely this was heaven. Surely the world could end right now and she would be content . . .

"Jeannette?"

She opened her eyes to see that he'd twisted his head to look up at her. "What?" She was wondering what he would do if she kissed him. He'd asked her to, not very long ago.

Her gaze dropped to his mouth, only inches away, and she remembered how wonderful his lips felt pressed to her own.

He drew a ragged breath. "What is it you want from me? What are you hoping to gain?"

His doubt and bitterness stabbed her to the heart. Did he think she was using him, trying to manipulate him? Regardless, he didn't trust her, couldn't trust her. And deep down, Jeannette knew he had no reason to. His mother had wronged him terribly, and he viewed her in the same light.

Summoning her pride, she pulled back out of reach. "I just wanted to make you forget," she said.

He watched her warily. "Forget what?"

"The past. The future. Who and what I am, too, I suppose. But that could never happen. You know me too well."

Treynor regretted his cutting words, especially when he witnessed the hurt they caused. Damn, Jeannette confused him. One minute she was defiant and the next she did something so sweet that he longed to pull her into his arms and hold her forever. He was angry at her for leaving him wanting, angry at himself for not being able to resist her effect on him and frustrated by the whole situation. He never should have helped her. He should have turned her in to the captain posthaste.

Except he didn't really feel that way. Not after learning what St. Ives had in store for her. He applauded her courage and determination and vowed to see her safely away from her powerful husband, but to do that meant he had to keep her safe from *him*. She'd never get an annulment if he took her virginity. It was the only weapon she possessed.

"I'm sorry," he said.

She didn't answer.

He dunked his head and washed his hair. Then he warned her that he was getting out and stepped over the edge of the tub to towel himself off. "The bath is yours."

He promptly dressed. He wanted to take Jeannette into his arms and kiss away the damage he'd done, but he told himself things were better this way. She would be safer if she kept him at a distance.

The way he was feeling, she couldn't get far enough away.

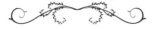

Jeannette waited for Treynor to dress and turn his back before she removed her clothes. It wasn't easy to ignore his presence, or his unkind words, but she concentrated on the water that would wash the grime from her body and give her a reprieve from her dirty boy's costume.

Treynor stood in the corner, feet spread wide, as he finished buttoning his shirt. His thick, wet hair fell partway down a back that was straight and true. He'd asked what she was doing to him, but Jeannette could have demanded the same of him. This so-called bastard had turned her whole world upside down. He invaded her thoughts, her dreams and sometimes even . . . her hopes.

She swallowed against the lump that had lodged itself in her throat and sank into the barrel. The water was tepid, as if some attempt had been made to warm it. Better than that, it was as fresh as he'd indicated.

"Did you really bribe everyone?" Hoping to establish a truce between them, she leaned back and closed her eyes. "Everyone else bathes and washes their clothes and hammocks in seawater, yes?"

Several seconds passed before he answered. "Not most of the officers. Mrs. Hawker collects rainwater for me. She uses it for my laundry, and I use it to bathe in." He sounded distant, composed.

For a moment, Jeannette resented his indifference, especially when her heart still raced at the memory of holding him in her arms. But it had been kind of him to share the luxury of his rainwater bath. She opened her eyes to thank him and caught him watching her in the mirror.

A slow smile curled his lips when their gazes met and locked in the glass. Evidently he wasn't so unaffected after all.

"At least have the decency to look away now that I have caught you." She gave her words plenty of starch, but the way she'd worshipped his body only minutes earlier stole any basis she had for real indignation—that and the relief that she wasn't the only one feeling what she was feeling.

"I have been quite the gentleman so far, despite my low birth. You certainly can't begrudge me a view of your loveliness in return for my bath."

Jeannette smiled. She was growing weary of Treynor's damned restraint and, perverse though it was, she somehow wanted to punish him for it. "As you wish." Standing, she lathered her body, purposefully ignoring him as she worked her hands around her breasts.

Treynor didn't say a word, but Jeannette caught him staring at her with slack-jawed appreciation.

"Do you not have work to do, Lieutenant?"

His eyes narrowed. "You are playing with fire, Jeannette. I am not one of your drooling beaux. I am used to getting what I want."

"I didn't ask you to stand there and ogle me."

"And yet you tempt me to do far more."

Finally embarrassed by her own behavior, she ducked down. He had her acting like a common whore one minute and a nun the next. She hardly knew herself anymore. But, when she pictured herself with child and returning to her parents, unable to hide her shame, she had sense enough left to know that she wouldn't thank him for taking advantage of the situation.

Something had to be done, before it was too late. "I am going to the captain," she said, her newfound resolution giving her strength. "Certainly we are far enough from England now."

A frown settled on Treynor's face. He looked as though he would argue with her, but he didn't. "Perhaps that is best for both of us," he said at last.

When Jeannette got out of the bath and dried off, she quickly pulled on her clothes and fled.

Chapter 14

A fire raged in the hearth of the drawing room at the baron's London town house. Percy sat before it with Thomas Villard, staring pensively into the flames. Jeannette had been gone for nearly four days. He had men scouring the teeming city and every route into it, but to no avail. They had given him a report as soon as he arrived an hour ago.

Something must have happened to her. Or had she outsmarted him after all?

Sir Thomas cleared his throat. "Providing your lady is alive and well, why not proceed with an annulment so you can seek a new wife? Hard as an annulment is to obtain, you might be better off," he said, lifting his glass of brandy to the light of the fire where he could better examine the golden liquid.

Percy turned a scowl on his friend. "And admit to being impotent? We both know that is likely what it would require, and I will do no such thing. How would I ever get an heir?" He shook his head. "No, I am committed to this path. Jeannette is ideal for my purposes. I knew it the moment Lord Darby contacted me about her."

"He contacted you?"

"Indeed. He was so eager to be rid of his poor French relations that he wrote to say he thought she would make me a perfect wife. He all but begged me to marry the chit." He watched Sir Thomas drain his glass. "And what we arranged is no less than fair. You have to give me that."

"I agree, of course."

"I ask Jeannette's forbearance for one night," Percy went on. "What is one night? In return she and her family are provided with financial security. Her sons will inherit all I have." He shifted to ease the pain in his foot. "She could never do better. She had no dowry besides a nominal amount from Darby."

Thomas reached for the brandy decanter on the table next to him. "I remember."

"And she is beautiful, which makes your job easier, does it not?" Percy imagined his wife's young, supple body lying naked on the sheets as Villard drove into her.

"The 'job,' as you call it, would be easy enough were you not going to be there watching every move." Thomas grimaced. "I have never had another man in the room before. I am not sure I will like it at all."

"Whether you like it or not is of no matter to me. I have to make sure I get what I am paying for." Percy admired Thomas's tall, thin build and the other physical characteristics he would like his son to have. "You were more than willing when I first approached you—eager enough to offer your brother a chance to participate. That foolish decision is at the root of all our problems."

Letting his gaze drop to the carpet, Sir Thomas loosened his cravat. "How was I to know he would refuse? You said you were looking for a number of men. I tried to help you find likely candidates, those with acceptable bloodlines."

"You should have known Richard better than that!"

"The money tempted him. I have no idea what went wrong. I think he refused just to spite me. Anyway, I did what I could to remedy the situation." Thomas's words had fallen to a mumble. "Her parents believed us, at least."

"That is what I am paying you for, is it not? Quick thinking and discretion? Unfortunately for me, those commodities do not come cheaply."

Sir Thomas smiled ruefully. "They come cheaply enough. The money goes too fast."

"Just remember that there is more where that came from when the deed is done."

"Then I shall do my part the moment you retrieve the sacrificial virgin." Thomas smiled and leaned his head back against the soft leather of his seat. "And what of Desmond?"

"He is with us still."

"I am not surprised. He is the type to enjoy you sitting next to the bed, urging him on when he lifts your wife's skirts. Putting on a show is his forte, not mine."

Just the mention of the spectacle he had anticipated ever since he'd met Jeannette caused a spark of arousal to leap through Percy's veins. Impotency was becoming a problem for him, but not when he pictured watching Sir Thomas with Jeannette. Perhaps he would be able to take a turn after all.

Thomas smiled at his silence. "Does the thought of having other men rock your marriage bed excite you, my lord?"

"Begetting an heir excites me," Percy snapped, irritated that he had been so transparent. "Do you think I will let Hawthorne House and all I own go to a distant cousin? And one I loathe at that?"

Sir Thomas covered his mouth against a belch. "Evidently not. But your new wife has certainly complicated our plans. I doubt her parents will give you the unbridled freedom they would have before."

Percy's desire turned to a dull ache in his joints, reminding him of his age and making him angrier still. "It won't be difficult to discredit her or her parents. When Lord Darby hears Jeannette's accusations, he might pay me a cursory visit, but he would hardly allow himself to lose face by trying to wrench her back. And by the time he does, it will all be over anyway. She will be with child, a child she will relinquish to me the moment it is born."

"Providing, of course, that we find her."

Percy rose from his chair and moved to where Sir Thomas sat, farther away from the fire. He grasped the man's arm, curling his nails, claw-like, into Villard's flesh. "No girl makes a fool of me. I will find her," he promised. "And when I do, she will cooperate. Then you will give me everything I have paid for, too."

Sir Thomas looked uneasy. "I have already given you my word. There is no need for any . . . unpleasantness."

"Very well." With a grunt, Percy pulled away and turned to pace—stiffly—on the expensive rug.

"Just because your first wife bore you no children does not mean you were at fault," Villard said. "Perhaps she was barren."

Percy faced his friend. He'd once thought the same thing, had blamed Elsie for everything—until years of bedding young servants, peasant women, prostitutes and the wives of several friends hadn't yielded him a single illegitimate child either. "It wasn't Elsie."

"But if this goes on much longer, our plan might not work. I mean—"

Percy swiped the glass from Thomas's hand, sending it crashing into the hearth. "It will work! The babe shall have the finest blood in all of England! And," he added, looking at it from a practical perspective, "no one will know who the father is, even the sires, which will protect my property from any future claims—"

A rap at the door halted Percy's tirade. "Damn you," he muttered, afraid Harripen, his butler, might have overheard. "What is it?" he called out.

Harripen entered, followed closely by Ralston Moore, the baron's solicitor.

"Moore, you were to meet us when we arrived," Percy growled. "Where have you been?"

"I came as soon as I could." Noticing the broken glass on the floor, he raised a questioning eyebrow, but Percy ignored it.

"Tell me you had good reason to be detained."

A smile crinkled the corners of the solicitor's eyes. "I believe I know where your wife is hiding, sir."

Percy's heart skipped a beat. "Where?"

Moore reached into his pocket and withdrew a small leather pouch. Wearing the same self-satisfied smile, he handed it to Percy.

Percy loosened the drawstrings and gazed inside, only to find a few long tresses of dark hair. "What is this?"

"Your lady's hair, I believe."

"What?" Percy felt a moment's confusion. "Where is the rest of her?"

"She may be aboard the *Tempest*, after all. One of my men found this in an alley behind a tavern where the sailors slept"—he paused for what Percy suspected was dramatic effect—"along with your wife's torn garments."

"What are you saying? That Jeannette has been ravished by sailors?"

"Let us hope not," Sir Thomas said, "or any brat she bears will certainly not have the finest blood in all of England."

Moore continued before Percy could respond to the snide comment. "I believe your wife stole aboard the *Tempest,* milord, just as we originally suspected. Only she did it dressed as a boy. I have spoken to a sailor who claims his clothes were stolen that night."

"But I sent a letter to the frigate! They searched for her and found nothing."

"That does not mean she wasn't there."

St. Ives fingered the silky tresses of his wife's hair. "The *Tempest* was bound for London, was it not?"

"It was, yes—until it received orders to join the blockade along the French coast," Moore explained.

"Which would explain why my wife never showed up to meet her family."

He gave a decisive nod. "Indeed."

Percy felt hope rise inside him. "Well, we are not without recourse. There are those at the Admiralty who owe me a favor or two."

"Yes, sir." Ralston Moore bowed deeply, and Percy turned to Sir Thomas.

"It is only a matter of time now," he promised.

Not wanting to explain her bath in Treynor's quarters, Jeannette skulked in the corridor outside the captain's cabin until her hair dried. Though the air was so cold she could see her breath, she doubted the weather was entirely to blame for the shivering that beset her. She had no idea how the taciturn old captain would receive the revelation of her identity. But she had to inform him. She dared not spend another night with Treynor.

Gathering her nerve, she knocked, and Captain Cruikshank bellowed for her to come in.

Jeannette's trepidation grew as she turned the knob and stepped inside.

The windows behind the captain glowed with the orange hue of sunset as he glanced up from where he sat at a wide wooden table. A journal lay open before him, a pair of spectacles rested low on his nose and he held a quill pen in his left hand. A look of expectation claimed his features as he recognized her, but he didn't immediately stand.

"What is it?" His gaze ranged over her short hair before systematically working its way down her body. Then his eyes jerked up to her face.

In her haste, she had left her hat and coat in Treynor's cabin, and the swell of her breasts was clearly visible beneath the white cotton of her shirt.

"God's teeth!" He came to his feet. "You are a woman!"

Jeannette cringed at the explosion. "Yes, sir."

His jaw worked several times before any sound emerged. When he finally spoke, his voice deepened almost to a roar. "Dammit! For once in his life, Cunnington was right. Who are you?"

Outside the drummer was beating to quarters. The rush of feet as all hands reported to their various stations for the officers' inspections wound Jeannette's nerves tighter with every thump. She swallowed hard. "I am the Baroness St. Ives. And I am afraid I have made a terrible *erreur*." She smiled sweetly in hopes of softening his heart. "I thought to escape my unwanted marriage by stealing aboard your vessel and only now do I realize how foolish that decision was."

"Indeed, madam." He dropped his pen, then toppled the ink when he tried to keep the quill from marking the page covered by his crooked script. Grumbling another curse, he quickly righted the jar, but had only his hands to dam the black puddle he'd created as he sent another disbelieving glance her way.

Jeannette crossed the room to offer him the use of her shirtsleeve. "Certainly a little ink can do no damage to this."

He jerked his head toward the cabinets that ran the length of the wall beneath the windows. "Under that bench is a towel."

Jeannette found it and mopped up the ink. While she worked, the captain watched her, glowering from beneath the ledge of his prominent brow and mumbling a string of expletives while shaking his head.

"Excuse my language, madam. I assure you it is a product of my intense surprise."

"You have every right to be angry, sir." Jeannette held the stained cloth away from her body until he took it, wiped his hands and dropped it onto the ruined pages of the journal. The sorrow in his countenance made her unsure which distressed him more: the loss of his journal or the appearance of a baroness on board his frigate.

"What now?" he asked. "If we turn back it could compromise the blockade. If we stay, your husband will be after my head for endangering your life. I cannot imagine whatever possessed you, but you have placed me in a very difficult position, madam!"

"Indeed, Captain." Head bowed, Jeannette kept her gaze fastened to the floor. "I can only apologize for my impulsive act—and beg your forbearance."

With a scowl, he began to pace. "You came aboard with Lieutenant Treynor. Did he assist you in this ruse?"

She shook her head. "Oh no, *monsieur*. I misled your lieutenant and the others with my charade. I am dreadfully sorry."

He considered her reply. "It is not often Treynor is fooled by anyone. How long has he known?"

"He does not know even now, sir." She lied, hoping to protect Treynor as he had protected her. "I thought it best to come directly to you."

"A wise decision, but one I wish you would have made long ago." He scratched his head and paced some more. "Why were you so desperate to flee?"

Unwilling to reveal the embarrassing truth, Jeannette told him something closer to what he might believe. "It was an arranged marriage. I was in love with another." She was thinking of an old beau, Lèfevre Campaigne, as she spoke, but she realized that, in reality, she had never felt anything beyond friendship for the kind, serious Lèfevre.

"I see." He rubbed his chin. "And how do you view your situation now?"

"I suppose you could say I have come to my senses, *monsieur.*" *Until we reach another port—any port—and I am able to disappear again . . .*

"A taste of the world has taught you much, no doubt."

"*Oui, monsieur.*"

"Well, then. I have invited my officers to join me in a late supper. We will address this issue more fully then. For now, I will have one of my servants prepare a bath for you and get you some decent clothes. My daughters have come aboard upon occasion. I believe we can find you a gown that fits, as well as a private cabin. It might take some shifting around, but we'll manage."

Trying to appear properly cowed, Jeannette nodded. This man held her future in his hands. If he chose to keep his position in the blockade, days, weeks, even months could pass, possibly giving her the opportunity to disembark at a port far from Plymouth.

But if Cruikshank took her back to St. Ives, she would know no more of freedom.

The wardroom was rather elegantly appointed with a black-and-white-checked floor, rich paneling and a long solid dining table. Seats for ten surrounded the table. Two small chests, providing a flat top for games, waited to the side, along with several more chairs.

Jeannette had plenty of time to study the furnishings as she walked the floor in her newly acquired slippers, waiting for the captain and his officers to arrive.

Already a handful of servants were busy bringing a variety of dishes to the table. Jeannette was hungry, but could take no interest in the food, despite the tantalizing aromas that drifted from the covered plates. She was thinking about Amelia, wondering how the girl fared.

She would find a way to visit her as soon as supper ended . . .

Self-consciously smoothing the green watered silk of her gown, Jeannette turned toward the silvered mirror that hung on one wall. She was finally dressed as befitted a lady, but she scarcely recognized herself. With a pair of scissors and a much smaller mirror, she'd managed to improve the state of her hair until it curled softly to her head, making her eyes look larger and more violet than ever. But the sun had tanned her face. Fortunately she'd been used to being outdoors already or she would have burnt.

She considered her lips and, for a moment, remembered the velvety feel of Treynor's mouth against them. Closing her eyes, she experienced again his sinewy arms as they encircled her—

"The captain says 'e'll be with ye right away, milady."

Startled out of her thoughts, she found a boy, no older than ten or eleven, standing behind her. *"Merci."*

He hesitated, then bobbed forward in a little bow. His awkward gallantry made her smile, but as soon as he ran off she glanced back toward the mirror, the last vestiges of Treynor's embrace still hanging on the fringes of her mind. Would the lieutenant find her attractive in her borrowed finery?

Jeannette shrugged and turned away. She normally wasn't one to worry about her appearance. What Treynor thought didn't matter anyway, she told herself, and tried hard to believe it. Her family had probably reached London by now. Or they soon would. She had to figure out a way to get there herself—if Cruikshank didn't take her back to the baron first.

"Lady St. Ives." The captain had entered the room, freshly shaved and garbed for supper. He bowed to kiss her hand, then the long sword that dangled from his hip swung in its scabbard as he stood to one side and introduced the officers who came behind him. "I believe you know Lieutenant Cunnington."

Except for the enigmatic smile on his face, Cunnington behaved as though they were being introduced for the first time. He bowed deeply, kissing her hand just as the captain had done.

"A pleasure, my lady," he said, all traces of harshness replaced by a humble, solicitous manner. "My parents attended your wedding, I believe."

"Did they?" Jeannette's skin crawled beneath his touch.

"You might remember them. My father is the Viscount Lounsbury, my mother Lady Eleanor. They are very good friends of your husband's."

Jeannette marked his emphasis, but smiled for the sake of propriety. "Then they are friends of mine," she lied, pulling her hand away. She had no wish to abuse the captain's hospitality, but wanted to dispense with Cunnington as soon as possible. Treynor had entered the room, and she couldn't keep her gaze from gliding over the handsome spectacle he made.

Dressed like the other officers, in a blue-and-gold uniform, white waistcoat and knee-length breeches, Treynor wore his clothes with an ease that most men lacked. His coat tapered in from his broad shoulders to hug his narrow waist and lean hips. His stockings revealed the muscular cut of his calves. His tanned face and honey-colored hair contrasted nicely with the blue of his eyes, making Jeannette wonder if she would ever meet another man who appealed to her half as much.

Following her gaze, the captain drew Treynor to her side, chuckling as he slapped him on the back. "Did you ever dream we would find such a jewel lurking beneath your servant's rags?" he asked, his eyes sparkling with appreciation. "Come, let me introduce the two of you."

Jeannette's breath caught as Treynor took her hand. The warmth of his fingers traveled up her arm with lightning speed, quickening her pulse.

"Treynor, this is Lady St. Ives. My lady, Lieutenant Crawford Treynor."

Their eyes met and held, then Treynor's gaze dipped to her low décolletage, which revealed much of the soft, curving flesh of her breasts. Jeannette's nipples hardened in response, tingling beneath his regard almost as though his hands, and not his gaze, caressed them.

"You are a vision, my lady." He gave her a roué's smile, as if he were aware of the immediate change in her body. Then, with a bow, he pressed his lips to the back of her hand. "I could go days without a meal if only I were allowed to feast upon your beauty."

"*Merci,* Lieutenant." Supremely self-conscious, she noted the close regard of Cunnington, who still looked on. "You are most kind, considering that I have put you and the rest of the crew in a most difficult position."

"Lieutenant Treynor is not a man to hold a grudge." Cunnington's tone was smooth, but edged with a subtle hint of malice.

His smile never wavering, Treynor's eyes flicked to the first lieutenant. "Not if I can get even instead." He looked back at Jeannette. "My charge for being duped is no less than a dance or two this evening."

A fifer had entered the room. Seating himself in the corner, he began to play.

Jeannette enjoyed music and felt a momentary thrill at the prospect of being swept across the floor in Treynor's arms. She acquiesced with a slight nod. Certainly she couldn't be tempted beyond the bounds of propriety inside a room full of people.

"*Avec plaisir*, Lieutenant," she said and turned her attention to the officer awaiting an introduction behind him.

The captain introduced the third and fourth lieutenants and the warrant officers, beginning with the master, John Borrows, whom Jeannette had seen upon occasion.

She greeted Mr. Borrows, then Bosun Hawker, who winked before bowing over her hand. "Not many 'ighborn ladies would brave goin' ter sea on a frigate," he said. "Ye 'ave pluck, I'll give ye that."

At the moment, Jeannette felt anything but courageous. Her knees knocked at the thought of facing St. Ives again, but she prayed she wouldn't have to. "I must thank you for all your kindness to me. And please, give my regards to Mrs. Hawker."

"Indeed I will. An' I still think ye'd make a right smart bosun."

"Perhaps you will lend me your pipe sometime."

He chuckled and turned away, allowing Cruikshank to finish the introductions. After Jeannette exchanged a few words with the carpenter, surgeon and purser, the captain escorted her to the seat on his right.

The others gathered around the long table, which was now laden with food. Lieutenant Cunnington sat directly across from Jeannette, Lieutenant Treynor next to him, and the others in order of descending rank until the purser, Roddie Gillman, took his place on her other side.

The captain sampled the wine, then nodded, ordering the servants to fill the goblets.

Remembering her earlier experience with the rum, Jeannette was careful to drink sparingly. The light, fruity flavor of the wine was certainly not the same quality that had once stocked her parents' cellars, but at least it didn't taste slimy and brackish like the ship's water.

"My lady, I was hoping you might regale us with the happier occurrences at home these days," Cruikshank said. "We get little news, as I am sure you can imagine. When we are in port, we hear mostly of the war."

The servants removed the covers from the hot dishes in the center of the table, and the aroma of lamb, veal and various meat pies wafted to Jeannette's nostrils in a small puff of steam.

While one of the captain's lads ladled food onto her plate, she said, "I am afraid I can tell you little. I was in Liskeard for the past several weeks, and nothing amusing happened there."

"Which leads me to the subject that has been uppermost in my mind. Perhaps we should address it now and be done with it."

The hubbub died down when he clinked his crystal glass with his knife and raised his voice so that those at the opposite end of the table could better hear him. "I have been hard-pressed, gentlemen, trying to decide whether or not we should immediately return the baroness to Plymouth. I am mindful of our duty, and the coming grain convoy from America, but a frigate is an unsafe place for a woman. Not only that, but the baron is no doubt, eager to see his wife return home."

Jeannette's heart sank. She'd been expecting such a conversation but certainly wasn't looking forward to it.

The captain's gaze circled the table. "I would hear your opinions on the matter, if you please."

Cunnington spoke first. "As a friend of the baron's, I feel it my duty to try and persuade you to return her immediately, sir. Lady St. Ives made our decision for us when she stole aboard this ship, especially when we consider that the baron tried to reclaim her before we left port."

Cruikshank grunted. "Yes, I have thought of that. It certainly does not reflect well on us that she escaped notice for so long. The baron has friends in high places who will no doubt wonder what kind of ship we are running here."

"Indeed," Cunnington agreed. "The only way to avoid further embarrassment is by returning her posthaste."

Jeannette tried to swallow the food in her mouth, but her throat seemed to have closed off.

Several of the others nodded their approval.

"Shall we return on the morrow then?" the captain asked.

Jeannette's gaze lifted to find Cunnington smiling at her as if he knew she'd rather be dragged behind horses than return to Plymouth. And his smile widened when Treynor spoke.

"At the risk of being the only dissenting voice, I feel it is imperative that we keep our position along the coast until after the grain convoy tries to break through to France. Our squadron is counting on us to help hold a line that is already too thin."

"Hear, hear," someone muttered, but Treynor continued with scarcely a pause.

"Although I share everyone's concern for the baroness"—he nodded his head politely in her direction—"I should hate to sacrifice the integrity of the blockade. We are, after all, at war."

Jeannette lowered her lashes, refusing to study the lieutenant as she longed to do. Was he trying to help her yet again? Or did he care only for the blockade, as he made it sound?

Regardless, his words garnered immediate support from the master, the purser and Toddy Pratt. For that, Jeannette was grateful.

"How noble of you, Lieutenant, to be so mindful of your duty," Cunnington said. "Somehow I thought you might disagree. You have made a habit of looking out for the lady's interests since you brought her aboard."

"Meaning what, Lieutenant Cunnington?" the captain asked.

"Meaning that the two of them are playing us for fools, sir. Can you not see it? They are lovers."

Forks stilled around the table. Even the captain looked as though he had to force down his last bite with a swallow of wine. "Excuse me," he sputtered after a hacking cough, but his attention never left Cunnington. "On what grounds do you make such an accusation?"

The first lieutenant shrugged and picked up his glass. "I have observed both of them quite closely, sir. I would wager Lieutenant Treynor knew Jean Vicard's true identity from the start."

The captain's bloodshot eyes widened and shifted, first toward Jeannette and then his second lieutenant.

Cunnington continued, "You all saw him step in and allow himself to be tied to the grate. He wanted to save her from more than a whipping. Her honor and her modesty were both at grave risk—"

Treynor interrupted him, but calmly. "You are forgetting one thing, Mr. Cunnington. As you are so fond of pointing out, I am a mere bastard. How could I convince a baron's wife to run away with me when I can offer her nothing more than boy's rags, a small cabin and my nominal navy pay? What is more, *why* would I do it? Not only would it ruin her life and my career, but the legal implications are enormous. A marriage contract is no small thing."

The others at the table were listening with rapt attention. Jeannette could feel their attention rest on her as if they were weighing the two arguments and did her best not to show her fear.

"Regardless," Cunnington responded. "You are infatuated with her. I have seen how your gaze trails after her, how you protect her at any cost—"

"That is all very romantic, Mr. Cunnington, but I am afraid you overrate my powers of seduction." Treynor smiled indulgently, as though Cunnington's words entertained him rather than upset him. "If the two of us are lovers, why would Lady St. Ives suddenly give herself up to the captain?"

"That is the question, is it not?" Cunnington raised his glass in silent acknowledgment of the shocked faces around the table. "Perhaps you knew discovery was not far away. I would have figured it out eventually. The fact remains that the lady spent three nights in your cabin, and I am sure the baron will not be pleased to learn that."

"The lieutenant had no idea the boy he sheltered was a woman, let alone the baron's wife," Jeannette argued.

"Forgive me if I find that difficult to believe, my lady." Cunnington saluted her with his glass.

She attempted to stare him down. "The truth is not judged by its plausibility, sir. The truth is simply the truth."

"Then, pray, tell us the truth for once," he scoffed.

"Cunnington, that is enough," the captain said. "We will get to the bottom of this when we have a bit of privacy, I assure you. But I will not have my supper ruined."

Her appetite lost, Jeannette pushed her plate away. If Cunnington discredited her by spreading his lies to his parents and their friends, she would never get her annulment.

Strictly speaking, perhaps she didn't deserve one. She hadn't physically succumbed to Treynor, but she had him to thank for that fact more than herself.

"I apologize, Lady St. Ives." A wry smile twisted Treynor's lips. "Lieutenant Cunnington is suspicious by nature. He seems to consider you compromised merely by my reputation as a rake."

"Which reputation is not completely undeserved," Toddy Pratt volunteered.

Pratt's jest seemed to ease the tension, and the conversation moved on to the possibility of a storm, but Jeannette could feel the men watching her when they thought she wasn't looking. Even the captain became morose, saying nothing while drinking plenty.

As the servants cleared away the dishes, the fife player struck up another tune. The light, airy notes contrasted sharply with Jeannette's mood. She wanted to excuse herself, to escape the vile Cunnington as soon as possible, yet she awaited the captain's word. She had no idea where she was to spend the night, or what his final decision regarding their return to Plymouth would be.

The purser intruded upon her thoughts as he pushed away from the table. "I think a game of whist is in order. Can I entice anyone to join me?"

Toddy Pratt, Cunnington and Bosun Hawker accepted his invitation, and the four moved to a small table along the canvas wall that separated the wardroom from the cabins beyond it. Those who remained enjoyed the last of their wine. Once Captain Cruikshank emptied his glass, he slid his chair back and stood, then bowed to Jeannette.

"Will you do me the honor of a dance, my lady? It is not often we have the pleasure of feminine companionship."

Jeannette accepted the captain's hand. She wanted to glance Treynor's way, but settled for singling out the deep timbre of his voice as he spoke with the ship's master across the table, discussing matters of navigation.

As Jeannette wondered what type of dance the captain might choose, he slid his arm around her back and gripped her right hand high. So it was to be a waltz, she realized, surprised that the unpolished captain would know how to execute a dance that most of the English considered quite scandalous. Not only that, but there was only the fife to provide music. The player began with a run of notes that gave Jeannette a burst of energy—but slowed to a stately pace when the captain began to tire and glared his way.

Fast or slow, the steps she followed were far from a waltz, or any other dance Jeannette knew. They were more of a modified version of several that left her constantly wondering what the next move might be.

"You dance well, my lady," he told her.

"*Merci, monsieur.*"

They turned about the floor for a few moments before he lowered his voice. "Tell me, is there anything to what Cunnington has said?"

Willing him to believe her, Jeannette forced her gaze to his face. "None, sir. I can assure you that Lieutenant Treynor was as ignorant of my identity when he brought me aboard as you were yourself."

"Indeed."

"As a matter of fact, I had never met him before signing on. I lived in London for only a year after arriving from France, and as I said, I was in Liskeard for the past month while awaiting my wedding. I doubt the lieutenant has had occasion to visit London, at least in a capacity that would bring the two of us together."

This seemed to bolster the captain's confidence, and his steps quickened again. He even began to smile. "As I thought. Treynor's conduct has always been exemplary."

Mention of Treynor drew Jeannette's attention to where he stood, leaning idly against one wall. As she and the captain moved, his gaze followed them, but he remained engaged in conversation with the fourth lieutenant and the ship's master.

"Lieutenant Cunnington must bear some sort of grudge against Mr. Treynor, sir," she said. "Why else would he spew such thoughtless slander?"

"They have always been at odds," he answered simply. "But now that the accusation has been publicly stated I feel, for the welfare of all involved, we should return to Plymouth with all due haste. I hope you understand."

He seemed intent on her reaction despite his earlier words in support of Treynor.

Jeannette prayed her smile looked far less brittle than it felt. "Certainly, *monsieur*."

Winded, the captain stopped and released her. "I apologize for my first lieutenant, madam, but you can rest assured that you will soon be safely ensconced in your husband's home."

"Merci," Jeannette replied, but silently cursed Cunnington. At Hawthorne House, there would be no one to stop St. Ives from doing whatever he wanted with her. By the time she could get help from Lord Darby in London, it would be too late. But she swallowed her panic and curtsied politely, knowing that arguing with Cruikshank would only make him doubt her credibility.

With a responding bow, the captain thanked Jeannette for the dance and told her he would have one of the midshipmen show her to a cabin when she was ready to retire. But before he had so much as straightened to his full height, which was several inches shorter than most of the other men in the room, the ship's master approached and asked Jeannette for the next dance.

She turned about the floor with the master twice and the fourth lieutenant once before Treynor approached. Bowing, an enigmatic smile on his face, he extended his hand. "I believe the next dance is mine."

And although Cunnington stared at them from the whist table by the wall, Jeannette could not bring herself to deny him.

Chapter 15

As Treynor took her into his arms, Jeannette couldn't help noticing the difference between his erect posture and firm, confident embrace and the other men's nearly apologetic stances. He moved about the floor with purpose, leading her with skill, his energy seeming to flow into her body at every point of contact.

"Do you think this is wise?" she murmured under cover of Pratt and Hawker's raised voices as they wrangled over their card game.

He cocked an eyebrow at her. "I always claim what is mine."

Staring at the buttons of his waistcoat so that their conversation would not be readily detected by the others, Jeannette lowered her voice. "I am not yours!" she protested hotly.

A fleeting glance revealed a sardonic smile on his full lips. "Easy, my lady. I meant the dance. You owed me a dance, remember?"

Jeannette felt her cheeks flame with embarrassment. She was too aware of Treynor, especially now, with his fingers threaded through her own, his palm on her back. She knew those hands could stir a deep longing, the memory of which would always plague her.

"What of Cunnington?" she asked. "I doubt he will let his accusations lie."

"It is not you he is after, my dear. It is me he wants to destroy."

"But his parents know my husband. If Cunnington discredits me, my cousin, Lord Darby, may not assist me. My hopes for an annulment will be lost."

"We can prove we are not lovers. You are yet a virgin—although how we have managed that, I cannot say. I have been entertaining the idea of dispensing with your maidenhead ever since I met you."

Afraid he might have been overheard, Jeannette glanced toward the others. "You risk much, *monsieur*."

"I would risk more if I thought we could get away with it." He grinned.

The melody continued and they fell silent, but Jeannette couldn't help worrying her lip. "Cunnington frightens me," she admitted. "He hates us both."

"My beautiful Jeannette, there is a solution to every problem."

"And you found one for the man who beat me." It was not quite a question.

Treynor squeezed her hand. "He deserved more than a bucket around his neck."

It was as she had suspected then. Treynor had punished the petty officer for what he had done to her. "How did you know it was he?"

"I have ways of getting what I want."

"Are you ever denied?"

"Not if I am determined."

Exhausted, the fifer came to the end of his tune and ceased to play, saving Jeannette from having to make a reply. She didn't know what to say anyway; she was glad she had left Treynor's cabin and turned herself in to the captain. The way he looked at her made her knees buckle and brought visions of his hard, naked chest. She wanted to trail kisses over the entire expanse of it, pausing only to feel the strong beat of his heart at the hollow of his throat.

The room suddenly felt far too warm. "Thank you, Lieutenant."

The captain approached, and Treynor released her with a simple, "My lady."

Cruikshank and the others bid her good night, but Jeannette barely heard their words. Instead Treynor's voice echoed in her ears. *Not if I am determined.*

She would have to be as well, she decided. Or she would become his next conquest—and any hope of an annulment would slip away.

Jeannette tossed and turned in the narrow cabin the captain had reserved for her use. Besides the dress, he'd had his steward bring over a nightgown fit for a lady and some smaller items, no doubt also left behind by his daughters. She was grateful for his kindness, and for the privacy afforded by the lock on her door. Cunnington's smug look as she'd bid the officers farewell haunted her still.

Unwilling to put out the lamp just yet, she stared miserably at the cannon below and to the right of her hammock. With its cold, dark muzzle pointed at the closed gunport, the wooden apparatus that cradled it tied securely into place, it became a symbol of how far she had come since leaving France only a year ago.

How had she gotten herself into such a terrible mess? She'd wanted only to help her family, to restore their happiness. But instead of being a dutiful daughter, she was letting Lieutenant Treynor consume more and more of her thoughts and dreams, torturing herself by wanting something she could never have.

"All's well." The sentry's cry echoed more and more faintly from the various stations on the deck above.

Jeannette gave up trying to sleep and climbed out of her hammock. Rather than feel sorry for herself, she would see to Amelia. She hated to venture out alone so late at night, but she was under the captain's protection now. No one would dare harm her.

She dressed, making sure to take a shawl against the cold and a handkerchief. As she headed out with her lamp, she listened carefully for footsteps that would indicate she had company. She knew the master-at-arms made a series of nightly rounds. She cared not if she saw him, but captain's protection or no, she had no desire to run into Cunnington.

Everything was quiet and dark. Most of the lanterns were extinguished at night so the ship could not be seen from a distance. She walked as quickly as possible to the galley, where she filched a bit of cooked salt pork saved from someone's dinner. Managing to garner a chunk of bread, as well, she wrapped it in her handkerchief.

Anyone else risked the cat-o'-nine for the theft of food—the theft of anything—but she knew she had no reason to fear the lash. Not anymore.

After descending two decks, she arrived at the hold, where the smell was no less pungent for being expected. Jeannette nearly gagged as she hesitated at the entrance, but managed to swallow her revulsion long enough to call Amelia's name.

No answer. Thinking herself alone in the hollow-sounding hull, she was about to give up. She hoped Amelia's beau had taken her elsewhere, found her a better place to hide. But she knew that wasn't the case when she heard a soft moan.

"Amelia? Is that you?" Fear caused a shiver that had nothing to do with the cold, dank air.

"Over 'ere," someone croaked.

Jeannette lifted her lamp high, using it to help search between the towering barrels.

"'Elp me. Please."

The voice was weak. What was wrong? Fear raced through Jeannette's veins like wildfire. "I am coming, my friend."

"Here . . ."

Jeannette wove her way through the maze to find Amelia lying on the floor, curled up on one side. She had Treynor's blanket bunched beneath her head, but her face looked ashen in the yellow glow of the lamplight.

"What is wrong? What has happened?" Jeannette knelt to feel the girl's forehead. It was hot and glistening with moisture.

"The baby . . . the baby's comin'."

"Now?" Jeannette set the food aside. "How long have you been like this?"

"Hours. I 'eard the bells."

Jeannette swallowed hard. "This is it, then."

Amelia nodded, a short feeble movement.

"We have to get you out of here. Who is your man? Where can I find him?"

Breathing shallowly through parted lips, Amelia closed her eyes.

"Amelia!"

The girl's eyelids fluttered open.

"You must tell me who he is." Jeannette felt certain Amelia would die if she didn't get her to a warm, dry place.

Amelia's breathing quickened as she struggled to speak. "Jones. Rulon Jones."

Jeannette smoothed the hair out of her young friend's face. "I will find him and return immediately."

Unable to speak, Amelia gave a slight nod and Jeannette raced away. Where could she find the man named Rulon Jones? And how would they spirit Amelia out of the hold?

By the time Jeannette climbed the companionway to the deck above, however, she knew she wasn't going in search of Rulon Jones. She was traveling as quickly as her feet could carry her to Treynor's cabin.

He answered her brisk knock almost as soon as her hand hit the panel. She might have thought he'd been awake, except his hair was tousled, and most of his clothes were removed. He wore only a pair of breeches that weren't entirely fastened.

Poking his head outside, he glanced down the hall before pulling her inside and closing the door.

"What are you doing here?" he snapped. "As much as I want you, it is far too dangerous for you to come to me. Cunnington is waiting and watching for just such an event, and he will ruin you along with me if he can."

"I know, but . . . I had no choice."

He seemed to realize this wasn't about them. "What is it?" he asked.

"There is a girl in the hold. I met her when I hid there myself. A man named Jones—Rulon Jones—has been keeping her, but she is very sick. We must help her!"

Understanding dawned. "So that is where my blanket went."

"Yes."

Treynor whirled around to find his shirt, coat and boots, which he threw on, reaching for the buttons as he headed for the door. "Stay here and wait for me. I will be back."

"No!" Jeannette restrained him with a hand on his arm. "I know where she is. It will be much quicker for me to take you to her."

"We cannot be seen together."

"Be that as it may, we cannot let this girl die!"

Confusion and surprise evident in his face, he studied her for a moment. Then he tenderly touched her cheek. "You are willing to take such a risk?"

"Oui."

"Then let's go."

He grabbed hold of her lantern and headed out, and Jeannette had to hurry to catch up.

Treynor used the lamp he held to search every dark corner as they reached the orlop deck and started down into the hold. Even if Cunnington was asleep in his cabin, Treynor knew there were men in the crew who would gladly share news of his and Jeannette's late-night venture if they thought it would buy them leniency at some critical point in the future. Cunnington and his whip had put the fear of God into the entire crew—and the enmity between the first and second lieutenants was no secret.

Jeannette panted softly behind him, so he slowed his steps for her benefit. Her skirts hampered her movement. Although she raised them high, revealing small feet and a shapely bit of calf, she had to take two steps for every one of his.

"How often do you go down to this girl?" he asked as they walked.

"I have only done it once, on the day I was almost tattooed."

"No wonder you wouldn't tell me what you were up to."

They'd arrived at the hold. "I had to take her some food. Her man promised to care for her, but he has not."

"Then I shall deal with him later."

A step behind him, she touched his shoulder and turned to the right. "This way."

"Amelia?" she called out. "Do not worry. I have brought help."

"Rulon?" The voice sounded exhausted yet hopeful.

"No. It is Lieutenant Treynor."

Taking his hand, Jeannette led him around the barrels. Her soft skin and small, delicate fingers made him want to lift her palm to his lips. But then they rounded a corner and the light lapped over a female form lying on the floor and all such thoughts fled his mind. The young woman's filthy state and tattered dress marked her as another of the many prostitutes Treynor had seen before, carousing with the men while they were in port. But her extended abdomen was obvious, made more so by the way she gripped it and moaned, rolling miserably from side to side.

He shot Jeannette an astonished glance. "She is having a *baby*?"

"I-I cannot say, for sure." She passed a hand over her worried brow. "I think she is *malade*—ill, and perhaps it is time for the *bébé*. I mean, how does one know?"

"*This* is a good indication." He nodded toward the girl writhing in pain. "We have to get her to the surgeon."

Amelia, for the most part, seemed oblivious to their presence, until Treynor bent to pick her up. Then she let out a piercing wail and tried to shove him away. "No," she panted. "The baby. There is no time."

Jeannette stared at him with wide eyes. "Shall I fetch the surgeon then?"

Amelia's hand shot out and clamped onto Jeannette's arm. "Don't leave me again. Please. The baby is—"

A gut-wrenching sob tore out of the girl's throat and she began to bear down, making Treynor's decision a simple but harrowing one.

"Here, hold this." He handed Jeannette the lamp while he pushed barrels back to give them more room. Creating a ledge on which he could set the light, he removed his coat. Then he spread out the blanket and lifted her onto it. "My God, she is little more than a child herself," he muttered.

Jeannette held Amelia's hand and coaxed her to cooperate. "It will all be over with soon," she crooned and looked up at him as if expecting him to confirm her words.

Treynor drew Amelia's skirts up above her waist, completely baring her bottom. The sight, along with a trickle of blood, drew a small gasp from Jeannette.

"This is unseemly," she said, flustered. "I mean . . . you are a man. What are you doing?" Her eyes darted from him to Amelia and back again. "She—"

"She is having a baby and, despite your delicate sensibilities, this is where it comes out. I am afraid I see no midwife, though I would trade my weight in gold for one right now. Unless, of course, you would like to try your hand at birthing . . ." He backed away, motioning her to replace him between Amelia's knees, which Amelia had instinctively raised and parted.

The spasm racking Amelia's belly subsided, leaving the girl gasping for air but able to utter a response of her own. "I've 'ad worse than 'im see it all."

She attempted to laugh, but the pain returned, and she had to force the rest through her teeth. "An' I assure ye, I don't rightly care at this bloody moment. I'd let 'im cut me 'ead off if I thought it'd heeeeeeelp."

The last word extended into another keening wail, and Jeannette shoved Treynor back in place. "Do whatever you can. Just help her."

Treynor knelt at the ready. He intended for his nonchalance to calm Jeannette, to calm them both, but inside, he felt as nervous as they appeared to be. He had never witnessed a human birth. He could only draw from what he had witnessed on the Abbott farm. Once, he'd assisted a mare in delivering her foal.

He hoped it would make him of some use. "Relax, everything will be fine." He regretted that his words sounded far less convincing than he meant them to be.

"What can I do?" Jeannette rolled back her sleeves as far as they would go. Now that propriety ranked somewhere below necessity and practicality, she seemed eager to take any instructions he was willing to give.

Treynor admired her courage—and her kindness. Jeannette had endangered herself more than once to help Amelia.

"I am not exactly sure," he admitted. "We will just have to hope it becomes apparent."

No sooner had he said that than Amelia bore down in earnest. A glimpse of what looked like a bald head made his heart thud until he could feel its vibration in his fingertips. He was about to help a new life enter the world.

He looked at Jeannette, who was holding Amelia's hand and whispering encouragement. *I would like to see her give birth to my son.* The idea came unbidden, out of nowhere, and he squelched it as quickly as it dawned on his consciousness. What foolishness was that?

Amelia's next push produced a fresh gush of water and blood. He could see the baby, but it wasn't the head, as he had thought. It was a set of pink buttocks.

Fear coursed through him. He knew little about birthing babies, but it wasn't hard to guess that this was unusual—and not in the least desirable. Again, he considered sending Jeannette for the surgeon. It might all be over by the time Sivern arrived, but then it might not. Mother and child could easily lose their lives . . .

His uncertainty drew Jeannette's attention. She searched his face, then mirrored his worry. "What is it?"

Amelia's eyes flew open. "Is somethin' wrong?"

"No." Treynor masked his concern with a calm smile. "Nothing. I was just thinking that Jeannette should go for Surgeon Sivern. He can only be a help to us."

"Not 'im!" Amelia tried to sit up, but Jeannette held her down. "That sawbones is not goin' ter lay a 'and on me or me baby! I've seen 'is work before. Ain't worth nothin' to the 'ealthy, an' the sick and dyin' dread 'im even more."

Treynor knew then that, despite her youth, Amelia was a seasoned stowaway and had witnessed the frigate in action. Surgeon Sivern's work was notorious and consisted mostly of hacking off the limbs of those who required such treatment due to injuries sustained during battle. The man prided himself on his speed and efficiency, and there were times he received plenty of practice. But, in all probability, he'd never delivered a baby. Would he be able to help? Or was Treynor simply trying to divorce himself from the awesome responsibility before him?

"At least he is somewhat educated in these matters," he argued.

Another pain was coming on. He wanted this to be the last one, the one that delivered the baby. Amelia was tiring fast, was probably not strong enough to last much longer—not after living in the inhospitable hold.

Amelia bore down again, but weakly.

He had to do something. Fortunately, instinct took over as the tiny buttocks appeared. Slipping one hand inside, he found and gripped the babe's foot and gently turned the child. "Push," he commanded Amelia.

She obeyed with a guttural moan, and he pulled at the same time. Amazingly, he saw more of the infant as the buttocks slid all the way out, revealing a tiny penis and testicles.

But the baby's head didn't appear. Would it suffocate before he could get it out?

"Push!" he cried, but Amelia only squirmed and twisted and moaned.

"I can't. I 'ave nothin' left." Tears ran from her eyes. "No more. Just . . . let me die."

"Of course we won't! You can do it." Jeannette smoothed her hair away from her face. "You are almost done, *mon amie*. Please. One more push."

With a surge of effort born of desperation, Amelia's belly contracted, and Treynor held on.

There was the baby's back. Then the shoulders. An oblong head finally appeared, plastered with wet, curly dark hair.

Treynor felt a lump rise in his throat. He'd managed to get the child from its mother's womb, but the babe's face was purple. He wasn't breathing.

Acting as swiftly as possible, Treynor cleared the mucus out of the baby's small mouth with the tail of his shirt.

And then . . . at last . . . Amelia's son burst into a hearty cry.

"It's a boy," he said as relief washed over him. "He's awfully tiny—not half a stone, I'd guess—and very angry. But he's alive."

Tears sparkled in Jeannette's eyes as she stared at the straining little body he cradled in his hands. Still connected to his mother via the umbilical cord and covered with her blood, water and membranes, he wasn't much to look at. Yet Treynor had never seen anything more beautiful.

"You have a son," Jeannette whispered to her friend.

Treynor moved to set the child in Amelia's arms, but the exhausted girl turned her face away, refusing to even look at the crying child.

"Take 'im away," she sobbed. "I don't want 'im."

Chapter 16

Treynor could not have been more surprised if Amelia had spit in his face. He cut the cord, tied it off and pulled the baby against his own chest, heedless of the blood that would stain his shirt. "What do you mean?" he demanded.

"Ye 'eard me," she said. "I don't want 'im."

Unable to escape the suspicion that his mother had said something similar on his own birthday, Treynor swallowed hard. "But he's your son."

"'E's a nuisance, that's all." She curled into a ball on the floor, rocking herself back and forth, the afterbirth now a bloody puddle near her feet.

"And his father?" Treynor knew the answer before he asked the question. She probably didn't know who the father was.

"'E doesn't want us. Ye don't see 'im 'ere, do ye?"

Treynor felt Jeannette at his side. "Let me take him," she murmured. "Perhaps she fears the babe will die anyway. She has nothing to give him."

He sat back, weary despite the rapid progress of the birth. "But how can a mother turn her back on her own son?"

Jeannette's expression softened, telling him she knew he was asking the question that had tormented him his whole life. Empathy filled her eyes, making him want to strike out, simply because she saw beyond the barricade that kept everyone else at a safe distance.

But then she touched his arm and he wanted to stand and enfold her in his embrace instead.

"At least now you can see that the blame doesn't lie with the child," she said.

Treynor felt raw, completely exposed. Deep down, he'd always believed that there had to have been something terribly wrong with him to make his own mother reject him. He'd never been able to outdistance that doubt, no matter the years that passed, no matter how hard he tried to forget the past, no matter what he achieved.

Jeannette took the child and wrapped it snugly in her shawl. "Sometimes we simply make poor choices."

"Maybe," he admitted. "But I would never walk away from a son of mine."

"Oh?" she replied evenly. "And does that apply equally to his mother?"

Treynor had no ready answer. He'd sworn never to marry, never to fall in love, even if he were to find a woman he admired enough, which he hadn't. Until now. Jeannette was the first woman he'd ever wanted in such a way, and they didn't stand a chance.

"I will get Surgeon Sivern," he said. Amelia and the baby needed medical care. And he was no longer the man to provide it.

Joints aching from the time on his knees, he rose and headed back the way he had come.

Jeannette watched Treynor go. She longed to soothe him, but she could not. What he'd been through as a boy made it impossible for him to extend the same feelings of loyalty he'd expressed toward a child to that child's mother. And although Jeannette wanted to gain the lieutenant's confidence, she knew, ultimately, she could only betray it—or betray her family's trust.

Sighing heavily, she felt the baby's tiny mouth against her arm. She gave him a finger to suck, something she had seen her brother's nurse do long, long ago. What would this child encounter? What kind of chance did he have?

None, if his mother continued to reject him. A frigate was not the easiest place to find a wet nurse. It was possible she could get some goat's milk. But would that do?

Jeannette eyed the now silent form of Amelia. She lay on her side, her face averted. But unless Jeannette missed her guess, the babe's sucking sounds affected her. The girl glanced back once, twice, then folded her arms across her chest.

"Take 'im away, I told ye. I don't want ter see 'im."

There were plenty of logical arguments Jeannette could use to convince Amelia to care for her son, but she feared none of them would work. So she tried another tack. "That is probably for the best," she said, keeping her voice somber. "He probably won't live long, anyway, ailing the way that he is."

Amelia's head popped up. "What do ye mean, ailin'? 'E was screamin' 'is lungs out a moment ago. 'E's a strong one, 'e is."

Jeannette conjured a skeptical expression. "But he is awfully small. That may not bode well."

"'E's a newborn. 'E's supposed to be small."

"Still . . . now that he will have nothing to eat . . ." She let her words fall away. "It is just a matter of time. But, as I said, it is for the best. It will make things easier for you."

Amelia propped herself up on her elbows and gave her baby a dubious look. "'E wouldn't want a life with me, anyway. 'Ow would I work?"

"You wouldn't be able to continue in your current profession. But . . . do you like it so well?"

"I 'ave to eat occasionally, and so will he."

"Then perhaps you could obtain a position as—as a laundress for a large household."

Amelia gave her a look that said she must be daft. "Oh? An' with what references?" She slumped back down, laying her head on her arms.

"My own. I come from a good family and my English cousin is a nobleman who could be persuaded to speak for you."

"It won't work," Amelia muttered. "I 'ardly look respectable. An' I'll not end up in a work'ouse with a passel of brats. I was raised in one of them 'ell 'oles."

"No need. Truly, you could earn your bread and a shilling or two besides." Hoping she'd be able to keep the promises she was making, Jeannette gave the unhappy new mother a confident smile. She was already planning to throw herself on Lord Darby's mercy. How much more could he take? "Why not nurse the baby, just for now?" she asked. "We will manage something."

Having gained no nourishment from her finger, the baby began rooting for something more productive. A distinctive squall rang out when he couldn't find anything.

"'E's 'ungry, no doubt," Amelia said.

Now that the pains of childbirth were behind her, and she'd had a chance to regain her breath, Amelia seemed to have recovered a bit of her usual aplomb. Jeannette took this as a good sign.

"*Quel bon bébé*," she cooed, moving closer so Amelia could better see her child.

The other woman's expression softened. "'E's red and shriveled, that's what 'e is. But 'e's lookin' for 'is mum."

Jeannette held out the infant.

Still skeptical, Amelia looked from her to the child but allowed Jeannette to place him in her arms. "Look at 'is toes," she said, marveling over the tiny, perfect features.

"He is hungry, no? Why not feed him?"

Amelia fumbled with her dress, unbuttoning it far enough to reach her breast—and gasped when the babe latched on.

"He knew what he wanted, did he not?" Jeannette asked in the sudden absence of his crying.

"Aye. 'E did at that." Amelia's voice sounded wistful and her eyes filled with wonder.

Doing what she could to clean up, Jeannette hid a smile. Her friend would never be able to refuse the child again.

As dawn stained the eastern sky a shimmering magenta, Jeannette fell, exhausted, into her hammock. It had been a long night, one that could easily have turned out to be a complete disaster.

As it was, she felt good about seeing Amelia nurse her child. Even after Treynor and the surgeon had arrived, the girl had continued to examine the tiny body, unwrapping the shawl here and there for a peek.

The surgeon provided her with some folded cotton cloth for both mother and child, and charged Treynor with the practical task of commandeering more. Even the aspect of diapering the babe seemed to interest Amelia. The powerful bond between mother and child was already forming.

It had been almost as gratifying to see Treynor's reaction to Amelia holding her baby. His weary confusion had vanished as his gaze returned to the pair again and again. When he'd noticed Jeannette's interest, the crooked smile he offered her caused something inside her to twist and yearn.

From there, they'd been occupied moving Amelia and her child to the sick bay, but Jeannette could still feel the warm blush that rose to her face when the lieutenant looked at her. Something in his gaze struck her as personal and full of meaning. But any woman would be flattered by the appreciation in his expression. Lieutenant Treynor was a remarkable man.

Jeannette slept until one of the captain's servants woke her with a knock. After she unlocked the door, he bid her a polite good morning and carried in a tray for her midday meal.

Still tired, she waited for him to leave with less than her usual good cheer. Her dreams had been plagued by visions of a wedding—her own, evidently, as she was once again wearing the sheer muslin over silk dress she'd worn at the chapel with St. Ives. She didn't recognize the man with whom she made her vows. He was as old and decrepit as the baron.

But she knew it wasn't a stranger who came to her bed that night. It was Lieutenant Treynor. He thrilled her with the touch and taste of him, with the passion of their love, then disappeared into thin air.

Closing her eyes, she kneaded her forehead until the door closed and she was once again alone. Then she cut into the meat pie and steamed vegetables the captain's servant had delivered. Because of Cunnington, the *Tempest* was taking her back to Plymouth. The first lieutenant had baited Treynor into defending her and was now using it against them both.

A card rested next to her plate. Jeannette turned it over and read a brief note from Captain Cruikshank. He wished her well, thanked her for her part in delivering the baby and informed her that the situation was well in hand—which meant, she surmised, that both mother and baby were being properly cared for.

Perhaps it also indicated that Rulon Jones would be punished. How well he deserved a few lashes! Jeannette wondered if Amelia might still object, but she felt no leniency toward Mr. Jones. Amelia could have lost her life because of him, as well as her baby.

Jeannette chewed her vegetables without really tasting them as her thoughts circled back to her own worries. What would St. Ives do when he had her in his control again? What would her parents do?

A poignant longing to see her family rose up in her, nearly bringing tears to her eyes. They had to be worried about her. No doubt they feared something terrible had happened. And it had. Jeannette had met a man she could love. But she could no sooner have him than the land she had once called home.

She reached up to touch her hair. Would her shorn locks distress her mother? Or would the fact that she had stowed aboard an English frigate overshadow all else? She smiled ruefully at the thought that she was no longer the protected innocent she once had been.

The rest of the day passed uneventfully. Claiming a headache, Jeannette declined the captain's invitation to sup at his table. Instead, she remained in her cabin and spent the time pacing and reading, although once the officers convened in the wardroom on the other side of the canvas wall, she couldn't concentrate on anything except Lieutenant Treynor's voice. He spoke with the others about the war, the ship, the weather—nothing particularly riveting. Just the sound of his voice was enough to hold her spellbound.

When they finished eating and said their farewells for the night, Jeannette tried to distract herself by reading poetry. The captain had given her a tattered volume by William Cowper, but she had to read each line, even those of her favorites, over and over to grasp the meaning. Her time with Treynor was dwindling to a close. The more minutes that ticked by, the greater Jeannette's sense of urgency.

Eight bells signaled the hour to retire. The captain's servant had delivered a light repast for her supper, along with tea, which she had enjoyed. But the food was long gone, and there was nothing to do now except sleep.

Scarcely tired, but depressed enough to climb back into her hammock anyway, Jeannette proceeded to shift and fidget. The lieutenant's face, with his knowing grin, appeared every time she closed her eyes.

Finally, with a groan of despair, she rose and lit a lamp, determined to muddle through a last bit of Cowper.

> *There is a fountain filled with blood*
> *Drawn from Emmanuel's veins;*
> *And sinners, plung'd beneath that flood,*
> *Lose all their guilty stains—*

A light knock on the door made Jeannette drop her book. Ever mindful of the night Cunnington had visited her outside Treynor's cabin, she drew the wrap the captain had provided tightly around herself, left the poems where they'd fallen and moved to the portal.

"Who's there?"

"It's me."

Lieutenant Treynor's voice was unmistakable. Fleetingly Jeannette wondered if something was wrong with Amelia or the baby, but deep down she knew he hadn't come to bear her news of their welfare.

The lock clicked loudly in Jeannette's ears as her trembling fingers slid back the bolt. Sure enough, when she swung the door open, she found the lieutenant in the hall.

"We dock in Plymouth tomorrow evening." He watched her as if he could feel her crumbling resolve, as if he offered her one last chance to take what she wanted. A trace of vulnerability in his face revealed how much he craved the same thing.

The light from her lamp threw shadows across his chiseled features, the cleft chin, the square jaw, the high cheekbones, the full lips. Jeannette's gaze rested on that sensuous mouth. The memory of it slanting across her own was enough to steal her breath.

She moved back, allowing him to enter.

He stepped cautiously past her, as though he longed to touch her yet feared the moment of contact almost as much as she did.

"You weren't sleeping?" He bent to retrieve the book she'd dropped on the floor.

Jeannette shook her head. "I could not."

He set the poems on the bureau and turned to face her. "Neither could I. I missed you at dinner."

"I was able to hear you," she replied with a shaky smile. "I hung on every word you said."

Holding her gaze with his own, he closed the distance between them. "Then I was a fool not to have spoken of your beauty."

"There is still time," she teased, her tone light.

He gave her a wry smile. "I am no poet, Jeannette. But I could tell you how your eyes turn into pools of amethyst when you want to be kissed, how your lashes lower to your cheeks and you arch toward me . . ." He ran a finger along her jaw.

The slight touch was enough to make Jeannette's heart pound. "You should not have come," she whispered.

"Then tell me to go." He stared at her for a long moment before his arms went around her. Then he pulled her up against the hard length of him. She could feel the corded muscles of his legs through her thin wrap and nightgown, his perfectly molded shoulders and arms beneath her hands.

His eyelids lowered as his mouth met hers. Softly, gently, his tongue explored the sensitive skin of her lips until she parted them and gave herself up to his kiss.

"Jeannette." He spoke her name hoarsely but with meaning before his mouth trailed down the column of her throat.

Her fingers found and delved into the thickness of his hair as she clung to him. Soon she could feel nothing except the inexplicable need to know more of Treynor, to touch him everywhere, to taste his salty skin and revel in his manliness. Her body began to tremble beneath his hands, hands that were expert in heightening her pleasure. He molded her to him, letting her feel his desire and the strength of his body as he bent over her.

But somewhere in the back of her mind the memory of every reason not to yield came back to her. "We can't," she said.

"But you want this as badly as I do."

"I won't deny it," she admitted. "It's my family—"

"Do you think I would steal your innocence? The one thing that might protect you from the likes of St. Ives?" He moved his lips to her ear so his next words came as a whisper. "There are other things we can do. Let me teach you."

She could scarcely breathe. "And what of tomorrow?"

"Tomorrow I would want more of the same."

"But when we reach Plymouth there will be no more tomorrows."

He tilted her chin up so she had to look into his eyes. "We have now. Or are you unwilling to trust me?"

"I would trust you with my life, but I would be a fool to do so with my virginity," she said.

A laugh escaped him as he glanced at her hammock, which swung with the movement of the ship, only inches away. "Must you be so wise?

Let me stay with you tonight. Let me feel the softness of your body against mine—"

"To circle the flame and hover close would only torment us."

"I look at it as taking what we can get."

Jeannette drew a deep breath. Fortunately, he hadn't mentioned anything of love. She longed to hear him speak some word of it and yet she was relieved, for she feared it would be her undoing. As long as she could convince herself he felt nothing more than a physical attraction to her, she could hold him off. Only because of that, she dared steal one small concession from the fate that awaited her.

Reaching up, she unbuttoned the top part of his coat. He watched her curiously until her hands slipped beneath the cloth to feel his bare skin. Then his eyes slid closed.

"I have never known another man like you," she whispered, parting the fabric and raising up on tiptoe to press her lips to the hollow of his throat.

The steady thrum of his heart pounded against her lips until it throbbed throughout her body. She turned her cheek to the warmth of him and closed her eyes as he held her close.

"Let me stay," he begged. "We have only one night."

"I cannot. Do you think I could then settle for what awaits me at Plymouth?"

Suddenly, Treynor's face lost all remnants of the roguish grin he'd used to charm her, and his voice took on a somber note. "I don't know, little Jeannette, which of us will be more hard-pressed to forget the other. Sometimes I highly doubt it will be you."

His lips brushed hers, quickly but without intent, then he turned to go. But when he opened the door to step into the hall, Lieutenant Cunnington's voice broke the silence.

From Jeannette's place in the room, she could see the first lieutenant, dressed as carefully as always, his hand raised as if to knock.

"I thought I might find you here, Lieutenant Treynor," he said.

Chapter 17

"What is it?" To shield Jeannette from Cunnington's direct regard and the smug expression on his face, Treynor stepped between them.

"Captain Cruikshank would like to see you in his cabin, immediately," the other man replied, a victorious smile curling his lips.

Treynor glanced back at Jeannette. Noting her embarrassment, he regretted the impulse that had led him to her quarters. His preoccupation with the baron's wife might well cost him his career. And, if he wasn't careful, it could cost her even more.

"If you will excuse me, my lady." He gave her an apologetic smile.

"Certainly." She nodded as he bowed and let himself out.

With the door shut behind him, he strode ahead of Cunnington, hoping to avoid conversation.

Predictably, the first lieutenant was not to be put off. "You surprise me, Treynor. I never thought to see you so besotted."

Treynor paused midstep. "More of your romantic illusions, Mr. Cunnington?"

"Hardly. Perhaps the others cannot see it, but I know you better than most."

Treynor picked up his pace. "Not if you think me besotted."

"You are a fool to involve yourself with Lord St. Ives's new wife, no matter how tempting you find her," Cunnington persisted. "There has to be a reason the baroness is willing to waste her favors on a bastard. Is she looking for someone she can use to further her own interests? Perhaps she hopes you will protect her from her husband."

Cunnington's dig stung more than usual, but Treynor attempted to shrug it off. "I thought she and I were partners in her escape from the beginning. It was you who told the captain I brought her aboard as my paramour, was it not?"

"Yes, and I will wager I was far closer to the truth than the captain and the others want to believe. If she wasn't warming your bed before, she is now."

"Your interest in my well-being is appreciated, Lieutenant, but I am not romantically involved with the baroness. I merely stopped in to thank her for her help with the birth of the stowaway's child. No doubt you have heard of the event by now—"

"Indeed. But do you think the captain, or the baron, for that matter, will believe such a flimsy excuse when I tell them I found the two of you alone in her cabin?"

Tempted to let the first lieutenant know, in no uncertain terms, that he would defend Jeannette's honor and his own in every way, Treynor whirled to face him. But such a declaration would only confirm Cunnington's suspicions. "I doubt the captain will involve himself beyond returning the baroness to her husband. But if you do anything to discredit or harm her—"

"You will . . . what?" Cunnington looked disgustingly hopeful.

"I will expose you for the meddling fool that you are. Lady St. Ives is still a virgin. And she can prove it if she must." Treynor walked away, knowing if he stayed another second he'd tear Cunnington apart with his bare hands.

The first lieutenant's laugh followed him. "Such admirable control, Treynor. Evidently you care far more for the baroness than even I believed. But you will never be able to have her for yourself. You know that, do you not?"

Treynor ignored him.

"She is as far above you as the stars in the sky. And when I tell the baron that it was you who hid her from him, you will be lucky to survive with your post," Cunnington called after him.

The desire to plunge a fist into Cunnington's face surged within Treynor. His fingers curled and his jaw clenched but, by sheer dint of will, he kept walking. He cared for the baroness, but he didn't love her. He couldn't love her. He had always held himself aloof from the entanglements of such enslaving emotion.

But almost as soon as the denial flitted through his mind, another part of his brain retorted with a question: He couldn't love her, or he couldn't have her? The line between the two had turned from black to gray. Even Treynor had to admit that.

"You are wrong," he flung over his shoulder, but he didn't sound very convincing, even to himself.

"We will see," Cunnington scoffed. "Soon, we will see."

Hours later, the tramp of footsteps going up and down the corridor woke Jeannette from a restless sleep. She could tell, even from her hammock, that something had changed. The sounds of the ship were different, the excess movement unusual. She sat up, trying to determine what time it was and just what such changes might signify.

Her cabin was located on the ship's gun deck, well above the waterline, which allowed some natural light to filter in when the porthole was open. After climbing out of her bed, she reached around the cannon that took up a large portion of the room and swung out the heavy block of wood that covered the gunport.

Dawn had already broken across the water. The sun pierced the hazy, gray clouds that had covered the sky for days, and nearly blinded her. She blinked several times in an effort to cut the glare when she saw what looked to be another ship in the distance.

Was it flying the French Republic's new tricolor, or was that her imagination?

Deep voices rose, loud and charged with expectation. There was more pounding in the corridor. Then someone banged on her door.

She dropped the porthole cover, but before she could don her wrap, a man called through the panel. "M'lady? I'm sorry to disturb you, but I'm afraid we must come in so we can prepare the cannon. Captain's orders."

Then the flag had indeed been a tricolor . . .

"I must dress," she called back and forced herself to move despite the fear clawing at her gut. Pulling on the gown the captain had loaned her from his daughter's wardrobe, she grimaced at the memory of Cunnington finding Treynor in her cabin only a few hours earlier. But she had even worse things to worry about now, so she shoved the memory away and opened the panel to see five men and one boy waiting in the hall.

A tall fellow with a thick dusting of whiskers spoke. "Lytle of the gun crew, madam . . . I mean m'lady. Lookout has spotted an enemy frigate. We been chasing her most of the night. The captain means to engage her as soon as we're close enough."

"I see." Their eagerness to assemble at their station, Jeannette could understand. Their apparent excitement she could not. Feeling nothing but dread, she stared at the gunner who had delivered this terse message.

He cleared his throat. "If you will excuse us then . . ."

"*Oui*. Just give me a moment." She closed the panel and leaned her head against it. The *Tempest* would fire upon the French, the French would respond in kind and men would die—men with wives and children. Only one side could win, and even then, the victory would likely cost all parties.

She hoped to God the *Tempest* would prevail. She couldn't bear to see the sailors she'd come to know hurt or killed. And if she became a prisoner of war, she would face the guillotine, just as many of her friends and more distant relations had already done. The Bouchers, along with the rest of the French aristocracy, were considered no better than criminals now.

Jeannette opened the door and allowed the gun crew to file in just as a boy arrived carrying a folded missive. He handed it to her without a word, then hurried away.

Inside, she found a hastily scrawled message.

> *My Dear Lady St. Ives:*
> *We are to engage an enemy ship at any moment. For your own*
> *safety, please stay below the gun deck, yet well away from the pow-*
> *der stores, in case of fire. Amelia and the baby are ensconced in*
> *the Hawkers' cabin on the orlop deck.*
>
> *Your Most Obedient Servant,*
> *Lieutenant T.*

Jeannette let her fingers pass over the words as though she could touch the hand that had written them. The same hands she'd watched deliver a baby with infinite care; the same that had thrilled her with the pleasure they could so easily evoke. She wished he'd written a more personal word, or salutation, but she knew he couldn't risk revealing their intimacy lest someone get hold of it.

The enemy ship seemed significantly closer already. She had expected this day to herald her return to Plymouth, not her initiation into naval warfare. Still, postponing her parting from the second lieutenant, for whatever reason, brought a measure of peace and rightness, despite the ominous portent of what lay ahead.

Folding the paper into a small square, she slid it into her bodice for safekeeping. The message would probably be the only thing she would ever own in connection with Crawford Treynor.

She headed topside, but before she reached the last companionway, one of the captain's servants came after her.

"M'lady! M'lady! The captain sent me for ye. 'E asks that ye await the outcome of the battle in 'is cabin, where 'e can be assured of yer safety."

Jeannette was reluctant to closet herself away at the stern. She wouldn't be able to see anything or know how the battle progressed. Nor would she be able to determine whether or not Lieutenant Treynor was safe. He would be on deck, a target for the enemy in his uniform, as officers always were.

"It's this way, m'lady," the servant pressed.

"I know where the captain's quarters are, and I will go there shortly. But I need to . . . I only want to . . ." Jeannette found herself at a complete loss for words. She couldn't tell the truth: that she wanted to see Lieutenant Treynor, whole and well, one more time. She had no desire to face that fact herself.

Turning away despite the doubtful look on the servant's face, she mumbled, "I will go there in a moment," and headed off.

"I don't think it wise to delay!" the boy argued, but he didn't follow and she ignored him.

Jeannette caught sight of the enemy the instant she stepped out on deck. The ship that had been nothing but a distant speck now loomed to starboard. It appeared to be a frigate, as she'd been told, not the more dangerous ship of the line, but looked considerably larger than the *Tempest*. And it had its gunports open. Judging from the long line of black muzzles pointed directly at them, it carried significant firepower, too.

Chattering about prize money, some crew members rolled up hammocks and stuffed them into nets at the gunwale to form a breastwork against enemy pistol fire. Others hurried to spread damp sand on the polished deck to keep the gun crews from slipping on the blood that would be spilled.

Jeannette watched in awe. Canvas sails snapping in the chill February wind, the *Tempest* raced toward her enemy. There wasn't much time now . . .

Suddenly, the lookout cried out from above. "It's the *Superbe*, Cap'n. I've 'eard of her. Her cap'n's a smart man, that he is, but we can take her. I know we can."

Jeannette certainly hoped that was the case. And that it would happen quickly.

Struggling to keep her footing on the pitching deck, she searched the crowd for the man she longed to see. Lieutenant Treynor couldn't be far. Another lieutenant stood close by, barking orders to a group of men who were busy cleaning cannon muzzles.

Cunnington was easy to spot, too. He happened to glance up and see her, reminding her that she had enough enemies already—and much closer to home.

"My lady, what are you doing up here?"

Jeannette recognized the gravelly voice of the captain before she turned to see his seamed face.

"I thought I sent Joseph to take you to my cabin."

"You did, sir." She tried to smile through her fear. "I apologize for not following orders as well as your men. I had to see what was happening before the battle started and I was left to await the outcome."

"You do not want to stay here. 'Tis no place for a woman."

"No, I am going."

"Very well. It shouldn't take long."

Did he mean it shouldn't take long to make quick work of the battle? Or it shouldn't be long before the fighting broke out?

"What are we waiting for?" she asked.

He stared across the water without answering. Didn't he hear her?

"Captain?"

Blinking, he returned his attention to her. "My lady, we must hold our fire until we are sure it will be deadly. And they"—he nodded toward the enemy ship—"must do the same."

"Captain!" The master approached and Cruikshank turned away.

Still unable to find Lieutenant Treynor, Jeannette went to the bow. She needed one glimpse, just one glimpse of him. Then she'd go below. But there were so many men and so much activity. And the enemy was drawing close . . .

Her nerves taut as the sails overhead, she hugged the forward mast. A hush fell over the entire deck. With five men and a small boy, the powder monkey, surrounding each cannon, the gun crews stood ready. The officers seemed to be sniffing the air, waiting to get close enough to their quarry while hoping not to miss the perfect moment to unleash a broadside before the enemy beat them to it.

And then she saw him. Treynor stood across the deck, braced for action. His eyes, as deeply blue as the ocean that churned and dipped as they sped through its roiling waves, were riveted on the other ship. His body, tense with expectation, stood straight and true, reminding Jeannette of an ancient warrior.

She'd had her glimpse—but still she couldn't make herself leave. Somehow it felt as if nothing could happen to him as long as she was there to be sure of it.

The other ship drew so close Jeannette began to fear they'd collide, and still there hadn't been a single shot. Even Treynor seemed to grow impatient. He flung an anxious glance back to where the captain stood, as if he longed to give the command himself.

Then the roar of guns deafened her and several iron balls smashed into the hull of the *Tempest*. Cruikshank had missed his chance to launch the first volley; he'd waited too long.

With a stab of foreboding, she clung to the mast as the *Tempest* fired in response. The gun crews, their members known by numbers to simplify orders, worked almost in unison from that point on. They hurried to clean muzzles, damp down sparks to prevent an explosion during reloading, and pack the guns with shot and powder before inserting a powder-packed quill as a fuse. Using handspikes and ropes to lever the guns back into firing position, they breathlessly awaited their officer's next command.

From what Jeannette could tell amid the smoke that soon hovered over the deck, Lieutenant Treynor's station included the carronades in the forecastle. Occasionally she could hear his voice, telling his crews to wait for the *Tempest*'s roll to help them aim their guns.

Other voices muttered, grumbled, cursed, groaned and cried out as they got off another few rounds.

"Come on! Come on, ye froggy bastards!"

"We'll show ye what we got!"

"Aim for the wheel . . ."

The smell of gunpowder gagged Jeannette, and smoke stung her eyes and throat. She managed to glimpse the lieutenant again, expected to see him deep in concentration but found him looking directly at her instead. Eyebrows drawn, his face set in anger, he motioned her toward the forward hatch.

Jeannette nodded to assure him of her compliance, and felt his attention shift back to the battle. She intended to act on her silent promise, but an explosion sent her sprawling.

A member of one of the gun crews landed on top of her. His weight threatened to suffocate her, as did the fresh wall of smoke that descended. She called for him to get off, but received no response.

The wails of the injured rose, silencing her own strangled cries. Spitting out the sand she'd gotten in her mouth when she hit the deck, Jeannette struggled to get free, but she couldn't budge the sailor.

Slowly she became aware of a warm, sticky substance leaking onto her face and arms. Turning the man's head to the side to see why he wouldn't respond, she felt a jolt of revulsion at the sight of his open, glassy eyes.

"Dead! Dead! Get him off me!" Panic gave her strength. She freed herself, but the carnage around her nearly made her retch.

Another enemy ball landed close by, and a boy fell several feet away, moaning, clutching an injured foot.

Jeannette tried to reach him amid the violent rocking of the deck, but the gun crews, feverishly loading, firing and reloading, were unwilling to clear a path. She dodged several powder monkeys that were rushing cartridges of gunpowder up from the handling chambers below while the gun captain of the crew closest to her lit a fresh fuse.

The men covered their ears and jumped out of the way as the violent explosion blasted the cannon backward into the ship, almost knocking her down again. Then a mad scramble ensued as the men leaped forward to reload.

She pressed on. "I am coming," she shouted to the boy. Huddled over a small pool of his own blood, he gave no indication that he heard her. The cannon blasts had deafened them all, but she kept calling to him, for her own peace of mind, if for no other reason.

By the time she neared the wounded powder monkey, the tattoo artist named Smedley was carrying him off. Like many of the other sailors, Smedley had removed his shirt. She followed, letting the rose tattooed on his shoulder guide her. They squeezed past a line of sailors passing leather buckets of water from the ship's pump, trying to put out a small fire caused by a red-hot cannonball.

"Are you taking him to the surgery?" she asked when they reached the hatch and started down the ladder.

Smedley responded with a slight nod and kept shouldering his way through men whose chests and pants were smeared with blood.

Located aft of the orlop deck, the sick bay was below the waterline, less in danger of enemy fire than the gun deck. The surgeon's table consisted of the crew's sea chests. Beyond that, only a small table along the wall, containing an assortment of knives and instruments, occupied the large room, which smelled more ripely of blood and less of gunpowder than anywhere else. Injured men and boys lined one wall as more poured in, like a steady stream running into a lake.

The surgeon helped to settle a sailor with a nasty gash in his leg on the table. Beneath and around them sat half barrels containing different items, a vat of tar, the smell of which made Jeannette wrinkle her nose, and water heated on a portable stove. One of the surgeon's mates oversaw that as well as the inventory of rolled bandages.

Already Surgeon Sivern looked tired. Sweat dampened his gray hair and caused his face to glisten as he barked out an order for Smedley to deposit the boy at the end of the line, near the door. Although painful, the powder monkey's injury was probably not life-threatening, which made him less of a priority, despite his tender age.

"Can I help?" Jeannette asked Sivern as Smedley headed out. "Perhaps I can do something for the boy or some of these other men . . ."

A look of annoyance claimed Sivern's face. "I haven't the time to coddle a woman, my lady. An attack of the vapors is the last thing I need."

"I won't faint. It looks like you can use all the help you can get."

"You deliver a baby and you think that makes you a surgeon, eh?" The man on the table cried out as Sivern probed a gash on his thigh to see how deep it was, but the surgeon ignored him. "Stay if you like, but keep out of the way. After this, you will be eager to return to your parlor, I guarantee you." He nodded to a barrel containing someone's sawed-off leg, and for the first time, Jeannette realized what it was.

Forcing back the bile that threatened, as the surgeon had no doubt expected it would, Jeannette stood straighter, more determined than ever to brave it out. Sick bay needed more hands, and hers were capable enough.

Swallowing hard, she stepped up to the table, only to wince and turn away when Sivern put a stick sideways between the man's lips for him to bite, and brandished a saw. "Perhaps I can help with the water and bandages," she mumbled.

"Suit yourself."

The sound of Sivern's blade hitting bone made Jeannette blanch. The man on the table screamed again, his voice muffled by the stick. With nothing but rum to ease the pain, the patient—or victim, Jeannette thought sadly—could only hope Sivern would do his work quickly.

In this, the surgeon obliged. The man's amputated leg thumped the bottom of the barrel. Then Sivern cauterized the bloody stump with hot tar, and Jeannette helped bandage the wound.

The smell of burned flesh almost incited her already weakened stomach to mutiny. Jeannette tried to keep her mind off the battle as a whole and her work in particular, but the fear that Lieutenant Treynor might soon be carried down to have a limb sawed off was ever at the back of her mind.

The surgery took on an unreal quality as the blasts above continued and more men stumbled or were carried in, some barely alive. Rocked by cannonballs and barrages of smaller shot, the *Tempest* tossed about on the sea as though it weighed a mere fraction of its several tons. And still the two ships pounded away at each other, making it difficult at times for Jeannette to keep her balance.

From the number of sailors swamping the sick bay, she could hardly believe there were men left to fight. But she had yet to see an injured Lieutenant Treynor, or hear of his death, and for that, she was eternally grateful.

"He's dead. Throw him overboard." Sivern indicated a man along the wall.

Jeannette cringed at the thought of a lifeless body floating in the briny water. So many bodies. But she knew they had no choice. Not in battle.

The surgeon's mate left to dump the barrel of severed arms and legs over the side and was followed by another man who carried the dead sailor. The container was brought back to be filled again, a process that continued for over an hour.

The advent of two sailors, barking for the others to move aside, broke the routine when they entered carrying the captain.

A hush claimed the room as the surgeon motioned for the man on his table to be returned to the line so he could care for Cruikshank, who was bleeding from the right shoulder.

"How do you feel, Captain, sir?" the surgeon questioned as he examined the wound.

"Like hell," Cruikshank groaned. "Give me a pull of that."

Cruikshank took a gulp of the rum Jeannette provided. Then he gritted his teeth and refused to cry out as the surgeon went to work.

Once Sivern determined that the captain's injury had been caused by a ball, which had passed clear through his shoulder, he washed the blood away and set Jeannette to bandaging the wound.

"What are you doing down here?" Cruikshank asked, as though seeing her for the first time. "Now I understand why the baron can't keep track of you. I can do no better."

"Well said." Jeannette laughed. "You are going to be all right, sir."

The captain grew serious and contemplative. "It is not my shoulder that worries me, beyond the fact that it keeps me from my duty." He turned his head to stare out the door, obviously wishing he were back on deck.

Cruikshank's words were Jeannette's first indication that the fighting wasn't going well. Although she knew they'd sustained a great many casualties, and even more injuries, she had no idea what was to be expected, or whether the French crew wasn't suffering worse death and injury. Now she worried about losing the battle.

"Is Cunnington in charge then?" she asked.

"Aye," he said, but the sigh that followed told her more than his words.

Her fate—and that of all those on board—now rested in Cunnington's hands.

It was a terrifying thought.

Chapter 18

Had the last blast of the *Tempest*'s guns hit their mark?

The pepper of gunfire sounded in Lieutenant Treynor's ears as he squinted through the smoke. The *Superbe*'s mizzenmast showed damage, but besides a few broken yards, it remained intact. He needed one more lucky round—just one.

"Wait . . . wait . . . wait . . . and fire!" he cried.

With another deep belch of the cannons there was a loud crack, as if the earth itself was dividing asunder. Then the French ship's entire mizzenmast fell onto their deck, forcing those below it to scatter.

A cheer rose from Treynor's men, but their exuberance did little to relieve the nagging worry at the back of his mind. Cruikshank had fallen among the injured. Now Lieutenant Cunnington was in charge, a man who had little experience and, in Treynor's opinion, even less sense.

He threw a glance toward the wheel. Cunnington strutted where the captain usually stood, behaving as if the battle had already been won, the continuing volleys of gunfire superfluous in some way.

They were outmanned, outgunned, and the French crew had already proven themselves better trained and more experienced than any Treynor had faced in the past. They had to do something decisive.

Putting one of his gun captains in charge, Treynor made his way amidships.

"What do you want?" Cunnington hollered above the din.

Treynor suppressed his irritation; Cunnington was, after all, his superior officer. "With all due respect, Lieutenant, judging from the condition of the *Superbe*'s quarterdeck, I think we may have injured or possibly killed their captain."

"They certainly do not appear to have a lack of leadership," he sneered.

Ignoring his response, Treynor lifted a hand. "Listen—do you hear that?"

Cunnington looked bewildered. "What?" he snapped impatiently.

"The silence since that mast went. If we capitalize on their confusion, we might board, turn their own guns upon them and capture the ship."

"Have you gone mad?" A staccato laugh punctuated Cunnington's question. "Our crew is smaller than theirs."

"They not only have more men, they have bigger guns," Treynor pointed out.

"So?" He shrugged. "The bloody frogs are idiots."

Treynor bit back a curse. "I beg your pardon, sir, but we have to do something before those 'idiots' blow us out of the water."

"We *are* doing something, Lieutenant. They haven't the mettle of Englishmen, as you know. If we keep at it, we will pound them into the sea." He fisted his hand as though it were that easy.

Again, Treynor struggled with his temper and raised his voice. "A little difficult when so many of our crew are awaiting the surgeon's attentions, don't you think?"

He'd been unable to keep the sarcasm from his voice. "Watch yourself," Cunnington warned, "or I will have you court-martialed after I return home with our prize. Although your idea shows a certain amount of . . . daring, by your own account of our injured, we haven't the men to pull it off."

"Already our carpenters are overworked and unable to fix the damage we have sustained," Treynor argued. "We are taking on water despite the pumps. Several fires have broken out and are barely contained. Once the *Superbe* starts firing again, she will continue to lob eighteen-pounders into our hull—"

"*If* they get going again."

"—while we respond with fewer and fewer twelve-pounders. It is only a matter of time. Do you not see that?"

"I see that you haven't enough confidence in our men. I think the battle is going quite well. Some difficulty is to be expected, as well as a certain number of casualties. If we won the battle easily, there would be no glory in it."

"Glory? Are you blind?" Fearing he might throttle Cunnington yet, Treynor took a deep breath. "My God, man, you are talking about running up an impressive butcher bill, a bloody battle to brag about back home, when we should be trying to swarm their ship so we can win while there is yet time!"

Cunnington narrowed his eyes. "Get back to your station, Lieutenant. Now! I will not have you tell me how to run this ship or win this battle! Do you hear?"

Even more convinced that the injured captain had left the ship in the hands of an inept fool, Treynor stepped forward. "You are asking for a miracle—"

"No, you are. Board their ship! Swarm the deck! Evidently you—"

There was an explosion, followed by a loud crack.

The mainmast fell toward them. It might have killed them both, but Treynor threw himself against Cunnington and knocked him far enough to the side to avoid one of the broken spars that stabbed the deck like a spear.

As Treynor got to his feet, a dazed Cunnington followed suit. Brushing off his uniform, the first lieutenant stared about himself in amazement, as though he'd only now awakened to find himself amid such chaos.

Treynor almost wished his reaction when the mast went hadn't been quite so quick nor half so instinctual. "We must board!"

Cunnington's brow furrowed. "I cannot go charging off. I must stay with the ship."

"Then I will lead the men. May I do so? Now?"

The first lieutenant stared at the *Superbe* while wringing his hands.

Treynor wanted to shake him. Cunnington was wasting precious time. Only the sure knowledge that a quarrel would most certainly take its toll in lives kept him speaking civilly. "If we do not act, and soon, we will all be killed," he reasoned. "Or taken prisoner. They are probably planning to board us just as I am hoping to board them. They shall not beat us a second time today!"

"Yes." Cunnington nodded. "Yes. Very well. A preemptive strike. We will board. But Lawson will lead the charge."

Treynor felt his jaw tighten. "What? He is not the man for the job, and you know it. Let me do it!"

"No! You would love nothing more than the chance to come out of this a hero, to reap the glory and praise of our superiors, to beat me to post-captain, but—"

"Think of this, Cunnington"—Treynor's hands balled into fists—"chances are far better I will be killed."

When Cunnington almost smiled, Treynor could tolerate no more. "I am going," he snapped, "and nothing you say will stop me."

"I shall have you hanged for mutiny!" Cunnington screamed after him. "How dare you defy my authority!"

"Go to the devil!" Treynor tossed those words over his shoulder. He would not stand by and let hundreds of Englishmen die because of Cunnington's ignorance and blind jealousy. Neither could he expect the soft-spoken Lawson to do what needed to be done.

Sparks flashed through the haze of battle as another boom, coming from the *Superbe*, rent the air. Splinters flew in every direction, several shards of which entered the flesh of Treynor's arm, knocking him back like a meaty fist. At the same time, Lieutenant Cunnington fell, writhing, to the deck—and one glance told Treynor that the steersman, who'd been standing next to them both only moments before, was dead, the wheel blown to bits. Now they couldn't steer the ship or angle the *Tempest* to send off another broadside. Whatever damage they could inflict with their chasers would never be enough.

A cry of *"Vive la nation!"* rose from the other ship, and Treynor guessed the French were about to board.

Oh God . . .

Red rings of blood fanned out from the splinters that pierced his left arm, but there was nothing he could do about that right now. Forcing himself to move in spite of the agonizing pain, he knelt to examine Cunnington's wounds.

"Take him to the surgeon," he said to the two closest sailors. Cunnington had a nasty gash on the head, a large piece of wood protruding from his middle, and a smaller one sticking out of his leg.

"No!" Fighting them off, Cunnington tried, unsuccessfully, to stand. "I am in charge here. Lower the flag."

Treynor gritted his teeth. The wounded, moaning seamen and the wreckage made him sick. If not for the captain's poor timing at the onset, and Cunnington's incompetence thereafter, the day could have ended much differently. They had beaten themselves. The battle had been decided the moment their wheel was destroyed. But Treynor wasn't willing to give up yet.

"Not now." Treynor fought to keep his feet despite his dizziness. "I will need all able-bodied men, pistols at the ready. We shall board. Like us, they have lost their mast, and perhaps their wheel. They will not get off another blast as square as the last."

A weak cheer met his words.

"Anyone who follows him will be hanged for mutiny," Cunnington groaned. With one hand grasping his stomach, he looked to the closest junior officer. "Did you hear me? Lower the flag. I am still in charge here."

The man glanced uncertainly toward the flag locker where all flags, including those used for signals, were separated into pigeonholes. Then he looked at Treynor. "Nay. I think it's time ye relinquish command, Lieutenant Cunnington," he said, only to be interrupted by a shout of alarm.

"We're goin' down!"

Those from the handling chambers and shot lockers below began to swarm the deck. They dived into the foaming sea as they abandoned ship, some clinging to wreckage while others, who couldn't swim, screamed until they drowned.

It was too late. Treynor hung his head as he tried to comprehend the magnitude of what had happened. They had lost the battle and the ship and far too many men.

And they stood to lose a lot more . . .

Calling for Lawson to lower the flag from the gaff and to see the wounded Cruikshank and Cunnington safely away in one of the few sound boats on the chocks abaft, Treynor headed to the hatch. He'd sent Jeannette below decks. Imagining her fear and confusion, he knew he had to find her. The battle had been lost. There was nothing more he could do for his men. But he would not lose her.

Shoving his way through what remained of the panic-ridden crew, Treynor looked first in her cabin and then, in a futile yet hopeful attempt, in his own.

Both were empty.

Remembering his note telling her to stay below the gun deck, he descended to the bowels of the ship, where he sloshed through the rising water that was already causing the *Tempest* to tilt at an odd angle. "Jeannette!"

His voice echoed back to him without answer.

Treynor saw Bosun Hawker hurrying his wife, along with Amelia, her new baby and Jeannette's dog, out of their small cabin.

"Have you seen Lady St. Ives?" he asked.

"No, sir. An' ye 'aven't the time to search for 'er unless ye're longin' fer a watery grave yerself. Chances are, the lady 'as already jumped ship."

Treynor thought that unlikely. He'd not seen her topside since the outbreak of the battle, at least that he'd noticed. And he hadn't passed her on his way below. But amid so many, he could easily have missed her . . .

Intending to search the water from the deck, he started to follow the Hawkers. The bosun claimed someone was holding a boat for them.

But then Treynor turned back. There would be no second chance to visit the farthest reaches of the ship. The *Tempest* would soon be awash and foundering in the rough sea. Then it would sink.

The thought of Jeannette going down with it caused fear to squeeze his chest, gripping so tightly he could scarcely breathe.

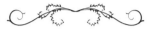

Jeannette tried not to panic amid the clamoring voices and pushing, frantic men. Filled with many who couldn't move, the surgery resounded with cries of doom and misery as water seeped into the room like icy fingers of death, grabbing at their ankles.

Clamping her hands over her ears, Jeannette hoped to block out the sound long enough to think of a way to get the injured topside. But there were far too many helpless sailors.

"Go!" The surgeon herded his mates out ahead of him. Each man supported one among the injured who could stand. They left behind those who were unconscious or unable to walk, along with the mortally wounded.

"What about the others?" Jeannette cried.

The surgeon barely spared her a glance. "There is nothing we can do. Get out unless you want to go down with them!"

When she didn't move, he shrugged and pushed through the portal. Half carrying a tall, thin seaman with a bandage circling his bare chest, he left Jeannette alone amid the cries for help.

The *Tempest* shifted, knocking her into the surgery table and the blood still puddled there. It stained her dress. No doubt her face and hair were speckled with it, as well. She could smell the freshness of that vital substance along with the sweat of the men who'd left it behind—just as she could smell the fear of those who remained.

It was the odor of death.

"Ma'am, don't leave me, please!"

Steadying herself, Jeannette turned to see the powder boy with the hurt foot, his large brown eyes glazed with fright.

"I can't walk. 'Elp me, please!"

The water level inched higher as Jeannette waded over to him, the weight of her wet skirts slowing her progress. It broke her heart that she couldn't save all those who reached toward her. But without help or more time, there was little she could do.

"I will come back for you," she promised the others as she helped the boy to stand. For most, her words would prove a lie, but she fully intended to rescue as many as she could. Hope was the only thing she could offer them at the moment.

The boy grimaced in pain as they worked their way to the door. Jeannette encouraged him as best she could, but was only half aware of what she was saying and was soon breathing too hard to continue speaking.

When they reached the top deck, she stared in horror.

The wet sand that had covered the wood was now a mixture of water, sand and blood—the blood of those lying prostrate on the deck or slumped over cannons, mouths gaping open in a forever scream. Portions of the deck were missing altogether. Scattered cannons were trapped among the considerable wreckage.

Instinctively she turned her face toward the place she'd last seen Treynor. With the slant of the ship, many of those who had died on deck tumbled toward the forecastle. Some had been snagged by the fallen mast or the broken boats.

Little remained near Treynor's post besides an overturned cannon that had come loose from its moorings. It had slid across the wood, gathering speed and smashing everything in its path until striking the foremast, which had held fast and stopped its forward momentum.

Forcing herself to examine the faces of those bodies strewn across the deck, she searched for Treynor, praying he had somehow escaped such a fate. "Have you heard word of the second lieutenant?" she asked the men who ran by her.

Few responded. Those who did, merely shook their heads.

"Every man for himself! Swim fer yer lives, ye—"

A French pistol popped as the man who was yelling that leaped over the side, and his words died with him. Then the gunfire ceased, leaving only human cries to echo against the sky.

Jeannette cursed the revolutionaries, the suffering caused by war and the feeling of loss that swamped her, and tried to bear more of the injured boy's weight. But her strength was giving out. Had she saved the boy from going down with the ship only to watch him drown? There were no serviceable boats, and she doubted he'd last long in the water.

"Can you swim?" she asked hopefully.

"Aye . . . a bit."

She let go of him long enough to slide a broken beam to the edge of the deck. Most of the bulwarks had been shot away. "Grab onto this as soon as you can after you hit the water," she said, struggling to shove it into the sea. "But be careful where you jump."

"Are ye not comin'?" he asked.

The acrid, smoky air caused her to cough. "Not yet."

"But the surgery will be under water."

She nodded as guilt and sadness welled up inside her. "I know. I am not going back."

His somber face looked far older than his years. "Thanks for 'elpin' me."

Glancing uncertainly at the dark swells dotted with men and floating debris, she sent him over the side. She didn't wait to see whether or not he managed to grab hold of the beam she'd pushed into the water. The fear that Treynor lay on deck, somehow not dead but injured, gave her new purpose.

Taking another deep breath, she set out to examine the bodies.

Gray, brown and a few pairs of blue eyes stared sightlessly up at her as she searched. Stepping in and around the bodies and blown-off limbs, she fought off renewed fear as the bloody sand swallowed her shoes. Only one thought drove her: the hope that Treynor lived, that she could find him.

When she spotted polished black boots beneath the tangled rigging and yards of the mast, that hope faltered.

Gingerly she pried some of the wreckage loose and lifted the man's shoulder to glimpse his downturned face. It was the purser. She recognized his dark, matted hair and his face—what there was of it. His jaw had been shot away.

Overcome, Jeannette slumped next to him.

The enemy's guns had fallen silent, but her ears still rang.

As she wiped Gillman's blood off her hands and onto her dress, she shivered uncontrollably. The sun had climbed high in the sky, but it offered little warmth to combat the cutting breeze. Considering the death and destruction before her, she wondered if she would ever be warm again.

Water lapped farther and farther up the deck. She was so tired, so discouraged, she could hardly feel fear. Where was Treynor? Dead, probably, swallowed by the cold, hungry sea, just as she would soon be . . .

A moan reached her ears, but amid the cries of so many, she scarcely noticed the sound until she realized it wasn't just a moan. It was her name.

Turning, she caught sight of Lieutenant Cunnington lying a few feet away, as pale as death. Blood trickled from his temple and from the corner of his mouth, but his eyes were fixed on her with the single-minded determination of a survivor.

"Help me," he groaned.

Jeannette stood but drew no closer. She had no time to help him. He was badly injured, would probably not live—and Treynor might need her.

Choking back a sob, she shook her head. "I will not let Treynor die while I save you!"

She spun around, renewing her search with less concern for who or what she touched. If she was going to die, she was going to die searching. She would not give up, would not give in to despair.

"Treynor!" she called, digging through the corpses. A jagged piece of wood cut her hand, but she scarcely felt it. "Treynor!"

"Come on!" A seaman, obviously assuming her to be out of her mind with fright, waved her toward the edge. "The sea is your only chance. The French are fishing those they can out of the water."

When she didn't budge, he grabbed her arm and tried to drag her to the side with him, but Jeannette jerked away. "I cannot. I have to find him."

"Who?"

"Lieutenant Treynor." Then she remembered Cunnington. "Wait! The first lieutenant needs your help. Over there—he is wounded."

The sailor shook his head. "I'll not bother with that cruel bastard. Or ye, neither, if ye'll not listen ter reason," he said, and hurried off without her.

Cunnington had done little to endear himself to anyone, but Jeannette couldn't leave him as she'd thought she could. She'd just started back for the first lieutenant when she heard Treynor call her name.

Nearly collapsing in relief, she turned to see him emerge from the hatch, soaked to the skin. His sun-darkened face had a grayish cast, and blood dripped from several pieces of wood piercing his left arm. But he was alive, and he was still standing.

"Thank God!" She covered her mouth to stifle a sob.

He crossed to her. "Are you all right?" His gaze ranged over her bloody gown as worry creased his brow.

Unable to staunch the tears that slid down her cheeks, she nodded. "The blood's not mine."

His good arm circled her waist and pulled her against him. "Shhh," he coaxed above her head. "We will survive. Somehow we will survive this."

Jeannette pressed her face into his chest. "I was afraid you were dead already."

"Alive enough, my sweet. But we must go." He pointed to a beam and tangled rigging bobbing in the sea not far away, supporting two men already. "See that?"

She nodded.

"After we get your clothes off, I will give you a big push. Keep your eye on that beam and swim like hell. You can swim?"

"Yes, but the sea is full of men. And the French, when they come for me—"

"Will find the most beautiful woman they have ever seen—in all her glory." He tore her bodice away when the buttons proved too stubborn. For a brief moment his eyes feasted on her breasts straining against the sheer fabric of her shift as though he might never see such a sight again. Then his voice dropped to a whisper in her ear. "And she will be alive, which is the only thing I care about."

"Treynor? Is that you?" Cunnington cried out. "For God's sake, man, help me!" He tried to shove himself into a sitting position, but failed.

"Do not go back for him," Jeannette whispered fiercely. "He will drown you. You are hurt. Come on. We will jump together. Now!"

The ship groaned as it sank lower in the water, the stern angling up by at least two feet.

A fresh surge of water gushed up the companionway and spewed over the deck, and Jeannette felt her feet begin to slip.

"Jump!" The lines of Treynor's face were hard and intent as he launched her out over the side.

Jeannette felt the chill wind grab hold of the hem of her chemise, making it billow out just before the cold water engulfed her.

Chapter 19

To keep from sliding across the deck and falling into the water, Lieutenant Treynor grasped what remained of the bulwarks as he watched Jeannette splash into the sea. He hoped her quick mind and strong body would serve her now, as the French had few boats with which to collect the survivors. Only a fraction of those in the sea would ever come out.

He prayed Jeannette would be one of them.

As soon as he saw her resurface and begin to swim, he went back for Lieutenant Cunnington, who'd managed to crawl away from the damaged wheel.

"Treynor." Cunnington clung to the tarry cable that secured the mizzenmast. "Thank God." He tried to laugh. "They left me. The bloody fools . . . left me lying in my . . ." Treynor took Cunnington's arm and pulled him into a sitting position, which elicited a groan. " . . . my own blood."

Treynor didn't reply. Nearly swooning from the pain, he used his injured arm to hold on to the mast while he hefted Cunnington across his shoulders. He fought to keep his footing, clinging to anything he could while he crept slowly to where he'd pushed Jeannette into the sea. "I hope you know how to swim, Lieutenant," he said.

"You could not have done it any better." Cunnington's throat worked as he swallowed. "You could not have won the battle—"

Treynor groaned as he slid Cunnington off. "Save your breath," he muttered. "You will soon need it."

"What are you doing?" The first lieutenant blinked in confusion, squinting into the sun. For a moment, Treynor wondered if Cunnington would die then and there, and spare him the trouble of trying to save him. But the first lieutenant still breathed, and Treynor could delay no longer.

"Hang on," he told him. With agonizing effort, he gripped Cunnington with his wounded arm and jumped.

The sudden cold stole Treynor's breath. Instinctively he let go of Cunnington and stretched both arms out, parting the water until he burst through the surface and filled his lungs with air.

Somehow Cunnington managed to surface as well a few feet away. "Treynor! Help me!" His head disappeared in the frothy waves, but his hands flailed against the water. Eventually, he came up and gurgled Treynor's name again.

Blast the man. He deserved to drown . . .

Treynor scanned the sea, looking for Jeannette. He didn't want to waste his time with Cunnington if she needed him. Holding his head above the swells, he searched, but to no avail. "Jeannette!"

The voices of desperate men answered him: the cries of those who were drowning, the last of those jumping ship, the cheers of the French sailors.

Had she drowned? Treynor's heart pounded hard and fast, fear for her life somehow lending him strength.

"Treynor!" Cunnington grabbed hold of him, nearly pulling him under.

Treynor gasped for breath and foundered before he could turn Cunnington on his back and begin towing him toward flotsam that might save them.

When Cunnington quit struggling and shut up, his pale lids lowering to cover his eyes, Treynor considered it a blessing. He was easier to maneuver this way. But as the *Tempest* sank behind them, it threatened to pull down everything close to it. Treynor had to use all his strength to swim away from the lethal force of the vast whirlpool that sucked at their legs.

He managed to break free from the ship's invisible hold just as Cunnington regained consciousness and began mumbling, but the floating debris that had appeared so plentiful from the ship now seemed miles away. Treynor wasn't sure how long they could survive with only his one good arm to propel them forward. The darkening sky and frothy waves promised a storm.

Squinting against the saltwater that stung his eyes, Treynor hoped to distinguish between the shades of gray surrounding them.

Behind him, the *Tempest* was gone.

Larger and larger waves curled over their heads, causing them to sputter time and again. They passed other sailors as Treynor struggled on, some drowned but still floating. Bits of debris swirled around them, too, but none large enough to support one man, let alone two.

Still, Treynor swam toward the enemy frigate that appeared and disappeared on the horizon like an elusive phantom ship. He could hear the French call to each other in their native tongue as they lifted survivors out of the water. But they seemed in no particular hurry.

Using only enough effort to keep them afloat, which was taxing enough, he paused to stare at Cunnington's thin, white face. The first lieutenant was responsible for a massacre of good men, a true loss to England, but a shipmate was a shipmate. Treynor could no sooner condemn Cunnington to die than he could willingly forfeit his own life. But that didn't mean he wanted to save him.

More determined than ever to survive, he swam on.

So now . . . the battle's over . . . we will drink a can of wine . . . and you will drink to your love . . . and I will drink to mine . . . He sang inside his head to keep his mind off the numbness invading his limbs.

I'm coming, Jeannette. Don't give up.

As if he'd spoken those words aloud, he heard her voice, shaky but otherwise true, "Treynor! Over here!"

Treynor had not the breath to answer loudly enough to be heard, but the knowledge that Jeannette lived and was only yards away kept him swimming. He pulled Cunnington in her direction as she maneuvered a portion of the ship's broken mast toward them.

You will . . . drink to your love . . . and I will drink to mine.

"Are you all right?" she gasped when he came within reach.

"Aye," he whispered and allowed her to pull him closer. With one last surge of effort, he threw his good arm over the mast and lowered his head to the wet wood.

Jeannette slid around it until she clung next to him. "You look t-t-terrible," she said, her teeth chattering through her words. "D-damn if you . . . didn't rescue . . . that d-devil." Shivering violently, she reached out to help support Cunnington.

Treynor didn't protest. Too exhausted to utter another syllable, he could only close his eyes in relief as she wiped seawater off his face.

"Don't you dare . . . d-drown, Lieutenant," she warned through blue lips. "You have p-promised me something . . . and I intend . . . t-to collect it."

The French lieutenant stood in front of the ragtag line of prisoners huddled together, sopping wet and shaking, on the deck of the frigate *Superbe*. Short and stocky, with dark hair and a long mustache, he strutted before them, preening like a rooster.

"I am Lieutenant Favre," he announced in passable English. "Your captain has not survived. His small boat capsized, and he died before we reached him. We lost our own captain when the mast fell, our first and second lieutenants as well. So you can officially surrender to me. Who is your most senior officer?"

"I . . . am," Cunnington responded as best he could from where he sat next to Treynor and Jeannette. Propped against the forward mast, he looked no better than a talking corpse. "We . . . surrender, sir."

He tried to stand but couldn't manage it, and Favre didn't move to help him.

Treynor watched, cradling his wounded arm. Jeannette wondered if he, like her, was taking stock of the ship's damage and the dirt-streaked faces of the surviving French crew, who were far less numerous than she had supposed.

Evidently, the battle had been brutal on both sides.

"It was close, no?" As the French lieutenant addressed Cunnington, his words echoed Jeannette's thoughts. "Only a fraction of our men are left." He nodded toward several of his crew who stood close by, pistols drawn. "Unfortunately, our Breton navigator has been killed. Has your navigator, by chance, survived?"

"No." Treynor answered for Cunnington; Cunnington didn't seem to know.

"Then we shall keep to the open sea to the north of us until after this storm has passed." Favre squinted at the hazy sky. "I have no desire to end up shipwrecked along our own rocky coast."

"Meanwhile, may we have some blankets to keep the wounded among us warm?" Treynor asked. "And the lady?"

Jeannette crossed her arms in front of her in an effort to hide her near nudity as Favre turned his attention her way.

"Ah yes. The lady. I was coming to her." He strode across the five or six feet between them to stop in front of her. "Who are you? A stowaway? A whore? The captain's daughter or mistress?"

Jeannette bit her lip. Her accent would give her away as soon as she opened her mouth.

"She is the wife of a powerful English baron who will pay handsomely for her safe return," Treynor answered for her.

Favre raised his dark eyebrows. "Indeed! Then I should like to hear the lady tell me who he is."

When Jeannette hesitated, Treynor once again filled the silence. "She is married to the Baron St. Ives of Cornwall. Perhaps you have heard of him?"

The French lieutenant kept his eyes on Jeannette, but raised his pistol at Treynor. "I said I would like to hear from the lady."

Jeannette did her best to eradicate the accent from her speech, but she knew the moment she heard her own voice that she had failed. "Lieutenant Treynor speaks the truth. My husband is the Baron St. Ives."

"Aha, a Frenchwoman, no?"

Jeannette didn't respond.

"I suspect there is more to this." He looked to Treynor. "Who is she really?"

"I just told you."

Favre's jaw tightened. "So you did, *monsieur*. But I want to know how this woman came to be where she is."

"By abandoning ship and swimming for all she was worth, like the rest of us." Treynor's sarcasm did little to endear him to Favre. The French lieutenant's finger tightened on the trigger.

"You will not make a fool of me. Answer my question!"

Treynor glared up at him without response.

Afraid Favre would shoot him, Jeannette opened her mouth to tell the truth, but the report of his pistol deafened her before she could speak. She screamed and lurched toward Treynor, but Cunnington had beaten her to it. With a groan of anguish, the first lieutenant had taken the ball in the chest.

"Cunnington!" Treynor cried as Cunnington's body sagged on top of him, eyes wide as he gasped for air.

Treynor eased him to the deck. Bright red blood spread over the first lieutenant's shirt to mingle with the crimson of his earlier injury.

"Cunnington, can you hear me?" Treynor asked.

Cunnington licked his lips. "Had to do something"—he swallowed—"to make it worth . . . your effort in saving me, Treynor."

"You should not have done it," Treynor said.

"No? Ah well"—a gasp and a groan—"I am the son of . . . a viscount, remember? I must live up . . . to my station."

"Indeed." When Cunnington's eyelids closed, Treynor gently shook him. "Hold on, man. This isn't over yet. We will make it, you and I."

The first lieutenant's eyelids fluttered open again. "No. It is better that I . . . die. You are so"—he coughed—"so much better at living." He tried to laugh, but groaned instead.

Treynor stripped off his shirt and wadded it up to plug the hole in Cunnington's chest, applying pressure to stop the bleeding. "Concentrate on catching your breath."

"I am dying . . . an honorable death, am I not?" he asked, his voice wobbling as his chest started to jerk.

"Yes." Jeannette took his hand. "We are witnesses to that."

At her words, his face lit up with the most genuine smile she had ever seen him wear. "Tell my father," he whispered, and with one final gasp, he was gone.

Jeannette's throat constricted and her eyes stung as she stared at Cunnington's face. "Thank you," she told him.

Releasing the first lieutenant's hand, she stood and faced Favre, who watched dispassionately. It was beginning to rain, which only made their situation more untenable. "I am Lady Jeannette Boucher, daughter of Jacques Boucher, Comte de Lumfere," she said proudly. "I shall appreciate your taking any further revenge on me and not these injured men."

The French officer saluted her, his dark eyes shining like pieces of obsidian. "So it is as I thought! We have managed to reclaim one of our own."

"It matters not who she used to be," Treynor said. "She is now the wife of an English baron. He would happily line your pockets with gold to get her back."

The Frenchman reached out to finger a lock of Jeannette's cropped hair.

When she pulled away, he dropped his hand, but his eyes warmed as they took in the generous amount of flesh revealed by her gauzy shift.

"Hmmm . . . the only thing I hate worse than an Englishman is a former member of our own aristocracy," he mused. "But I must say, she is a rare beauty, even for a Frenchwoman."

"Do you not hear, man?" Treynor argued. "St. Ives—"

"I have heard enough about this baron," Favre snapped. "What is he to me? Would you have me sacrifice my principles for a few francs?"

"But you have nothing to gain by taking her back to France!"

"This woman has missed her rendezvous with the guillotine, *monsieur*. Justice must be served. But how would you know? You English still labor under the control of the rich and powerful, while we . . . we are free." He lifted his chin and paced in front of them. "And then there is the pleasure of her company on the voyage home," he added with a lewd smile. "The English baron would certainly hold me accountable for any liberties I might take. The guillotine will not."

Treynor shoved himself to his feet. "She would be worth much more—"

"I have been at sea a long time, *monsieur*. Nothing could be worth more than what I plan to enjoy at her expense. And the fact that she is a highborn lady will make our time together all the more . . . stimulating. Perhaps it will teach her how a real man takes a woman. We all know the English make love only to their money!"

Some of the French sailors sniggered.

Lieutenant Favre seemed to enjoy their mirth, but he didn't laugh with them. Instead, his teeth gleamed beneath his mustache as he smiled, his eyes wandering back to Jeannette. "I will provide you with what clothing I can find," he told her. "You will bathe and dress, then join me and the other officers at supper."

"And if I refuse?" she asked.

Favre's eyes sliced to Treynor. "Then I will kill this man here."

A muscle twitched in Treynor's cheek. "My life means nothing to her."

The Frenchman cocked one eyebrow. "What I have observed tells me differently," he told Treynor. "And I can assure you your life means even less to *me*." He nodded to one of his men, who moved forward and put a newly primed pistol to Treynor's head.

His body tense, his eyes mere slits of hatred, Treynor glared at Favre.

"No!" Jeannette's pulse raced, making her blood rush in her ears until she could hear nothing else. The soldier with the gun grinned, but before he could pull the trigger, she sank to her knees. "Please. I will do anything. Just spare him."

Treynor's injured arm began to throb as soon as he grew warm enough to feel it. Propping himself against a cannon on the badly battered gun deck, where three of the French crew guarded him and the other prisoners with pistols, he proceeded to extract the splinters, gasping from the pain with every jerk.

Blessed darkness hovered at the corners of his mind as he worked, but the thought of Jeannette, frightened and alone in Lieutenant Favre's quarters, kept him from succumbing to oblivion.

Laying his head back and breathing deeply as the rain fell on his face, he let himself rest when his grasp on consciousness became too tenuous. Then he started again.

The French had given them blankets, but brought no food or drink. Treynor longed for a bit of rum or brandy to steady his hand and ease the pain. Or some nourishment to rebuild his strength. His only respite from the gruesome, bloody business with his arm turned out to be Smedley, who moaned next to him, gut-shot.

"Smedley." He gently shook the man's shoulder. "Hey!"

The tattoo artist peered up at him. "Sir?"

Still trying to avoid the light-headedness that plagued him, Treynor breathed through his nose. "We have to do something."

"Aye, sir." Smedley's exhale was accompanied by a rattle in his chest. "You don't fancy the thought of prison, eh?"

"I have too much to do in England." Treynor was thinking of his mother at that moment. For the first time in his life, he regretted having been so hard on her. She had caused him a great deal of pain, but somehow what had happened before didn't matter so much anymore. He was a man now, and lucky to be alive. The time had come to make peace with his past.

Smedley pulled him from his thoughts. "What do you suggest?"

Treynor focused again on the urgency of their situation. The three French guards, huddled together against the rain and the penetrating cold, were talking and laughing. From the smell of it, they were drinking, too. They ignored their prisoners.

Treynor doubted they spoke English, but he lowered his voice, just in case. "I would guess there are fifty or sixty of the French. Maybe more below. There are almost forty of us, though many are injured."

"Don't look good, eh?" Smedley grimaced as he licked dry, cracked lips.

"No. But you feel the rain. A storm's coming on, and I am not so sure the *Superbe* won't suffer the same fate as the *Tempest*. Did you hear Favre say they have lost their Breton navigator?"

Smedley's nod was almost imperceptible, but Treynor continued. "He thinks we have open sea to the north of us, which means we are probably somewhere off the approaches to Brest, west of the peninsula, maybe beyond the Passage du Raz and the Pointe de Saints. Only I think we are closer to the coast than he expects. The wind carried us due east throughout the battle."

With a curse, Treynor shifted to relieve the throb in his arm, but to no avail. "With the sky so overcast, there is no way to know for sure."

It was several moments before Smedley could respond. "I'm sorry we couldn't take 'em, sir," he said. "We should've blasted 'em out of the water—"

"What is lost is lost," Treynor broke in as he glanced toward the French sailors. They were still talking and laughing. He could hear snatches of their conversation on the wind, but he was too tired to translate their words into English. "Favre seems more interested in savoring his sudden command and the spoils of war than in keeping a sharp lookout. He thinks he need only wait out the storm, then dock at Brest, probably tomorrow, when he can use daylight to his advantage."

"Meanwhile, he's planning to entertain the baron's wife—at your expense, eh?" Smedley said.

When Treynor scowled, Smedley chuckled.

"You don't have to admit it, sir. I saw it in your face back there." Clutching his stomach, he fell silent.

Treynor didn't relish the thought of being so transparent. "This has as much to do with saving our hides as it does hers." He kept his voice even, kept working at the splinters in his arm, but he longed to tear Favre's heart out with his bare hands.

Noticing that he was busy, Smedley lifted his head and indicated Treynor's arm. "What are you up to there?"

"A little surgery of my own." The words were more of a grunt, spoken as he pulled out a large piece of wood.

The world spun, then went black, but he must not have been out for long, because Smedley's next question made sense and seemed to follow.

"What do you think we should do, sir?"

"How are you feeling?"

"Wet. And I could use a drink."

"I promise you will get one."

Drawn by the sound of Treynor's voice, some of the other prisoners stirred and moved closer, although most were nursing injuries of their own—or despair. After a time, the officers could expect to be traded for French prisoners of war. But the rank and file often faced long stretches in prison barges.

"What ye sayin', Lieutenant?" Mrs. Hawker asked. Her taciturn husband stood behind her. Amelia hovered nearby, trying to shelter her baby from the cold. Bonnie lay on the deck with her tongue lolling out, the picture of canine exhaustion.

Having extracted the last of the wood from his arm, Treynor couldn't answer right away. When he did, he spoke through his teeth as he wound his shirt, already sopped in Cunnington's blood, around his arm to staunch the bleeding.

"'Ere, let me 'elp ye with that." Mrs. Hawker had her husband give up his own shirt and tear it into strips. Then she bandaged Treynor's arm as best she could under the circumstances.

"There's not many of them, and they have lost their senior officers, so they are not well organized," Treynor said when she finished. "The ship is steering wildly, the rain is coming harder and the sea is getting rougher. Soon they will have to turn their attention to the storm if they want to survive it. When they do, we will have an opportunity."

"How so?" Mrs. Hawker asked. "They know this coast better'n we do."

"But they don't know where we are in relation to it."

"I'm willin' to take any chance, no matter 'ow slim," her husband chimed in. "We will not see the inside of a French prison. Not if I can 'elp it."

"Good." Treynor searched the deck for any sign of Favre. "Then pass the word to the other men. They must be ready to grab any weapon they can find and put it to good use as soon as I give the word."

He looked at Smedley, but the tattoo artist gave no sign he'd heard, making Treynor wonder if he'd slipped into unconsciousness. "Smed?"

The man nodded. "Just tell me what and when," he breathed, his face ashen, "I will do what I can."

"Your task will be a simple one," Treynor told him. "We just have to wait for the right moment."

Wearing the boy's clothes Favre had brought her, Jeannette sat alone, silent and still as a stone, staring at her reflection in a basin of water.

She hardly recognized the tired face staring back at her. Never had she dreamed she would find herself sitting in the captain's quarters of an enemy ship, awaiting a complete stranger, a man who made no secret of his salacious intentions.

But preserving the second lieutenant's life outweighed her fear for her own safety. She didn't regret, couldn't regret, what she'd done.

Numbly, her gaze circled the room. Rich wooden paneling and cabinetry covered every wall. An abundance of Louis IV furniture sat on thick rugs and competed for dominance.

There had to be something amid the clutter she could use to defend herself, she thought, but she'd gone through all the cabinets and drawers, even searched the armoire—and found nothing.

She dipped a rag in the basin of water, destroying her pale reflection, and began to bathe. Beyond her fear for the immediate future, she felt a strong sense of loss for her way of life and the France she once knew.

The crew of the *Superbe* called themselves Frenchmen, but they were strangers to her. Part of a new breed. The enemy.

The sparkle of a shiny object in the mirror stole Jeannette's attention from her ablutions. She crossed the room to investigate and discovered what looked to be a table knife on the floor beneath the captain's desk.

Favre had made a cursory search of the cabin, to make sure it was safe to leave her alone, but if he'd seen the knife, he'd not thought it enough of a threat to remove it.

Jeannette fingered the blade. If it was sharp enough to cut meat . . .

The knife might be sufficient for the job, but was she capable of stabbing a man?

She shuddered at the thought.

A knock on the door nearly made her drop the potential weapon.

"Madame? Shall we eat?" Favre called.

Jeannette shoved the knife into her right boot just before he entered, wearing a fresh uniform. "*Oui*. I am ready." She inclined her head, hoping to look demure.

With a bow, he held the door for her.

As she passed through the door her trousers fell in baggy folds. But her short, low-heeled boots fit far more tightly, holding the knife securely to her ankle. Favre must have taken them from a boy—most likely a victim of the battle.

The French lieutenant led her to the wardroom, where four other men waited around a rectangular table. Several seats remained empty, attesting to the number of casualties among the officers.

Jeannette didn't speak as Favre seated her next to him and the French cook served supper. By then, the rain was pounding out of the sky and the *Superbe* was rocking so violently she could scarcely eat for the roiling in her stomach. She wanted to slip her bread, at the very least, into her pocket and somehow convey it to Treynor, in case the prisoners hadn't been fed. But Lieutenant Favre watched every move she made with growing interest.

"Do you not like the fare, madame?" he asked. "I assure you our cook is one of the best."

"It is excellent," she murmured, speaking in her native tongue, as was he. "It is the rocking of the ship that disturbs me."

"One grows accustomed to it." He smiled confidently, although at least two of those who dined with them looked nearly as green as she was herself. "So, tell me, how is it that an English baron has captured the heart of such a beautiful French lady?"

"Love knows no bounds," Jeannette replied, thinking of Treynor. Her parents would never consider him a viable suitor, but she couldn't tell her heart not to love him.

"Spoken like a true Frenchwoman." He toyed with his mustache as he considered her. "However, I would guess your marriage had much more to do with saving your neck than love."

Jeannette shrugged. "And if it did?"

"Then we are fortunate to have you back."

A young man with fair hair and a fuzzy upper lip cleared his throat. "Lieutenant Favre, sir. I hesitate to interrupt, and I mean no disrespect, but . . ." He glanced at those around the table, all of whom gazed back at him, chewing in silence. Taking a deep breath, he continued, "But the storm worsens, sir. And many repairs are necessary—"

"Are they not being made at this very moment?" Favre snapped, swilling his wine and studying the burgundy liquid.

"Yes. But we are so short-handed, sir. Certainly there are better things for us to be doing than dining as though—"

Favre scowled. "We've got to *eat*. Even the captain *ate*, did he not?"

"Yes, sir. But . . ."

"But what, Mr. Croutier?" Favre set his glass back on the table and fixed his eyes on Croutier's reddening face. "Am I not in charge here? Are you accusing me of not knowing what I am doing?"

Croutier looked to those around him again, but no one dared offer their support. "No, sir. Of course you do, sir. It is just that the rain is coming so hard now. And I thought that—well, perhaps we should hurry."

"Then hurry, Croutier. You can have the first watch." Favre smirked at Jeannette. "I will be busy for a while."

Jeannette tried to swallow another tasteless bite and nearly gagged. She set her silver back on the table so the men wouldn't notice how badly her hands were shaking, and concentrated on the feel of the knife in her boot. She would have to use it. There was no one else to save her.

After Mr. Croutier's comments, the meal passed quickly and in silence. Evidently Favre's intention to show her off as a prize of war hadn't brought him quite the satisfaction he'd anticipated. His men were too concerned with other things—the storm above all.

Lightning flashed across the sky as the French lieutenant led Jeannette from the wardroom to the deck. He kept her elbow gently but firmly in his grasp as he spoke with the steersman and put Mr. Croutier in charge. Shielding his face from the rain, he called to the lookout, who cried back that he saw nothing but gray and didn't expect to see more until after the storm lifted.

Finally, he bowed to Jeannette. "Shall we retire to the captain's cabin, my lady?"

Jeannette couldn't bring herself to nod. "If we could just look in on the prisoners," she said, raising hopeful eyes to the lieutenant's face.

He shook his head. "It's too wet out here. And it could get much worse. Croutier might be right. We should hurry."

For the first time, Favre's face held a glimmer of doubt as he stared at the mountainous waves that tossed the *Superbe* like a child's toy. "I might be needed on deck," he added.

"But it will only take a moment. Then I will go with you willingly."

"You have no choice, regardless," he told her and pressed his lips to hers in a sloppy kiss.

Jeannette couldn't help wrenching away. Her reaction far more instinctual than calculated, she wiped his saliva from her mouth, and Favre slapped her.

"I will have none of that, my pretty whore," he gritted out, but Jeannette's ears were ringing so badly she could scarcely hear him. "You will give me all you gave your English husband and you will act like you enjoy doing it. Do you understand?"

Getting wetter by the moment, Jeannette stared at him, numbly fingering her cheek. The motion of the ship, combined with her stint in the ocean and her own anxiety, left her almost too weak to stand. "Yes, sir. What you want is plain enough, but you will get nothing from me unless you allow me to assure myself of the prisoners' safety. If they are dead, there is certainly no reason for me not to join them."

"They are alive."

"Am I to take your word?"

He cursed, but relented. "As you wish. A quick turn past them is all, however. And you will have my promise that they will shortly receive some food."

She tilted her head. "That is enough."

Wanting to get in out of the rain, Favre kept his promise to the letter and made their stop at the prisoners a mere second. Jeannette scarcely had time to find Treynor. When she did, she noticed that he watched her and her escort with the eyes of a stalking cat.

Not wanting him to worry, she nodded slightly to tell him she was all right.

Lieutenant Favre commanded one of the guards to bring bread to the prisoners, and Jeannette turned her face away. Remembering the glint in Treynor's eyes and the hard planes of his face, she moved forward. Crawford Treynor might die this night, she thought, but if she had anything to do with it, Favre would not be the man to take his life.

Nor would the Frenchman rape her.

When they arrived at the captain's cabin, Favre waved her inside. "After you, madame."

Jeannette walked through the portal, her mind focused on the blade pressed to her ankle—and a fervent prayer that her nerve wouldn't fail her.

Chapter 20

The wind made short work of the *Superbe*'s sails. Already shot through and nearly in tatters, their poor condition hindered the steersman who struggled to keep the damaged frigate under control. The loss of her mizzenmast only compounded the problem.

Silent and pensive, Treynor listened to the howl of the wind, wanting to lend his own voice to its keening wail—to sound a battle cry as ancient as any on earth. The sight of Jeannette with Favre had nearly driven him to desperate measures. He longed to kill the Frenchman and free her, but he had no chance of getting more than ten paces from the spot on which he sat. That his opportunity might arrive too late, if it arrived at all, only caused his rage to mount.

Finally Mrs. Hawker placed a hand on his arm. "Ye'll be no good ter 'er if ye don't use yer 'ead, Lieutenant," she cautioned.

"Good advice," he responded. But it didn't erase the vision of Favre forcing himself on Jeannette.

"What means more to ye, 'er life, or 'er virtue?" she asked.

Her life. That meant everything to him—but still he couldn't bear the thought of her being hurt, especially in that way.

"She's strong," the bosun's wife continued. "'Ave no fear of that."

Far past the point of calm reason, he said, "I will kill him." He could see only red, feel nothing but the desire to wring the breath from the French lieutenant's body. "Just give me one chance," he said, "and Favre is a dead man."

"Now you know what it feels like to be kissed by a real man, a French-man." Lieutenant Favre pulled back from pressing his lips to Jeannette's to look in her eyes as they stood next to the bed.

She cringed at the sour smell of his breath, wishing she could wipe away the moist imprint of his mouth. One of his hands clutched her breast through her shirt while the other cupped her buttocks and pressed her against him.

He released her long enough to remove his shirt, and she stumbled back, nearly falling onto the bed.

I can do it. I won't look at him. It's not real. She stared at the design on the carpet as the lieutenant's outer garments hit the floor with a soft *poof*, and almost pulled her knife from its hiding place right then.

But it was too soon. Favre would only wrestle it from her. Difficult though it was, she had to be patient.

The sight of the lieutenant's bare chest, pale beneath the thick black hair that covered it as well as his shoulders and arms, increased her terror by a staggering degree. Only the vision of Treynor held hostage by surly guards not far away made her control the impulse to protect herself or flee. Treynor needed her to have his kind of courage. They all did.

She gave Lieutenant Favre a shaky smile before he could remove his breeches. "Are you not going to help me first?"

The lieutenant's eyes gleamed with lust and anticipation. "You are far more eager than I had hoped, *ma petite*. I am glad to see you are a woman of your word." He closed the gap between them in a single stride and pulled her into his arms for another revolting kiss, gagging her with his tongue. Then he fumbled with her buttons.

Jeannette steeled herself beneath his groping fingers. She had to wait until they were both on the bed and she could use her weight to bear down on him with the knife. But when his hand delved beneath her clothing, she pulled away.

"What?" His eyes narrowed at the loathing and disgust that she struggled to hide. "Is something wrong?"

The lies Jeannette planned to utter froze in her throat. She couldn't pretend; it was beyond her. "You are worse than a pig," she spat. "My skin crawls beneath your touch."

Jeannette hadn't expected her words to be well received, but the immediate violence of the blow he struck caught her by surprise. She blinked as bells and whistles seemed to explode in her head, then stared at him, dazed, as he advanced upon her.

"I am not doing this for *you*." Gripping her by the hand, he yanked her forward and tossed her onto the bed, where he grabbed a handful of her shirt and tried to rip it away. But by then Jeannette had regained enough of her senses to fight.

"No!" She struggled to free herself, but he claimed her wrists and pinned them above her head. His overlong nails grazed her skin from collarbone to breast as he tore open her shirt. Jeannette could see the crest of her own nipple, bouncing as her chest heaved beneath his weight.

"Beautiful," he murmured, letting go of her hands in his eagerness to feel her flesh.

Jeannette groaned, not caring whether he'd interpret the sound as pleasure or pain, and reached for the knife. It was time. Time to claim her weapon. If only she could reach it . . .

The tips of Jeannette's fingers brushed the hilt several times before she managed to pull it from her shoe. By then the lieutenant had shifted to fumble with his belt and unknowingly knocked the knife from her shaking hand onto the bed along with them.

Oh God, help me. Frantically patting the bedclothes, Jeannette searched for the cool steel of the blade.

Finished undoing his pants, the lieutenant turned his attention to stripping off the rest of her clothes.

"Treynor," she whimpered. "Treynor . . ." And then her fingers found the knife.

"Breakers dead ahead! The rocks!" The lookout's cry caused the entire ship to take notice. "Heave to! Heave to!"

Some of the French sailors scrambled up the wet rigging. Others raised the ship's blue lights and fired the warning rockets. The three men guarding Treynor and the other English prisoners peered questioningly at each other. They'd been given strict orders not to leave their posts, but the emergency of the situation clearly confused them.

"All hands to stations!" someone else shouted. *"Vite! Vite!"*

Treynor felt Smedley slump against him and glanced down. The man had drawn his last breath without Treynor knowing it. Another loss—but there was nothing Treynor could do. And, with any luck, Smedley could still be of help.

"This man is about to die! We need a surgeon! Have pity!" he cried above the roar of the wind and waves.

His yells destroyed the last vestiges of the guards' resolve to remain. Injured and dying English prisoners were of no importance when the ship would wreck if they did not act in time.

The rocks along the coast seemed to rise from the foaming breakers a quarter mile away, growing larger by the second.

Lowering their pistols, the guards ran off, some slipping across the deck in their efforts to help with the sails and keep the *Superbe* from certain doom.

Treynor blinked against the rain. "Let's go!" he called and sprang into action. "Now is our chance!"

Had another man led the charge, perhaps the *Tempest*'s battered crew would not have followed, but they were used to his voice. Some grabbed slabs of wood as a weapon. Many went at the French with nothing more than their fists and sheer fury.

Favre had to have heard the alarm. But he was nowhere in sight. And Treynor couldn't look for him. Despite the wind buffeting every move they made and the rain slashing into their faces, they had to subdue the French and gain control of the ship or they would all die.

The rocks rose higher on their leeward side, backed by the humped shadow of land. From the ship, the jagged coast looked like the teeth of some great serpent slithering through the water to devour them.

After knocking away the Frenchman who tried to stop him, he rushed the steersman with single-minded determination and slugged him until he let go of the wheel.

Without someone at the helm, the *Superbe* swayed even more dramatically. Treynor planned to take control, but the steersman wasn't about to let him. They grappled for several seconds, fighting on the slippery deck, before Treynor managed to get enough space to knock him out.

Pushing the limp man aside, he rose unsteadily to his feet, wincing. Many of the wounds on his arm had reopened in the struggle. Fresh blood soaked through the makeshift bandages, but he ignored it along with the damp, windy weather and the pain.

Jeannette . . .

He had to reach her. But at that moment he could do nothing other than steer the ship out of danger. Wiping the water from his eyes, he grasped the wheel and turned it with unthinking skill, hoping to save them all.

The others, still locked in battle, were fighting with equal parts rage and desperation. But it wasn't long before they sent up the cry of "Long live the king!" The French had been taken by surprise by both the rocks and their English prisoners. Without someone to lead them, they soon gave up, begging to surrender.

But Treynor intended to take no prisoners. He couldn't risk an uprising later, would need all hands from the *Tempest* just to sail the ship. He shouted an order for any Frenchman yet alive to be thrown overboard, and soon the *Superbe*'s crew jumped ship and swam for the very rocks Treynor worked so hard to avoid. Then his men, shouting to each other and to him, swarmed the rigging and regained control despite the rain.

But the switch had cost them time, too much time. The ship began to swing the wrong way again . . .

Treynor cast a glance over his shoulder toward the captain's cabin where he'd seen Favre take Jeannette. Its portal was still closed. To rescue her he would have to let go of the wheel. But they were not out of danger. He couldn't risk drifting any closer to the rocks. Already, it appeared too late to avoid such a calamity.

Despite the fact that he was using all his skill, the frigate yawed one way and then the other. The wind seemed determined to dash them against the French coast, but then . . . it shifted. With a shudder, the *Superbe* settled, rocking in swells that would take them away from the rocky coast.

Marveling at the miracle that had just saved them, Treynor called Bosun Hawker to the wheel the second they were clear.

"Take this," he shouted above the storm. "And hold her steady."

Hawker used his wet sleeve to wipe the water from his face. "I don't think anyone can. Not in 'er condition," he cried. But he complied.

As soon as the older man's hands closed about the wheel, Treynor made a dash for the captain's cabin. Slowing as he reached the door, he pressed his ear to the wooden panel, hoping to get some indication of what went on inside. His strength was fading—he needed the advantage of surprise.

The sound of the rain hitting the deck, the shouting of his men, the rigging whistling above and the water churning about them echoed in Treynor's ears, but he could hear nothing from inside.

He tried the knob.

Locked.

Damnation. He stepped back and used his shoulder as a battering ram. But the door held fast. He was just getting ready to slam into it again when it opened and Jeannette's pale face appeared.

"Treynor?" Tears swelled in her eyes and splashed over her thick lashes to run down her cheeks as she blinked up at him.

"Are you all right?" She was still wearing the clothes she'd had on when she'd gone away with Favre. Her shirt was torn, revealing several scratches on one lovely breast, but it was the abundance of blood farther down that made Treynor's fists clench.

"What happened? Are you hurt?"

Shaking visibly now, Jeannette stood back and swung the door wide.

Water dripped off him as Treynor entered and searched the room with his eyes until he found Lieutenant Favre lying on his back, staring at the ceiling, a knife plunged deep in his bare chest.

Blinking in surprise, Treynor moved closer. Favre still wore his pants. But his belt was unbuckled, his shirt and shoes tossed to the side as though removed in haste.

"Are you hurt?" he asked again, turning to take Jeannette into his arms.

She shook her head and collapsed against him, sobbing quietly into his shoulder.

The smell of bile permeated the room, indicating she'd been sick, but he couldn't help marveling at her courage. Pulling back, he tilted her chin up long enough to catch and hold her gaze. He had never known a woman of such spirit.

"You did only what you had to do. It was you or him," he told her sternly. "Had you not killed him, he might have rallied his crew and finished us."

"It was terrible," she whispered. "I was so afraid. And then, after I was sure he was"—she swallowed—"dead . . . that I had actually . . . k-killed him, I dared not come out for fear of what his men might do."

He took her by the shoulders as gently as he could. "You are safe, little Jeannette. The French are even now swimming toward their own coast. Our worst enemy has become the sea."

"I felt the ship heave to. I wondered why." Her voice trembled.

"We nearly wrecked upon the rocks. But they are no danger to us now. As soon as we ride out this storm, we will sail to England. As damaged as the ship is, it may take us several days, but we will make it. Both of us."

Jeannette nodded and turned her face back into his shoulder. "How is your arm?" she asked as he stroked her hair.

"It has felt better." He grinned down at her. "But I can tell you this: I am glad I never tried to force myself on you."

Jeannette looked to the bed, and though Treynor felt her flinch at the sight of the dead man, a small, victorious smile curled the corners of her lips.

"He deserved what he got," she stated with conviction. "But it was certainly more than he expected." And then, because there was nothing else they could do, they laughed.

The storm lessened an hour later, enabling the *Tempest*'s crew to pump the hold and mend some of the rigging and sails. By nightfall, the rain had stopped and the heavy cloud cover had thinned into wisps that allowed the moon's light to shine through.

Still concerned about the damage the ship had sustained, Jeannette watched as they sewed the French lieutenant's body into a tattered sail. With a cannonball at his head and at his feet, they threw him into the sea. Treynor stayed on deck, overseeing everything to that point. But then he collapsed. Bosun Hawker took command of the *Superbe* while Jeannette, feeling a strong aversion to the cabin where so much had happened that she would rather forget, cared for the fallen lieutenant in some lesser officer's quarters.

Bone-weary, she slumped against him as her vigil lengthened into the wee hours of the morning. She longed to succumb to sleep, but worry, and the many sailors who poked their heads in to see how their leader fared, kept her from nodding off.

When those not on duty finally searched out a hammock for a few hours' rest, and the ship began to quiet down, she studied Treynor with a freedom she had never allowed herself.

The sight of his half-naked body mesmerized and thrilled her, quickly chasing away any thoughts of sleep. Leaning over, she touched his forehead and then his cheek, checking for fever, but felt none.

Never had she known a more virile man. Even in repose, Treynor's powerful arms, square at the shoulder, dipped and then bulged again with the line of his muscle. His bronze-colored skin was so smooth—at least where he had not been wounded.

Laying her head over his heart, Jeannette said a prayer for him as she listened to its steady beat. Then she let her hands trail over his chest.

How would she go on without him? He stirred such fierce passion in her with the merest glance, was everything she admired, everything she held dear . . . almost.

Jeannette sighed. There was still her family. She couldn't shirk her duty to them. Her sense of responsibility was too strong, too much a part of her.

But for now, she forced them from her mind. She'd been given this time alone with Treynor, and the memory of it would have to last her a lifetime.

Tentatively, she kneaded the corded muscles beneath her hands. When he didn't stir, she grew bolder, letting herself luxuriate in touching him with as much abandon as she had dreamed of doing.

Delving her fingers into his thick hair, she kissed his still lips, then each eyelid before moving lower to taste the salt on his breast. Her fingers trailed over the lean flesh that rippled over his ribs. Laying her palms on the flat plane of his stomach, she played with the line of hair that extended down, below his breeches.

"Just the thought of your touch kindles my desire," she breathed, committing to memory every contour of his body. "The sight of you makes me long to forget everything else—"

A subtle change in his breathing caused Jeannette to glance up. A pair of deep blue eyes, now open, watched her quizzically.

"Don't tell me a count's daughter wants to bed a mere bastard?" His words were slurred, but the jaunty arch of one eyebrow made his meaning clear.

Jeannette felt her face grow hot under his regard. "How long have you been awake?"

He frowned and pretended to search his memory. "The first thing I heard was something about the sight of me making you want to surrender everything."

Averting her face in an effort to shield her embarrassment, Jeannette tried to move away, but he reached out to stop her.

"Still, I am not sure exactly. Why not tell me again, my little coward, now that I am capable of a response?"

"You are incorrigible."

"I wasn't the one kissing your breast, although I would certainly like the opportunity."

A roguish smile revealed his teeth as he tried to shift himself in the bed, but ended up sinking back with a groan. "If you plan to make love to me when I am insensible, Jeannette, at least make sure I truly am. Otherwise, allow me to participate. I assure you, it is much more fun that way."

"You are in no condition to—"

"I think I could manage." He laughed. "It is, after all, a factor of motivation."

She rolled her eyes. "You are delirious."

"I must be. How I could be so . . ." He paused. " . . . attracted to an aristocrat's brat, I cannot fathom. It is the ultimate irony. Perhaps God is playing a joke on us both."

"Attracted?" Jeannette studied him for a moment. "I would say you feel more for me than that, no?"

She saw something flicker in his eyes, something warm and soft and compelling, but then his smile turned into a scowl. "Do not put words in my mouth, Jeannette. I have no room in my life for a woman. An aristocrat least of all."

A sharp pain lanced through her. He didn't want her? Could she have misread the look in his eyes, his concern for her safety? It was difficult to tell. He wouldn't meet her gaze now. "But you have plenty of room in your bed," she said softly, testing him.

"If you want." His Adam's apple bobbed as he swallowed, and Jeannette could have sworn he winced when he added, "I have never promised you anything more."

Struggling to keep her composure, she took a deep breath. After everything they had been through together, he still wasn't willing to open himself to the possibility of love.

It didn't matter, she told herself. They each had to keep an eye on their duty. But deep down, his denial did matter, far more than she would ever let him know.

"Perhaps you should approach a woman who is willing to settle for a few hours of pleasure at your hands." She stood and avoided him when he tried to reach out to stop her from going.

"Don't turn your nose up at something you know nothing about," he called after her.

"I think I know more than you give me credit for," she said.

Before he could see how deeply he'd hurt her, she marched out and slammed the door behind her.

Bosun Hawker cleared his throat, drawing Treynor's attention away from the porthole where the morning's sun filtered into the room.

"Sir, most of the leaks 'ave been fixed, at least temporarily," he repeated. "An' the men at the pumps are takin' care of the rest."

Treynor nodded, trying to forget Jeannette long enough to concentrate on the business at hand. She'd stormed out of his room the night before and hadn't returned. He'd done only what he had to do, but his rebuff had pained him far worse than it could have hurt her. It angered him that his heart would betray him so completely.

"Sir?"

Treynor looked at him. "Very good, Hawker. How are we for supplies?"

"Most of the food's ruined."

"How many days do you think it will last?"

"Long enough ter reach 'ome, I 'ope. The wind's been comin' from too far north to steer for England until today, an' we've got three 'undred miles to sail. Given a fair wind it could take three days. If the weather turns, who knows?"

"And the sails?"

Hawker's weathered face broke into a smile. "They're 'olding up nicely. We found plenty of spares, an' repaired most o' the riggin'. If we 'adn't lost the mizzenmast, we'd be 'alfway ter London by now."

"What speed are we making?"

"Maybe three knots."

Treynor smiled. "Not exactly racing home, are we, Hawker?"

"No, sir, but we're movin' steadily, thanks to ye. If ye 'adn't done what ye did . . . well, we'd all be in France right now—and 'Is Majesty would not own this froggy excuse for a frigate."

"The credit belongs to all of us." Waving away the bosun's offer of help, Treynor blanched as he sat up. Jealousy—he refused to call it love—had motivated him as much as patriotism to act as he did, but he wasn't about to volunteer that information to Hawker.

The bosun harrumphed. "I don't give credit where credit ain't due. Like Mrs. 'Awker says, ye played the 'and what was dealt ye like the man of 'onor we know ye to be."

Treynor's mouth twisted in a sardonic smile. A man of honor didn't try to seduce a lady. There were prostitutes enough to exhaust one's lust. He had never lacked for female companionship. Yet the thought of taking anyone other than Jeannette to his bed no longer appealed to him. Somehow, he had gotten caught in his own web. A man of honor didn't do that either, only a fool.

"I can see ye don't like ter 'ear such praise," Hawker went on. "But ye are what ye are, sir. No one can take that away from ye."

Treynor tried to ignore the prick of guilt the bosun's words caused. Fortunately, a flash of color at the door caught his eye. He turned, but was disappointed to see Mrs. Hawker, and not Jeannette, push her way into the room, carrying a tray of food.

"Where is Lady St. Ives?" he asked.

Mrs. Hawker's expression let him know she did not approve. "Ah, Lieutenant. An 'ighborn lady like 'er can only spell trouble for the likes of a sailor, lieutenant or no. Ye'd best forget 'er."

He didn't need someone else to echo his own opinion. He held up a hand to stop the outspoken bosun's wife before she had a chance to get started. "Please, don't bother," he grumbled. "I plan to do exactly that."

Mrs. Hawker fisted her hands on her hips. "I'm glad to 'ear it, but gettin' over 'er won't be easy."

Treynor let his irritation show. He knew Jeannette had managed to gain possession of a small piece of his heart—actually, she possessed the whole of it. But he was determined to reclaim it and get on with his life. She had to go back to England and get an annulment from the baron; he had a war to fight. The fact that he couldn't get her out of his mind was merely fate's revenge for laughing at other romantic fools.

"I have never had a hard time forgetting a woman before," he told Mrs. Hawker. "And I do not plan to start now."

The four days it took to get to England were the longest of Jeannette's life. The *Superbe* limped along, barely moving in the water while Jeannette waited impatiently to see her parents and to reach Lord Darby so she could plead with him to help her annul her marriage.

Meanwhile, the memory of the sinking of the *Tempest* haunted her at night, as did her encounter with Lieutenant Favre. She yearned to visit Treynor's cabin and let Treynor make her forget. But his words when she'd last spoken to him, and the knowledge that they would soon be home, forced her to concentrate on her future and forget about the second lieutenant.

"There ye be." Amelia startled Jeannette while she stared out over the choppy water near the bow.

Jeannette was surprised to see Amelia without her baby. "Where is little Denton?" It had taken Amelia some time to name her baby, but Jeannette had learned just that morning that she'd decided on an uncle's name.

"Mrs. 'Awker dotes on 'im. She insisted I take a turn out in the sunshine while she rocks 'im."

Jeannette smiled. The Hawkers had taken Amelia in like a long-lost daughter.

"I've never thanked ye proper for yer 'elp." Amelia shifted on her feet, looking awkward. "Ye know . . . with the baby an' all."

"There is no need. I am happy you are both doing so well."

"Aye. We're thrivin', that we are. But yer lookin' more miserable by the day."

Jeannette turned her face away from Amelia's shrewd gaze. "I am tired of mildewy biscuits," she said, attempting to lighten the mood.

"Yer lovesick. That's what ye are. An' if the lieutenant 'ad any sense, 'e'd see 'e loves ye, too."

"The lieutenant knows exactly what he wants. And it is not love."

"Trust me. I know men better than ye think. I knew Denton's father didn't love me, but I wanted 'im to so badly I chose to believe anythin' 'e told me. But the lieutenant is quite another sort o' man."

With a laugh, Jeannette gave Amelia a shake of her head. "And how do you know the lieutenant so well?"

Amelia pursed her lips. "The 'Awkers talk about him all the time. And they say 'e's always askin' about ye, that 'e's gettin' right angry ye won't answer 'is summons."

"Summons! As if he is royalty!"

"'E is around 'ere."

"Well, I don't care who he is. I don't want anything to do with him."

Amelia gave her an exaggerated wink. "I think 'e's met 'is match. That's what I think."

"Jeannette!"

Jeannette turned to see Mrs. Hawker trudging across the deck, carrying Amelia's baby.

"The lieutenant would like ter see ye."

"I am afraid I have other plans," Jeannette responded.

"Then perhaps we can exchange a word out here."

Despite Mrs. Hawker's frown and her wagging finger, Lieutenant Treynor made his way to the bulwarks. The bosun's wife started to scold him for leaving his bed, but Amelia snickered and put her arm around the older woman, dragging her and the babe away.

"I think the two of 'em are just stubborn enough to deserve each other," she said.

Mrs. Hawker cast a doubtful glance over her shoulder. "She can only bring 'im 'eartache. She's married ter a baron, for the love of Mary."

Amelia prodded her on. "The lieutenant can manage for 'imself, right enough."

As Treynor watched them go, Jeannette tried to dodge him and follow in their wake, but he stepped in front of her. "Avoiding me, my dear?"

Jeannette threw back her shoulders. "What would you have me do? Crawl into your hammock, then go home to tell my parents I am no longer a virgin?"

"Is a visit to my sickbed too much to ask?" he asked with a scowl.

Jeannette didn't answer. She couldn't sit primly beside him and pretend she didn't care about him.

The stubble on his chin gave him a more rugged appearance than usual. He rubbed it with one hand, his face growing thoughtful when she remained silent. "What will you do once you reach London?"

"Apply to my father's cousin, Lord Darby."

"And if he won't help you?"

Treynor had just voiced her secret fear, but Jeannette tried to sound confident when she replied. "He will."

"Will your parents support you in this?"

"*Oui.*"

"So you will receive an annulment and then what?"

"Remarry, of course. I can hardly support my family by becoming a nun or a governess, although such a life has its appeal."

Anger darkened Treynor's face. "And what if your new husband is as old and twisted as the baron? What will you think when a man like that takes you to his bed?"

Of a broad chest covered with golden hair that swirls into a single line as it lowers to his navel and beyond . . . Her mouth suddenly dry, Jeannette closed her eyes. "That I did my duty."

"To your family perhaps." He studied her carefully. "What if I help you? Set you up in London? Provide for you and your family's needs? I will probably receive more than two thousand pounds in prize money for this ship. I know it is not a lot to someone who has lived the kind of life you have, but if we are careful, it could last for several years."

Set her up in London? But he had said nothing of marriage. Was he asking her to be his mistress? "In exchange for what?" she asked evenly, almost afraid to hear his answer.

"At this juncture, I don't know, but . . . we will see where it leads."

Her heart constricted with pain. "You know where it will lead. I suppose you expect me to thank you for that kind offer. But I will not disgrace myself or my family by being your whore or anyone else's. Who knows? Perhaps after the annulment, my parents and I will find a man who can love me. Is that so difficult to believe?"

His nostrils flared as a pained expression crossed his face, an expression that told Jeannette he wasn't as indifferent as he'd like her to believe. "Not so difficult, no."

Then why is it too much to ask that you *love me?*

The lookout gave a shout from high in the rigging. England was upon them.

Jeannette bit her lip to keep from crying and turned away. The battle between her and St. Ives was waiting to be fought. Even if she freed herself from the baron's grasp, there would be another loveless marriage behind the first. For all her brave words about marrying another, she had little hope of finding happiness with any one of the motley group of nobles who had shown interest in her before.

But Treynor didn't love her. He desired her, yes, even cared about her. She saw it in his eyes. But he didn't feel as strongly for her as she did him. If he had asked her, she would have married him without a second thought.

They stood together and watched the green jewel that was England grow larger and larger. Eventually, the *Superbe* entered the mouth of the Thames. Then Treynor spoke.

"I will see you safely to your parents when we disembark."

"There is no need. I can make my own way."

"No." From the corner of her eye, she saw Treynor's jaw tighten. "You will allow me that much."

Chapter 21

As soon as they reached solid ground, Treynor took firm hold of Jeannette's elbow. He did not look back at the *Superbe*—the ship was now one among many in a forest of masts, her sails furled. The wharves near the Tower were a hive of activity. Dockmen and sailors mingled with officials and prostitutes, both looking to do business.

News of the *Superbe* had arrived well before they did and a group had gathered to raise a cheer for her capture. But Treynor barely acknowledged their excitement. He had other things on his mind—like the saucy little lady who stalked down the street at his side.

"We will get you out of those sailor's clothes and back into a dress first thing," he said as they dodged this way and that to avoid all the foot traffic and carts.

"But where will we get a dress?" she asked. "To have one made would take days."

"I know a shop that sells used clothing." He glanced at her attire as he hoisted the bag with his kit higher on his shoulder.

She wrinkled her nose. "Used clothing?"

"Don't worry. The proprietor is a good friend. I am sure she has something that once belonged to a lady, kept clean and in good repair. There is a market for such things."

Jeannette frowned but followed his lead, her boot heels clacking above the various noises floating around them.

"Afterward, we will get a room at an inn so we can bathe and have some supper," he continued.

"And then?"

"We will get a good night's sleep."

Jeannette looked at him for the first time, wariness in her eyes.

"In separate rooms, if you like," he added.

"And tomorrow?" she pressed.

"Tomorrow I will hire a carriage and take you to your cousin's house so you can be reunited with your family."

"Certainly you have better things to do with your time, Lieutenant. I can take care of myself."

"I don't think you realize how dangerous the city can be."

"I am not that innocent."

Treynor didn't say anything. He couldn't explain how important it was to him that she be kept safe.

Jeannette glanced around as though she expected the baron, or the baron's solicitor, to reach out and grab her. Lowering her eyes to the dirty street, she picked up her pace. "What will happen to the *Superbe*?"

"Most likely the government will have her repaired and reoutfitted. Then she will receive a new name and head back out to sea, this time carrying an English crew."

"Will you be among them?"

They passed Tower Hill and headed toward Aldgate. "I cannot say at this point. If I am lucky, I will be promoted to first lieutenant or possibly post-captain. There is even the remote possibility of a knighthood." He shrugged. "It has happened to others. In any case, I will receive a significant share of the prize money derived from the *Superbe*."

"Wonderful. You must be very pleased."

Treynor ignored the sarcasm in her voice. Why, now that he had achieved all he had hoped for, did he feel emptier than before? He knew his lack of enthusiasm had much to do with the woman walking beside him, but he told himself she deserved more than a bastard.

If she went back to her family, her life would follow the course it was meant to follow.

Their time together was nearly over.

St. Ives heard the knocker clang against the brass plate on the front door from his study, where he was going over the household accounts. It was too late for visitors. But when the sound came again, louder and more insistent, he removed his spectacles and waited, wondering how long Harripen would take to rouse himself and answer the door.

Too long, he decided when the knocker sounded again. Getting up, he hobbled to the gold-tasseled bellpull on the wall by his desk and gave it a yank, hoping to wake him. The butler slept in a room at the back of the house so he could guard the plate and silver—theft of such items was far more common in the city—but Harripen was older than St. Ives, and the baron feared the man was losing his hearing.

Outside, whoever waited gave up on the knocker and began to bang on the door itself.

"Lord St. Ives! Lord St. Ives! I bear a message for Lord St. Ives!"

"Damn Harripen." Percy winced at the pain his gout caused him as he grabbed his cane, took the candle that burned on his desk and made his way down the stairs. It was possible that the messenger had brought word of his missing bride.

Percy cracked open the door, then felt a moment's trepidation at his own impulsiveness. It was late, and he carried no weapon. He could be opening his home to a band of thieves or murderers. But the deed was done. The wind whooshed into the house, tearing the door out of his grasp. It slammed against the interior wall, startling both him and the young man waiting on the other side.

Bundled up in a thick coat and long scarf, with a hat pulled low over his brow, a lad of about sixteen blinked at him in surprise. "I bear a message for the baron," he announced before Percy could gather his wits enough to speak.

"From whom?"

"I must deliver it to Lord St. Ives himself."

"I *am* Lord St. Ives, you little fool," Percy snapped, irritated that Harripen had left him to do the job of a common servant. What good was a butler if he had to answer his own door during the most dangerous hours of the night?

Obviously doubtful, the messenger paused as though measuring the richness of St. Ives's robe against the small, balding man inside it. "My apologies, milord," he said at last.

Without his wig, St. Ives felt as old and shriveled as he knew he must look, which only made him angrier. "Well? Out with it!"

"Your solicitor bid me tell you to come to the King's Arms in Aldgate—immediately. And bring some men with you. He has found your wife."

Percy's irritation evaporated. "Indeed! Then tell Mr. Moore I am coming."

The boy hesitated, waiting for a stipend.

"I am in my damned robe. I haven't got a halfpenny," he snapped and slammed the door.

"Milord? What is the matter?" The crash of the door had roused Harripen. The butler shuffled forward, holding a candelabra with one shaking hand while squinting against its light.

If his night visitor had been bent on murder or mayhem, the venerable butler was hardly able to defend him. Harripen carried a pistol, but he seemed more intent on shielding the flame of his candle with it than in protecting anyone.

"Nothing now," he replied. "But you can rouse Price and tell him to bring the carriage round. I am going to Aldgate."

"At this hour, sir?"

"Indeed. My lady will not escape me again."

"Lady St. Ives has been found, milord?"

"She has." Feeling more energetic than he had in years, he made his way up the stairs to dress.

"I do hope she is unhurt, milord," Harripen called after him.

St. Ives paused. "Yes, so do I."

The butler shuffled back toward the kitchen as, satisfied at last, St. Ives hurried up to his room. He would have his head footman hire some muscle off the docks, which was what he guessed Moore meant by men.

His lovely young wife would be home by morning.

Jeannette paced before the fire in her room at the King's Arms, unable to sleep. Finally full and clean and wearing some decent clothes, she told herself she should be in high spirits. But dinner had been miserable. The atmosphere between her and Treynor had been tense, and when it had come time to retire, he had brushed a quick kiss across her brow and left as though relieved to be away.

With a sigh, she made another pass. She wanted nothing more than to see her family again. And yet . . . she dreaded the moment she would have to part ways with Treynor and face St. Ives.

Perhaps in her absence the baron had decided he didn't want a wife who would fly from his home . . .

It was tempting to hope, but Jeannette suspected St. Ives would not let her out of the marriage so easily. A man who would resort to such extreme measures to acquire an heir wouldn't give up simply because he met with resistance.

Jeannette heard Treynor's movements in the room next door and realized he wasn't sleeping either. She longed to go to him, to seek the comfort and reassurance she lacked.

Perhaps she had been foolish to deny them the pleasure of being in each other's arms.

Ignoring her better judgment, she padded out into the hall and knocked softly at his door.

"Treynor?" she murmured through the panel. "Are you asleep?"

"Hardly." The door opened immediately. He wore breeches but nothing else. "Is something wrong?"

Jeannette was almost too afraid to go through with the plan taking shape in the back of her mind. She simply stared into his face, her heart thudding until he pulled her inside, shut the door and gathered her in his arms.

"Are you frightened, dearest?" he breathed into her hair.

She hated to admit that fear had driven her to his door. She wasn't sure, exactly, what she felt. "I just want to talk," she lied.

"I think you mean to drive me mad."

Jeannette pulled away and moved to gaze out at the moonlit snow, which had nearly melted away. The rain had come and gone all evening, creating a muddy mess.

"What is it, Jeannette?" Treynor came to stand behind her as if ready, should she give him any kind of sign, to take her back into his arms.

She glanced at the bed, then closed her eyes. "All right."

He turned her to face him. "I don't understand."

"Tomorrow I must return to my parents, but tonight is ours."

He gaped at her while holding himself rigidly in control. "But the annulment—"

"The baron chose me for my pedigree. No doubt he chose his sires according to the same criteria. If I give myself to you, if there is a chance I might be with child, your child, he will not want me."

Treynor's eyes narrowed. "But what if he does?"

"We both know how slim my chance is of getting an annulment, even with my virginity intact."

"I will not let him hurt you."

"There is nothing you can do," she whispered.

He lifted a hand to touch her cheek. "Go back to your own room, where you are safe."

"Treynor." She wrapped her arms around his neck. "You cannot talk me out of it. Who knows what tomorrow will bring? At least I will have this night."

"I cannot let you tempt me. What kind of man would I be—"

"Just a man," she said, kissing the indentation above his collarbone.

His muscles went taut. She thought he'd set her from him again, but he didn't move. "Jeannette—"

"Now, Treynor, take me now."

Something akin to a growl sounded low in his throat. In one quick movement, he crushed her to him. His lips moved over her cheek, then paused to mold her mouth to his.

She didn't refuse when his fingers hungrily worked the laces of the dress he had bought her earlier. He stood back to pull her bodice and shift down, baring her to the waist. Then his head descended, and he took one nipple and then the other into his mouth.

"You are beautiful, Jeannette. God, how I want you. I have wanted you since that first night."

Jeannette thought she'd melt in his hands. He trailed kisses up her throat, causing her to drop her head back as she abandoned herself to his caress. She had never felt anything so vital as his lips moving over her skin or his heart beating beneath her hands.

"How I wish we had forever," he whispered hoarsely.

Closing her eyes, Jeannette allowed herself to believe in forever as he placed one arm under her knees, swung her up and carried her to his bed.

"Your arm is hurt. You will start it bleeding again," she protested, only half-mindful of such practicalities.

He ignored her efforts to make him put her down. "I feel nothing but desire."

As Jeannette slid down Treynor's body, she felt the hardness that attested to his words. A small tremor of fear passed through her as she wondered what she had started and where it would end. But it no longer mattered. She could sooner turn the tide or deny the moon than leave Treynor at this moment.

Eager now that the decision had been made, Jeannette reached for the buttons of his breeches. He watched her as she began to undo each one—then the door seemed to explode.

Jeannette screamed and covered herself as best she could, and Treynor spun to protect her from whatever was coming. But it was too late. The Baron St. Ives stood in the hall between two burly giants. Ralston Moore followed in their wake.

"How dare you!" he thundered, entering the room. "Get away from my wife!"

Treynor tossed a blanket over Jeannette and moved to stand in front of her without bothering to fasten the top buttons of his breeches. "She plans to annul your marriage. You have no claim upon her."

St. Ives's eyes nearly bulged from his head. "What are you talking about? I own her! She is as much mine as Hawthorne House or any of my other properties. I will have you thrown into prison if you dare stand in my way."

On the verge of tears, Jeannette did her best to make herself decent.

"Then I will be forced to protect her any way I can." The rough edge to Treynor's voice indicated his words were no bluff, but she feared there was little he could do. He was outnumbered four to one—and injured on top of that.

"I will not have them hurt you, Trey. I will go." Finished lacing up her dress, she threw off the blanket and moved toward St. Ives, even though the ugly glint in his eyes frightened her more than the presence of his hired help.

Ralston Moore stayed in the background, as if reluctant to become involved. But Jeannette had no doubt where his loyalties lay.

She stopped to look once more at Treynor. "We can appeal to Lord Darby in the morning and—"

"By then it will be too late and you know it." Treynor caught her by the wrist and pulled her with him toward his pistol and sword, which rested on the bureau.

"Make one more move toward that, an' I'll drop ye where ye stand." One of the hired brutes pointed a gun at Treynor's chest.

"Whatever he is paying you fellows isn't enough," Treynor said.

"You are a fool!" St. Ives snapped.

"A gambling fool, perhaps. I am willing to wager I can kill you before they get me. Are you willing to bet against me?"

The tough spoke again. "An' ye with a wounded arm. I'd like ter see that."

"Wait." Making a soothing gesture, Moore spoke for the first time. "This is getting out of hand, and there are . . . legal implications. Perhaps we can arrange a meeting in the morning. It is late after all, my lord—"

"Silence! I will wait no longer." St. Ives studied Treynor as though trying to gauge just how determined he was. "Name your price," he said at last. "A good toss is only worth so much. You could buy a hundred whores for what I am willing to pay to have Jeannette back."

"I have no interest in your dirty bargain," Treynor responded. "Like your man said, come back in the morning, preferably after we have had a chance to meet with the Earl of Darby and a man of the cloth who knows something about how to achieve an annulment."

"You are an insolent dog. I have heard enough." St. Ives snapped his fingers.

There was the click of a trigger, then a deafening roar.

Jeannette screamed in horror, fearing the worst as a ball went through the window, shattering one of its diamond-shaped panes.

Shoving her to the floor, Treynor whirled around for his gun. Another boom rent the air as the lieutenant shot the man coming toward him.

The brute collapsed, howling, clutching at the blood spurting from his thigh.

Treynor dropped his pistol and wielded his sword instead, forcing the other brawny hireling and the baron to step back. "That could just as easily have been you," he told St. Ives. "Now get out."

The uninjured man the baron had brought took one look at the shiny steel of Treynor's blade and ventured forth just long enough to help his wounded comrade to stand. "I only wanted enough coin for a drink or two," he complained, lugging his groaning burden toward the door. "I'm not willin' ter 'ave me arse carved up for it, nor me brother's neither, be ye baron or the bleedin' king 'imself!"

Ralston Moore looked ready to flee, too. He glanced after the men as they staggered off. Then his eyes widened, and he tapped the baron's shoulder to draw his attention to something in the hall.

Irritated by the distraction, Lord St. Ives scowled in the direction indicated. But when he turned back, his weathered face wore a glacial smile. "Ah. We shall have that audience with Lord Darby a little sooner than we anticipated," he said, and stepped aside so the earl and Jeannette's parents could enter.

"Jeannette!" Rose Marie started across the room, arms outstretched to enfold her daughter. But then she saw Treynor and stopped dead. Red suffused her cheeks as she eyed his near-naked state and Jeannette's disheveled hair and gown. "*Mon Dieu!* We have been so worried about you, *ma petite*. But there must be some mistake. Tell me this is not what it appears."

Jeannette's mother turned to her husband, who looked as stunned as she did.

"You see, my lord?" The baron's voice turned shrill as he addressed Darby. "This is why your pretty cousin fled my house. And this is how she has thanked you for your efforts on her behalf, by accepting a young, virile man in her bed."

The earl's jaw sagged as he looked from Jeannette to Treynor. "She did not strike me as . . . I mean, you have me at quite a disadvantage, sir. I apologize profusely, of course. And from this moment, I will support whatever is required to help you obtain an annulment."

The baron drew himself up straighter. "I daresay you have been too forgiving in your opinions of the chit, but I remain enamored of her, even after this. If she will but return with me this night to Hawthorne House—"

"The baron is in error," Treynor interrupted. "Forgive me for speaking so bluntly, but Jeannette's maidenhead is intact. And she did not run away with me."

Rose Marie's eyelids fluttered; Jeannette thought she might faint. "Who is this man?" Her gaze latched onto the jacket of Treynor's uniform, slung over one of the bedposts. "A navy rat? Jacques, tell me our daughter is not such a fool as that!"

Jeannette's father struggled for a moment to find the right words. "*C'est impossible!* How would she have met him? And where?"

"I met him only after I left Hawthorne House," Jeannette said. "Did Henri not tell you what he heard?"

"Indeed he did." The count reached out to calm his flustered wife. "I can understand that you were frightened, *ma petite,* but the outland- ish tales Henri carried to you are completely false. We are convinced of that."

"Just as your parents are in agreement with Lord Darby that you should honor your vows and return to Hawthorne House with me," St. Ives added.

"Indeed." The earl cleared his throat. "It is most kind of Lord St. Ives to take you back, my girl, and that he means to . . . to say nothing of this unfortunate event is gallant beyond measure. Your father and I have spoken to the man Henri overheard that night. Mr. Manville assures me that your beauty, combined with too much drink, prompted him toward such nonsense."

Jeannette separated herself from the others. Considering all that had occurred, Darby would never believe in her innocence. And her parents would, very possibly, fear the damage to her reputation enough to turn a deaf ear to her pleas. What had she done?

Treynor's hand closed over her own, somehow lending her the strength she lacked.

"No, Lord Darby," she said. "My brother told the truth. I know it in my soul. I can still remember the way those men looked at me." She shuddered, glaring at St. Ives from her position halfway behind Treynor. "Trust me, I beg you. I must obtain an annulment—"

"I am afraid I cannot ignore what I have seen with my own eyes," Darby said. "How could I support an annulment? It would take months, possibly years. And the scandal would be all over London! We could never get you another husband—"

"But I won't go back. Nothing anyone says will convince me. *Mon père,* please!"

"I know not what to do," her father admitted. "Right now I am just glad to have you back safe."

Feeling some hope, she turned her attention his way. "How did you find me, Papa?"

"Mr. Moore sent us word not more than an hour ago."

St. Ives's solicitor squirmed near the door. "It was only right to relieve their anxiety as soon as possible," he explained when the baron sent him a damning look.

Maybe St. Ives was upset with him, but Jeannette was eternally grateful. "Maman, Papa, this is Lieutenant Crawford Treynor, of His Majesty's frigate the *Tempest*. I do not know how I would have survived the past few weeks without him."

Treynor bowed. "I am sorry we meet under such unfortunate circumstances."

"What have you done to my daughter?" Rose Marie asked. "She is ruined." Tears ran down her cheeks, but she wiped them away. "You are no one. You have nothing to offer her."

Jeannette's heart gave a painful squeeze. She was about to defend him when her father stepped forward.

"Forgive my wife. She is upset and does not mean what she says," he said. "We know not what role you have played, Lieutenant Treynor, but if you have indeed been our daughter's champion, we owe you a great debt." His eyes lingered on the rumpled bed before settling again on Treynor's face. "We cannot undo what has been done. But I beg you to let us take Jeannette away from this place without further incident. My wife has been through enough already."

"Indeed, sir." Treynor tilted his head to indicate the red-faced baron. "I will make no move to stop you, as long as you and Lord Darby promise me one thing."

Her father's surprise that he would make any stipulation was evident. "And that is?"

"That you will not send her back to Hawthorne House under any circumstances."

"How dare you involve yourself—" Lord Darby began, but the baron interrupted.

"Jeannette is my wife!" he thundered. "No matter what liberties you have taken with her body, she bears my name. I will not be denied that which is mine!"

"You will not practice your debauchery on her," Treynor responded, his voice low. "Not as long as I am here to stop you."

"I assure you that can be remedied." The baron bowed stiffly. "I extend a challenge to you, sir. A duel between gentlemen, although you are no gentleman. Three days hence, just beyond the city by a quarter mile, at Lambsdell. There's an old beech tree there that is unmistakable. Meet me at dawn, and bring your second."

Treynor gaped at him. "My lord, I am half your age and you have just seen me wield both pistol and sword. Though you may choose your weapon, you have little chance of besting me."

"I choose pistols. Perhaps your confidence will be your undoing. I have no intention of being beaten by anyone. You least of all." He appealed to the earl. "Do you support me in this, Lord Darby?"

Ill at ease, Darby shifted. "Can we not settle this without violence?"

"This is the quickest way to bring the situation to a decisive end," the baron insisted.

Darby fidgeted, obviously uncomfortable with the idea, but then he sighed. "I am also anxious for a resolution, so allow me to state the terms. Should Lord St. Ives come out the victor, Jeannette will go back with him to Hawthorne House. Should Lieutenant Treynor prevail and Lord St. Ives survive, he will not seek to prevent the annulment. Do you both agree?"

They each nodded assent.

"May I have your word as gentlemen that you will fight fairly and fulfill your end of the bargain?"

Treynor bowed. "As you wish, my lord."

"No!" Jeannette tried to move forward, but Treynor held her back. "The lieutenant is injured, and he has nothing to do with this," she said. "I ran away on my own. He has merely kept me safe."

Lord St. Ives gazed at her, eyes gleaming with righteous indignation. "And you have, no doubt, repaid him generously." He tapped his cane on the floor as if to emphasize his words. "I give my word, *as a gentleman*," he said to Darby.

Then, with Ralston Moore dogging his footsteps, he left.

Chapter 22

Snowflakes twirled lazily past the window as Treynor gazed out, watching the sunrise on another cold day. He had slept little. After the baron left, Jeannette had departed with her parents and Lord Darby, throwing him a last look of regret and apprehension.

Then the inn's proprietor had stormed up the stairs to demand an explanation for gunfire in his establishment. The man had wanted to throw Treynor out—which reminded him of his stay at The Stag the first night he met Jeannette—but after a sincere apology and some fast-talking to convince him that he had every intention of paying for the broken window, Treynor had been left to sleep in peace.

Only he hadn't closed his eyes. The night had dragged by like a ship snagged in a narrow channel until Treynor thought he would go mad, especially because his thoughts seemed to make one continuous round.

He should feel relieved, he told himself. Jeannette was back with her family, her future dependent on a fight he knew he could win. What more could he ask for? Why did he feel so dissatisfied?

Because he wanted Jeannette for himself.

He knew he should walk away and never see her again. It was the kindest thing he could do for her. The wife of a naval officer was lonely indeed. He would return to sea in a few weeks and remain away for months at a time, even if the war ended soon. And should she be free to wed again, her family would certainly discourage a match to a bastard with no name and no inheritance. Jeannette had once been accustomed to the wealth and status his mother enjoyed. Whether the king knighted him or not, he could provide her with neither.

She was better off with someone else.

But that thought brought him no comfort.

Gingerly, he pulled the jacket of his uniform over his injured arm and buttoned it. Regardless of what he could or could not have, he hoped to rid England, and Jeannette, of one worthless baron. But first he had a promise to keep.

After a day and a half of riding in the drizzling rain, Treynor arrived at his mother's estate. He'd almost turned back time and again, except he owed his mother an apology. And he had decided while on the *Superbe* that if he ever had the chance, he would deliver it in person.

A stablehand spied him through the rain and came out to hold the reins while he dismounted, then led the horse away with a tip of his hat.

Treynor watched him before approaching the grand columns of the front entrance.

He rang the bell, wondering as he waited how his mother would receive him. Would she rebuff him? Mock his sudden change of heart? For how could she not think it sudden after all these years?

He wished he could explain what had happened to him the day Amelia gave birth. How watching her baby be born had touched something deep in his soul. How coming so close to death on the *Superbe* had taught him the value of life. How all the changes in him seemed to be wrapped up in loving Jeannette—

The door creaked open and his mother's elderly butler peered out at him. "Master Treynor. It is a pleasure to see you, sir."

"Thank you, Godfrey," he said. "Is my mother in?"

"Indeed, sir. She told me you were here. She can see the drive from her study."

The butler showed him inside a luxurious entry hall with mahogany paneling and marble-topped tables, tapestry-covered chairs and an ancient mural of the Last Supper. "Lady Bedford asked me to show you upstairs. She has not been feeling well," Godfrey announced, taking his wet coat and giving it to a silent maid. "Put that by the downstairs fire, Agnes," he said.

With a quick, shy smile, she bobbed a curtsy and folded the coat over her arm before scurrying off.

Treynor followed Godfrey to the top of a grand staircase, then down a hall to a balcony overlooking a ballroom. Eventually, they came to a small sitting room where his mother stood gazing out the window.

"I am surprised to see you." Once Godfrey had withdrawn and closed the door, she turned to face him. "I read of your daring naval battle in the paper today. There was even mention of a possible knighthood. I thought you would be glorying in your success, not traveling out in the cold to visit me." She offered him a thin smile. "What brings you here?"

Not knowing where to begin, Treynor ignored the question. "Godfrey tells me you are not feeling well."

She laughed softly. "It is nothing. Old age and bad weather, both of which sneak up on the unsuspecting."

"It is warm enough in here." He strode to the fireplace, collected the poker and jabbed the fiery logs. They sparked and popped before falling into a pile of glowing embers. "Is your husband home?"

"He is visiting a lady friend in Exeter. It seems they have something to celebrate."

"A lady friend?"

His mother shrugged. "May I offer you some tea?" Obviously, she was more interested in trying to unravel the riddle of his presence than in talking about the marquess.

"I would enjoy that. Thank you." He saw her confusion as he set the poker aside, but she moved dutifully to the bellpull to summon a servant.

"Do you want to tell me about the capture of the *Superbe*?"

Treynor gave her a wry smile. "Mother, I didn't come here in hopes of earning your approval, at least in the sense that used to be important to me."

Her eyes widened. "Something has changed. What?"

Treynor cleared his throat. "I came to offer you an apology."

She didn't respond, but her eyes lingered on his face. While waiting for him to explain, she seemed to falter and took a seat on a rose-damask settee.

"Perhaps I have been unfair to you." He ran a hand through his damp hair, feeling more self-conscious than he'd imagined.

"I beg your pardon?"

He soldiered on. "Since I became a man, I have never given you a chance to know me, or to care for me. Nor have I opened my heart to you." Unable to read his mother's face, he swallowed hard. "I have been too busy holding grudges. I am sorry."

His mother closed her eyes and covered her mouth with a hand that shook ever so slightly. After a moment, she stood, holding her head at a proud angle. "I have always admired you so. If I have done nothing in this life but give you birth, I have achieved one success." She stopped talking long enough to control the quaver that had crept into her voice. "And although I bitterly regret some of the decisions I have made, I am grateful that I can call you my son."

Treynor had never touched his mother before, had not been permitted more than a brief, formal kiss on the cheek. But for a moment he took her in his arms and held her close, feeling the fledgling tenderness inside him grow stronger, healthier.

"I love you, my son," she murmured. "I have always loved you."

Pulling back, she wiped away the tears that streamed unheeded down her cheeks. Then she crossed to a tall secretary and opened its doors.

After withdrawing something Treynor could, at first, not see, she turned and handed him a folded paper sealed with red wax. "This is for you."

"Do you love him?" Jeannette's mother sat across from her in the earl's well-appointed drawing room, peering over the rim of the delicate china cup she held to her lips.

"Love whom?" Jeannette kept her eyes cast down. Her father and Lord Darby were out, and Henri had gone searching for a book upstairs in the library. She and her mother were alone for almost the first time since she had returned nearly two days ago.

"The lieutenant, of course."

"I barely know him, Maman."

"Nonsense." Rose Marie set her cup on its saucer and scooted her chair back. "We found you in his room. Barely dressed."

Jeannette felt herself blush. "I am sorry for that, Maman. I know it distresses you. I was . . . I was frightened and lonely, and the lieutenant had been good to me."

"He is not even a first lieutenant, Jeannette. And England is at war. Truly, is that the sort of man you wish to become involved with? To think you once dazzled every young aristocrat in France."

The balls and soirees she had attended, her ardent admirers, her pampered life—none of that mattered to her anymore. Her sentimental longing for the past had vanished. Were she given a chance to marry Lieutenant Treynor or reclaim what she had lost in France, she would marry the lieutenant without a backward glance.

But he hadn't asked for her hand, so there was no use discussing the subject with Maman.

"Those days are gone. I wish I could get them back, for the sake of you and Papa and Henri, but I cannot."

"Ah, Jeannette. Fate has conspired against us."

"Indeed. We are now merely poor relations to an English earl. Should St. Ives let me go, I must settle for whatever new suitor Lord Darby can find."

"He did not do so well the first time," her mother said tartly.

Jeannette had to agree. "No, but he had no way of knowing St. Ives was a dishonorable fellow. A proper marriage to a man of means and good family would allow me to provide for you and Papa. And there is Henri to think about—he will need entrée to society and a gentleman's education. I care about nothing beyond that."

Rose Marie smiled patiently. "Your father and I are getting old and have lived our lives. Henri is young and can make his own way. Do not choose a husband for what he can do for us, my child. You made that mistake with St. Ives, no? We were fools to go against our better judgment. After what has happened, I shall never put you at risk again."

"But you have so little here in England!"

"We have you and Henri and each other. Is there anything more important? Our dearest friends were not so blessed when they went to the guillotine."

Jeannette fell silent. Those final days in France had been terrifying. "Still," she ventured after a moment, "if I make the right match, you will know no want in your old age—"

"And you may know no happiness. I have thought so since meeting Treynor at the King's Arms."

Jeannette's eyes widened with surprise.

"Choose your lieutenant, Jeannette. That is what your heart tells you, is it not?"

"He-he is a bastard, Maman. Would that bother you?"

Rose Marie grimaced, but laughed. "*Ma chérie*, if you love him, you love him."

"Thank you, Maman," she began, "but . . . you need not worry about my marrying him. He does not . . . care for me in the same way."

"He is risking his life for you."

Jeannette winced at the reminder. She had been trying not to think about the coming duel. St. Ives walked with a cane. His movements revealed stiffness and pain in every joint. It was unthinkable that the baron dared challenge Treynor—unless he planned to ensure his own success. "I fear St. Ives will not fight fairly."

Rose Marie considered her words. "He risks much if he does not. Surely the lieutenant will walk away unscathed. You need not worry."

"I would have said the same thing not more than an hour ago." Lord Darby had just entered the room with Jeannette's father.

Jeannette looked up in surprise, then followed the earl with her eyes. "And now?"

"Your father and I learned some interesting news today." Doffing his hat, he sank onto the sofa. "Evidently the baron likes to duel. He has been at it for years."

"But the gout—"

"Is in his leg," the earl finished.

Jeannette and her mother glanced at each other. "There must be some mistake—"

"I am afraid not." With a sigh, Darby crossed one leg over the other. "He nearly killed a young upstart not too long ago. Boasted of it all over the gaming hells. And there are . . . rumors as to how he accomplished it."

"He cheats?" Jeannette cried.

Darby's eyebrows went up. "No one dares accuse such a powerful man, but . . . the rumors suggest that, yes."

"Then we must warn the lieutenant!"

"I already sent my coachman to the King's Arms to deliver the news. I felt it only fair that Treynor know what he might be up against."

"What if that isn't enough?" Jeannette asked.

"The rest resides in God's hands," her father said.

"No," she argued. "We must go to the duel, make sure the baron fights fairly."

He gave her a pointed glance. "We will do no such thing."

That night, Jeannette tossed and turned as thoughts of the duel at dawn faded into nightmares of Treynor being killed. She told herself she worried for nothing. The lieutenant was well trained and capable. If he won, she would be free of the baron. But if he lost . . . it was too frightening to consider.

Burying her head beneath the pillow, she tried to block the memory of Darby's haunting words.

He nearly killed a young upstart not too long ago. Boasted of it all over the gaming hells. And there are . . . rumors as to how he accomplished it . . .

He cheats?

No one dares accuse such a powerful man, but . . . the rumors suggest that, yes.

He would not fight fairly. She knew it. Would a mere warning be enough to save Treynor?

There was no way to be sure. She could do nothing to stop the duel. Treynor had given his word and would keep it, regardless.

Her father might have sufficient faith to leave it in the hands of God, but she could not sit back and do nothing. Leaving the warmth of her bed, Jeannette hurried down the corridor to her brother's room. Henri was sleeping soundly, one arm thrown over his head. The sight of him looking so young again, so innocent, tugged at her heart, making her grateful to be reunited with her family.

But she dared not linger. Treynor needed her.

She put on a shirt and breeches from Henri's wardrobe. Then she grabbed one of her brother's coats and covered her head with a hat. She would need to move without notice. This time of night, a boy could certainly do so more easily than a young woman.

Cringing as the floor creaked beneath her feet, she made her way to her parents' rooms. Since the revolutionaries had stormed their house in Paris, her father kept a gun close by.

She found his powder flask and bullet bag, which she shoved in her pocket. The gun was there, too. Securing it between Henri's belt and the bare skin of her stomach, she gave her parents one last look, said a silent good-bye and headed outside.

The soggy grass squished beneath her feet as the long barrel of her father's pistol pressed against her hip and leg, extending almost to her knee. She had nearly achieved St. James's Square, which was empty this time of night, when she heard a drunken voice singing an old ballad.

Someone was making their way home from the pubs.

Ash trees grew at the side of the road. Her breath misting in front of her, she ducked into them, using the fog for cover as well, while she waited for the stranger to stumble by. But it wasn't easy to waste the time. She had at least two miles to walk to make the duel site before the baron or the lieutenant arrived.

As soon as the man was gone, she trudged on and on—endlessly, it seemed. Fortunately, Oxford Road was easy to find. So was Lambsdell and the old beech tree with its massive trunk and giant spread of branches.

But how would she watch unobserved? The fog would help cloak her, but she could not rely on that alone. And if she had to hide herself too far away, she would not be in a position to help if something went wrong . . .

As she circled the beech where the duel was to take place, the snap of a twig brought Jeannette to a halt. She tried to hear beyond the soft rush of her own breathing, listened for the sounds of some small animal, which it probably was, but heard . . . nothing. Silence reigned, broken only by the sudden trill of a bird.

She was just considering a thick stand of trees as her hiding place— she might be able to view the action despite the thick fog from there— when the ground began to vibrate.

Someone was coming. Moving deeper into the surrounding woods, she found an icy ditch and climbed into it.

Peering over the lip of her hiding place, she caught a glimpse of black through the branches and the dense gray of a stormy-looking dawn: the baron's carriage. It sped so confidently toward her, she began to feel more and more justified in her fear for Treynor's safety.

"My, you are eager for this meeting with the lieutenant, *monsieur*," she murmured to herself. "What, exactly, do you have planned?"

Chapter 23

The carriage pulled to a stop so close to her hiding place that Jeannette could almost reach out and touch the wheel. She wished she had managed to find a spot a little farther away—something that would give her more room to maneuver, if necessary. But it was too late. She couldn't risk moving. Not now.

St. Ives's shoes came into view as he descended from his carriage. Ralston Moore climbed out next. Jeannette recognized him as he walked in front and gazed down the road as if he thought he should be able to see Treynor coming toward them in spite of the fog. Evidently, the solicitor was playing the role of the baron's second.

"Are you sure this is the place?" Moore rubbed his temples as though trying to relieve a headache.

The baron came to stand next to him. "He can't miss the tree."

"But . . . did you want to get under the branches or—"

"The road is fine. There isn't a soul around."

Moore kicked at the ice-hardened mud. "Is it truly needful to go through with this? I mean, certainly there must—"

"There is no other way! This is where Lieutenant Treynor draws his last breath. And I, for one, cannot wait."

"But—"

"Silence!" St. Ives glared at him, then tossed a glance at his liveried driver and lowered his voice. "Do you think I wanted any part of this? I have no choice. It is all Richard Manville's fault. If not for him, I would have my wife with child and tucked safely away at Hawthorne House even now."

Moore shook his head. "But death is so . . . permanent."

"Always a good thing to keep in mind."

"You are not threatening *me* . . ."

St. Ives lifted his head in an imperious manner. "Merely telling you that your concern is unwarranted. You need only watch"—he smiled— "and report what I told you."

Moore hesitated, but ultimately acquiesced. "Yes, my lord."

"Now." The baron clapped his hands. "My pistols."

With a sigh, Moore returned to the carriage. When Jeannette saw him next, he was holding a velvet box from which he took two ivory-handled guns. "Here they are."

"And just in time." St. Ives gestured toward the road. Two men approached on horseback, coming from the city. Jeannette couldn't see them, but the clopping of hooves and the whinnying of their horses carried to her ears.

It had to be Treynor. She strained to catch a glimpse of him and the man with him, but the fog was too thick. It wasn't until he was nearly upon them that she could make him out—and what a vision he made sitting astride his horse, his back straight, his shoulders square, the brass buttons of his uniform shining despite the dull, overcast sky. Bosun Hawker was his second. Although they appeared at ease, there was a predatory awareness about them that made Jeannette feel slightly reassured. Had they gotten the message?

There was no way to be sure . . .

Treynor's eyes scanned the dark, foggy woods on either side of him, causing Jeannette to hunch down. "I see you have chosen a spot with plenty of cover," he said as soon as they were close enough for him to speak. "Somehow, I thought you might."

The baron didn't respond to his sarcasm. "This need not take long." He walked to meet the lieutenant, his steps jerky without the aid of his cane.

"It need not take place at all," Treynor responded. "I have no desire to kill an old man who is ill-equipped to face me."

St. Ives's voice revealed his eagerness. "I have had my share of success with a pistol. Take heed for your own hide, Lieutenant Treynor. Your minutes on this earth are numbered."

Treynor chuckled, but didn't get off his horse. "Is there no way to talk you out of this madness?"

"My lord, it might serve you well to listen—" Moore started. Jeannette could tell he was hopeful the duel would be canceled, but St. Ives squelched any talk of forgoing the bloodshed.

"A pity my wife is not here to see what a sniveling coward you really are," he snapped at Treynor, and Moore's shoulders slumped in defeat.

Bosun Hawker mumbled something, and he and Treynor dismounted.

Jeannette crawled down the ditch, trying to get a better view, but the rustling of her movements sounded far too loud. Afraid the foursome would turn and see her, or at least investigate, she held still.

They didn't even glance over.

The cumbersome gun wedged inside her belt poked into her stomach, which was uncomfortable. She was just reaching for it when she sensed that she had company and froze. Someone or something had come up from behind. Who or what? St. Ives, Ralston Moore, Bosun Hawker and Treynor were already marking off their paces, oblivious to her presence.

The hair on the back of her neck rose as she braved a glance over her shoulder. Sir Thomas, the baron's filthy-minded friend, crouched beside her, wearing a sinister smile beneath the shadow of his big nose. The other man she'd met at her wedding, Desmond Something, if she remembered right. He crept out of the fog on her other side, trapping her between them. Bringing a pistol into view, Sir Thomas pointed it at her head and motioned her to silence.

Jeannette began to sweat despite the cold, damp air as Desmond put a hand on her shoulder to hold her in place.

"Four . . . five . . . six . . ." Moore counted as Treynor and the baron walked.

Jeannette watched the men move apart. According to the rules set by their seconds, at ten, they would turn and shoot. Only Treynor would be dead before he could pull the trigger. Sir Thomas was already taking aim.

"Seven . . . eight . . . nine . . ."

Jeannette's nerves stretched so taut she tingled all over. Taking short, quick breaths, she prayed for the opportunity to do what she must.

Sir Thomas watched the men on the road as carefully as she did, waiting for the right time. She could see his finger tighten on the trigger, knew she had to stop him or Treynor would die, just as St. Ives intended.

As soon as Ralston Moore cried, "Ten!" everything happened at once. Using all the energy she possessed, she broke free from Desmond and knocked Sir Thomas off balance.

His gun exploded in spite of her efforts.

She pulled out her father's pistol, but several more shots rent the air before she could fire, and Sir Thomas and Desmond both fell.

Scrambling up and out of the ditch, she took no time to wonder who had shot them. Frantically, she looked around for Treynor, half expecting to find him in a heap on the ground. But he wasn't dead; he was striding toward his opponent with his gun raised. Amazingly, the baron stood, unhurt, as well.

"Evidently you do not understand the rules of a duel, my lord," Treynor said. "No doubt the tactics you have employed this morning is how you have won so many." He motioned for St. Ives to drop his pistol as men from the *Tempest* came out of the foggy thicket behind Jeannette.

The baron complied, his eyes daggers of hate.

"You see," Treynor continued, "having a hidden accomplice shoot your opponent is against an Englishman's code of honor. Or, at least, that is what I have been told. But I am just a bastard. Hawker, have you ever heard otherwise?"

"Not me, sir, no." The bosun held a gun to the frightened Ralston

Moore to keep him from going anywhere. "But then I'm not a bloody aristocrat, either. Seems the baron thinks 'e can murder in cold blood whenever it suits 'im."

"I tried to stop him," Moore said, his voice filled with regret. "I told him it was wrong."

The baron sent his solicitor a disgusted glance for this betrayal, one that said he was lower than a dog.

"Fortunately for me, I brought a little insurance," Treynor said.

"Sorry we was late, Lieutenant." A pig-tailed sailor dragged a sullen Sir Thomas into the open; another man did the same with Desmond. They'd both been shot and were in a great deal of pain, but they did not seem near death. "We 'ad a 'ell of a time findin' these blokes after we watched 'em go in. But the lad here—" He nodded at Jeannette, then blinked in surprise when he recognized her. "Blimey! 'Tis Jean Vicard! I mean Lady St. Ives, if ye'll forgive me language!"

Treynor's steady gaze pinned Jeannette to the spot where she stood.

She looked down at the gun in her hands, only now remembering that amid her fear and worry, she had forgotten to load and prime it.

"She's a right brave lass, sir," said the man at her side.

"That she is," Treynor acknowledged, but he hardly seemed pleased. "I still say you deserve a good spanking," he told her. "And I know just the man to give it to you."

His lips curved into a wry grin that Jeannette answered with one of her own. "Proceed with caution, Lieutenant. This time I am armed."

"May you both rot in hell!" the baron growled.

Treynor raised a sardonic eyebrow as he turned back to St. Ives and reached into his jacket to withdraw a packet of papers. "I believe you have an agreement to fulfill, sir. I happen to have all the paperwork right here."

At the mention of a document, Ralston Moore craned his head around to have a better look. "What is it? A confession?"

"It's a promise to seek an annulment, you idiot." St. Ives visually checked with his driver as though considering the possibility of escape, but his man sat slack-jawed on the seat, stunned. He definitely didn't seem to be thinking about going anywhere. Even if he was, the tars surrounding him stepped closer.

Moore brushed himself off. "I recommend you sign it."

St. Ives gave his solicitor a scathing look When he turned his attention to Jeannette, she could almost hear his thoughts, feel his desire for revenge.

Sign it, she silently willed him.

"You are a fool," he said to her. "You have given up everything. And for what? For *him*?" He motioned to Treynor. "What will he be able to give you? Nothing. Nothing at all."

"At least I will be free of *you*," she spat.

Reluctantly taking the quill Treynor handed him, St. Ives moved to dip the nib into a jar of ink held by one of the other sailors, but fumbled and dropped it. Immediately, he bent as if to retrieve it, but pulled a hidden pistol from his coat instead.

A shot rang out, the sound deafening at such close range. Jeannette blinked at the men, fearing the baron had shot Treynor after all, but it was St. Ives who crumbled to the ground.

Throwing down his pistol, Hawker stared at the man he'd just shot.

"Blast you to hell!" The baron clasped one hand to his chest as if he could hold back the blood that seeped through his clothing.

"My lord!" Moore rushed to kneel at his patron's side and tried to help him staunch the bleeding.

Sir Thomas and Desmond stopped writhing from the misery of their wounds long enough to gape in horror.

The solicitor blinked at Sir Thomas and Desmond, then at St. Ives. "I will get help. Don't worry." He looked back at the road, but before he could even stand, a gurgle came out of the baron's throat, and he died.

The gruesome spectacle sickened Jeannette. She averted her eyes as Treynor sent two of his men to town to bring medical help and a constable.

"It's over now," he murmured, pulling her into his arms.

The others gathered around, staring at the dead man.

"You will hang for murder," Sir Thomas told Bosun Hawker. "Maybe you all will."

Treynor made a negating sound. "Not when we have so many witnesses to tell what really happened." He cocked an eyebrow at St. Ives's driver and his solicitor, who was still trying to wipe the baron's blood off his hands. "Is that not true, Mr. Moore?"

Moore's eyes darted to Sir Thomas, who was shot in the arm, and Desmond, who was shot in the shoulder a little higher and seemed worse off, before looking at Treynor. "I want no more trouble." He sounded relieved. "I will tell the truth. I swear I will."

His words seemed to drain the anger out of Sir Thomas, as well. St. Ives's friend studied the solicitor for a moment, then nudged Desmond. "So will we," he said at last. "Just get us a damn doctor."

"Where will you go from here?" Jeannette asked Treynor as she rode behind him in the saddle.

The chestnut gelding's hooves rang out on the cobblestone streets that led to the square where Darby lived. "I have some matters to attend to."

She tried to ignore the feel of his lean waist beneath the circle of her arms, but couldn't stop her nerves from responding to him any more than she could stop her heart from loving him. "Are you to be knighted, then?"

He glanced back, his brows raised. "What?"

"I asked if you will receive a knighthood."

"It's a possibility."

"Are you not excited?"

He nodded. "But I have other issues to deal with that might prove less enjoyable."

Jeannette waited, thinking he might elaborate. When he didn't, she decided not to press him. "I suppose you will be going back to sea shortly."

"Yes. I am to be promoted to post-captain." He said it matter-of-factly, as though it wasn't a monumental accomplishment, but Jeannette knew better.

"Good. You make an admirable leader." She didn't add how much she'd miss him, or how frightened she was at the thought of him going back to fight more battles like the one she had witnessed on the *Tempest*.

They fell a few paces behind Bosun Hawker and the others, who had been riding in a group around them. "Hopefully I will get a decent ship. And you? What will you do?" he asked, his body tensing as though he feared her answer.

"I have been thinking about becoming a governess. I could teach French."

He turned to see her face. "No more marriage contracts?"

She tried to laugh. "I hope not."

Treynor halted the horse in front of Darby's town house, and one of his men helped her dismount. "Perhaps our paths will cross again."

Jeannette tried not to wince at the casual remark. "No, I think not." She allowed him to help her down, then gave him a brief smile. "Thank you, Lieutenant. I wish you health and happiness," she murmured and turned to move away, but he called her back.

"Jeannette?"

She glanced over her shoulder, her heart nearly stopping at the sight of him sitting tall in the saddle, watching her. A weak sun, the only sun they would likely see all day, gleamed off his hair and lighted the chiseled planes of his face, drawing her attention to his lips.

What she wouldn't give for one more kiss.

"I . . . never mind." He stayed on the horse, unbending. Then he smiled a good-bye and rode away.

"So. I am officially a widow." Jeannette, still wearing Henri's clothes, faced her parents as they sat at breakfast. Fortunately Darby hadn't yet descended from his room, or Jeannette knew he'd be scandalized by her attire and her devil-may-care attitude. But she couldn't find it in her to worry about such trivialities anymore.

"What happened?" Her mother took in her disheveled hair and boy's clothes with minute precision.

Ignoring the food on his plate, her father shoved his chair back and stood. "You didn't go to the duel . . ."

Jeannette nodded, too tired after her sleepless night to remain standing. She was not inclined to placate her parents for having disobeyed her father. She sank into a seat at the end of the table and propped her chin on her fist.

A frown punctuated her father's disapproval. "You are getting far too willful for your own good, young lady—"

Rose Marie cut him off with a restraining hand on his arm. "Jacques, she loves him. Can you not see how miserable she is? What good is your fussing now? She is back, no? And whole enough."

He opened his mouth as though he would berate her anyway, then shut it. "At least tell us what happened," he said at last.

"What is this?" Henri entered the room and gawked at her. "Since when have you started wearing my clothes?"

"Never mind, Henri," Rose Marie told him. "Fill your plate and sit down. We are in the middle of something." Her gaze returned to Jeannette, but Henri would not be put off so easily.

"You went to the duel!" he exclaimed. "I cannot believe it! And Maman would not let me watch."

"Henri!" Rose Marie snapped, her voice a warning. "Eat your breakfast."

"Yes, Maman." Henri shot his sister a sulky look as he helped himself to the food on the sideboard before taking a seat across from Jacques.

"Well?" Jeannette's mother prompted. "Are you going to tell us how your lieutenant killed the baron?"

"He didn't kill him, Maman. His second did." Jeannette quickly explained everything that had happened, cringing at the memory. She had come so close to losing Treynor . . .

What was she thinking? She *had* lost him. He was going back to sea, moving on with his life.

"And what of the lieutenant?" her mother asked when she'd finished the tale.

"He has been made post-captain and will be receiving his own ship. He does not yet know which one—"

Rose Marie set her napkin aside. "So he is returning to sea?"

Jeannette swallowed against the lump in her throat and nodded.

"And you, my poor daughter?"

"I think I shall become a governess, Maman."

Worry etched deep lines in her mother's face. "Surely, you cannot be seriously considering going into *service*."

"I am."

"But why? You could run a girl's school or do charitable service, either of which would be far more befitting your station—"

"I no longer care about station, Maman. At this moment, teaching children appeals to me more than anything else."

"Are you sure? Being a governess, living with others, is not an easy thing. I hate to see you give up the idea of marriage and a family of your own—"

"I am sure," Jeannette interrupted.

Rose Marie nodded. "I see. Well, it is a respectable way to live, *ma petite*. You would make an excellent governess. Perhaps the earl can recommend you to a good family."

"I shall speak to him, Maman."

"No, I will take care of it," her father said.

"Thank you, Papa."

"Why is everyone so sad?" Henri asked. "We knew the baron wouldn't live forever. We arranged a marriage contract, did we not?"

"We did," Rose Marie confirmed. "Jeannette will receive a goodly widow's portion. And she deserves it after what that miserable wretch has put her through."

"Then what is wrong?" His childish gaze moved from face to face. "Jeannette, you are glad to be rid of the baron, *n'est-ce pas*?"

Jeannette nodded. "Indeed, Henri. I have never been happier," she said. And then she burst into tears.

Chapter 24

The Earl of Darby's study, with its dark paneling, leather furniture and the scent of pipe tobacco lingering in the air, was a somber place. It didn't help that the earl's father, a severe-looking man, glared down from his portrait high on the wall.

Having been a widower for nearly twenty years, Lord Darby had transformed the house into a wholly male domain, this room more than any other. Newspapers were stacked on chairs; various files, documents and law books lay open on the floor or on the side table; and a pile of mail awaited his attention in front of him. Jeannette saw Darby frowning over an invitation of some sort as she knocked tentatively on the open door.

"Excuse me, Lord Darby. Do you have a moment?"

He glanced up, looking puzzled at the interruption, as though he had forgotten his houseguests. Indeed, the way he went about his business as though she and her family weren't there made Jeannette suspect he had.

He cleared his throat. "Yes, please, come in. Make yourself comfortable."

Standing, he rounded his desk to clear off a chair for her, then glanced helplessly at the clutter as if he didn't know where to put the pile of papers now that her visit had disturbed its normal resting place.

"I will not allow the maids in here," he explained, his color rising. "My fondness for finding what I want the moment I need it is too great."

How he could find anything on his overburdened desk or in the avalanche of paper growing toward the center of the floor was a puzzle, but Jeannette smiled as he solved his dilemma by simply adding to the pile in the chair next to her.

"A man's study should be exactly as he would like it," she said as he returned to his seat. "I apologize for disturbing you here. It is just that . . . I have had something on my mind of late, and wish to discuss it with you."

"Of course. I am afraid I have been neglectful of you. Those damn Tories in Parliament, you know. They keep me hopping. Every good Whig needs to do his civic duty—indeed more, during these trying times."

"In comparison, this is a trifling matter, but . . . I spoke to my father about the possibility of my becoming a governess nearly a fortnight ago." She toyed with the edges of her shawl. "He assured me he would ask you for a letter of recommendation, but I fear the matter has completely slipped his mind."

That Jacques was holding out, hoping she would change her mind was more likely, but Jeannette had no intention of speaking more of the truth than necessary.

"A governess?" The earl pursed his lips. "But your mother hopes you will marry again and have a family. Another few years and—"

"I know. I might be too old to make a favorable match."

He didn't argue with her. "You have considered that?"

Jeannette took a deep breath. She had thought about nothing else in the two weeks since the duel. Part of her had secretly hoped she would hear from Treynor, but when no word came, she knew she had to go on and build something with her life.

"Thanks to my widow's portion, we shall not want for money. My family and I plan to let a small house here in London where we can once again stand on our own, and I—"

"You and your family have been no trouble," he interrupted.

Jeannette knew he was merely being polite. Kind but basically practical, the earl would be glad, whether he admitted it or not, to rid himself of his impoverished relatives and be left to devote himself exclusively to his political causes. "And you have been most generous, my lord, but I feel it is time we adjust to this new country and make our own way in it."

"An admirable attitude, but has your experience with the baron so poisoned you against marriage that you are unwilling to try again?"

Jeannette frowned. "No, not that, exactly. I have come to the conclusion that I cannot be happy with a man I do not love."

"But many times love, or at least a mutual respect, comes later."

It had for her parents, but . . .

"For me, it will be marriage that comes later—much later. I am quite set on my decision. Teaching will give me something worthwhile to devote my life to."

"Very well, then. I shall speak to my friends and acquaintances and see if I can find you a good post."

"Thank you, sir. You can tell them I am ready to start immediately."

"And how long might you stay on?"

Jeannette thought of the years that loomed before her, long, lonely years without Treynor. "Two to four, to start, I should think."

"I shall see what I can do."

"You have my gratitude." She stood to go, and he turned his attention back to the work on his desk. But before she passed into the hall, he called her back.

"Yes?"

He lifted the square sheet of paper he'd been reading when she entered. "The Duke of Ellsborough is having a ball. He knows that I rarely attend such events, but he has sent me an invitation nonetheless and asks that I bring my French relatives. Are you interested in going?"

Jeannette thought of all the balls and masques she had attended before St. Ives extended his proposal, and didn't think she could endure another one. She refused to go into mourning for the baron, a man she scarcely knew and didn't love, but was hardly ready to return to polite society and the gossip that would face her there. She longed only for a quiet post where she could bury the hopes and dreams that were now lost to her. "No, sir."

"I will send His Grace a polite refusal and see you at dinner, then."

"Yes, my lord."

"And Jeannette?"

"Yes, sir?"

"Do not worry. I shall find you a two-year post as governess within a fortnight."

Jeannette gave him a smile that was decidedly wobbly. "Thank you, Lord Darby. You are most kind."

A week later Henri burst into her bedroom without so much as a knock. "Jeannette!"

Irritated, Jeannette looked up from the book she had been reading. "What is it, Henri?"

"The Duke of Ellsborough is here."

"*Who?*" Where had she heard that name before?

"The Duke of Ellsborough! And he wants to see *you*."

"Me! But why?"

"He didn't say. Lord Darby has already introduced Maman and Papa and myself, so I suppose His Grace simply wants to meet the rest of the family."

Jeannette tossed him a disbelieving look. "That makes no sense, Henri. A duke would not stoop to introduce himself to a family of poor French immigrants."

Henri looked insulted. "Papa is a gentleman!"

"I know." Jeannette gave him a weak smile in apology for her dour mood and tossed her book on the bureau. The last thing she had expected was a visitor. But she could not refuse to meet a duke.

With a quick glance in the mirror, she did what she could to tame her short, curly hair—which was, thank goodness, growing out—and ran a hand over her dress to smooth away the wrinkles.

"Come on, Jeannette. We cannot keep him waiting," Henri said.

"Does the duke seem to know Lord Darby well?" She followed him from the room, still trying to figure out the reason for this unexpected visit.

"I think so."

Then it hit her, where she'd heard Ellsborough's name before. Lord Darby had mentioned it during their interview a week ago. From the sound of it, he and the duke were friends. Perhaps Ellsborough wanted to meet her because he was looking for a governess.

Of course! Darby had promised she would have a post inside of two weeks, but so far she had heard nothing. The duke's visit signified that the earl was remaining true to his word, after all.

She felt a tremor of excitement, the first since Treynor had left her to go on his merry way. If she must work, she could do no better than to school a duke's children.

Her parents were sitting on the sofa when she entered the drawing room. Darby stood next to a wingback chair, his back to the windows that overlooked the fashionable houses across the square. A tall, older gentleman with flowing dark hair and graying temples sat closest to the door. He regarded her with thoughtful blue eyes the moment she stepped into the room.

"There you are, Jeannette," Darby turned to the older man. "Allow me to introduce Lady St. Ives, my cousin's lovely daughter." To her, with a nod, he said, "His Grace, the Duke of Ellsborough."

Jeannette dipped into a deep curtsy. "It is truly a pleasure, Your Grace."

"The pleasure is all mine. I see that I have not been misled. You are beautiful indeed."

Blushing at the thought of her unconventional hairstyle, she smiled. "Thank you, Your Grace. You are very kind."

"His Grace has come to insist we attend his ball next week, Jeannette," the earl announced.

Her mother added, "And I told him we would be happy to."

"Then of course we will come," she responded immediately.

"Now, concerning the matter of a governess," the Duke began.

Jeannette didn't have to look at her frowning parents to know they hoped she would change her mind.

His gaze flicked to Darby. "Lord Darby has mentioned your interest in such a post, Lady St. Ives. Are you convinced you shall enjoy such work?"

"Indeed, Your Grace. I have no prior experience as a governess, but I am well educated and long for the opportunity to be useful."

His eyebrows rose. "You appear quite determined."

"I am, sir."

"Well then"—he paused and rubbed his chin—"I have no young children at home, but my oldest daughter is married with three girls of her own. She is looking for a good governess. I will happily recommend you for the post, if you still want it after the ball."

"Thank you."

"It will be my pleasure. And now, I am off to Bath. The duchess has been ill for months. I shall accompany her there to take the waters, and I will not be back until the day before the event."

"I am sorry to hear Her Grace is ill. Is she hoping to attend the ball herself?" Rose Marie asked.

"No, she will be staying in Bath for at least a month."

"We will certainly miss her."

"Alas." He turned his attention back to Jeannette. "After the ball, with your permission, I shall arrange an interview for you with my daughter."

Jeannette inclined her head in a graceful nod. "I would be most grateful."

"Then we are agreed." The duke rose. "I look forward to it with the utmost anticipation."

Jeannette struggled to keep her bemusement from revealing itself on her face. Why had this duke suddenly taken a personal interest in her? And why should he care whether or not she attended his ball?

Ellsborough gave a slight bow. "Until next week," he said to the room at large, and with a strange smile, he let the butler show him out.

The night of the ball, Jeannette dressed in a new lavender silk gown, deeply décolleté, with puff sleeves that fell off her shoulders. With matching slippers, long white gloves and some of the first flowers of spring in her hair, she had to admit she felt better, and more feminine, than she had in a long time.

The ride to the duke's house at St. James's Square took only fifteen minutes. Jeannette sat in the carriage next to Darby, facing her parents.

"Are you nervous, dear?" her mother asked as they rocked and swayed over the cobblestones. A light rain had begun to fall, just enough to wet the ground, but the weather was surprisingly warm.

"No." Jeannette smiled in an effort to show some enthusiasm, but she could feel a headache coming on and wished the ball were over. After the preceding months, she knew it would be difficult to go back to the stilted, polite conversations that would be required of her this night.

The carriage came to a stop behind a row of similar conveyances. The earl grumbled something under his breath and tugged at his cravat. Jeannette felt sorry for him, knowing he had no more desire to attend the ball than she did. "We do not have to stay long," she assured him.

He gave her a quick, grateful smile. "Simply say the word, and we will leave."

Feeling better for knowing she had an ally, Jeannette allowed the waiting footman to help her down. When they had all alighted, she took the earl's arm and walked with him and her parents to the line of guests waiting at the door.

The women around them tittered and gossiped, making Jeannette's head hurt more. Many of them were near her age; she should have felt a natural kinship to them. But she felt removed, apart, older. Rubbing her temples, she determined to help the earl escape his social duties in record time. Then she caught sight of a tall man with sandy-colored hair standing farther up the line—a man who looked remarkably like Lieutenant Treynor.

Just the thought that it might be him made Jeannette's heart pound against her ribs. She stood on tiptoe to see for sure, but surely her eyes were playing tricks on her.

Those in front jostled and moved, making it difficult for her to see. When the man passed through the door and disappeared, she groaned in frustration.

"Is something wrong, my dear?" her mother asked.

Jeannette blinked at Rose Marie, her mind too busy to answer. Treynor didn't generally circulate among the ton. According to the *Times*, he had been knighted, but she still didn't expect to find him at a duke's ball.

She craned her head to see inside the double doors ahead of them.

Her mother grasped her arm. "What is it?"

"Nothing," she replied. "I am a bit cold."

"Then pull your cloak tighter, dear. It is this cursed rain. I swear, I shall never get used to it."

Her father patted her mother's shoulder, then glanced down at Jeannette. "You look lovely, *ma petite*. You will be the toast of the evening."

"Merci," she replied, curbing the more instinctive, *I hope not*! For once, she wasn't interested in generating attention or gathering beaux. Not like before. If the man she saw wasn't Treynor, there was no one here to interest her. And if he was . . . How would she face the lieutenant without giving her heartbreak away?

The servant at the door announced them, and Jeannette reluctantly followed her parents through the portal.

A man with fine brown hair and eyes the same color stood next to the Duke of Ellsborough, helping him greet the guests.

"Ah, there you are." The duke smiled when he saw them. "Lord Darby, you know my son. Comte de Lumfere, Lady Lumfere and Lady St. Ives, this is my heir, Lord Baldwin."

The duke was far more distinguished-looking than Baldwin was. Ellsborough stood several inches taller and carried himself with an athletic grace Jeannette couldn't help but admire. But his son was not unhandsome.

She smiled as he kissed her hand. "*Tout le plaisir était le mien*, Lord Baldwin."

"So this is the one," he replied, sending a glance at his father. "I can certainly understand the attraction."

"*Pardon,* my lord?" Jeannette asked.

"You are a vision of loveliness, my lady. If you would be so kind as to save me a dance or two, I would be most honored," he replied.

"Of course she will." Rose Marie spoke with a blatant eagerness that caused heat to shoot up Jeannette's neck and pool in her cheeks. Evidently her mother hadn't given up hope that Jeannette would marry again instead of becoming a governess.

She sent her a pointed look before responding. "Who can refuse such flattery, Lord Baldwin?"

"I will anxiously await the moment."

The liveried servant at the door announced the next guests and Jeannette followed her parents deeper into the ballroom. Large chandeliers, blazing with candles, hung from the ceiling over a marble floor. The orchestra played from their place in the far corner, but was nearly drowned out by the low roar of voices.

The women were dressed in fine, jewel-colored gowns. Most of the men wore brocade waistcoats of similar hues with black tailcoats and knee-length breeches. Jeannette searched for another glimpse of the man with the sandy hair, but the room was already crowded. She could see only those immediately surrounding her.

A maid passed, carrying a tray of drinks, and her father paused to sample the champagne. "Excellent," he murmured, and they moved on, occasionally stopping to visit with some of those they had met at other soirees.

Many raised their fans to whisper about Jeannette as she passed, but she ignored them. She was too preoccupied to be annoyed by the gossip over her ordeal with St. Ives.

Hair the color of Treynor's caught her eye again. She made her way toward it, only to discover a man too fat to resemble the lieutenant in any other way.

"Lady Lumfere, is that you?"

Jeannette glanced back to see a rotund woman push past a couple of young ladies to reach her mother's side. Wearing a yellow gown bedecked with gathers, frills and ribbons, the woman smiled in obvious pleasure when Rose Marie turned and recognized her.

"Lady Hafton! It has been too long! How wonderful to see you looking so well. I had heard you were ill."

"Oh, deathly so." The woman fluttered her fan. "I thought I would die for certain."

As Lady Hafton expounded upon the details of her ailment and her subsequent recovery, Jeannette watched others mingle about the Hepplewhite tables and chairs, which were strategically placed so those too old or too tired to dance could sit and enjoy the sights. Only a few heeded the music this early in the night. Most were too busy greeting old friends, taking note of the new arrivals or admiring what the fashionable wore.

Jeannette's eyes sought the sides of the room, the corners, every nook or cranny, hoping to locate the man she had glimpsed earlier, but she found him not ten feet away, on the dance floor.

Evidently her mother caught sight of him at the same time. "*Ma petite*, look who is here. It is none other than your friend, Lieutenant Treynor, *n'est-ce pas?*"

Jeannette struggled to keep her mouth from gaping open as she gazed at Treynor moving in step with a tall blonde wearing a green velvet gown. An exceptionally attractive woman, his partner had a voluptuous figure to rival her porcelain-pale face. And she turned a dimpled smile on him every time he spoke.

"Did you say something about the lieutenant?" Lady Hafton asked.

A definite numbness began to deaden Jeannette's fingers and toes, making her wonder if her heart had stopped beating altogether.

"He is the latest rage, you know," Lady Hafton continued, without waiting for an answer, "a bit of a war hero. That is my niece Maude he is dancing with now. They make a divine couple, do they not?"

Jeannette forced herself to nod and smile along with her mother. "You know him, then?"

"Yes. He is courting Maude. He has been to the house a number of times over the past week."

Jeannette purposely ignored the look of sympathy and understanding her mother gave her. She had been mooning over Treynor for nearly six weeks. And here he was, looking as fit and handsome as ever in a single-breasted black coat over a double-breasted blue silk waistcoat, making his debut with the aristocracy.

Throwing her shoulders back, she forced her eyes from the woman who touched Treynor with a familiarity that lent credence to Lady Hafton's words. She couldn't watch them together, or she would cry. And she refused to shed any tears over him—not here, not now.

Rose Marie nudged her again. "You are too good for him anyway, *ma petite*."

"He made me no promises, *ma mère*. I expected nothing more." The falter in her voice gave away her true emotions and solicited a gentle squeeze from her mother.

"What is it?" her father asked. "Jeannette, you look so pale."

"I have a headache, Papa. Perhaps we can go." She started toward the door, but her mother pulled her back.

"Wait." Rose Marie nodded at Lord Baldwin, who was making his way toward them, and Jeannette felt her heart sink even further. The music had stopped. Those on the floor were getting ready to start another quadrille, but she wasn't up to smiling and dancing and talking.

"Is something wrong, Lady St. Ives?" Lord Baldwin asked as those around her parted to let him through. "You seem distressed."

Jeannette shook her head. She dared not speak.

"Would you care to dance, then?"

Forcing a shaky smile, she nodded and curtsied before taking the arm he offered. She wouldn't make a fool of herself and humiliate the duke's son by pulling away and fleeing the ball in front of everyone. She would dance one dance, then slip out before Treynor saw her.

Unfortunately, however, Lord Baldwin lined up right next to the lieutenant and the blond woman, and it was only a moment before she heard Treynor's unmistakable voice.

"Lady St. Ives, what a surprise to see you here."

The fact that he had greeted her forced her to acknowledge him. She nodded, using every ounce of self-control to appear indifferent. "I might say the same, Lieutenant Treynor."

He smiled, but his gaze sparked with anger. "Indeed. May I introduce Lady Ambrose? Lady Ambrose, this is Lady St. Ives."

Jeannette felt the tightness of her own smile but did her best to be pleasant. "Lady Ambrose."

As Treynor's lady friend nodded, her gaze ranged over Jeannette from head to foot with little effort to hide the perusal. "I have heard a great deal about you."

"I am sure you are not the only one," Jeannette said.

Lady Ambrose's eyes widened, but the music started, cutting off any reply.

Jeannette endeavored to keep her mind on the dance, which moved her down a line of men and presented her with a new partner every few moments. Treynor was the last to take her hand, and try as she might, she could not stop herself from feeling the warm vibrancy that coursed down her arm when he touched her.

"The duke is playing games with me, I see," he said, his voice curt, as though something had upset him.

"*Pardonnez-moi*, Lieutenant?" She and the other women turned a full circle before they came close enough to their partners to speak again.

"Nothing. How are you, anyway?"

"As well as could be expected. His Grace, the Duke of Ellsborough, has promised me a recommendation. It seems that his granddaughters are in need of a governess."

"He has, has he?"

Jeannette ignored his wry tone. "I should be well engaged in teaching before long." She didn't know why she added that, except she wanted him to think she had her life well in hand. "Are you now a captain?"

Again she turned around and came back to face him before he could answer. "Yes, but I am still awaiting word of my ship."

"The wait must be very frustrating. It is a good thing you have had Lady Ambrose to entertain you."

"Jeannette—"

It was time to switch partners again. Gratefully, Jeannette released her hold on the lieutenant and returned to her beginning position across from Lord Baldwin. As they started through the line again, she heard Lady Ambrose say, "You promised to tell me more of the battle that won you such honors, Sir Crawford."

Jeannette wished she could tell Lady Ambrose about the rats, the lice, the smell of blood and what it was like to see a man die, but Treynor merely shrugged.

"The weather turned and allowed us to gain the upper hand."

"Surely you are being modest," Lady Ambrose responded. "Men are not knighted for a lucky turn in the weather."

"Are you enjoying your stay in London?" Lord Baldwin intruded upon Jeannette's awareness of Treynor and his partner, causing her to lose the thread of their conversation.

"*Oui*, my lord. Do you like it here, as well?"

"At this time of year, I do. But when August hits, the heat drives me to our country home farther north."

"I see." Jeannette's eyes flicked toward Treynor every few moments despite a supreme effort to stop them. Once their gazes clashed, and she looked quickly away.

"Have you known Captain Treynor long?"

If the duke's son wasn't privy to the latest gossip, she had no intention of enlightening him. "No. We are merely acquaintances."

"I thought we had graduated to friends, at the very least," Treynor interrupted, overhearing her words.

Jeannette ignored him as the music ended. Turning, she headed off the floor almost before Lord Baldwin could escort her. "I am warm," she said, feeling a desperate need to escape the room without having to negotiate her departure with her parents. "Perhaps a walk in the gardens would be nice. Would you care to join me, Lord Baldwin?"

He shot a glance over his shoulder at a glowering Treynor and smiled. "I would be delighted. Perhaps you would like something to drink first?"

Jeannette thought of dulling the razor-sharp edge of her emotions with wine, then decided against it. The last thing she needed was to lose one shred of her control. Pride was all she had left. "No, thank you."

The garden offered the cool, quiet respite Jeannette needed. She turned about the well-manicured bushes and freshly blooming flowers, breathing in the heady scent of the roses that scaled the white lattice as she tried to clear her head.

"Are you feeling better, Lady St. Ives?"

"A little." Jeannette bit back a sigh and kept walking, hoping she didn't appear as pensive as she felt. "You have a lovely home," she said in an attempt to provide at least some pleasant conversation.

"And never has a more beautiful woman graced it. I had heard tell of you, I must admit, but the realization is far better than the original promise."

"Merci." She knew such a compliment deserved better than a tired thank-you, but couldn't rouse herself to the occasion. Gentle strains of music filled the air; she focused on trying to let it ease her misery.

The duke's son paused near a white iron chair. "Would you care to sit down for a moment?"

Jeannette felt no great need to sit and rest, but to accommodate him, she agreed.

Baldwin made a few comments about the weather and the war, which she tried to answer coherently, but her mind was consumed by the memory of Lady Hafton's words. *He is courting Maude . . . he has been to the house several times over the past few weeks.*

She could see a corner of the ballroom through the open doors of the house. The silhouette of a tall form, standing in the shadows and gazing out, suddenly claimed her attention and made her miss what the duke's son had said last.

"My apologies, Lord Baldwin. I am afraid I am not very good company tonight. What did you say?"

He laughed. "Nothing important. I merely mentioned that my father tells me you want to become a governess. I would tell you that it is a waste of your beauty and talents, but it is not my place. So I will settle for warning you that Catherine's girls are hardly what you might expect."

"My lord?"

"One would picture three little girls of only ten, eight and six as sweet and subdued."

"Are they not?"

"No. Nor are they studious. All three have a rather, shall we say, tempestuous nature. And I am not sure my father mentioned this, but Catherine is demanding a four-year commitment." He laughed. "She hopes the children's next governess—yes, they have chased off quite a few already—will seriously apply herself instead of giving up on the girls."

Lord Baldwin's words were discouraging, but not overwhelmingly so, not when Jeannette remembered growing up with a similar "tempestuous nature." "I consider such children a challenge, *monsieur,* nothing more."

She glanced back at the house again. The man hovering near the doors had to be Treynor, for no one else stood so tall or so straight. Where was Lady Ambrose?

"What would motivate a woman like you to throw away her youth?" he persisted.

She did not reply.

"Forgive my impertinence, but governesses should be plain and without better option. You come from a good family. I know you have experienced difficult times, but you have a sponsor here in England. Lord Darby would see you remarried, I dare say, if you but gave the word. Is there not someone here you have met?"

The thought of Lord Darby selecting another husband for her chilled Jeannette to the bone. "Marriage no longer appeals to me," she said simply, unwilling to lay her heart bare. "Shall we go back inside?"

As much as she wanted to flee the pain inflicted by Treynor's presence, Lord Baldwin's company and his pointed questions troubled her, too. Standing when he nodded, she allowed him to take her elbow and lead her back into the house.

They had scarcely entered the crush when Treynor cut them off. "There you are."

"Growing a bit hot, Lieutenant?" Lord Baldwin asked. "May I suggest a turn about the gardens? The weather is lovely."

"I am not interested in the gardens." Treynor's voice was a bit too brusque to warrant the chuckle that came from Baldwin. "I was wondering if Lady St. Ives would grant me the pleasure of the next dance."

Jeannette shook her head, but Treynor pulled her away from the duke's son before she could offer a refusal sufficient to stop him.

"I beg your pardon?" she snapped.

He led her almost forcibly to the dance floor. "A 'turn about the gardens' with Baldwin. Are you looking for another proposal, after all?"

"And if I was?" Jeannette challenged.

"You said you wanted to become a governess."

"And you said you were returning to sea. We are both free to do as we please."

"There you are, Sir Crawford." Lady Ambrose had placed herself in their path. "I have been looking all over for you. Do you not remember that you promised me another dance?"

Treynor opened his mouth to speak, but Jeannette answered before he could. "He was just on his way to find you, Lady Ambrose. Good night, Captain."

She pulled her elbow from his grasp and headed toward Lord Darby, who was standing next to the door and edging closer to it all the time. At least she wouldn't have to talk him into leaving. They would simply send the carriage back for her parents.

"Jeannette—"

Treynor called after her, but a backward glance revealed Lady Ambrose at his side, wrapping a possessive hand around his arm.

"There is nothing left for us to say," Jeannette muttered, mostly to herself. Then she hurried away—before the tears burning at the back of her eyes found their way down her cheeks.

Treynor cursed under his breath as he watched Jeannette and Darby pass through the door. Carefully detaching himself from Lady Ambrose, he mumbled an excuse he hoped wouldn't offend her, without really caring if it did, and attempted to follow.

Baldwin's hand on his arm stopped his forward motion. "The Lady St. Ives is a rare beauty," he said, looking after her. "Now I can see why you would fight a duel for her." He smiled. "But since you are so set on remaining unfettered by the fairer sex, perhaps you wouldn't mind if I—"

"Stay away from her," Treynor growled. The admiration on the other man's face was worthy of a fight.

Baldwin laughed. "So Father was right. I thought so."

"Right about what?"

"You are smitten with Lady St. Ives, and she with you. Now, you can continue to deny the truth and try to distract yourself with other women, fickle women like Lady Ambrose there, who would not have the warmth to capture a dog's heart. Or you can make Lady St. Ives your wife and have her waiting for you, warm in your bed, every time you put in."

Not wanting to let the thought of Jeannette waiting for him in any bed influence the decision he had made to go on without her, Treynor scowled. "I am trying to do the kindest thing I possibly can. She deserves more than what I can give her. What kind of life would she have, always waiting for me to return from sea?"

"The war will not last forever, my friend. Besides, there are worse things than being married to a sea captain. Teaching Catherine's girls is one of them." A mischievous sparkle entered Baldwin's dark eyes as he shrugged. "It seems an easy decision to me, but then, I inherited my mother's good judgment and not my father's stubborn streak." Bowing, he gave Treynor a jaunty smile and took himself off.

Treynor watched him go, then slipped through the crowd and out into the garden. Baldwin was right. For weeks he had immersed himself in trying to forget Jeannette. But just the sight of her was enough to let him know that all his efforts, especially the time he'd spent with Lady Ambrose, had been wasted.

He wanted Lady St. Ives. And now that he knew what he wanted, he had to decide how to get it.

Chapter 25

"Maman, the duke has sent me a message. I am to meet him and his daughter, Catherine, this afternoon." Jeannette put the elegant stationery the butler had delivered to her just a few moments earlier on her mother's dressing table.

Sitting before the mirror in her wrap, Rose Marie glanced at the note as though it were a snake. "So soon, *ma petite*?"

"*Oui*. Why not? You, Father and Henri will be busy settling into the house you found last week. I will beg a few days to help you, but then there is nothing to stop me from working. A post like this is very difficult to find."

Her mother picked up the brush she had been using and went back to work on her hair. It was early, not yet time for breakfast, but the men had already left for Black's Coffee House, where they liked to sit and read the newspaper. "I am afraid your father will not be pleased. He is convinced you will be happier with a husband and children."

Jeannette sighed. "And I can tell that you agree with him. But who would you have me marry, Maman? Another old man? Another stranger?"

"The duke's son seemed quite taken with you last night."

"He was merely being polite. I do not exactly understand his and the duke's sudden interest, but I am no longer in the market for marriage."

"Jeannette, I know how you feel about the lieutenant—or is it captain now?—but with time—"

"Time is exactly what I am giving myself, Maman."

"How much time?"

"Lady Catherine wants a four-year commitment."

Rose Marie's brush clattered onto the table. "*Four years*, Jeannette? You will be an old maid before you are free to carry on with your life."

"I will only be twenty-three."

Her mother rubbed her face before looking at Jeannette in the mirror. "If I cannot talk you out of it, then I will support you in it."

Jeannette knew it took considerable effort for her to say those words. They were enough.

"Thank you, Maman." Dropping a kiss on the top of her head, Jeannette smiled. "This will be a good thing for me. You will see."

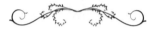

Brought to the door by Darby's footman, Jeannette entered the duke's house feeling conspicuous without a lady's maid. One had always accompanied her in France. But Lord Darby ran his house with a minimum of servants. Short of taking a scullery maid, Jeannette had no one to attend her.

There were worse things to worry about, however. She excused the footman to wait with the coach and followed the duke's butler through a large marble entry into a front parlor tastefully decorated with brocade furniture, several family portraits, fabric-covered walls and a high ceiling with thick crown molding.

Fresh-cut peonies filled several vases, perfuming the air and adding to the room's spacious elegance.

"His Grace and Lady Catherine will be with you shortly, madame," the butler said and bowed himself out.

Dressed in a purposely plain blue dress, Jeannette perched on a settee in the center of the room and told herself that she was doing the right thing. She wanted a husband and a family, eventually, but she couldn't think of that now, not after Treynor.

The door clicked and Jeannette looked up, expecting to see the Duke of Ellsborough and Lady Catherine. Instead, the butler came to stand before her. "Madame, before His Grace and Lady Catherine come down, the duke's son begs a word with you."

Surprised, Jeannette inclined her head. "Of course, I would be pleased to speak with Lord Baldwin."

"Oh, but it isn't Lord Baldwin, madame, it is Captain Sir—"

"I will take over from here, Hodges," a familiar voice drawled, coming from the entrance.

"Yes, sir."

Jeannette looked around the butler to see Lieutenant—no, Captain—Treynor walk into the room. The surprise of it nearly knocked her from her perch. What was he doing here?

The butler's steps receded in the hall outside as Treynor stood looking at her with an inscrutable expression on his face. "My father tells me—"

"Your *father*?" Jeannette echoed. The last she had heard, he didn't know who his father was. Evidently that had changed.

He gave her a wry smile. "Yes, my mother finally told me the truth—I thought the gossip was all over the ball last night, but evidently you left before you heard the news. The Duke of Ellsborough is my father." His grin widened. "A bastard could do worse, eh?"

Jeannette felt some of the tension leave her and smiled, hoping, for Treynor's sake, that he had been able to put the devils of his past behind him at last. "I am happy for you," she admitted. "Truly happy."

He shrugged as though this latest development didn't affect him, but she could tell it did, deeply, and that he was pleased. "Nothing essential has changed."

"He is publicly recognizing you as his son. That is something."

"Now that he knows I exist, he is willing to do what he can, but legally I am still a bastard. That will never change." He paused, watching her. "Does it bother you, Jeannette?"

Jeannette considered the question. From the first, Treynor had proven himself to be an extraordinary man. What difference did the circumstances of his birth make?

She shook her head. "If I have learned one thing since the Revolution, Captain Treynor, it is that high birth and wealth are not the measure of a man."

"And what is the measure of a man, to you, my lovely Jeannette?" He dropped down on one knee in front of her, and Jeannette thought she would drown in the depths of his eyes as he took her hand and gazed up at her.

"His heart, of course."

"And my heart, Jeannette? Is it good enough for you?"

Jeannette felt her throat tighten. How could he doubt that it was? "You are a man of honor," she told him honestly. "I care not whether your heart is perfect, Treynor. The only thing that matters to me is whether it is mine."

He raised both her hands to his lips and kissed each one in turn. "Ah, Jeannette. What have you done to me? My heart was yours the night you left me writhing in my bed, and though I have done my best to wrest it back, I have finally realized there is no hope of that. Not ever."

His eyes appealed to her, holding a wealth of emotions: hope, admiration, vulnerability. "Will you marry me? Wait for me when I am at sea? Welcome me when I come eagerly home to your arms?"

If not for the solid feel of him touching her and the intensity of his gaze, Jeannette might have thought she were dreaming. She had come to the duke's to give four years of her life away as a governess and instead found the fulfillment of her fondest hopes. "Is marriage really what you want, Captain?"

"*You* are what I want," he replied, "as my wife and the mother of my children."

"But you once told me you have no use for a virgin," she teased.

"That is a problem I shall fix at the first opportunity." Reaching up to palm the back of her head, he drew her to him for a searching kiss.

Jeannette parted her lips, welcoming the warm, velvety sensation of his tongue as it entered her mouth and delved deeper and deeper still, until she felt completely consumed with him and could imagine nothing better on earth.

After a moment, he pulled away. "Tell me you love me, that you will be my wife," he said, his breathing ragged. "I want to hear the words from your lips, not just the welcome of your body."

Jeannette tried to laugh, but her heart was pounding too hard and her lungs hadn't the air for it. "My body does not lie, Sir Crawford," she said. "I will love you always and forever. I am already praying that the war will end so you will never have to leave me."

"Then I will tell my father that Catherine will have to find another governess."

She laughed and abandoned herself to the joy of feeling his arms close tightly about her, never to let her go again.

Jeannette waited with her parents and Henri at the fine old church on Piccadilly. She wore a watered-silk gown of the palest pink and held a simple bouquet in her hands. That her wedding was to be a quick, private affair suited her. Indeed, she doubted she could have waited a second longer.

The door boomed shut, and the Duke of Ellsborough and Lord Baldwin made their way up the aisle, but they weren't whom Jeannette wanted to see. Where was Treynor?

Her mother patted her arm. "He will be here, *ma petite*. He is not even late. Calm down."

Her parents stood to greet the duke and his son. They bowed over her mother's hand before kissing Jeannette's as well.

"I can see you are as eager for this marriage as the groom, young lady, and I cannot tell you how well it pleases me," the duke said. "I knew you were perfect for each other the moment I met you."

Jeannette smiled. "Without your matchmaking efforts, I fear we would not be here, Your Grace. Treynor and I both owe you a great debt."

"Just make him happy," he said. "That is all I ask."

Another thud signaled the entrance of someone else and drew Jeannette's attention once again to the door. There, dressed in a black cloth coat, an embroidered waistcoat and a white, lace-trimmed neckcloth above a snug-fitting pair of knee breeches, was Captain Sir Crawford Treynor.

As he strode up the aisle, Jeannette thought he had never looked more handsome. His hair was neatly groomed, his face tan and clean shaven. A ready smile showed his teeth.

He bowed when he reached her parents, but his eyes strayed to her as though she were the only one in the church. "Good morning, Lord and Lady Lumfere. I trust you slept well?"

"Better now that we know our daughter will not spend her life pining away," Jacques said. "You will treat her well, no?"

"Indeed I shall." He turned to Jeannette and lifted her hand to his lips. "Are you happy, my love?"

"How could I be anything less?" she asked as the warmth of his strong fingers gently caressing her own sent shivers up her arm.

Treynor cleared his throat. "Shall we get on with it?" he asked the others.

The duke laughed. "I am glad you are so eager, my son, but I fear we must wait for the vicar, special license or no."

Treynor scowled, but the vicar soon appeared and greeted them all. "Have a seat everyone. Are we ready to begin?"

Just then light came streaming into the dim interior as the door opened again and the Marchioness of Bedford entered.

"Mother." Treynor left Jeannette's side to meet the stately woman coming up the aisle. He placed a gentle kiss on her cheek. "I thought you couldn't make it."

The marchioness held him for a few moments, smiling. "I wouldn't have missed it for the world."

"Lady Bedford." The duke stood, drawing the woman's attention at last from her son.

"Your Grace."

Their eyes held for a moment as something passed between them. Then the duke took and kissed her hand. "We created a fine son, despite everyone and everything," he said. "Thank you for letting us know each other at last."

She nodded. "The truth has brought me peace."

"Then let us begin."

She greeted Jeannette and Jeannette's family, took a seat next to the duke and Lord Baldwin and turned an expectant smile on the vicar.

The ceremony began and Treynor's hand, warm and powerful, closed around Jeannette's. He towered at her side, his energy filling her at that single point of contact, fusing them together as if they were already one.

Jeannette reveled in the sight and the feel of him, and in the tingle of anticipation that came with knowing they would soon be man and wife.

"Wilt thou have this man to be thy wedded husband, to live together after God's ordinance in the holy state of matrimony? Wilt thou obey him and serve him, love, honor and keep him in sickness and in health? And forsaking all others, keep thee only to him so long as you both shall live?" the vicar asked.

Jeannette looked at Treynor and thought her heart would burst with loving him. "I will."

ABOUT THE AUTHOR

PHOTO BY MICAH KANDROS

When Brenda Novak caught her daycare provider drugging her young children with cough medicine to get them to sleep all day while she was away at work, she quit her job as a loan officer to stay home with them. She felt she could no longer trust others with their care. But she still had to find some way to make a living. That was when she picked up one of her favorite books. She was looking for a brief escape from the stress and worry—and found the inspiration to become a novelist.

Since her first sale to HarperCollins in 1998 (*Of Noble Birth*), Brenda has written fifty books in a variety of genres. Now a *New York Times* and *USA Today* bestselling author, she still juggles her writing career with the demands of her large family and interests such as cycling, traveling and reading. A four-time RITA nominee, Brenda has won many awards for her books, including the National Reader's Choice, the Booksellers' Best, the Book Buyer's Best and the Holt Medallion. She also runs an annual online auction for diabetes research every May at www.brendanovak.com (her youngest son suffers from this disease). To date, she's raised over $2 million.

3 1170 00965 7143